NOFORN

D0534986

DESCRIPTION		
VERSION LAMBDA TOP ASSEMBLY PERSPECTIVE	**Aerosystems Unlimited** Coast Facility	
RELEASE *B. Ulmu*	PRINT SIZE	SC-4136-1
NEXT ASSY CADVERSION	**A**	DRAFTSMAN *Don Thomas*

Also by Dean Ing

The Big Lifters
Blood of Eagles
Butcher Bird
The Nemesis Mission
The Ransom of Black Stealth One
Silent Thunder
Single Combat
Systemic Shock
Wild Country

DEAN ING

LOCAL AUTHOR

BUTCHER BIRD

FORGE

A TOM DOHERTY ASSOCIATES BOOK
NEW YORK

BUTCHER BIRD

Copyright © 1993 by Dean Ing

This book is printed on acid-free paper.

A Forge Book
Published by Tom Doherty Associates, Inc.
175 Fifth Avenue
New York, N.Y. 10010

Library of Congress Cataloging-in-Publication Data

Ing, Dean.
    Butcher bird / Dean Ing.
        p.   cm.
    "A Tom Doherty Assocation book."
    ISBN 0-312-85397-1
    1. International relations—Fiction. 2. Military weapons—Fiction. 3. High Technology—Fiction. I. Title.
PS3559.N37B87   1993
813'.54—dc20   93-26553
                                                          CIP

First edition: November 1993

Printed in the United States of America

0 9 8 7 6 5 4 3 2 1

For Tom, who keeps me ticking,
and for Al, who keeps me talking.

ACKNOWLEDGMENTS

Recent advances in unmanned flight, on both sides of the Atlantic, gave me a rich—even bewildering—fund of facts on which I hung this tale of the barely possible. Could I help it if many of those very real flying robots look like UFOs? The curious skeptic can verify this with such texts as Peter Bowers's *Unconventional Aircraft* and, especially, Bill Siuru's *Planes Without Pilots.*

While full responsibility for the Butcher Bird lies, of course, with me, I could not have reached even its preliminary design stage without the good-humored help of Dr. Doug Elerath. I became convinced that Doug could easily have designed a better version—but wouldn't have been free to describe it! Thanks, too, to the little team of retired Ullmers who helped me with the design critique. As always, I deviated from expert counsel wherever I had to fudge the numbers in the interests of a good yarn.

As for the model: again, thanks to Bill Fletcher for some of the advanced composites work. This one, we won't even try to fly. We don't want it to. . . .

PROLOGUE

JANUARY 1991

THE HUGE BIRD passed California's northern border late on a Sunday afternoon, each pinion feather clearly distinct against the sky. Later, near Oregon's Cape Sebastian, a surf fisherman turned away from the spray to dismantle his rig, and glanced up. He stared past the tip of his casting rod and estimated the creature's altitude as a thousand feet, give or take. It must be heading for home too, he decided; a six-foot buzzard usually swept in arcs, yet this one's path was arrow-straight.

The fisherman would not have believed the simple truth: the silent giant's home was a hangar, not an eyrie of sticks. Its altitude was not a thousand feet, but almost ten thousand. Its wings spanned over sixty feet, and this synthetic creature was hurled forward at more than a hundred and fifty miles an hour by a muffled ducted fan hidden in its guts. The plumage, electronically "painted" onto its surfaces by a process familiar to very few, was known as a pixel skin. Computer-run, that skin could imitate its own background so well it became invisible to the eye or, as it did now at cruise altitude, could mimic a solitary vulture. Virtually the only surfaces not covered by that pixel skin were the clear twin bulges of the canopy that made it look not so much birdlike as insectile. But from below, those bulging "eyes" were not visible.

The ultralight craft had a name, Black Stealth One, and a nickname: Hellbug. It was virtually invisible to radar, and in 1989 it had answered a question asked by its developers, the National Security Agency. That question went as follows: *If someone stole a two-place aircraft that could fool the eye, infrared sensors, and radar as well, how would you get it back?* They knew the answer now: you wouldn't. Black Stealth One, the first of its kind, became the most expensive prototype ever stolen from America's spymasters.

Presently the Hellbug ghosted northward past Port Orford, perhaps Oregon's loveliest setting, the copilot peering dreamily through the bulbous starboard eye of the canopy. The young woman sighed and abandoned her pensive slump. "Hey. Can I take her from Bandon to Coos Bay?"

"Thought you were asleep, Petra," said the stocky pilot beside her. "And how many times must I tell you—"

"The Hellbug's not a 'she,'" the young woman finished for him, gently mocking. "Ri-ight. Better not be, mister. If I ever find out it is," she pointed a forefinger at him and snapped her thumb forward, "powie. Come on, let me take the stick."

He nodded, grinning at her, his squint lines hidden by sunglasses that took years from his age. He flexed arms and fingers to relax, studying his companion as she banked the great wings for a sweep inland. She no longer held herself rigid, white knuckled, when holding the stick as she once had. Given enough time, Petra might even be as capable as he in a vertical landing or takeoff. *She's sure got the calves for it,* he admitted silently. Those foot-operated hover controls had no power assists but then, he reflected, when designing the Hellbug he hadn't dreamed this honey-haired little heller would be flying it.

For that matter, Black Stealth One was literally the only aircraft she had ever flown. When that thought led to another, he laughed aloud.

Her glance was puzzled, darting from his face to the console. "Dammit! What am I doing?"

"I often wonder," he rumbled in that aging whiskey baritone of his. "You're doing fine. Actually, you reminded me of my grandmother."

"My God but you're a weird old man," she muttered.

This taunt about the disparity in their ages had become a running joke between them, their way of dealing with the fact. This time he ignored it. "Happened when I was still a kid. Grandma had never learned to drive a car," he told her. "Didn't like men yelling at her, she said. Nobody ever thought she cared until one day when she complained about it with my dad in his Porsche. One of the classic bathtub coupes, a '53, I think."

"Jurassic era. Before my time."

"Watch your mouth, kid. So Dad stopped the car and wouldn't go another foot unless she drove. Well, she did, and ground a half-pound of synchromesh transmission outa that poor coupe while my dad bit his tongue and talked her through it. But by the end of that day, by God, my grandmother could drive a four-speed Porsche. When he got a raise from Rockwell he bought a 'Vette and gave Grandma the Porsche. As long as she lived, the only car my grandmother ever drove was a red '53 Porsche coupe. And she never got a license either. Ain't that a pisser?"

"That is a bona fide pisser." She smiled, her New England accent making the phrase more ludicrous. "I get the connection now. Can't you just see me, getting some flight instructor to check me out in the Hellbug?"

"Nope. I keep seeing you in handcuffs."

"That's a roj," she said, unconsciously borrowing his vintage pilot jargon, then falling serenely quiet. Gradually she reduced the engine's power to idle, letting the Hellbug float downward on gentle evening currents. In unspoken agreement they removed their sunglasses and watched the sun's image quenched by an endless ocean. At last, seeing headlights appear on a thread of highway far below, she spoke again. "This has been a wonderful weekend, luv. You were right, after a couple of months of an Oregon rainy season, Barstow has real charm."

"Figured you needed a break from stress calculations. People see Oregon on its best behavior and accept jobs in the Northwest and *then* they learn about the rain. I hear it isn't really logging that endangers the spotted owl. Poor little buggers just drown in the treetops," he said.

The young woman dutifully chuckled, glancing at him, noting the lines of his face etched more deeply by the dusk. "I think you need some rest too, hon. You're working too hard."

"Oh bullshit," he growled. "Who gave you that idea? Speedy?"

"No; one of our other many mutual friends," she said with obvious sarcasm. "But it wasn't him, it was you."

"You worry too much," he said, spotting a familiar cliff formation near the beach. He reached for his control stick. "I'll take it now, we're nearly there. Punch up the IR display, will you? I don't want to squash some lust-maddened teenagers out here in the sand."

"That's my Cherokee," she said, knowing his real reason for the infrared display.

He was fairly certain he had correctly identified her old Cherokee parked alone near the beach but, well into his fifties, he no longer had youthful night vision. *I could've asked her to be my eyes. Yeah, and then to bring my cane and help me into my La-Z-Boy. No dice. Petra's not going to remember me that way. . . .* He'd been right about the Cherokee after all. While Petra scanned the bleached bones of driftwood nearby, he engaged the wastegates of Black Stealth One and used its three diverter nozzles to settle the craft vertically into tuft grass on those columns of cool air. Together, they began flicking switches until finally, with nothing left to do, they clasped hands in silence for a long five minutes.

Then: "You mustn't stay long," she murmured.

"Why? Late date with Ullmer tonight?"

"That too," she replied, accepting that absurd notion to prolong the joke, "but it'll be midnight before you raise Barstow, as it is." She opened the starboard hatch, the cockpit filling instantly with the rank odor of kelp and a vagrant tang of wood smoke. She pulled a shapeless overnight bag from behind her seat back, leaned toward him, kissed him gently. "Kidnap me again soon?"

He had done that, once. "Count on it. Seduce me in revenge?"

She had tried that, once. "Oh yeah. Ohhh, *yeah.*" She chuckled, because it was no longer an issue, and stepped from the aircraft.

"Give old Ben my love," he called, starting to energize the Hellbug again. She heard him over the soft chuff of the rotary engine, and laughed. That was perhaps the biggest joke they shared. Ben Ullmer, now president of his own aircraft factory, had once sworn to recover Black Stealth One, and then, unknowingly, had hired the only woman on earth who might have led him to it. The pilot waited until he saw the Cherokee's lights blink before he levitated the Hellbug, knowing how Petra loved to see it rise, ghostly as some prehistoric monster, to blot out the stars. The possibility that she might force a meeting with Ben Ullmer never really entered his thoughts.

ONE

—

FEBRUARY 1991

BECAUSE THE UPTURNED bucket wasn't much of a reviewing stand, the Kurdish colonel did not have far to fall. And because of the way he staggered and lost his footing in midharangue, some of his *Peshmerga* warriors whispered that the colonel's pratfall was Allah's warning to the arrogant. Scanning bare, goat-nibbled slopes to the nearest snowy ridge line, others suspected a Turk marksman and sent a few rounds buzzing in the general direction of the nearby Turkish border. Of course it need not have been a Turk; the Syrian border was only a day's march to the west and Syria, too, had her reasons. These half-starved Iraqi Kurds were also targets of Saddam Hussein, dictator of their own country. Even the Americans who brought them food and arms were not true allies.

Once the colonel's boots had quit twitching in cold dust and a young officer noticed the trickle of blood at the juncture of neck and collarbone, the sharpshooter theory seemed proven. Moments later, the colonel stopped breathing. All three hundred of the colonel's guerrillas just inside the northern border of Iraq agreed on one thing: it was one hell of a shot.

Just how special a shot became obvious late that afternoon. Working under a tent of camel hair, the battalion doctor found no slug in the colonel's body; only a shallow wound the diameter of a fingertip, penetrating perhaps two centimeters. Stranger still, the penetration had been almost straight down. No one had heard the shot—but the Peshmerga troops had been noisy in the manner of Kurdish nomads. It was possible that the kill had been made accidentally by a pebble fired from afar, as children sometimes did, from a vintage black powder smoothbore. Perhaps the pebble had simply fallen to the ground after finding its target of opportunity. If so, the colonel's death could have been simple shock; it did not seem very likely, but stranger things had happened.

The doctor muttered these observations to an assistant as his innocent fingers probed the wound. Then, finding grit that did not feel quite like sand, he performed the kind of analysis that physicians have performed since the time of Mohammed: he tested the grit with his tongue and found it bitter as quinine. Finally he pronounced the colonel dead of a sniper round and took his prayer rug outside for devotions. The physician was a solitary man, and that is why no one found his body until nightfall. The rumor of a hostile *djinni* surfaced around Kurdish campfires that night.

Though a belief in the devil is common among Moslems, in the major cities very few Moslems still believe in minor demons such as the invisible djinn. When a djinni surfaces, it is almost always among people with primitive beliefs; Kurds, for example, who do not even speak Arabic though they remain Moslems. But old ideas will sometimes return to modern men, when such men find themselves in ancient settings, faced with the unexplainable.

Al Qimishli, Syria, lies roughly one hundred miles to the west of that Peshmerga camp. Six days later, a Syrian civilian deplaned at the Al Qimishli airport and hired a driver to visit, so he said, a ruin of antiquity an hour's drive distant. He took pains to satisfy himself that the driver did not speak French. Naturally, as a scholar in good standing, he had official permission from Mukhabarat, the intelligence service in faraway Damascus. And naturally, as a Syrian born and bred, he had a bit of special business to transact. He knew the rules of the game but thought his gunrunning business had not yet come to the attention of President Assad's men in Mukhabarat.

Waiting for his contact, hat snugged down as he listened to the whine of wind through long-defeated walls at the ruin, the scholar risked the shine on his fine low-quarter shoes in a stroll. An educated man, he did not believe in the djinn that were supposed by simpler men to inhabit such ruins, and imagined that the soft distant whirr he heard for one brief moment was, perhaps, a flight of pigeons. In any case he saw nothing in this desolate sky, and presently he stopped to relieve himself in privacy.

Later, the driver claimed he had heard one hoarse, strangled cry before leaving the shade of his battered Peugeot; nothing more.

Nothing, he added to Mukhabarat nabobs, but a dead man lying in piss-damped sand, still unzipped, with a hole in his hat and another drilled down into his skull. He knew better than to show inconsistency to his questioners and was certain, he said, that he had seen no one else at the ruin. He was equally certain that he had neither seen nor heard any aircraft. A Sunni Moslem, he was privately certain that he wanted nothing further to do with these Alawite thugs with their newfangled, barely Moslem ways. Much later, recounting it with friends in the *souk,* he pointed out that the dead man was defiling a ruin, and wondered aloud if that ruin had harbored a djinni.

These rumors of ancient demons might have grown instantly popular if Operation Desert Storm had not, at the time, occupied every tongue in every bazaar in the Middle East. The Mukhabarat noted each rumor on their computers in Damascus, passing their findings to a well-disguised desert research laboratory, and watched foreign devils on CNN as Western technology turned Iraq's legions into a marmalade of flesh.

With the end of Iraq's defeat, tongues wagged again on the subject of djinn. More evidence bolstered those claims: a Sunni leader in Syria's port city of Aleppo fell dead within arm's length of his confederates, with a shallow wound high on his forehead. Near Damascus, a Shiite moderate suffered the same fate. In the souks, old fears found new life.

And in their desert lab, a few men smiled. In two cases, physicians had forwarded reports about those djinn victims in which traces of a violent alkaloid had been found in the wounds. The reports were promptly suppressed and the physicians got forcible reminders about national security. That was enough; everyone in Syria knew that Hafez Assad played by Hama rules.

Nine years before, Hama had been a thriving Syrian city known for the pervasive squeal of its many waterwheels, but that was before Assad sent his special forces with attack helicopters to quell dissent among his reluctant people. They followed up with bulldozers. Much of the city, today, exists in eerie quiet as fist-sized rubble, a parking lot for the dead, a lingering reminder to other dissenters that Hama rules means no rules at all; no quarter, no compassion, no limits.

If any Syrian noticed that each of the djinni incidents befell an enemy of Hafez Assad, he did not say it aloud. For a time, the connection went unnoticed in foreign capitals. And in the desert lab, a new, more potent sibling of that djinni learned new tricks.

TWO

February 1991

I N SOME WAYS, the djinni validated ancient legend. To all but the sharpest eyes, it was invisible in flight. And like traditional djinn its home was a dead city, an underground lair near the magnificent ruin of Palmyra in central Syria. Before the Christian era, camel caravans had taken water from Palmyra's springs before the waterless five-day trek to the Euphrates. Now that same water could be used for industrial processes to create a modern demon. Satellite photography would reveal little because the site was disguised as an archaeological dig. Heavy crates could be moved from the highway, or from the nearby airstrip that served an oil pipeline pump station, without alerting Western curiosity. It would have been perfectly natural for archaeologists to erect permanent tents near the excavation, and to bring some of their work to the tents before midday heat drove them inside. On this morning, two men worked methodically at a shaded workbench outside the underground lab.

"Tell me about Palmyra's archers," said Clement, adjusting the tiny setscrew that positioned a sliding cover plate. His motions were quick, exact, the gestures of a man with vast self-confidence. When energized, the cover plate was designed to slide away from an aerodynamic duct of very special shape. Setscrew, plate and duct were all miniatures, which was not to say they were toys. Any aircraft designer would have recognized that duct as a highly efficient inlet developed by the Americans at NASA. Many new aircraft still did not sport this high-tech NASA inlet. Roland Clement had specified this one because, very soon, the djinni would need all the ram air it could get to cool its new weapon. He said "Energize" as though it were part of his previous request.

Selim Mansour paused before toggling the switch. It was so like Roland Clement to keep several topics rattling around in his head at once! And here in this sun-stunned wilderness at the desert's edge, Clement had found no one else whose mind was as swift as his own. Mansour sometimes wished he did not know so much; indeed, wished that neither of them did.

Still, Mansour tried manfully to play Clement's game. "Energizing," he said, and saw the cover plate jam in its slide. "The Romans found that Palmyran archers were wonderful sharpshooters," Mansour said quickly, hoping to divert Clement from one of his sudden furies, "and used them as far away as Britain even after the emperor Aurelian destroyed Palmyra. Power off." As usual, they spoke French; Clement's Arabic was villainous, and there were many technical topics in which Arabic simply would not serve.

Now Mansour looked away, as if he had not noticed the maladjusted setscrew, while Clement changed its setting. Though Clement's work was brilliant and quick, he was prone to mistakes. And when the thickset French scientist became frustrated, as he was now, his mood could turn ugly in a flash. Weeks before, a low-level Syrian technician had dropped a crate of delicate instruments in the lab, and the commotion had made Clement spill some of the etching acid he held. The rest of that acid went into the hapless Syrian's face. The incident, Clement said later, was just the sort of object lesson in lab safety that Arabs understood.

Mansour understood, all right. Now, watching Clement adjust that setscrew, he went on. "Some say that Palmyra's archers might have saved the city from the Romans if they had not fought as Romans taught them, against their own people."

A vagrant midmorning breeze toyed with the canopy of their tent. Clement stared into the distance, toward the pillars that had once marked a major stage on the spice route to India. "Must be in the genes," he said.

To this, Mansour said nothing. For one thing, Clement might even be right; in Syria alone, the Sunni Moslem majority squirmed under the rule of Assad's Alawite Moslems, and Shiites hated them both. An Alawite himself, with the swarthy slender carriage of his people and a nose like a ship's prow, Selim Mansour was very much a modern man. A good thing, too, else he would never have earned such freedom in his own country.

Mansour felt that President Assad was the only hope for a modern Syria. He had never swayed in his loyalty, even when he began to realize that his scientific work would pinpoint other Syrians for assassination. Assad boasted few followers who combined that kind of loyalty with such an excellent Western education. Undergraduate work at the *Ecole Polytechnique* in Paris, graduate work at MIT, speaker of four languages—but Mansour did not delude himself. He lacked the creative genius of a Roland Clement. The man might be erratic, but few technical minds on the planet could compete with his in sheer brilliance.

Clement interrupted this reverie with, "We really should send the Americans a thank-you note. A man can hear himself think, now that the damned pumping station is quiet." He straightened, scowling at his work. "Energize," he repeated.

Mansour nodded, with a flick of the toggle. The rhythmic chug of diesel pumps had never been very loud here at the "dig," but these days they had fallen utterly silent. Crude oil no longer flowed from Iraq across the Syrian desert to Mediterranean ports. In this desert stillness, the *snick* of the cover plate proclaimed success.

"Thus far, good," Clement said. "Now we must run two hundred replications. See to it." Then that bewildering change of pace again, expecting his Arab colleague to understand instantly that he was no longer talking about NASA inlets. "It's much too large, you know."

Mansour did know. His design for the particle bed reactor was both too large and too heavy to be carried by Clement's djinni in its present form. "You know as well as I, it is the nature of nuclear reactors to be heavy," he replied. His first phrase was not strictly true; in the field of nuclear engineering, at least, Mansour knew more than Clement. "The enriched uranium alone weighs several kilos, and without the heat exchanger you would have a meltdown in midair, my friend."

"If I am to remain your friend, you must simply think harder, and quicker," Clement growled. Without another word, he strode off toward a lab entrance that, to external appearances, was no more complex than a horizontal mineshaft. A mineshaft containing the most deadly robotic devices ever built. Given another year and a handful of uprated djinn, Syria might become the only Islamic nation with a seasoned leader. Jordan's Hussein and Iraq's as well; Egypt's Mubarak; Iranians, Lebanese, even Libya's Khaddafi if necessary: any and all could be dispatched at will. And all this without tipping the Syrian hand. Anyone who suspected advanced weapons would hardly be squinting at Syria.

Mansour knew better than to reply to his superior and moved about beneath the tent, setting up for the replication tests, gazing toward the great freestanding stone pillars of the ruin on his near horizon. Ever since late January, when that Iraqi had defected across the border from his Abu Gharaib facility with a saddlebag full of lead-wrapped uranium rods, Mansour had known the pangs of stress. It had been one thing to theorize with Clement about stuffing a nuclear-driven laser beam into the djinni. It was becoming something wildly different to actually do it. Particle bed reactors had been built for space applications, but even those no larger than a suitcase had weighed nearly as much as a small man. And none of them, to Mansour's knowledge, had produced such brief ravening bursts of energy as Clement demanded. Of course, there was no denying that a laser would be a far more potent weapon for a djinni.

The original weapon, a rifle powered by compressed gas, weighed only five kilos and fired a pellet of bonemeal and sugar impregnated with a Bulgarian poison, chiefly ricin doped with curare. But its range was only two hundred meters or so, which meant that the djinni must descend so close that, in a quiet setting, its rotors might be faintly heard. It might even be seen, though as nothing more than a mote in the heavens. And any of its victims could protect himself from it with nothing more than a helmet and plastic armor. Oh yes, Clement was right to uprate the weapon; but with a nuclear-pumped sting?

Selim Mansour sighed and turned toward the lab entrance. He already knew two things that Roland Clement would eventually decree, and Mansour did not like either of them. One, the basket-sized djinni must be enlarged before it could carry anything like— the very phrase awed him—an invisible death ray.

And two, he must discard some of the failsafe devices that weighed down his tiny nuclear reactor.

THREE

March 1991

WHEN "SENIOR STAFF briefing in five minutes" resounded through the hangar's speaker system, Wes Hardin cursed under his breath. *Never enough time to build our spookships on schedule, but always time to get reamed out by Ullmer,* he thought, wriggling carefully from the unfinished fuselage of Spook 14.

His bitching was only halfhearted; his troubles might have been worse, and Hardin knew it. In most aircraft companies the senior staff included a dozen number-crunchers who'd mostly forgotten what it was like to bond a wing panel or take a brand-new bird for a test flight. Ben Ullmer often said that Aerosystems Unlimited couldn't afford to keep such expensive folks on its payroll, which is why senior staff numbered exactly four people. Old Ben was not only the president of the firm, he was also the principal designer of its high-tech aircraft. Hardin, still in his forties, held down several hifalutin' titles but spent most of his time running an assembly team. That's how you did it, Ullmer would drawl to anybody within earshot, if you cared more about building airchines than building empires. And through development of the silent, hovering Black Stealth One while a government employee and, later, producing the Coast Guard's high-flying Nemesis surveillance aircraft, Ben Ullmer had proven himself one of the world's best at building his beloved "airchines."

Stripping off thin latex gloves, Hardin ducked under the wing of Spook 14. Those throwaway gloves, used with advanced adhesives, had become as common in building ultralight aircraft as rivets

had been a few years previous. He made his way across the concrete floor of the climate-controlled building known to them all
simply as "the hangar." "Morrison," he called—softly, because
Colleen Morrison did not respond well to sharp tones—"I reckon
it's ream time."

She popped up beside him from behind a mold, tugging at a
glove with her teeth. A pilot and engineer with a background that
challenged Hardin's, Morrison led another assembly team. "I
heard," she said. She had to look up at him though Hardin himself
was of less than average height. "You know something I don't?"

"As always," he lied, and lifted a suggestive eyebrow.

"You don't know shit, Tex," she said, slapping his wrist with
the other glove.

He started up the stairs ahead of her, leering back. "I like to
keep my women ignorant," he half-whispered.

Morrison checked her riposte and Hardin chuckled, knowing
that Ben Ullmer found no charm in their constant sparring. Not
that the old Georgia cracker could have any doubts about the
fact that Hardin and Morrison split a duplex between them, nor
that they often emerged from the same half of that duplex on their
way to work. *He'd rather see us making calf eyes at each other. Like hell,*
he told himself, and stopped in the outer office long enough to grab
a chilled near-beer from the decrepit Amana.

Marie Duchaine, Ullmer's assistant, solved Hardin's questioning look with a glance away from her computer terminal. "Go on
in, you two. Be with you in a sec." Old Ben had stolen Marie from
the National Security Agency when he'd left, and no one doubted
that she was as senior as staff ever gets. Hardin twisted the top from
his Sharp's and then gestured for Morrison to precede him into
Ullmer's office.

Ben Ullmer, nearing seventy, had lost most of his hair but
none of his alertness. He had been staring out of a window toward
rain-sogged trees, a dependable view in early spring near Coos Bay,
Oregon. Now he teetered his swivel chair around and snagged his
desk with both hands, tieless in the usual dress shirt with sleeves
rolled, an antique Breitling chronomat on one corded forearm.
Peering over his half-glasses, he saw Hardin wait for Morrison to
enter. "Decorum? You must've lost a bet, Hardin."

"Nope. Just figured I could duck behind Morrison if you start
throwin' things," the little Texan said.

Morrison's grin, as she sought a chair, made her seem younger.
"He always hides behind my big heart," she confided to Ullmer.

Hardin snorted. "A chinchbug couldn't hide behind—" he began, then saw something ignite in Ullmer's eyes and raised his voice. "Marie! Mayday, Mayday. I'm declaring an emergency."

Marie swept in, svelte for a woman of her years and long accustomed to this family of hers. "I'll bet it was pilot error," she said without smiling. Marie also knew the game these men played: if you grinned, you lost. She played it well herself.

"Before you start, Marie," rumbled old Ullmer, "I've had my pill." He saw her nod. "Don't think I'll need it today, though; the news is good."

"Be still my heart," Hardin muttered, and Morrison kicked him, smiling all the while.

"But I'm still gonna throw something," Ullmer went on. "Unless you bozos can find some excuse why not, I'm throwing you a study contract."

"No sh— foolin'," Hardin said in surprise. Marie, he thought, must already know.

Morrison: "Who's prime?"

"It's not like that." Ullmer waved her concern away. "This is eyes-only stuff, strictly software, and there's no competition."

"That means government," Morrison guessed, her tone wary.

"That means very good money for two months' work," Marie put in. Oh yes, she already knew. . . .

Hardin cleared his throat for attention. "We talking just good ol' generic government or," he finished in a stage whisper, *"government?"*

Now Ullmer burst out, hands on his knees, glowering: "Awright, goddammit, it's NSA! And it could mean bonuses."

"Last time I worked for those honchos," Morrison said with a Nutrasweet smile, "I wound up crashing my spookship into a jungle lake. For a bonus I had to nursemaid Tex's collarbone—but hey," she said, the smile broadening to an idiot's rictus, "it's your shop, Ben."

Wes Hardin decided he couldn't have said it any better and merely said, "Ditto," with a casual salute toward his housemate. That little disaster in the Central American highlands had brought the two of them together, but their Nemesis mission had almost killed them both.

"I hope you two were listening when I said it's only software. A family of designs. Period. The worst risk you take is leaving some floppies out where the security guard can nail you. Or dropping a hint about it beyond the team members. I also told you it's eyes-only stuff," Ullmer finished.

"And you already have the team picked," Hardin accused.

As if switched on, Marie Duchaine consulted her Gregg notes and said, "Team manager, one Wesley Hardin; deputy, and propulsion, a certain Colleen Morrison; Jared Cutter can sign off for weapon subsystems and—well, Ben, I'm sure you know what you're doing on stress analysis."

Ullmer sat back with a wry glance toward Marie. "She thinks good stress folks all have to be old and gray, just because I am," he said to the ceiling. "And Petra Leigh is still in her twenties. She is also," he speared Marie with that gaze again, "quicker'n scat with a CAD program."

"Oh, yeah, that preppie from Brown with the legs and the heavy connections," Colleen said, her head tilting from side to side as if weighing an argument and finding it not worth the effort.

She knows Leigh as well as I do, Hardin mused to himself. *Why the sudd—aha: the legs, huh? Jeez, Colleen, give the kid a break.* All he said was, "Does she have a hot clearance?"

Ullmer paused, looking past them with some thought he did not voice. Then: "Oh, sure. Morrison, I grant that she got the job with pull. But that's not how she's keepin' it. She's good; just don't tell her I said so." He slapped his chair arms briskly. "Well, how 'bout it? I know we'll have some schedule slippage, but my thought was to split your shifts, half-days on your assembly teams and the other half on the, uh, drone study."

"That's what I was gonna suggest," Hardin said, and swigged at his bottle.

Morrison: "Sixty calendar days?"

Ullmer: "Yep, or less if the customer is happy with our stuff before that. Bonus country."

Wes Hardin waited for Morrison's decision, knowing what it would be, knowing too that she liked to think she led. When she gave a judicious nod, he said, "Like the lady says, it's your shop." He leaned forward, the fabric of his coverall stretched tightly across shoulders meant for a taller man. "So what's all this about a drone?"

"Well," Ullmer said, wagging his hand from side to side, "it is and it isn't. We'll get the parameters on scrambler line from Fort Meade when I accept the job. What NSA wants, according to Bill Sheppard, is a set of designs that describe a flying gizmo."

Morrison cocked her head. "You're telling us the No Such

Agency doesn't *know* whatthehell they want? I know those guys think they're so secret they barely exist, but this is carrying it to extremes, wouldn't you say?''

Now Ullmer began to chuckle, an almost falsetto squeak that they seldom heard. "I'll lay that one on Sheppard," he said. "I guess the answer is yes and no. We have enough to start: minimum payload and range, loiter and hover capability. They know they want it small and stealthy, too. But where flight surfaces are concerned, we can blue-sky it. That's why they offered us the study."

"If it's a drone, it won't have a pilot aboard," Hardin said, pointing with the neck of his Sharp's. "Not even a mission specialist playing Spam-in-a-can games?"

"I think your team will have to decide. I said a *family* of designs. Some may, and—"

"And some may not," Hardin finished for him. "There's a crapload, 'scuse me, Marie, of yes and no in this."

Marie shrugged while taking notes as if only mildly insulted, indeed as if she hadn't heard far worse in that office. "We'll know more when they scramble the fax stuff," Ullmer admitted, then frowned. "So what the Sam Hill are you two lounging around here for? Go build an airchine!"

Morrison had reached the doorway, Hardin on her heels, when she turned. "Tell you what: don't tell the Never Say Anything boys we accept: tell 'em maybe, and then again maybe not."

"Wouldn't even slow 'em down," Ullmer said morosely. "They understand that better'n anybody. But I have an idea Bill Sheppard knows exactly what this stealthy bird is s'posed to do. He just wants us to tell him *how.*''

FOUR

MARCH 1991

ROLAND CLEMENT WATCHED the white Mercedes stop below the slope leading to his lab entrance, forewarned that it was carrying Islam's most successful terrorist. Though he sat at his private console fifty yards inside the hillock, the same remote sensors that identified targets could give Clement a commanding view of the outside world. Rooms and corridors had been carved into the sandstone, then made secure with a bombproof ferroconcrete liner. The effect was that of living inside huge interlocking bubbles with flat floors, the rounded pastel walls glowing softly with indirect lights.

Clement recognized only one of the men who emerged from the Mercedes a hundred yards from the entrance tent. He had met the man no more than twice, but he had been carefully briefed on this visit and its hidden agenda. In any event he could not mistake that bulging high forehead, the pouty lower lip, the strong chin and the straight dark hair cut Western style. President Hafez Assad, once seen, was not to be forgotten. "Which of them will it be?" Clement muttered aloud, tapping at his keyboard as Selim Mansour left his side, hurrying to the entrance. A heavy scent of coffee wafted through the office.

The orders he had received from Assad had been a bit cryptic, but as a fifth man unfolded from the limo, Clement smiled. The stranger was dressed like a conservative Western businessman, taller than most and, like Assad, displayed no weapons. The other three would be bodyguards, then. A kilometer distant, two more white sedans blocked the road leading from the highway, an effective security tactic. In response to Clement's dancing fingers a set of red crosshairs appeared on the screen, proceeding at Clement's directions to rest on the image of the tall stranger, and Clement pressed *Enter* on his keyboard. He waited long enough to make certain the cross hairs had locked on, the tall man craning his neck to view the surrounding desolation. Then Clement saw the figure of Selim Mansour on the screen, striding into sunlight, a one-man greeting party. Enough; the target acquisition system needed no more data.

Clement blanked his screen before moving quickly to face his office mirror. The white lab coat, spotless, with sleeves turned back exactly two folds, brown hair neatly parted, a fresh shave; and as a final flourish, he hung safety goggles rakishly at his breast. If he delayed any further, he thought, he might give offense to the one man he must not yet offend.

Clement knew the importance of the next few moments. On this first visit to the lab, Assad must take home the impression of a flawless operation run by a world-class technical mind—which was, of course, nothing less than the truth. Had Clement stood outside waiting for the limo's arrival, one might think he took his research schedule casually. Had he waited for Syria's president to come to him in the lab, one might infer another truth: that Assad was important only as a means to Roland Clement's ends.

He strode down the main corridor unhurriedly because it pleased him to do so, silently counting off the seconds, then sped up so that he would emerge past the blast doors with all appearances of a hurry. His timing, as usual, was flawless. Preceded by two bodyguards, followed by a third, Mansour and the visitors were within twenty paces of the tent, Mansour doing most of the talking as they navigated the slope. *It's really disgusting the way Selim toadies to the man,* Clement reflected.

He met Assad with a hearty "salaam," following it with *"Ahlan was sahlan,"* my house is your house, and assumed that his Arabic accent worked. Assad, however, quickly responded in French. The Syrian waved his guards away before they could pat Clement down. "I hope you can feed an extra belly," he said—hardly a traditional suggestion, but the sort of gesture to mark him as modern—and clapped his hand on the tall man's shoulder. "Hamid Kharameh, with our Ministry of Economics. Doctor Clement is the man I have been filling your ear about all morning, Hamid."

Kharameh murmured his deference, though Clement thought

the man's bow showed that his awe, if any, was minimal. Modern handshakes completed their ritual before Clement noticed the unwavering stare of his patron tyrant, fixed on the tent.

"One of my assistants, Odile Marchant," Clement said softly as an attractive and slumbrous-eyed, olive-skinned young woman, her contours sleek in her lab smock, slid a tray onto the largest table under the tent awning. Assad remained still and silent as he watched the woman whisk a damask cloth from the tray, so the others paused as well. Then, "Odile followed me from France. She is the most meticulous computer technician I ever had; I would be lost without her," Clement added casually.

The spell broken, Hafez Assad programmed a man-to-man smile for the Frenchman. "A familiar touch in foreign climes? You are wise," said Assad.

He thought Odile was an Arab at first, Clement told himself. *And if he had hinted that he wanted her, what then?* Abruptly, he was angry because he knew the answer. He would have offered Odile Marchant's services without hesitation. Hating it, he would have nonetheless done it. His was a dependable fury; it followed each occasion when he must accept inferiority, as surely as thunder follows lightning. This time, he contained it.

Clement could feel a flush spreading across his ruddy features. He turned his face toward the tent with, "She also brews fine coffee," and led the way to the table as Odile, with downcast eyes, waited to serve them. Clement waited for his flash of rage to pass, focusing instead on Odile's demeanor. He had coached her in correct behavior with regard to Islam, and she was acting her part wonderfully. That was Odile, all right, able to play any role that pleased her. In sexual roles, she could entice a man in ways downright bewildering. Not that Roland Clement made frequent demands on her; he found more excitement in the right catenary curve he could master than in the sweet curve of an instep or a thigh that captured *him.*

With coffee came the inevitable small talk of Palmyra and Syria's faded glory, a topic on which Assad was as well versed as Mansour. The economist, Kharameh, chiefly kept his silence.

Clement found his opening when Assad spoke of the glory to come. "And with the most ancient weapon of all: superstition," Clement said.

Assad's brow clouded, then cleared. "Ah. The djinni? You may be sure, Doctor Clement, that educated Syrians will not be put off with that explanation. No, the real value of our weapon lies in its ability to eliminate a crucial man, at the time and place of our choosing. Not only for the man, but for the movement he leads, it amounts," he hacked downward with the edge of his hand, "to decapitation." His smile was gentle, almost euphoric.

"And no one will know whose hand wields the axe," Mansour put in.

"Sooner or later they will," Assad grumbled. "Western intelligence agencies, I am told, have begun to take more interest in a few isolated, ah, mishaps in these parts." He looked hard at the Frenchman. "I am a man without illusions, Clement. The West and the Soviets have their wizards too, and once they know enough about our djinni they will not be long in countering it."

My God, he is making my argument for me, Clement enthused, but the glance he turned on Assad seemed to be full of fresh surmise. "If that is the case, any outsider who knows my work too well might be considered an enemy of Syria."

Assad said nothing, but his openhanded gesture said, *There you have it.*

"There is such a man." Clement wished he could feign fear, though such ploys were the province of Odile. He did his best with an offhanded gesture of dismissal. "I can only hope no one approaches him about the djinni."

Suddenly, Assad became absolutely still. When he spoke, it was a whisper. "You have told some foreigner?"

"No, certainly not; that is, not after I developed it. But years ago in France, we shared ideas about weapons of the future. It was his conclusion that even the French government would not desire such a weapon as our djinni."

"You were both naive," Assad grunted; "you in your way, he in his. Who is he?"

"His name is Didier; I have known him since our student days in the *Ecole Polytechnique.* To sacrifice Claude Didier would be a great pity," he lied, with a sorrowful headshake.

Assad paused for a moment before asking, "Do you know where he might be—reached?"

Of course I know, you blundering raghead. "Not at the moment, but he could probably be located." Clement shrugged, and let hesitance creep into his question. "Are you certain it's necessary? Claude and I were quite close when I worked in Matra's development facility." *Close enough for the* salaud *to finally slander me.*

"He is a scientist like yourself, then," Assad guessed.

"Attached to the French government, but Claude Didier is

very much at home both in Matra and Aérospatiale of France. I fear that he would be a difficult target for, ah, conventional means."

"But not for a djinni," Assad replied, and looked at nothing for a moment. "Still, I am not ready to commit your operation that far from Syrian soil. Your own reports tell me you must launch and recover a djinni from some remote, isolated place. The entire country of France is too urbanized for a secure launch, I should think."

"Quite right. Except for French Guiana," Clement said. "Didier spends a good part of his time there when the European Space Agency is planning launches. That is where the orbital Ariane rockets are launched, virtually in a jungle on the northern coast of South America."

"Kourou, if I am not mistaken," said the despot, as if to remind them that he knew his current events.

"Near Kourou. I was born near there in Cayenne, you know," Clement said dreamily. "My father and sister are there yet."

"That, I did not know," Assad murmured, studying the scientist with fresh interest. "You maintain your connections there?"

Clement's shrug was perfectly French. "They are my family, m'sieur," he said. "Since my father cannot legally leave that province—a matter of youthful indiscretions that sent him there—he has made the best of it." No need to mention the archipelago of prisons that foreigners once knew, and Frenchmen feared, as Devil's Island; and besides, Clement did not relish discussing that part of ancient history.

"I will be blunt, Clement. Make no mistake: I am not pleased that Syria's most potent weapon may already be known to a foreign—an outsider," he amended. "Though that was before you came to us, therefore no crime I suppose. But this is a serious matter. We must settle this without delay and if you shade the truth, I will eventually know it. And I shall not like it."

"I understand," Clement answered, his gaze unwavering. "But why would I lie about such things? I have never tried to hide the fact that I was raised in Cayenne. After French Guiana became a province in full standing, I left with a full scholarship to Paris; the *Polytechnique*, in fact. I met Didier there. But I spent my first eighteen years between a humid jungle and the Caribbean, and of course while with Matra I returned home several times for research rocket launches."

Assad ended a long, pregnant pause with, "Do not take this as a commitment, but as a possible option for you to consider at some later date: how much help would you need shipping the djinni to Kourou?''

Not too glib, now. This is supposed to be a fresh idea for me. ''Well—I suppose it could be flown there in secret by a cargo aircraft. As you will see, the new djinni is larger to accept its new weapon, almost as broad as a man is tall. Better still, many firms ship odd devices to Kourou by surface shipping. One could let it be inspected at a port of entry without giving much away—so long as the nuclear material and the laser are not in the crate, of course. And it should be possible to reach some arrangement with shippers in Marseilles. Switch some papers to disguise its original port, I imagine. I am not expert in such things; your security men doubtless know more about that end of it than I.''

Assad toyed with his cup, nodding to himself. ''Could you move freely in the region?''

''I believe no one would consider it odd. I am not under suspicion there, if that's what you mean,'' Clement said with a smile. ''For that matter, Mansour or even Odile could sign for a few heavy crates of, say, a dismantled wind-powered generator. I would need a minimal crew, naturally. Four, including myself.''

''And you are certain this man Didier will be there?''

''No; I only know that he often flies there for extended periods, as I myself did.'' Clement timed his pause beautifully, as if reluctant. ''Are you quite sure this needs doing? And are you sure it would not be more easily done in conventional ways?''

''I am certain of very few things, Doctor. But on the heels of Saddam Hussein's great defeat, I am strengthening ties with France. Yet as surely as you are in line to lead all my armament research, the man Didier must go. As a practical matter, I think the work should be handled by Mukhabarat; as you say, they are the experts in such matters.'' Mukhabarat's expertise was aided by links to Libya, whose state security agency carried the same title as Syria's. Now musing, stroking his chin, Assad smiled. ''Still, I like the idea of him meeting his fate in South America. It would divert suspicious minds from Syria, you see.''

Clement registered mild dismay. ''Ah. Poor Claude. Well, I am sure your men will be able to do their work, even with a man as well protected as Didier.'' *And I shall simply have to seek other ways to escape this barren hell with my brainchild.* ''Have you a list of people for me that, perhaps, they have not been able to—reach?''

''Perhaps the madman Hussein himself,'' Mansour suggested.

Though Assad's eyes glittered with surmise at the mere impli-

FIVE

MARCH 1991

THE DJINNI WAS already humming like an animal, its gyros and the tiny propulsion turbine operating, when Assad reached the launch bay. "You may have noticed the crumbling stone tower atop this hillock," the Frenchman told him, without needing to raise his voice. "Well, it is not as old as it looks. This is what lies at its bottom." Assad's bodyguards fanned out into the well-lit bay, ever watchful, ever silent, curious only as to possible dangers to Syria's leader. Assad felt quite safe. It was abundantly clear that if harm came to him, his host would suffer luxurious agonies.

Noting the discomfort of the tall bureaucrat he had brought with him, Hafez Assad grinned in a way that was almost lascivious. Protected by sloping concrete walls, the vertical shaft before them was the width of a two-car garage, floored with concrete, surrounded by a many-sided enclosure of thick glass. Inside that enclosure, the patriot Mansour studied the digital readouts of a waist-high console through his safety goggles before reaching to detach a multiprong cable from its socket on the djinni weapon system. A similar console loomed on the near side of the glass within Clement's reach. The French scientist watched Mansour's operations carefully, judgmentally.

Assad was not watching Mansour. His eyes were roaming over the dull gray-blue contours of the djinni, which sat elevated on a fully ordinary plywood scaffold. That said two things to Assad, both of them good. *He is not wasting my money* and *this weapon system* cation of a better killing team than Mukhabarat, the big head shook slowly. "A defeated Saddam, still in place, is exactly what Syria needs," he said. "We have now become the pivotal power in this region, and I would rather have a weakened Saddam at my backside than a strong successor to him." He looked around him, with a glance toward Odile Marchant. "The coffee was excellent, and I am fully refreshed. Perhaps now we can have a demonstration of my invisible demon?"

"A sporting demonstration? Certainly," Clement replied. "Selim, prepare for launch. Odile, the target information is ready for input."

Though his staff hurried into the tunnel, Clement took his time as he followed, explaining the way pressure guns could spray repeated coats of concrete to line a set of underground cavities. The guards showed proper suspicion of side passages and Kharameh shuddered at the sudden drop in temperature.

Assad only looked, and nodded, and seemed to enjoy himself. "Very modern," he said. "Comfort without great expense. Somehow it seems entirely in keeping with a weapon that does with guile what the superpowers do only with enormous waste."

"Do you know what is most satisfying about it to me? Its efficiency," Clement said. "The absolute minimum of energy and expense. You need not pay a bureau of spies and assassins."

"Oh yes, I will always need an intelligence service. By the time a hostile leader surfaces, I need to know all about him. Including his face, eh, Hamid?"

Clement managed to avoid a glance toward the economist who, by now, seemed distinctly ill at ease. *He knows this is not kind of information he would ordinarily be trusted with*, Clement ized. Aloud he said, "Actually, we already have the face of S latest enemy. Quite recently," he added, and let his smile li Kharameh's gaze.

"I find it chilly in here," Kharameh complained.

"Perhaps I can make it warm enough for you," Cl At his side, Hafez Assad began to laugh.

does not need a vast array of support equipment. But the djinni itself occupied most of his attention.

In repose, the new version of the device appeared as a pair of perfectly circular, huge shallow bowls arranged to face each other lip to lip, perhaps an arm's depth from top to bottom. It sported a pair of rudders that reminded him of a Turk's scimitar, curving away from its upper surface, and it stood on three slender legs that scythed gracefully down from the lower bowl to support the little craft. Somehow those spindly legs gave it the look of an enormous insect—perhaps a scarab beetle. Several indentations in the ply-wood attested that the djinni's landing feet had made some heavy impacts when settling. No printed legends of any kind marred its dull finish, though Assad could see several slight protuberances and inlets on the shell and faint outlines that might hide access hatches in the djinni's skin. A man might have spanned the entire device with his arms, but in doing so he would lose both hands; where the two bowls met, the circumference was a blur of many short vanes, spinning like the blades of a very small windmill. "This is larger than I was led to believe," Assad murmured.

"Because the new weapon it carries is much heavier," Clement explained as the Syrian scientist, Mansour, left the enclosure and approached the little group, smiling. "If you bend your knees a bit, you can see the slot between the sets of levitator vanes."

A man looks ridiculous when squatting, Assad reminded himself, and ignored the suggestion. "Why more than one set, Doctor?"

"They spin in opposing directions and give much greater thrust. The term for that is contrarotation. Without it, torque—twisting force—would tend to make the entire lifting body spin, and we would need a small tail rotor to counter that torque. A much less elegant solution than this."

"Like helicopters." Assad nodded, pleased with himself.

"Exactly so. Though the djinni's planform is circular, it does have a front and a rear so that it is an efficient lifting body. To move forward in flight, the djinni's forward edge drops slightly—again, like a helicopter. The rudders steer from the rear, and those levita-tor vanes that lift our little demon have internal pitch adjustment. We have programmed the djinni for a local mission, as you di-rected, and I can send it on its way from this console, or from my office."

"How reliably can it accomplish those missions, Doctor? I have always noticed that the newer a technology, the more it is prone to failures." Assad, who considered himself an excellent reader of expressions, judged that this man Clement carried enough self-as-surance for a dozen men.

"The djinni"—Clement smiled—"is *my* design. We have tested it many times. It is powered by a well-developed French turbine scarcely larger than a bread baguette and its fuel supply lasts for perhaps four hours. Somewhat less, of course, if it must operate continuously at top speed."

Without glancing away from this bizarre device, so like the flying saucer of Sunday supplements, Assad said, "Top speed?"

"Limited, to conserve fuel and gain greater range."

"You have not answered my question," Assad remarked softly.

"Perhaps a hundred forty kilometers per hour," Clement replied. "Or ninety miles an hour, whichever you prefer. Normally it cruises at two-thirds that speed."

Assad cocked an eyebrow. "My Mercedes is faster."

"But perhaps a bit more easily spotted, a thousand meters above the ground?" Clement's riposte was barely a question.

Assad, long familiar with the kind of egotism that would challenge the will of Allah, thought this man's outlook a trifle too confident. Time enough to strip some of that arrogance from him—but this was not the time. "And its weapon; I do not see it."

"Fully enclosed," Clement said. "There could be a slight hazard to you if we exposed it this near. Part of the added weight in this new version is radiation shielding for the weapon's energy source. The reactor stays inside the lifting body, but the beam cavity and aiming laser must point at the target. It is always below, of course, but the djinni must stop and hover for a perfect shot. The beam weapon has its own little framework, and while hovering there is no reason why it cannot pivot out from the carbon filament casing—"

"And so that is what it does?" Assad interrupted with an impatient nod. "I would like to see it, ah, perform now," he said, with a glance toward Hamid Kharameh. "Wouldn't you, Hamid?"

The economist agreed, his expression suggesting that he was thoroughly ill at ease with the whole business. Clement seemed amused as he caught Assad's eye. "Would you like to dispatch your djinni? You launch it by flicking this," he urged, pulling a spring-loaded shield aside from an unmarked switch.

"I think," said Assad, "we will leave that honor to our friend Kharameh. Go on," he added to the reluctant Kharameh. "You are a man who likes to make things happen." Then, caressingly: "Or will you refuse me?"

Kharameh, after some hesitation, reached out and toggled the switch, and snatched his hand away at the result.

Only an iron will kept Assad himself from flinching. All three of the bodyguards snatched at their weapons, then relaxed. The djinni, no more than a few yards away, changed its hissing hum to a rising note and seemed to fairly leap from its platform, its landing feet snapping up to lie flush against its underbody. A swirl of dust motes contained by the glass enclosure dimmed their view somewhat as the djinni levitated straight up to disappear, accelerating steadily, up the shaft. Assad felt the faintest chill when he heard that muted wail rising up the shaft. *Now we know a djinni truly does howl*, he thought.

"We can watch from outside," Clement said. "Or from the video monitor in my office. The target, of course, must be outside."

As the men retraced their path through the lab, Assad twitted the foreigner again with, "I thought it would be more silent, Doctor. That is not exactly a stealth machine."

Clement, imperturbable: "Not in such a confined space, but in the open it is hardly noticeable. Actually, to identify a target among several similar shapes it will first make a low sweeping pass. That might barely be heard nearby, but at altitude . . ." He dismissed the complaint with a shrug.

Nearing the glassed-in office, Assad saw the Frenchwoman, Odile, intent on a console with a video screen. "Doctor, can you show us the target ahead of time?"

Clement paused, perplexed. "Why, yes, certainly. This is your wish?" At Assad's nod, his glance passed to Kharameh, then back to Assad as the men milled about just outside the office. "The reticle is already focused on that target in the video recording, however. There can be no doubt in anyone's mind, once I bring that video record to the screen. Ah—you understand, I hope."

But Hafez Assad found himself enjoying this game more as all the others became more reticent. "I understand perfectly, Doctor," he said, striding into the office with the others in tow. It was, after all, an office funded by his money. Ruling as absolutely as the ancient Syrian tyrant, Sennacherib, Assad moved with the confidence of a man who knew that this was *his* office, *his* lab, *his* weaponry.

The woman's fingers played at the keyboard for an instant, the screen now blank. She moved backward, eyes downcast, and murmured only, "Effendi."

"No, no, please proceed," he told her. "Marchant, is it?" The woman looked directly at him for a moment and nodded. *An ordinary man could lose himself in those soulful antelope eyes,* he decided, then smiled at her. "If Syria is to be modern," he went on, "she needs modern women. You do know what we are doing here?"

"I have been fully briefed," said Odile Marchant, her voice low and musical. Her glance swerved to that of Clement, who by now seemed to be awaiting orders.

Assad gave them. "Mademoiselle, please show us the recording of the target."

She hesitated, then gave Kharameh a wide berth as she moved back to the keyboard.

"Wait! It will please me if you direct Hamid's fingers. Let him operate the system," Assad exclaimed suddenly, in great good humor. He urged the tall man forward.

Hamid Kharameh moved like a sleepwalker, allowing the woman to take his hands, manipulating his forefingers although they were visibly shaking by now. At her bidding he punched several keys, then saw the screen flicker to synthetic life.

Assad moved nearer. "Ah; so that is the way of it," he said as he watched himself emerge from his car, then saw Kharameh as well. Presently a small set of red crosshairs winked into existence, proceeding jerkily to rest on the image of Kharameh. The crosshairs stayed on the tall man's image as it moved up the desert slope.

Kharameh turned, his mouth working, his face a grayish hue. "Effendi," he croaked. "I do not know—"

"The day you began to divert state funds to your own account, you knew." Assad chuckled. "Only a stupid man could fail to know the penalty, and you are highly intelligent, Hamid. You knew," he said again, nodding to himself.

"There has been a mistake," Kharameh said, now shaking so badly that he pulled his hands from the woman's and thrust them into his armpits. "Perhaps this is a great joke," he said, a shred of hope at the corners of his trembling mouth.

"Correct; the mistake was yours, and now the joke is mine." Assad smiled. He patted Kharameh's shoulder. "My friends must always be prepared to deal with my sense of humor, friend Hamid." Assad turned toward the Frenchman. "My compliments, Doctor, for a most instructive day. But I have much to do in Damascus," he added, glancing at his wrist as his gaze found the entrance tunnel.

His hand pressing gently against the back of Kharameh, Assad propelled him toward the entrance. He could feel the man practi-

cally vibrating with—what? Relief? Residual fright? By now Kharameh was mumbling to himself though Assad found the words inau-
dible. "In any case, Hamid, you may take this as a warning," said
Assad.

At the entrance, Assad paused beneath the tent and thrust his
hand out to the Frenchman. "I am more than pleased with what I
have seen, Doctor Clement," he began, then turned his head toward Kharameh. "Go on, Hamid. My men will see to your health."
He waved the men away, then turned back to Clement, who was
scanning the sky. Speaking softly, he asked, "Is this a good test for
our djinni?"

"Yes—unless he gets into that car. Those conditions could create problems of several kinds."

Now Assad turned again, and called out toward the retreating
men. "Hamid! Do not get into the car. If you try, you are to be shot
instantly."

If Hamid Kharameh had thought he was to receive only the
scare of his life, now he seemed to reach a new and horrifying conclusion. He jerked his head around, then began to scan the heavens
in a fruitless search, as the mouse might try to sense the descending
falcon. Then, suddenly, he was running; not toward the limousine
but in long bounds, heedless of the rocky footing, into the desert.
Hafez Assad began to laugh. Apparently, Kharameh had only just
realized that Assad's idea of a warning was not a verbal reprimand.
The city of Hama, now: *that* was a warning. . . .

Assad had to shout twice before his men lowered their weapons, his good humor fading with every step that Kharameh took.
"Doctor," he said after a moment, as the bureaucrat's legs continued to piston him away, "I do hope the joke is not to be on me.
If that thief gets away—"

Then he fell silent, the better to listen. A fluttering whirr
passed somewhere above, its source unseen. It might almost have
been the desert wind, but in any case it was gone in the space of two
heartbeats. The look Assad turned on the Frenchman must have
been too full of uncertainty, for Clement then strode from under
the tent into full sunlight as if to present an alternate target.

Clement: "The pattern recognition pass. It will fire from a
greater height."

Assad moved out to stand near the Frenchman. "Hamid has
turned an ankle, I see. If he covers his face now?"

"It will make no difference," Clement replied, watching as the
bureaucrat hobbled on, now hundreds of yards distant. "The djinni

is a true robot, you know; it interprets a target's behavior to predict its next movements. A target might just possibly avoid one bolt by a sudden move, but that has never happened yet."

When it came, the blast of ultraviolet energy from above was silent and invisible but its effects were dramatic. Kharameh, stumbling ahead, now reached both arms out; clasped his temples with both hands; took another step; then fell headlong, the long legs still driving. Now his left leg ceased moving, his left arm as well. Kharameh's right side seemed still to be functioning but in no useful way. In moments, the man lay still.

"A head shot, somewhat to the right of center," Clement said, coolly analytical. "The right side of the brain controls the left side of the body. A bolt of that power, impinging for less than a second, simply destroys much of the brain inside the skull, even liquifying it. The edema—swelling—is massive and sudden. Your target is already dead, even though the heart may continue to beat for a few moments. That is what we found with the goats we tested. Of course, a coroner would find the problem; but he would be unlikely to guess the whole truth."

Assad nodded, said, "Leave the corpse; they make the best warnings," and turned on his heel. He refused to look upward as he strode down the slope toward his car, thinking, *I wonder if Clement has a videotape of me in his files with cross hairs on my body. But I can find out easily enough. If he does, I will use him for target practice. Perhaps a wise move in any event, sooner or later—but not before I ascertain whether my Mukhabarat can, indeed, silence this fellow Didier. I shall give them two weeks to try.*

SIX

April 1991

PETRA LEIGH PUSHED away from her computer's keyboard to study the sketch on its screen, realized that she was chewing idly on a tuft of her honey-blond hair, and chided herself for keeping that juvenile habit. By far the most junior member of the Aerosystems study team, Petra remained self-conscious of her youth and worked hard to be taken seriously. "Hardin, how's this for dimensions? I've plugged in the stuff you gave me on the stub wings."

Jared Cutter, deep in some weapon calculation at his own desk, glanced at the figures on Petra's screen and then, evidently satisfied with what he saw, ignored them. Without getting up, Wes Hardin scooted his castered chair from his workstation to Petra's, passing Colleen Morrison en route. Though the team members could have worked farther apart, with headsets and networked computer stations, they had found that this more primitive and personal approach suited them best. It was Ben Ullmer who had said it: "Ignore any process like memos or daily schedule crap unless they work for you as a team. I'm keeping tabs, and when I cover your butt, it's bulletproof. Let me worry about progress reports, okay?" They had taken him at his word.

Hardin's shoulder brushed Petra's as he squinted at her handiwork. Morrison wouldn't like that, assuming she noticed. "Looks like the wing-loading could be a tad high, but go ahead and stress it out," he suggested. "Colleen will take it from there."

Colleen Morrison was not too intent on her own work to hear

every word. "I'm already waiting for that input," said Morrison, with the faintest edge on her words.

No you're not, Petra thought at her, nodding to Hardin as he moved away. *You're just sniping at me as a way of guarding your turf. As if I didn't have a man of my own. Oh, Morrison, if you only knew!* As Petra focused again on Beta Version, the odd-looking contraption on her screen, her mouth twitched at a private joke.

In some ways, she knew, the joke was on her. Two men were most influential in her life, and she would be childishly stupid ever to mention either of them. James Darlington Weston, her Uncle Dar, still had enough clout after his retirement from CIA Langley to get her hired by Aerosystems; the others probably knew, but to trade on that connection among the likes of Morrison would have marked Petra as a fool. To mention her other major influence would have been far worse. Most of her colleagues would simply not believe a word of it; and if they did, she might soon be facing a prison sentence.

Sure as God's my copilot, I wouldn't be allowed to keep this job. The job was crucial to Petra in two ways. It created the foundation for her career in high-tech design, which was obvious. But equally important, her position in Aerosystems brought her special priority items that, for most private citizens, were not to be had at any price. And priorities could not get more private than some of Petra's. . . .

The keeping of secrets came easily to Petra Leigh. It became more difficult when she grew intrigued about a gadget that just happened to be a matter of national security; tougher still when her lover was one of the few men who would have shared her enthusiasm. Beta Version, for example, was the second design by her team for a small unmanned aerial vehicle—in government jargon, a UAV. While Alpha Version had the look of a figure eight, like one wrecking ball sitting atop another with helicopter blades sticking out from its narrow middle, Beta Version was recognizably a scaled-down aircraft. At the tips of its stubby wings were long-bladed propellers that pivoted, so that it could hover with a helicopter or fly in the conventional way. *Very cute in principle,* she thought, *but as a structure it's a freewheeling bitch.* It was Petra's job to make sure their structures would not fail, and never mind that these odd little designs were similar to larger stuff. The Canadians had already flown something like Alpha; Boeing and Bell had proven that something resembling Beta could work. But here at Aerosystems, the team had already received fresh refinements from their customer, NSA. Those refinements made this study look more sinister by the day.

No doubt about it, their study no longer looked so much like designs for a prototype spy vehicle. Cutter had mentioned it first, with grudging agreement from Hardin after a lively debate. Morrison had suddenly agreed after the second ECO—engineering change order—from NSA. Now, Petra was catching whatever had infected them with suspicions. And to make it worse, she could not grumble about it outside that room.

But she could look ahead and wonder silently what Version Epsilon or Lambda might do, and with each of these Greek-lettered goblins she found that more of her enthusiasm was trickling away. Instead, she was starting to wonder whether she wanted any damned thing further to do with it.

SEVEN

APRIL 1991

O DILE MARCHANT HAD known little about Mukhabarat until Clement told her, chortling, that Syria's stellar thugs despaired of reaching one particular target in the immediate future. She knew even less about her impending trip to South America until three days before she began it. After a few seasons among a sea of sand dunes, she would have welcomed almost any change.

Unlike many programmers and mathematicians, Odile's soul remained more romantic than obsessive. While still in her twenties she had fallen, perhaps even crawled, beneath the spell of a brilliant technical man who filled her dreams with rosy visions, including the myth that he valued her as much for her computer work as for her real genius in bed. The fact that this man could be dangerously erratic lent excitement to a relationship that, she eventually realized, could have been a thundering bore. Though dreams die hard, they fade more easily. Perhaps, she reflected during her lone flight across the Atlantic, at last she would get a taste of the luxuries Roland Clement had been promising for so long.

When Odile's airliner reached the coast of French Guiana, she got only a distant glimpse of the famed Kourou launch complex—to all French-speaking scientists, the Centre Spatial Guyanais. Across this entire swath of equatorial South American jungle the common nuisance that defined the season, which would extend through May, was its leaking sponge of cloud blanket. Odile managed, through rips in that blanket, to discern the lush tropical rain forest. It seemed to carpet the whole region until her Airbus flared out for its landing at Rochambeau airport on the outskirts of Cayenne, a deep-water port sixty kilometers farther down the coast.

Because the airport and ground transport had profited hugely from the French space program, Odile's first impression was of a modern locale. Smartly turned out in a tailored suit, heels, and an expensive hairdo, she would have no trouble passing as a documentary filmmaker with Cinéma Recherche de France. Playing such elegant roles was Odile's métier, but the rain and the cloying heat had ruined the entire effect before she had walked fifty meters. Worse, Clement and the others were arriving separately so that she would have to see to all of her equipment by herself. Damn Clement anyway, for snarling that she had packed too many clothes! She had won that round by pointing out that she would have raised suspicions at Customs by *not* bringing several changes. The only good thing about her trip was that, flying directly from France, she would not suffer long delays at Customs. Still, Odile Marchant was cursing before she found a taxi large enough for her equipment.

Seated between suitcases nearly as large as she, Odile read directions off to the driver of the Citroen and settled back to enjoy the ride. They had not traveled far before she began to notice that, capital city or not, Cayenne's modern charms lay thin as veneer over an ancient colonial poverty. The driver earned his tip twice over, lugging her equipment through a constant drizzle into the lobby of the Hotel Epoque Deuxième, in the shadow of what passed for Cayenne's skyscrapers.

The Deuxième's concierge made it clear that it was her mountain of luggage, not her reservation, that gained her admittance to this flyblown palace. Odile kept her temper in check before the delicate insults of the concierge. The Deuxième, he said pointedly, was an old and respectable establishment.

It also had no hot water, she soon learned, but no one could have raised gooseflesh under a shower that was roughly blood temperature. Her third-story room had a window that did not open, facing windows of another hotel five meters away. *Perhaps,* she said to herself, *this is how guests amuse themselves when they discover there is no television.* When she had toweled off and donned fresh clothes it was still raining. Her wristwatch had evidently drowned in the downpour and could not be revived. When she felt perspiration trickling from her armpits ten minutes after a brisk toweling, Odile began to describe Roland Clement aloud in ways she had never considered before, and that was when she heard the knock at her door.

She opened the door a hand's breadth, exclaimed, "Roland," and then he was pushing inside, rain dripping from his hat-brim onto her shoulders.

"We have half an hour before Mansour arrives here," he husked, and reached for her as she bolted the door. "You know how prompt he is."

She knew. She also knew that Clement was randy as a goat, which meant all had gone well at the docks; and that Clement might have saved her a dozen maddening moments by having her travel with Mansour but for Clement's petty groundless fears that she might seduce the Syrian at first opportunity. And she knew above all that she had never been so infuriated at this infantile, brilliant, self-absorbed, manipulative genius as she was at this moment. "A half hour," she murmured, and moved against his barrel chest, pushing the coat from his shoulders until it lay in its own puddle on the floor. Take her for granted, would he? Well, he had handed her a velvet lash of time, and oh, how she would beat him with it!

"Not in these clammy rags," she whispered, still fully clothed after he stood before her, completely nude except for his Rolex, black oxfords, and black silk socks halfway up his shins. He had never been more ready than this, nor looked half so ludicrous, totally unaware of it as his gaze burned into her.

For many years, since her deflowering in student days, Odile had known her own genius: she could all but read the thoughts of a sexual partner. Once she had taken a man to her bed, or onto a bare floor, or into a pit of thistles if she chose, that man knew she was kinky as a box of fishhooks and would trust her to lead them both to ecstasy. Every time, and seldom quite the same way twice. Nor had she ever disappointed her lovers—until now. It was Odile's nature to be quiet, but not particularly forgiving.

After the long process of peeling his clothes off for him she began to strip for an audience of one, now lightly flicking the sleeve of her blouse against his erection, now evading his grasp with a giggle as she stepped from her skirt. When she took his hand and pushed him back on the squalling springs of the bed, he was trembling.

"Now," she said, stifling his objection with her fingers, "let me change into something special." He moaned with desire, but in this pastime he knew how to remain passive and lie there obediently. She rummaged among her clothes, with hot glances toward him now and then as she selected something lacy, something elastic, some things with heels like marlinspikes. Then she made a girlish wave, turning it into a stroking motion with languor that made his tip twitch. And swept quickly into the grimy bathroom with, "I'm all rank with sweat, *mon petit*. Let me wash the salt from your candy."

And with that, she took another shower. She soaped, and she sang a little ditty, and she made herself giggle like an ingenue, and all the while her mental clock was ticking. By the time she began toweling off, Odile was feeling much better, so much that her giggles were now unforced. Through the keyhole she could see Roland Clement, still reclining though part of him stayed erect, and now and then he would reach a hand down to toy with himself. Then she would rattle the doorknob to watch him jerk that hand away. *Manipulative* cochon, *I shall teach you manipulation*, she said silently, and now her rage had become joy.

Though a woman can dress herself as silently as a butterfly uncurls from its chrysalis, she can also give a listener an agenda with snaps of elastic, tic-tics of heels, and rustlings of cloth. Odile did these things as noisily as possible, with quick looks out the tiny bathroom window every minute or so. When at last she saw a familiar swarthy figure emerge from a panel truck a half block away, she opened the bathroom door.

She had once seen the German actress, Dietrich, make an entrance by first extending one long, elegant leg. Odile's legs were no less enticing, all the more so in a split skirt and opera-length stockings. By the time he saw the garter belt Clement was flexing his hands like a concert pianist; when she made her slow-motion prance to the bed she could barely see him through her slitted eyelids. And when she slithered astride his knees, someone's knuckles barked on the door to the hall. Her timing, she exulted, had been uncanny.

Even as Clement's forefinger flashed to his lips, Odile was calling, "A moment, please," to thwart him. She slid onto her side, giving him the most sorrowful look in her repertoire, followed by a perfect Gallic shrug. Then she was gathering his clothes swiftly while still lying down, and she managed to avoid laughing as she saw that Roland Clement's hands were now sticky.

She had seen his sudden furies before, but never vented at her. Teeth bared, his face crimson, Clement rolled onto her, one palm pressed against her mouth. His other hand flashed down her flanks, and during one blinding instant of pain she thought the man had torn her apart. Her scream, one gutteral bleat muffled by his hand, did not carry. Then he thrust away from her, and between the thumb and forefinger of that other cruel hand he held a single tuft of wiry blond ringlets: pubic hair, ripped from her body as if for a trophy.

His expression warned her not to cry, and she obeyed it, biting her upper lip. His pointing finger directed her to the bathroom, and she obeyed that order as fast as she was able. She found, to her surprise, only a few pinpricks of blood near the center of her pelvic arch. Her agony had been completely out of proportion to the physical damage, but in another way the injury was the sort that festers. Odile's weapons tortured sweetly. Clement's remained savagely primal. As she dressed, she told herself that he had acted without thinking. And knew that she lied.

EIGHT

April 1991

FOR THE HUNDREDTH time, Mohmed: I am desolated about your mother's condition, but you already know that you cannot call Syria from here," Mansour was saying as Clement approached the ramshackle work shed. Clement paused, listening.

Mohmed Ashraf, a lab assistant and the fourth member of Clement's team, replied in such rapid-fire Arabic that Clement missed half of it. He did catch *sick*, and *mother*, and *duty*, however, before the staccato blurt of a small chain saw interrupted.

Clement stuck his head into the shed as the chain saw died. "We will need those trees cleared by tonight," he said, and Ashraf grabbed a tank of fuel before hurrying toward the jungle that loomed like a shadowed green wall a hundred paces away. Between the shed and the jungle, giant ferns and young hardwoods were trying to obscure rotting stumps from the last human incursion, years before. Mansour watched the man go with relief etched on his face, then smiled toward Clement and shook his head. His expression suggested that Ashraf's complaint was trivial; that the new clearing inside the jungle would not be a problem.

Odile, still occupied in the pumice blockhouse with her breakfast chores, would complain as much as Ashraf if the converted farm shed was not made suitable for their electronic gadgetry. With few words, the two men began to line the inside of the shed with filmy plastic. The stuff had drawbacks, but there was no better way to create a dust-free, waterproof assembly bay on short notice. The term for such a place, a "clean room," was self-descriptive. The djinni, perhaps four feet in diameter without its vanes, squatted in the shed under its own plastic wrap. By dark, with luck, they would begin to insert vanes around its circumference to exact tolerances.

If Ashraf seemed genuinely upset to find that he would not have access to a telephone, Clement was not surprised. Nor had he been shocked to find a cellular telephone while reviewing Ashraf's equipment. It was a French unit, which might have made perfect sense in a French province, except that French Guiana's handful of cellular telephone users were restricted to a back-alley bandwidth maddeningly incompatible with anything else, anywhere. In any event, Clement had added smoothly, the possibility of interference with high-frequency telemetry for satellite equipment meant that personal radio-frequency traffic was monitored as well as restricted. Persons calling Syria on high-tech telephones from the jungle were likely to provoke interest from the DGSE, France's central intelligence group. In short, there must be no cellular transmissions from Clement's team.

Mohmed Ashraf had arrived in French Guiana the day before, two days after the others. Less voluble in Clement's presence, the man evidently was a nonstop complainer when Clement was out of earshot. In itself, this was hardly surprising; Arabs tended to grumble. But Hafez Assad's bureaucrats had found reasons to forbid Clement's other choices as a fourth member from his lab. It was clear to Clement that this fellow was performing double duty as an Assad spy, what the Russians called a political officer. Clement would have been surprised to find it any other way. When Ashraf finally found a telephone line to Damascus and explained his trouble with the cellular unit, some Mukhabarat flunky was going to be missing a few fingernails.

Ashraf, short and burly with a round shaven head, had been more useful in the lab for his brawn than for any special expertise. His French was good; his English, dreadful. And Roland Clement knew it would have been sheer madness to insist that his fourth member speak decent English. Assad would have wanted to know why.

Well, Clement would manage somehow. Already he had managed to relocate to this isolated Montsinery farm, property owned by his mother's family. It had electricity, but its lack of telephone service was a giant step in Clement's retreat from Syrian controllers. He ignored the drumming of rain on the shed's corrugated metal roof and smiled as he worked. He could almost sympathize with Ashraf's problem. A spy without even a telephone! In fact, that missing communication link might alert Damascus too soon, and so long as they stayed in French Guiana, Clement thought it might be well to allow a few calls to "Ashraf's mother." Meanwhile, Mohmed Ashraf had that hungry little chain saw, and all those thickset muscles, and a house-sized hole to clear in the jungle. There, they could prepare a launch site where it would not excite the curiosity of any passerby.

That rundown farm, a place he had vaguely remembered from childhood, had made everything simpler. Before he left Syria, Clement had known that his first base of operations would be here in the vicinity of Montsinery, some miles inland between Cayenne and Kourou. With the intelligence provided by Assad's people, he expected to locate his old colleague and betrayer Didier at the missile tracking site within the next few days. The space agency's tracking cameras, as Clement had known for years, were grouped on Isle Royale a few miles offshore from Kourou. And Clement's little band could locate Claude Didier without moving from the farm, letting the djinni create its own map from aloft before its more deadly mission.

Clement's Syrian lab contained adaptations of a very special bit of loot taken from the battlegrounds of Iraq: elements of the control system salvaged from an American cruise missile, perhaps the only stray from the Desert Storm conflict to fall without exploding. Clement, with Odile's help, had soon learned how the American robots found their targets. He had exulted to find that his own guidance system, while requiring many gigabytes of stored memory aboard a small vehicle, had certain tactical advantages.

The American cruise missile used on-board sensors to follow terrain features, creating a flight path already fed into its memory. This required a previous flight, either by high-flying aircraft or satellite, to create that memory. In Clement's system, the djinni itself created a visual memory with a preliminary flight. It did not need radar; it first followed a gyrocompass setting for a preset distance at roughly ten thousand foot altitude, letting its video camera record the entire flight path, which was instantly stored as well in its enormous electronic memory. Because its target area would be a few scores of miles distant at most, the small errors of the gyrocompass—perhaps three degrees or less—would certainly put the djinni within sight of the target area. Flying as a true robot entirely without external guidance, it could not be jammed by an enemy signal and it would return following the same path it had memorized on its way to the target.

Once the djinni had returned, visually recognized its launch site, and landed in its jungle clearing, they could remove its video camera and study the flight. It was Odile who would then feed in any necessary corrections to the djinni's visual memory. On its second trip, the djinni would be more heavily laden. It would proceed straight to the target area carrying its lethal weapon, to hover a half mile up while its optics scanned the area. This scanning pattern, called "rastering," would continue for hours if necessary. When the djinni recognized patterns close to its stored images of Claude Didier, it would make an identifying pass, climb again, hover—and scramble the brain of Didier like an omelette.

If Didier was very, very lucky, he would remain out of sight in the small buildings of Isle Royale until the djinni's clever little robotics sensed that its fuel reserve had become dangerously low. In that event the djinni would fly home without a kill, only to return with the dawn.

This need for ambient light was the djinni's major limitation. Clement found it a surpassing irony that his djinni fired an invisible laser beam with horrendous effects on a human skull, yet its optics needed *visible* light to recognize path and target patterns. A victim beneath a roof was no victim at all. A victim wandering about at night was equally safe. Clement knew there were ways around this, and fully intended to develop night vision for his stealthy demon. But that might take years, and he had waited long enough for his revenge against the arrogant fools in the scientific community who had labeled him dangerously out of control.

T hree more days passed, and with them another six inches of rain, before the djinni sat in its clearing, its levitator vanes a blur. "Have you ever seen anything so primitive?" Odile remarked as Ashraf helped remove the djinni's umbilical cable.

"All quite wonderful," Clement murmured, accepting her words as praise. The djinni's rough wooden platform rested on logs spiked to fresh tree stumps, and its rain cover was nothing more than plastic film stretched over a set of pivoting poles. *I can launch and recover my beauty in the worst of conditions,* he reminded himself, *without all the rigamarole that attends most launches.*

Then Mansour, kneeling at his makeshift console, called, "All systems nominal." Without being told, Ashraf swung the pole roof away.

"Goggles," Clement sang out, donning his own and, "Take

cover," kneeling behind the log barricade Ashraf had built. If the djinni should ever shed one of its composite vanes on takeoff, anyone in its path would suffer the equivalent of a tiny meat cleaver hurtling at hundreds of miles an hour. After a delicious pause, then: "Liftoff."

Mansour toggled a switch. The djinni's whirr became a soft howl that dopplered away as it climbed, leaving a momentary flurry of small particles—bits of bark, leaves, hapless insects—to whirl back to earth. Craning his neck, squinting into the overcast, Mansour said, "No ground winds to speak of."

During its vertical climb to cruise altitude, the djinni could drift with the wind. It was almost out of sight now, however, a faint blue circle dwindling silently to a dot overhead, then to nothing. Into his team's collective sigh, Clement made his announcement. "We will have most of this day for routine work. Each of you will tell me what is on your schedule." Odile, he thought, would probably want to clean that filthy house though he had other plans for her. Mansour, in all probability, would choose to assemble the tiny nuclear power plant. He knew beyond doubt what Ashraf wanted; indeed, he counted on it.

A half hour later, Clement sat in the truck with Odile, as Mansour leaned on the windowsill, his eyes troubled. "And how long must I remain here alone? The djinni will need maintenance when it returns, you know."

"It will survive with a rain cover," Clement replied, warming the truck's engine. "Ashraf," he nodded toward the shaven head in the front passenger seat, "claims he can catch a ride back from Cayenne after he sees to his mother's welfare." As the bald head nodded, Clement went on, "And Odile will accompany me to see my family. We may need a night or two, so that my visit will seem natural. It is absolutely essential that they know better than to call the authorities if some local farmer warns them of squatters here. You understand that, surely." *Of course he does, but Ashraf must understand it too.*

"And," said Mansour, "if I receive intruders I cannot handle in the meantime?"

"That should be simple," Clement replied. "Merely show them how the reactor works."

Mansour closed his eyes for a moment and sighed, understanding perfectly. "And then bury them, you mean. I will feel much better when Mohmed returns, but you are the director."

"And Mohmed will return before you miss him; eh, Mohmed?"

Ashraf's agreement had only begun, in traditional overstated fashion, when Odile leaned forward from the panel truck's interior. "If you delay us any further, Selim, I swear I will stifle in this thing."

Clement raised his brow and engaged reverse gear, and followed soft ruts out to the graveled road. For the moment the rain was in abeyance. Clement made good time for the fifteen miles into Cayenne.

The fidgeting Ashraf left them with ornate promises of his immediate return to the farm. "I would believe him sooner," said Odile, moving forward to occupy the front passenger seat, "if he did not swear to it so readily."

Clement lurched the truck up through its gears, smiling. "Arabic is a luxurious language, my dear, though you are right not to trust them. Loose-tongued, diseased, treacherous. Not like us at all." Clement did not care that his judgment included Selim Mansour, an excellent physicist who had never shown any of those unsavory qualities. Clement had spoken as a man wary of rivals.

Odile placed her hand on her director's thigh. "If you say so. I do hope we will have an hour or so before we meet your sister."

Her eyes were smoky with intent; perhaps she truly was as anxious as he to repair their little tragedy in that sleazy hotel. Reluctantly, he countered her suggestion. "That must wait, *ma coquette;* I have old business in Kourou. It may take a day or even two, possibly three. Meanwhile, we retain some luggage in your room in the Deuxième for emergencies. I want you to occupy that room until I call for you. No, no," he continued, seeing the sudden alarm in her face, "we have not been compromised." He went on in perfect calm, feeding her lies because he did not dare risk the whole truth yet. Neither of them would be welcome among his family due to old estrangements, he claimed, adding that he was only thinking of Odile. She had money, and a few days to enjoy Cayenne, he said. But on the stroke of even-numbered hours, she must be in the Deuxième room, in the event of a sudden change of plan. This, for Clement's paranoia, had the added advantage of making any trampish behavior on Odile's part an impractical matter.

When he had finished, they were a block from the hotel. Odile kissed him soundly before getting out, a sly smile on her lips. "I know why you want me here," she said, almost shyly.

"But I have told you," he said.

"That is not your reason, Roland. You simply do not trust me alone among those Syrians."

"Well," he said, and shrugged. "It is still for your own good."

She laughed, flirted her hair, and walked off down the street without looking back.

And an hour later, Clement had purchased his air passage from Cayenne by way of Caracas to Bogotá, Colombia, with a final leg by smaller aircraft to Medellín.

NINE

April 1991

I F THE NATION of Colombia were a pitcher full of drugs, its geographic spout would be neighboring Panama. The city of Medellín lies in a cordillera valley near that spout, pouring out enough cocaine annually to derange the Western Hemisphere while making a few Colombians staggeringly rich. Chief among those drug lords was, and remains, a curly-headed, potbellied fellow given to casual bright shirts and a villainous mustache. He is a legend among traffickers in Marseilles, where Roland Clement obtained a contact to the man's organization. Magazines preoccupied with money list him as one of the world's wealthiest men. At that time, he occupied a posh prison built to his own specifications by a government glad to have him behind bars on any terms. His name is Pablo Emilio Escobar Gaviria.

On the day Clement deplaned in Medellín, Pablo Escobar's people were in tender negotiations with Colombian authorities, hoping to avoid the billionaire's extradition to the United States. The U.S. charges ranged from drug traffic to premeditated murder. Clement did not care about those negotiations.

Clement cared about negotiations of his own, and about the nervous habits of the armed thugs who, within hours after his arrival in Medellín, had blindfolded him in a taxi, driven him to someone's villa, and subjected him to various indignities. Somehow Clement had never seriously considered hiding weapons inside his body, but Colombians obviously had. Either that, or they simply expected to make him feel dehumanized, less confident. If the latter, they grossly misjudged Roland Clement.

After a night locked in a windowless room, Clement gained an interview with a spiffy gentleman who may have been a lawyer, or simply a better grade of thug. He was clearly not the very best grade, however, for he spoke no French. He said, in excellent English, that there was positively no chance of a direct confrontation with el señor Escobar. However, this meeting was being videotaped. El señor would see the result. Over an excellent breakfast, Clement and his interviewer got down to cases. Yes, he really was Roland St. Helie Clement, a ranking scientist in the aerospace community. No, he was not currently acting for anyone more highly placed than himself. No, he had not been sent by any agency. And yes, he thought he might lend his talent to Señor Escobar's business.

What was his talent? Here, Clement faced the man with the silk tie and the recent shave with a self-deprecating smile. "I can cause a man to die instantly, a hundred kilometers distant, without hired assassins or telltale clues."

The man blinked, paused, and asked more questions. The victim, Clement admitted, would die with a tiny hole in his skull. No bullet, no noise, no smoking gun. A Colombian judge? Certainly, given enough pictures of the man—preferably closeup video footage. Without high-quality pictures this aerospace weapon could not function. And given two million dollars in cash, of course; half on assignment, half on its completion. Two million was the minimum for a group of topflight aerospace colleagues in work like this.

Now the spiffy dresser seemed to relax, having reached common ground. A Colombian judge could be had much more cheaply than this with *sicarios*, willing lads in the slums, but some victims might be more difficult. *El Presidente de los Estados Unidos?* Easily— but for a hundred million. Clement made it clear that he would be amenable to repeated contracts. Why come to this benefactor of the poor, el señor Escobar? Because, Clement replied, no one had a better reputation for payments due, or could pay a needy scientist better. No, not even the American mafia. And if such technology was indeed at Clement's fingertips, what might keep him from using it against Señor Escobar himself?

"My intelligent self-interest." Clement smiled. "Sooner or later, headlines alone would convince el señor to become my *patron*. It is not every man who can employ an invisible demon."

"*Un demonio,*" the fellow muttered, rubbing his forearms to make the hair lie back down. "And if my *jefe* chooses to decline this—business proposition?"

"Then in all probability I will not leave here alive," Clement admitted softly, following this with a lie: "And my colleagues will know we have been rebuffed. They will select a new leader, and do business elsewhere without me." He had not actually claimed his colleagues knew where he was; let the Colombians draw their own conclusions.

His interlocutor's smile was distant, though not unpleasant. Clement thought the man's aplomb faintly askew as the interview drew to a close, and this encouraged him. Without any question, the cartel would have voice stress analyzers to check that video-tape. *Well and good. I have told no lies, made no overt threats, given nothing away.* And if they drugged him to extract more information, that might be an advantage too. The most important thing they would learn was his absolute confidence that he could deliver.

Still, it was a pensive Roland Clement who spent the balance of his day alone, relaxing behind high walls in a lavish sunlit garden.

With the evening came another exquisite meal and to help him eat it, the man who had served as Escobar's proxy. Nothing of quite this sort had ever been offered, the man said, sampling a wilted lettuce salad. "But let us posit that a Colombian, a traitor to his friends, enjoys the safety of an American prison. Who knows what questions he is asked, or how damaging his answers?"

"That, I cannot say," Clement replied. "But if your traitor can be seen from far above, and if we have suitable photographs, I can say his answers need not continue." The squab really was excellent, Clement decided.

"We would prefer that they stop," said his dinner partner, allowing the succulent sauce to spot that silk tie. "His name is Guillermo Borges. He is held in a place called La Tuna, in the American state of *Tejas* near El Paso. Señor Borges has proven difficult to—ah, reach. My *patron* considers him an ideal test case. Do we understand one another?" Another spot from the sauce; but then, Clement judged, squab is notoriously difficult to handle using cutlery.

Clement, with surgical skill, dismembered his tender squab and smiled. He had known he would make his move northward eventually, where most of his enemies lived. But to receive funding so soon was beyond all expectation. "We have a contract," he said, "when I receive the advance and first-rate pictures. And you, of all people, will understand why I need safe passage for my little team at crucial points in our travels. After we fulfill the contract I shall contact you for the remainder. If we cannot fulfill the contract, the million will be returned."

They spoke of Guillermo Borges and of travel for a time, pursuing their meal as if food, and not a particularly barbarous form of murder, were their primary aim. By the time Clement had polished off his dessert soufflé, he felt sure that he would receive better treatment upon leaving than he had on arrival.

Clement declined the offers of women and his drug of choice before accepting the thing he wanted: a suitcase with twenty kilos of American cash. The following morning he accepted a VHS tape and several glossies, all featuring one Guillermo "Billy" Borges, whose capture by the Americans had resulted in much media play the previous year. Pablo Escobar, as a host, could not be faulted. His proxy offered free use of an executive jet back to French Guiana. This, too, Clement declined, preferring to keep a correct tally on his passport stamps. He did not mind carrying that suitcase with him. Thanks to the dependable lack of concern by South American airlines, he was not challenged when he flew back to Cayenne.

Though Clement kept watch as always for suspicious vehicles behind his panel truck as he drove away from the air terminal, a leisurely drive around the city convinced him that he was not followed. Only then did he call the Hotel Epoque Deuxième. He told Odile Marchant that he had never felt better in his life, and that this time they had more than a half hour. "All the same," he added, "please complete your toilette before I arrive, this time."

TEN

MAY 1991

I N HIS ROLE as deputy director for the National Security
Agency, Dr. William Sheppard had learned how to smell trouble
over a fax line. With a study contract, sometimes it stank like
incompetence. Now and then it reeked of dishonesty. In this case,
he did not believe it could be either of those because Ben Ullmer
was both competent and honest to a fault. It smelled, Sheppard
thought, like smoke. *And God knows, over the years Ullmer has built
enough fires,* Sheppard reminded himself. He did not wait to find out
what was burning, because that study contract was getting hotter
all by itself. He merely let Ullmer know he was coming.

He could have snagged a ride on fast military aircraft. Instead,
he chose the cheap option to the Oregon coast, a commercial flight
via O'Hare to Portland, then to North Bend Municipal on one of the
cramped little Horizon Airlines craft that Oregonians called "Air
Conduit." Because the Coast Guard and NSA are on very friendly
terms, the last leg of Sheppard's trip was a short hop in one of the
big helos stationed at the nearby North Bend coastie station.

It was hard to believe that the Coast Guard's high-flying
Nemesis planes, among the world's most sophisticated aircraft,
were built in Aerosystems Unlimited's dual-hangar structure that
squatted in the shadow of Douglas firs less than twenty miles from
North Bend. The simple blacktop airstrip was too short to accomodate anything but ultralight craft and, of course, helicopters. Sheppard snugged his tweedy old jacket lapels tight when deplaning and
walked quickly through a coastal sprinkle to the employee en-

trance. As usual, an Ullmer operation wasted no expense on facades.

The security at Aerosystems was spartan but good. Within seconds after he walked into the Black Box, the room where Ullmer's team dreamed up their unmentionable devices, Bill Sheppard knew that his nose for trouble had not misled him. He tried to ignore it. "Old home week," he said, grinning, using his trick memory to name people he had not seen for some time. "Wes; good to see you. And Colleen; feisty as ever?" If he had not thrust his hand out, he suspected, they would not have offered to shake it. *Good Lord, what now?*

"Doctor Sheppard," said young Petra Leigh, who looked as if she would have liked to hug him. Her handshake, at least, carried some enthusiasm.

Old connections are a mixed curse, he reflected, and beamed his approval as he took her hand. "Been a long time, Petra. And Cutter! I knew you were all on this study, but in person it's a bit overwhelming."

The *snick* of a door latch behind him said that Ben Ullmer had just entered, and Sheppard turned, the smile still working hard.

"Get ready to be underwhelmed," said the old man, his handshake more friendly than his face. "We're winding it up." Ullmer turned toward his team members, who seemed to be milling about in a room too small for it. "Siddown, for God's sake, the man thinks we're about to stone him."

Sheppard, physically a small man whose bow ties and academic clothing made him look more formal than he was, parked his rump on a vacant desk and let his smile dwindle to nothing. Ullmer waited until the others were seated, then took a seat of his own. "Just for the record, Doctor William Sheppard here is a deputy director at NSA. You've been working for him, as I'm sure you know. And now you don't want to. And I agree one hundred and one percent," he said, letting his glance glide to Sheppard. "My folks aren't dumb, Bill. You swore this was something we could do in good conscience; a surveillance drone."

"That's right." Sheppard nodded. And saw at least two heads shaking silently. *They know. But they can't know it all, not yet. I was hoping it wouldn't come to this. . . .* "Look, I can see you're all pretty glum about something. Forget titles and ceremony, and talk to me as plain Bill Sheppard. You've been doing great work up 'til now. Impressed my people at Fort Meade."

"But you're not plain Bill," Ullmer injected. "You're front man for an agency that can pretty much fund any damn' thing it wants to, without congressional approval. And now you've got us designing stuff none of us could sleep with.''

The least I can do is try. ''A lot of prelim schemes for surveillance,'' he began.

''Back-shooting robot soldiers, you mean,'' Ullmer accused. ''All those ECOs you've been faxing us: you think we're that dumb we can't spot a weapon system?''

Sheppard could feel the flush coming to his cheeks. ''Those engineering change orders aren't our idea, Ben. I can't even tell you whose they are.'' *Because I don't know!*

Now Ullmer was waving a forefinger back and forth, his words metronoming with that finger. ''A hundred times I've heard that crap, hiding behind need-to-know. Well, Bill, we've damn' near had some resignations over this. There are plenty of folks who'll design robot snipers for you, but Aerosystems doesn't seem to have any of 'em this season. Some things we don't wanta do, and a little bitty assassin bird is one of 'em.''

''Neither do we,'' Sheppard countered.

''That ol' dog won't hunt,'' said the Texan, Wes Hardin. ''You boys at Fort Meade have done lots of things you claim you don't want to—but you did 'em. See, *we know who you guys are,* Doc.''

''I was 'Bill' when you flew me over Mexico, Wes. I still am.''

''Wait a minute.'' Colleen Morrison's husky contralto was imperious. ''Are you telling us you don't expect anybody to build some verson of this thing?''

''I can't answer that, as phrased.''

Jared Cutter had been sitting back, hands clasped behind his head, and Sheppard knew Cutter was the weapons specialist. No wonder that Cutter took up the questions with: ''Doctor Sheppard, do you know about the ECO we got day before yesterday?''

Sheppard closed his eyes for two beats. ''Ah, seventeen, wasn't it? New volume and mass requirements.''

''Yes, for a nuclear-driven ultraviolet laser. Jesus Christ, Doc, an aerial nuke-powered zapper! Can't put it any plainer than this: I want out.''

A nod from Colleen, and after a moment's hesitation, from Petra. Ullmer cleared his throat for attention and got it. ''But we've done a lot of work, Bill, and certainly I intend for you to have it. We just don't want to pursue this any farther. Imagine having a fleet of those goddamn things hovering around. Now I know how Robert Oppenheimer felt when he wanted out of the H-bomb program. It get back. Not my idea of a stealthy bird. I take it the thing is stealthy enough that it's still a black mystery?"

"Deep black. In no case has any witness seen or heard any-thing—no, cancel that. HUMINT from a sister agency reports that a Syrian taxi driver supposedly heard the wind moan like a banshee, or the Arab equivalent, shortly before something killed his client in an abandoned ruin. That was one of the poison slug killings, we're pretty sure."

"Any eyewitnesses to the killing at Kourou?"

Sheppard folded his arms and stared at nothing, as if trying to place himself at the scene of the crime. He recited it slowly. "Actually, it was a dozen miles from the mainland. This man Didier was walking across uneven ground on Isle Royale, near Kourou, between two telemetry specialists. He was talking, and then suddenly he gasped in midsentence. When he fell, they thought he'd just turned an ankle. But a sprained ankle doesn't turn a man's brain to tapioca. His eyes were dilated, central nervous system failure, only brain-stem functions for a moment or so. And neither of his companions saw a beam, and neither of them picked up any residual radiation. Neither did Didier. While walking shoulder to shoulder with two friends, the man just died," he finished, indicating the event's abruptness with a finger-snap that made Petra jump.

"Mighty good shooting," Wes Hardin observed.

Cutter thought about that for a moment. Then: "So good, I think we can rule out a human marksman anywhere in the system. My guess is, maybe it's an optically aligned ultraviolet laser. Invisible beam, but more efficient than X ray. A lot more energy against the poor bastard's skull."

Ullmer maintained his own silence. *These kids are quick as scat, don't need me to bias their ideas. Hardin and Morrison now, they don't give a shit who I am.* There would be plenty of time later for critique, anyhow.

"Beta bird looks a bit large and gimmicky, but there's a reason for it," Sheppard was saying. Obviously, he knew what the aircraft looked like. "I'm just as interested in how the bird picks its target. A live operator nearby, for example, with a power designator beam."

"State-of-the-art stuff already," Hardin injected. "But it for this kind of mission, and the designator beam would by Captain Marvel. I think Cutter's right."

"There's got to be a simpler way," Colleen muttered. "I mean the hardware might be complex as hell."

wouldn't be long before somebody else got crackin' on something like it."

Well, I can make need-to-know decisions. Play it straight, Sheppard, he urged himself silently. He took a deep breath. "Ben, somebody else already has them. And we don't know who."

"Oh, my God," Petra whispered.

"We're finding out more about it because it's already in use. Every time they use it, we get a hint," Sheppard went on, dully, as if admitting some terrible misdeed of his own.

"Shit fire and save matches," Ullmer said softly. "These ECOs are to pass on what you're learning from day to day?"

Sheppard nodded. "Evidently there's more than one weapon system developed for it. We thought it was confined to very short range in the Middle East, shooting poison pellets, until a few days ago. And that's all I can tell you unless you're prepared to continue the study. Not even its code name. Oh yes, it already has a classified name," he added. "Savagely appropriate."

He offered to leave the room when the team members began to talk among themselves. To his relief, they seemed to want him present. For the next five minutes, Bill Sheppard worked hard to keep his silence unless directly addressed. Even then, he gave them little more.

Eventually Ullmer asked the crucial question: "So it looks like we're trying to dope out how the thing looks and what it can do, and maybe what it can't. Right?"

"Exactly."

"So we can figure out how to counter it?"

"I devoutly hope so," Sheppard said gently. "We don't intend to build anything like it. This country isn't in the assassination business. But can you see why the Secret Service people are having nightmares right now?"

Dead silence for a long moment. Petra broke it with, "I think I'd like to change my vote."

"From the mouths of babes," Colleen responded, but her nod toward Petra was approving. "I guess I'm convinced; my conscience insists," she finished.

Hardin and Cutter exchanged looks. Both ex-military pilots, they had struggled long and hard over their ethics. "Sorry, Wes," Cutter said at last. "I can't chicken out of this."

"Sorry, hell." Hardin snorted. "So we were wrong. So let's get right." He glanced at Ullmer. "If Ben will go along . . ."

"Couldn't have said it better myself," Ullmer replied. "But you can't leave us hanging out to dry like this, Bill. We really do need to know a lot of shit you haven't been sending us. For instance, we're gonna have to figure out which countries are capable of building this assassin robot. Certain hotshot designers have a kind of design signature. Just glance at a MiG and you know it's from Mikoyan's shop, you know?"

"You're absolutely right, Ben. We've just been trying to compartment this thing."

"To the point of paralysis," Ullmer charged.

"That's the risk," Sheppard agreed. "On thing you'll want to know is, five days ago a French subminister dropped dead near the ESA launch facility in French Guiana. Fellow named Didier."

Ullmer's head jerked up. "Claude Didier?"

"That's right. You knew him?"

"Met him a coupla times." Ullmer shrugged. "One of those froggy doubledomes who knew ever'body. More a generalist than a specialist; had a lot of admirers in Dassault and Matra. You attend enough international conferences, you get to know who's hot and who's not. I'd say Didier was middlin' hot."

"From the reports, we think it could have been an aerial assassination. That's why we're worrying about a really hideous little weapon system, Cutter. Something—different."

The weapons specialist opened his mouth; closed it; then glanced at the two women. "Mind telling me the effects?"

"Yes, but I will anyhow. A little hole, only millimeters wide, down through the skull. And it doesn't exactly burn its way down; with enough power, a laser sort of flakes things away."

"Spalling," Cutter supplied.

"Yes," said Sheppard, and swallowed hard. "It happens in a fraction of a second, apparently without much noise or visible light. When it gets down through the bone to gray matter—well, the shock wave literally homogenizes part of the brain."

Petra Leigh spoke quickly, perhaps to rid herself of a grotesque mental image. "So either it's an orbital weapon, or it can fly to South America."

"That, or it's now based there," Ullmer put in. "And by the way, what the hell is that code name?"

"At Meade," Sheppard told him, "we refer to it as the Butcher Bird."

ELEVEN

MAY 1991

BEN ULLMER DIDN'T recall which playwright had what's in a name, but he knew the answer was Once his team accepted that their job was to de Bird, not to promote some nameless horror, they b Sheppard with more friendly queries. Within had Sheppard watching a screen over Petra Le

"No, I hadn't seen these latest drawings ted, studying their new Beta version of a rotors at the tips of its stub wings now gine, buried in the fuselage, sat below the mouth of a manta ray. "Isn't th

"My input," Cutter told him kind of power source that's com energy, since lasers are ineff twenty thousand watts of la few *million* watts to drive

"And since efficien you're giving it a wa hurry," Sheppard sa

"Got to—or b ter went on, "I s to drive an X-ra nobody would be would not only atomiz mushroom cloud overhea

"You bet it would," Sheppard agreed with fervor. "Cutter, you might take a look at the optical resolution of our Keyhole satellites. If a KH-14 can read a license plate from orbit, what if someone else has something just as good in the Butcher Bird? That implies a very, very expensive bird," Sheppard said. "So pricey its owners wouldn't sacrifice it. And far too sophisticated for any but a handful of nations."

Petra, with a quick tapping of keys, invoked ghostly lines of internal structure to the drawing. "That's a roger," she said. The structure spoke for itself; complex, wildly expensive stuff.

For somebody who doesn't even own an airchine, thought Ullmer, *that kid talks a lot like a QB veteran. Oh yes, Petra Leigh is more seasoned than she lets on.* Aloud, Ben said, "What does an on-board nuclear power source do to its propulsion, Colleen?"

"The usual; more mass to carry means a bigger engine." The woman shrugged. "Bigger fuel tank, bigger everything. You know that old struggle better than I do, Ben; we sure had to fight it developing the Nemesis."

With a sigh, Sheppard stood up and rubbed the muscles in his neck. Pointing to the screen: "If that turns out to be close to the right planform, it may be the Israelis behind it. Some of their UAVs look a lot like that. The question is, how advanced are their laser optics?"

"That's a phase of this study we haven't even addressed," Hardin announced. "Bill, you say the damn' beam weapon is already operational. If you're abso-by-God-lutely sure it's not a U.S. product . . ."

"Sure as we can possibly be. Hughes, Lockheed, Boeing, Northrop, even Sandia and Lawrence Livermore. We've identified their people who might conceivably cobble up such a bird, we played the paranoid games right to the end, and there's just no way," Sheppard said with a smile that Ullmer thought a bit sad. "So let's try a new approach: if it's a Mikoyan bird, how is it likely to look? If it's Israeli, how would it differ? Every nation that could field a Butcher Bird would have its own unique range of options."

"Its own national signature," said Ullmer, who had been silently mulling that question over for some time. "And that has a political side to it. If I know the cover-yer-ass part of the equation, Bill, you guys at Meade already have some Company analyst figuring out which bunch of bastards wants to do what this bird is doing. We need to have their input," he added.

"CIA is in the loop. You wouldn't believe what they think."

"You'll just have to try us," Ullmer challenged.

Sheppard folded his arms, meeting that challenge with the faintest of smiles. "The Kourou anomaly, as they call it, doesn't seem to fit the previous events. But remember, there have been several earlier cases to factor in." With a headshake, as if to distance himself from what he was about to say: "Politically, they think it fits an Islamic pattern."

Ben Ullmer laughed outright. "Ayrabs?" he boomed in jovial disbelief.

"Not," said Petra, with a teen's drawled inflection that brought chuckles from the others.

"Let's hope you're right, Petra," Sheppard urged. "I admit it seems farfetched—even fanciful."

"Whole effin' scenario seems like it was fetched from the Oort Cloud," Ullmer growled.

It was Cutter who had to ask: "Fetched from which?"

And Sheppard who had to tell him, grinning, "The Oort Cloud—where comets come from. Barely in the Solar System, and that's pretty farfetched, I'd say."

"I gotta remember that one," Hardin said.

Sheppard's grin was fading now. "While you're at it, remember this: if the Butcher Bird has already crossed the Atlantic, who's to say it can't cross the Gulf of Mexico?"

TWELVE

MAY 1991

LOOKING BACK ON his first few days in the world of the infidel West, Mohmed Ashraf later decided that his misgivings had been omens. No wonder this far-flung piece of France had begun as an annex of an island penal colony! Sequestered on the edge of a steaming jungle, he longed for the familiar dry heat of his native Syria.

Worse than the climate, Mohmed felt torn between his priorities because he served two masters. It was almost as if he had no master, and Mohmed strongly endorsed the Arab proverb: *Better to live forty years under tyranny than one day in leaderless chaos.* Had French Guiana been a sovereign nation, he might at least have been able to contact a full-fledged Syrian embassy nearby, with its Mukhabarat officers and secure telephone lines to Damascus. Mohmed's mother, of course, was not sick. She had been dead for years. It was Mohmed who would become sick if he did not keep the illustrious Assad informed of what was really happening in French Guiana. On the other hand, Mohmed had found nothing seditious to report.

At least, he reflected as he helped Mansour repack the heavier parts of their equipment, in his second call he had been able to verify one piece of good news. There had been no doubt of their success when, after one fruitless mission by the djinni, the little weapon system had returned with traces of radioactivity on its hide and a videotape of its kill. As the videotape proved, the djinni had loitered over its target area for nearly two hours to make that kill. Its turbine fuel tank was almost empty when it landed.

Clement had replayed the tape several times, sharing his moment of success with his team. For a man forced to scramble the brains of an old friend, Clement had shown uncommon glee. The French scientist had lingered over the sight of a tubby little fellow in shirtsleeves, foreshortened by the steep angle of the camera's view, who abruptly collapsed between two companions while walking on Isle Royale.

Now it was Mohmed who felt a surge of hope, because he was helping dismantle the djinni's innards. Very soon now, Mohmed felt, he would relish the Syrian variety of heat again. "Bring up the magnification," Mansour said, his hands encased in remote manipulators like skeletal gloves. "I cannot see through walls, you know."

Mohmed watched his small video monitor and obeyed, acutely aware that they were working with the very heart of a tiny nuclear reactor. Mansour had his own monitor to help him, using slaved three-fingered manipulators, in placing a machined lead casing over a small metal object on the other side of that low wall. The wall was actually two parallel walls formed of several thicknesses of concrete blocks, the space between those blocks taken up by a metric ton of water in thickwalled plastic bags. Mohmed was technician enough to understand that a thick wall of water and concrete made a passable imitation of lead sheeting, where hard radiation was concerned. And they needed modest radiation barriers when preparing the djinni for shipment; the lead casings made close-fitting capsules over two carefully machined plates of enriched uranium.

The plates themselves weighed several kilos apiece but were not much broader than hockey pucks. Under Mansour's direction they had been cut with deep concentric grooves and ridges so that, when the plates were brought very near each other, the ridges fitted closely without touching. Mansour had once casually mentioned that those two circular grooved plates of uranium must never be allowed to touch, no matter what else failed. "But failsafe systems are all too heavy for Clement effendi," he had muttered. "So I must hope for perfection in those control linkages and trust to Allah for the rest."

With the encapsulation of the second uranium plate, Mansour heaved a huge sigh. "Now, brother Mohmed, we can secure those capsules by hand." By "we," he meant Mohmed himself, who was growing infernally tired of being the donkey of all heavy work.

Mohmed walked around their makeshift barrier and moved between the remote manipulator struts. "Shall we leave the bags of water here, or must I repack those as well, brother Selim?"

"Clement wants the concrete blocks moved to the jungle," Mansour replied. "You must repack the water bags. Count yourself fortunate that he wants them empty."

Both men snickered at Mansour's small jest. Clement's orders often sounded senseless though, Mohmed admitted to himself, they usually turned out to have some rational basis.

Presently, Mohmed finished sealing those capsules and began to disassemble the radiation barrier, carrying bags of water outside two at a time slung from a handmade neck yoke in the historic Arab manner. Mansour worked alone on removing the djinni's laser tube, a rectangular box with rounded edges that was an arm's span in length, but only as wide as a man's head. During a mission, it lay inside the shell until it pivoted downward to fire.

Mohmed was already distributing concrete blocks in the jungle when, returning to the shed, he heard Clement's voice inside. Mohmed promptly squatted down just outside and began to tinker with the wrapping of his neck yoke.

Now Selim Mansour was saying, "—terrible chance, putting that uranium in the hands of foreigners."

"In a Panamanian diplomatic pouch," Clement replied as if speaking to a child. "A business associate with connections in the Panamanian government has promised that whatever small items I choose to ship this way will not be questioned nor tampered with. And I have excellent assurances that our capsules will receive the most careful handling."

"Is that what we are to say when we arrive in Damas—"

"And it is my decision, Selim." The voice went on, imperturbable, implacable. "Let the lightnings flash on me. You are not responsible, and as you see I am completely confident. Our djinni will arrive with everything in order. By the way, where the devil is Ashraf?"

Mohmed did not hear the response, shuffling to his feet and shouldering the shed door open. "—exhausted, I should think," Mansour was saying.

Clement's gaze on Mohmed held no suspicion or rancor. "Tired, Ashraf? By all means, take a rest."

"*Kattr kheyrak*, my thanks to you, effendi," Mohmed exclaimed, feigning a weariness he did not feel. But overstatement, spoken or not, had been ingrained in Mohmed Ashraf as a legacy of his mother tongue.

Mohmed squatted on his heels to rest, arms folded over his knees, and closed his eyes. Because he often took his breaks in a light doze this way, he hoped to be ignored. Meanwhile, he kept alert.

As feet scuffed across the shed floor, he heard Clement ask about the packing of the djinni, and Selim's reply. "Another few hours tomorrow, and we shall have everything ready for shipment."

"Tonight" was Clement's rejoinder. "We must be on the wharf soon after dawn." Mohmed thought about the hours of work remaining to him that evening, and his heart fell.

"But why the hurry?" Selim wondered aloud. "If we transship by the same route—"

"But we shall do no such thing," Clement announced. "We cannot be certain, merely because we have not been arrested, that we remain undetected. The last thing we want is to have some Interpol snoop or French agent trace us back to Syria. No, while the uranium goes by air, we shall ship the djinni first to Tampico, in Mexico. Then by truck to Veracruz, and *then* onward. It launders our trail, you see."

"It seems out of our way," Selim said, his doubt palpable.

"It is indeed. It is also the safest route, and we will travel by air using our false passports. I know what our Syrian master expects, but we shall surprise him with our subtlety. Surely he will appreciate that."

Resting his forehead on his arms, Mohmed felt a twinge of alarm. Would this foreign devil never learn? Arab leaders appreciated subtlety when *they* practiced it. When Westerners did it, the reaction could be volcanic. Still, there was no denying that Clement's ploy was well reasoned. Whatever happened, it would be Mohmed's job, and his great pleasure, to pass this tidbit on to Damascus at first opportunity.

THIRTEEN

MAY 1991

HE U.S. DRUG Enforcement Administration learned about Roland Clement's stateside contract through sheer luck and from an unlikely source. Agent Juan Saltillo had worn his deep cover in Colombia for two years, earning his second salary as a corruptible warehouse official, without locating any major drug pipelines for his DEA bosses. Juan's warehouses lay behind twelve-foot fences near the Terminal Maritimo in Santa Marta, and on a special evening in May he tested every lock before signing himself out as usual.

Because Santa Marta is a port town near Cartagena, the local bars and cafes resound with the murmur of many accents. Juan's Spanish was perfect, but Puerto Rican; and he had spent many an off-duty hour developing the special language flavors that, he hoped, would eventually mark him as a native Colombian wharf ruffian. He looked the part in his stained tan whipcord pants, a work shirt covering the massive upper torso of a man who moved cargoes in those warehouses. An old scar across his chin completed the image. Juan had a hilarious story about that scar, and how he got it from a woman's razor in nearby Barranquilla. The truth was, he had got it climbing over a fence in Spanish Harlem.

On this evening, Juan hauled his little Emerson radio headset from his pocket and clapped its speakers over his ears without turning it on. In his experience, men in bars tended to talk more freely when the stranger nearby was snapping fingers to some popular tune only he could hear. Juan Saltillo, of course, was hearing them instead.

He lingered at a streetside stall for a moment and spent a few pesos on a pair of the small, fat bananas known locally as *manzanitas,* little apples. The vendor spoke a common argot that Juan copied, developing that cover of his at every opportunity. Those stalls sold food that Juan had never known in the States; fruits like curuma, zapote, and the delicious guanabana he relished. The skinned guinea pig and fried pork chicharrones he could do without, but one small banana and three blocks later he sniffed the breeze with real appreciation. Somewhere very near, a familiar odor was calling him.

Juan could not recall entering the little cafe before, but after two years in the area his stomach had adapted to most local foods. Of course he would not touch the water during this season; when the local rainy season was late and Santa Marta's reservoirs this low, that water fairly crawled with the kind of amoeba that churned a man's innards to treacle. He ordered a beer instead, with a plate of the *ají* that had lured him inside. He sat at a rear table, his back to the wall, and avoided eye contact with the others. Not until he put his head down to attack his *ají,* a dish of chicken pungent with coriander and chili, did the two men sit down near him. Juan Saltillo soon realized that he had turned his face down at exactly the right time.

From the first moment after the waiter left those two, Juan Saltillo knew why he must shift his seat a bit, turning further away from the newcomers. When a man has tuned his ear so carefully to accents, he also develops a memory for voices. One voice, low and gutteral, was new: Peruvian highlands, if Juan was any judge. The other voice raised hackles on his neck because, unless Juan was hallucinating, it belonged to one of the three men in Colombia who could make him as DEA.

The mere fact of hearing Morgan Delora's educated tones in such a place was not enough in itself to bring gooseflesh. Delora, who ranked well up in the Colombian security forces, was not one of those pale *blancito* bureaucrats who feared street action. It had been Delora who'd welcomed his DEA counterpart to the region and wangled him that warehouse job. The one word that had alerted Juan Saltillo was *mercancía,* merchandise. That word was rarely used by locals for anything but contraband, and that usually meant drugs.

Okay, he's meeting one of his undercover men, Juan told himself,

ELEVEN

MAY 1991

B EN ULLMER DIDN'T recall which playwright had first asked what's in a name, but he knew the answer was "electricity." Once his team accepted that their job was to defeat a Butcher Bird, not to promote some nameless horror, they began to bombard Sheppard with more friendly queries. Within five minutes, they had Sheppard watching a screen over Petra Leigh's shoulder.

"No, I hadn't seen these latest drawings," the NSA man admitted, studying their new Beta version of a flying killer robot. The rotors at the tips of its stub wings now were shrouded and its engine, buried in the fuselage, sat below an air intake that gaped like the mouth of a manta ray. "Isn't that airscoop awfully big?"

"My input," Cutter told him. "That last ECO requires some kind of power source that's compact but with a tremendous jolt of energy, since lasers are inefficient as hell. I mean, if you want twenty thousand watts of laser, you start by drawing a surge of a few *million* watts to drive it."

"And since efficiency losses show up mostly as waste heat, you're giving it a way to conduct all that heat overboard in a hurry," Sheppard said, making it not quite a question.

"Got to—or burn the bird up with its first shot. 'Course," Cutter went on, "I suppose that's an option. We know the popular way to drive an X-ray beam weapon is a small nuclear detonation. Well, nobody would be in any doubt as to where it came from, Doc. It would not only atomize the bird, naturally, but it would also put a mushroom cloud overhead. That's the kind of weapon you don't get back. Not my idea of a stealthy bird. I take it the thing is stealthy enough that it's still a black mystery?"

"Deep black. In no case has any witness seen or heard anything—no, cancel that. HUMINT from a sister agency reports that a Syrian taxi driver supposedly heard the wind moan like a banshee, or the Arab equivalent, shortly before something killed his client in an abandoned ruin. That was one of the poison slug killings, we're pretty sure."

"Any eyewitnesses to the killing at Kourou?"

Sheppard folded his arms and stared at nothing, as if trying to place himself at the scene of the crime. He recited it slowly. "Actually, it was a dozen miles from the mainland. This man Didier was walking across uneven ground on Isle Royale, near Kourou, between two telemetry specialists. He was talking, and then suddenly he gasped in midsentence. When he fell, they thought he'd just turned an ankle. But a sprained ankle doesn't turn a man's brain to tapioca. His eyes were dilated, central nervous system failure, only brain-stem functions for a moment or so. And neither of his companions saw a beam, and neither of them picked up any residual radiation. Neither did Didier. While walking shoulder to shoulder with two friends, the man just died," he finished, indicating the event's abruptness with a finger-snap that made Petra jump.

"Mighty good shooting," Wes Hardin observed.

Cutter thought about that for a moment. Then: "So good, I think we can rule out a human marksman anywhere in the system. My guess is, maybe it's an optically aligned ultraviolet laser. Invisible beam, but more efficient than X ray. A lot more energy against the poor bastard's skull."

Ullmer maintained his own silence. *These kids are quick as scat, they don't need me to bias their ideas. Hardin and Morrison now, they don't give a shit who I am.* There would be plenty of time later for Ullmer's critique, anyhow.

"Your Beta bird looks a bit large and gimmicky, but there's a precedent for it," Sheppard was saying. Obviously, he knew what existing UAV craft looked like. "I'm just as interested in how the Butcher Bird picks its target. A live operator nearby, for example, aiming a low-power designator beam."

"That's state-of-the-art stuff already," Hardin injected. "But it complicates this kind of mission, and the designator beam would have to be aimed by Captain Marvel. I think Cutter's right."

"There's got to be a simpler way," Colleen muttered. "I mean simpler tactics. The hardware might be complex as hell."

wouldn't be long before somebody else got crackin' on something like it."

Well, I can make need-to-know decisions. Play it straight, Sheppard, he urged himself silently. He took a deep breath. "Ben, somebody else already has them. And we don't know who."

"Oh, my God," Petra whispered.

"We're finding out more about it because it's already in use. Every time they use it, we get a hint," Sheppard went on, dully, as if admitting some terrible misdeed of his own.

"Shit fire and save matches," Ullmer said softly. "These ECOs are to pass on what you're learning from day to day?"

Sheppard nodded. "Evidently there's more than one weapon system developed for it. We thought it was confined to very short range in the Middle East, shooting poison pellets, until a few days ago. And that's all I can tell you unless you're prepared to continue the study. Not even its code name. Oh yes, it already has a classified name," he added. "Savagely appropriate."

He offered to leave the room when the team members began to talk among themselves. To his relief, they seemed to want him present. For the next five minutes, Bill Sheppard worked hard to keep his silence unless directly addressed. Even then, he gave them little more.

Eventually Ullmer asked the crucial question: "So it looks like we're trying to dope out how the thing looks and what it can do, and maybe what it can't. Right?"

"Exactly."

"So we can figure out how to counter it?"

"I devoutly hope so," Sheppard said gently. "We don't intend to build anything like it. This country isn't in the assassination business. But can you see why the Secret Service people are having nightmares right now?"

Dead silence for a long moment. Petra broke it with, "I think I'd like to change my vote."

"From the mouths of babes," Colleen responded, but her nod toward Petra was approving. "I guess I'm convinced; my conscience insists," she finished.

Hardin and Cutter exchanged looks. Both ex-military pilots, they had struggled long and hard over their ethics. "Sorry, Wes," Cutter said at last. "I can't chicken out of this."

"Sorry, hell." Hardin snorted. "So we were wrong. So let's get right." He glanced at Ullmer. "If Ben will go along . . ."

"Couldn't have said it better myself," Ullmer replied. "But you can't leave us hanging out to dry like this, Bill. We really do need to know a lot of shit you haven't been sending us. For instance, we're gonna have to figure out which countries are capable of building this assassin robot. Certain hotshot designers have a kind of design signature. Just glance at a MiG and you know it's from Mikoyan's shop, you know?"

"You're absolutely right, Ben. We've just been trying to compartment this thing."

"To the point of paralysis," Ullmer charged.

"That's the risk," Sheppard agreed. "On thing you'll want to know is, five days ago a French subminister dropped dead near the ESA launch facility in French Guiana. Fellow named Didier."

Ullmer's head jerked up. "Claude Didier?"

"That's right. You knew him?"

"Met him a coupla times." Ullmer shrugged. "One of those froggy doubledomes who knew ever'body. More a generalist than a specialist; had a lot of admirers in Dassault and Matra. You attend enough international conferences, you get to know who's hot and who's not. I'd say Didier was middlin' hot."

"From the reports, we think it could have been an aerial assassination. That's why we're worrying about a really hideous little weapon system, Cutter. Something—different."

The weapons specialist opened his mouth; closed it; then glanced at the two women. "Mind telling me the effects?"

"Yes, but I will anyhow. A little hole, only millimeters wide, down through the skull. And it doesn't exactly burn its way down; with enough power, a laser sort of flakes things away."

"Spalling," Cutter supplied.

"Yes," said Sheppard, and swallowed hard. "It happens in a fraction of a second, apparently without much noise or visible light. When it gets down through the bone to gray matter—well, the shock wave literally homogenizes part of the brain."

Petra Leigh spoke quickly, perhaps to rid herself of a grotesque mental image. "So either it's an orbital weapon, or it can fly to South America."

"That, or it's now based there," Ullmer put in. "And by the way, what the hell is that code name?"

"At Meade," Sheppard told him, "we refer to it as the Butcher Bird."

loitered over its target area for nearly two hours to make that kill.
Its turbine fuel tank was almost empty when it landed.

Clement had replayed the tape several times, sharing his moment of success with his team. For a man forced to scramble the
brains of an old friend, Clement had shown uncommon glee. The
French scientist had lingered over the sight of a tubby little fellow in
shirtsleeves, foreshortened by the steep angle of the camera's view,
who abruptly collapsed between two companions while walking
on Isle Royale.

Now it was Mohmed who felt a surge of hope, because he was
helping dismantle the djinni's innards. Very soon now, Mohmed
felt, he would relish the Syrian variety of heat again. "Bring up the
magnification," Mansour said, his hands encased in remote
manipulators like skeletal gloves. "I cannot see through walls, you
know."

Mohmed watched his small video monitor and obeyed, acutely
aware that they were working with the very heart of a tiny nuclear
reactor. Mansour had his own monitor to help him, using slaved
three-fingered manipulators, in placing a machined lead casing
over a small metal object on the other side of that low wall. The
wall was actually two parallel walls formed of several thicknesses of
concrete blocks, the space between those blocks taken up by a metric ton of water in thickwalled plastic bags. Mohmed was technician
enough to understand that a thick wall of water and concrete made
a passable imitation of lead sheeting, where hard radiation was
concerned. And they needed modest radiation barriers when preparing the djinni for shipment; the lead casings made close-fitting
capsules over two carefully machined plates of enriched uranium.

The plates themselves weighed several kilos apiece but were
not much broader than hockey pucks. Under Mansour's direction
they had been cut with deep concentric grooves and ridges so that,
when the plates were brought very near each other, the ridges fitted closely without touching. Mansour had once casually mentioned that those two circular grooved plates of uranium must
never be allowed to touch, no matter what else failed. "But failsafe
systems are all too heavy for Clement effendi," he had muttered.
"So I must hope for perfection in those control linkages and trust to
Allah for the rest."

With the encapsulation of the second uranium plate, Mansour
heaved a huge sigh. "Now, brother Mohmed, we can secure those
capsules by hand." By "we," he meant Mohmed himself, who was
growing infernally tired of being the donkey of all heavy work.

TWELVE

May 1991

LOOKING BACK ON his first few days in the world of the infidel West, Mohmed Ashraf later decided that his misgivings had been omens. No wonder this far-flung piece of France had begun as an annex of an island penal colony! Sequestered on the edge of a steaming jungle, he longed for the familiar dry heat of his native Syria.

Worse than the climate, Mohmed felt torn between his priorities because he served two masters. It was almost as if he had no master, and Mohmed strongly endorsed the Arab proverb: *Better to live forty years under tyranny than one day in leaderless chaos.* Had French Guiana been a sovereign nation, he might at least have been able to contact a full-fledged Syrian embassy nearby, with its Mukhabarat officers and secure telephone lines to Damascus. Mohmed's mother, of course, was not sick. She had been dead for years. It was Mohmed who would become sick if he did not keep the illustrious Assad informed of what was really happening in French Guiana. On the other hand, Mohmed had found nothing seditious to report.

At least, he reflected as he helped Mansour repack the heavier parts of their equipment, in his second call he had been able to verify one piece of good news. There had been no doubt of their success when, after one fruitless mission by the djinni, the little weapon system had returned with traces of radioactivity on its hide and a videotape of its kill. As the videotape proved, the djinni had

Mohmed walked around their makeshift barrier and moved between the remote manipulator struts. "Shall we leave the bags of water here, or must I repack those as well, brother Selim?"

"Clement wants the concrete blocks moved to the jungle," Mansour replied. "You must repack the water bags. Count yourself fortunate that he wants them empty."

Both men snickered at Mansour's small jest. Clement's orders often sounded senseless though, Mohmed admitted to himself, they usually turned out to have some rational basis.

Presently, Mohmed finished sealing those capsules and began to disassemble the radiation barrier, carrying bags of water outside two at a time slung from a handmade neck yoke in the historic Arab manner. Mansour worked alone on removing the djinni's laser tube, a rectangular box with rounded edges that was an arm's span in length, but only as wide as a man's head. During a mission, it lay inside the shell until it pivoted downward to fire.

Mohmed was already distributing concrete blocks in the jungle when, returning to the shed, he heard Clement's voice inside. Mohmed promptly squatted down just outside and began to tinker with the wrapping of his neck yoke.

Now Selim Mansour was saying, "—terrible chance, putting that uranium in the hands of foreigners."

"In a Panamanian diplomatic pouch," Clement replied as if speaking to a child. "A business associate with connections in the Panamanian government has promised that whatever small items I choose to ship this way will not be questioned nor tampered with. And I have excellent assurances that our capsules will receive the most careful handling."

"Is that what we are to say when we arrive in Damas—"

"And it is my decision, Selim." The voice went on, imperturbable, implacable. "Let the lightnings flash on me. You are not responsible, and as you see I am completely confident. Our djinni will arrive with everything in order. By the way, where the devil is Ashraf?"

Mohmed did not hear the response, shuffling to his feet and shouldering the shed door open. "—exhausted, I should think," Mansour was saying.

Clement's gaze on Mohmed held no suspicion or rancor. "Tired, Ashraf? By all means, take a rest."

"*Kattr kheyrak*, my thanks to you, effendi," Mohmed exclaimed, feigning a weariness he did not feel. But overstatement, spoken or not, had been ingrained in Mohmed Ashraf as a legacy of his mother tongue.

Mohmed squatted on his heels to rest, arms folded over his knees, and closed his eyes. Because he often took his breaks in a light doze this way, he hoped to be ignored. Meanwhile, he kept alert.

As feet scuffed across the shed floor, he heard Clement ask about the packing of the djinni, and Selim's reply. "Another few hours tomorrow, and we shall have everything ready for shipment."

"Tonight" was Clement's rejoinder. "We must be on the wharf soon after dawn." Mohmed thought about the hours of work remaining to him that evening, and his heart fell.

"But why the hurry?" Selim wondered aloud. "If we transship by the same route—"

"But we shall do no such thing," Clement announced. "We cannot be certain, merely because we have not been arrested, that we remain undetected. The last thing we want is to have some Interpol snoop or French agent trace us back to Syria. No, while the uranium goes by air, we shall ship the djinni first to Tampico, in Mexico. Then by truck to Veracruz, and *then* onward. It launders our trail, you see."

"It seems out of our way," Selim said, his doubt palpable.

"It is indeed. It is also the safest route, and we will travel by air using our false passports. I know what our Syrian master expects, but we shall surprise him with our subtlety. Surely he will appreciate that."

Resting his forehead on his arms, Mohmed felt a twinge of alarm. Would this foreign devil never learn? Arab leaders appreciated subtlety when *they* practiced it. When Westerners did it, the reaction could be volcanic. Still, there was no denying that Clement's ploy was well reasoned. Whatever happened, it would be Mohmed's job, and his great pleasure, to pass this tidbit on to Damascus at first opportunity.

THIRTEEN

MAY 1991

T HE U.S. DRUG Enforcement Administration learned about Roland Clement's stateside contract through sheer luck and from an unlikely source. Agent Juan Saltillo had worn his deep cover in Colombia for two years, earning his second salary as a corruptible warehouse official, without locating any major drug pipelines for his DEA bosses. Juan's warehouses lay behind twelve-foot fences near the Terminal Maritimo in Santa Marta, and on a special evening in May he tested every lock before signing himself out as usual.

Because Santa Marta is a port town near Cartagena, the local bars and cafes resound with the murmur of many accents. Juan's Spanish was perfect, but Puerto Rican; and he had spent many an off-duty hour developing the special language flavors that, he hoped, would eventually mark him as a native Colombian wharf ruffian. He looked the part in his stained tan whipcord pants, a work shirt covering the massive upper torso of a man who moved cargoes in those warehouses. An old scar across his chin completed the image. Juan had a hilarious story about that scar, and how he got it from a woman's razor in nearby Barranquilla. The truth was, he had got it climbing over a fence in Spanish Harlem.

On this evening, Juan hauled his little Emerson radio headset from his pocket and clapped its speakers over his ears without turning it on. In his experience, men in bars tended to talk more freely when the stranger nearby was snapping fingers to some popular tune only he could hear. Juan Saltillo, of course, was hearing them instead.

He lingered at a streetside stall for a moment and spent a few pesos on a pair of the small, fat bananas known locally as *manzanitas*, little apples. The vendor spoke a common argot that Juan copied, developing that cover of his at every opportunity. Those stalls sold food that Juan had never known in the States; fruits like curuma, zapote, and the delicious guanabana he relished. The skinned guinea pig and fried pork chicharrones he could do without, but one small banana and three blocks later he sniffed the breeze with real appreciation. Somewhere very near, a familiar odor was calling him.

Juan could not recall entering the little cafe before, but after two years in the area his stomach had adapted to most local foods. Of course he would not touch the water during this season; when the local rainy season was late and Santa Marta's reservoirs this low, that water fairly crawled with the kind of amoeba that churned a man's innards to treacle. He ordered a beer instead, with a plate of the *ají* that had lured him inside. He sat at a rear table, his back to the wall, and avoided eye contact with the others. Not until he put his head down to attack his *ají*, a dish of chicken pungent with coriander and chili, did the two men sit down near him. Juan Saltillo soon realized that he had turned his face down at exactly the right time.

From the first moment after the waiter left those two, Juan Saltillo knew why he must shift his seat a bit, turning further away from the newcomers. When a man has tuned his ear so carefully to accents, he also develops a memory for voices. One voice, low and gutteral, was new: Peruvian highlands, if Juan was any judge. The other voice raised hackles on his neck because, unless Juan was hallucinating, it belonged to one of the three men in Colombia who could make him as DEA.

The mere fact of hearing Morgan Delora's educated tones in such a place was not enough in itself to bring gooseflesh. Delora, who ranked well up in the Colombian security forces, was not one of those pale *blancito* bureaucrats who feared street action. It had been Delora who'd welcomed his DEA counterpart to the region and wangled him that warehouse job. The one word that had alerted Juan Saltillo was *mercancía*, merchandise. That word was rarely used by locals for anything but contraband, and that usually meant drugs.

Okay, he's meeting one of his undercover men, Juan told himself, even as the conversation told him otherwise. The Peruvian did not seem to know Delora well and obviously there was not a great deal of trust between them. It was Delora who insisted that they keep their cover long enough to eat the shrimp ceviche they had ordered, then make the exchange and leave one at a time. Neither of them made any mention of a later meeting, and that detail was usually among the first to be settled among men who expected to meet again. The Peruvian suggested flipping a coin to see who would leave first, and Delora agreed with a chuckle.

Juan Saltillo ate little and listened long while the men chewed their ceviche with a Reisling that Delora cursed even as he drank it. *There's just no way this is Seguridad business,* Juan finally decided. *And if Morgan Delora makes me now, he's got to suspect I know it. With him out to get me and my cover blown, I won't live a week—unless I take him in now. And Jesuchristo, I'm not even packing my Beretta!* With that in mind, Juan put up a silent hand with his empty beer bottle in it, waving for another. A full bottle packed a lot more weight than an empty one.

The place had filled up a bit now, the single waiter scurrying among patrons at the front tables. If all those goddamn calisthenics and the warehouse work had done their job, Juan figured, maybe he was physically capable of doing what had to be done and getting the hell out before he could be stopped. A defensive position in this matter would be suicidal, which meant he needed a good offense. That was when Juan reached up with one hand and pulled the sponge rubber from the right earpiece of his headset. The tiny bare speaker, he knew from experience, looked exactly like the mouthpiece of a transmitter. Juan needed to give the impression of having a team backing him. It might work; by Jesus it had better . . .

Juan's beer came, already open, naturally. He took a single swig and then quietly put down a bill large enough to pay for a dozen meals. Behind him, a muttered exchange included the soft stirrings and clicks that meant someone was inspecting a paper-wrapped package while someone else opened luggage fastenings.

Both men seemed pleased. Delora offered to pay for the meal, the Peruvian accepted, and then Juan heard someone push away from his chair. He put his head down again, but this time it must have alerted Delora.

The Colombian took two steps, then whacked Juan's tabletop with an attaché case. Any man would have looked up, and Juan did it, coming erect with the bottle in his fist.

Morgan Delora's jaw fell open as he recognized Juan, and because he stepped back without reaching for a weapon, Juan spun on his heel toward the second man, a well-dressed little fellow who was in the act of rising from his seat. Juan caught him squarely in the hollow of his temple, beer splashing everywhere, and the little man went over without even a grunt, a string-wrapped package in newspaper falling from his lap to the floor. Now people at nearby tables were staring, and Juan dropped into a squat at his own table, expecting gunfire.

But Morgan Delora was already sprinting for the front door, swinging that attaché case toward the face of the waiter, who was unlucky enough to be approaching with a loaded tray. And now, with food scattering through the air, the place was a pandemonium.

"*Alto,*" Juan cried, adding the dreaded police phrases. It worked perfectly and Juan snatched up that wrapped package before hurtling after Delora. And Holy Maria but the fucking thing was heavy as a window weight, far too massive for any illegal powder, including cocaine. Juan crashed through swinging doors into the street and saw Morgan Delora stepping high like a sprinter, but impeded by that attaché case as he ran.

Juan, slowed by his astonishingly heavy package, still managed to gain a few paces in the first block. "*Alto,* stop, or I'll fire," he croaked, begrudging the breath it took but knowing he had to maintain his illusion of power. Delora showed no sign of slowing until he tried to duck into a darkening alley and, in the dusk, misjudged the swing of his arm holding that attaché case. The case slammed into a cornerstone and then Delora was spinning on his heel, trailing a soft explosion of small bricks that cascaded into the alley. It was then that Morgan Delora used his favorite Anglo expression as he fell backward: "Son of the BITCH!"

Juan dropped his package into the shadows and came down on his old pal Delora in approved fashion, one knee in his back, his left hand grasping Delora's hair for a forward smash. He did not deliver the stunner because Morgan Delora made no resistance.

"The money, Juanito, *por Dios,* the *money,*" he stammered.

"Move and you're dead." Juan panted, getting up. He took his time patting the Colombian down, then rolled him over for another try. Now Delora was looking at him, and Juan wasn't sure there was enough light but gave it his best shot. He took the little Emerson from around his neck and murmured into the bared speaker, in English, "Subject evaded arrest. Searching now," and he named a street several blocks away. Then he made a show of turning the tuner before letting the headset fall around his throat. He continued, now in Spanish: "They can't hear us now, Morgan. Mean to say you aren't even armed?"

"For a Peruvian museum director, for God's sake? Of course not." In tones less filled with disgust, more with urgency, he went on. "Juanito, there are a lot of pesos scattered behind you. If anyone passes by there's going to be a riot."

Juan reached down and helped his friend to his feet. "Round it up, then." He decided that Morgan Delora was gasping harder for breath than he was himself, and reclaimed the wrapped package as he watched the Colombian scramble on hands and knees for bundles of Colombian money. He could not wait to see what was inside and tore at the package until he could see, in failing light, what he had been tossing around with such abandon. Poking from layers of old newsprint was the head of a statuette the size of a squirrel, grinning like a skull, with an intricately worked headdress. The damned thing gleamed an almost saffron yellow, as Peruvian gold sometimes did.

"Man, do you have some explaining to do," Juan said, his hands beginning to shake.

They walked together back to the warehouse area because it was perfectly clear that Delora could not avoid prosecution unless he killed his DEA friend, or made his explanation a thing of beauty. With their ID, they had the clout to go through any gates they liked at any hour. Once inside Bodega Dos, the second warehouse, Juan opened windows to let a breeze ventilate the place and sat down on a sack redolent of unroasted coffee beans. "I never heard of anybody smuggling ancient treasures back into South America. You say it belongs to the Peruvians; well, why couldn't that guy just carry it back and declare it?"

"Because, Juanito, it was stolen by his son." Delora fondled his scalp gently with spread fingers. "*Ay de mi*, you nearly scalped me like some wild west *indio*. I think, if I had been armed—well, *no se importa*." The smile, moonlit, seemed genuine. "I had it coming, I suppose."

Juan toyed with the Emerson at his throat. "You did, for a fact. Hold on, now. You brought this damned little Inca figurine back yourself to avoid the paper trail and the embarrassment, you say. Nice guy, hands across the border and all that shit. So how do you explain this attaché case?"

"He brought it in himself."

"The money, Morgan, the fucking *money*, don't pull on my erection," said Juan, making excellent use of the local idiom.

"No." A long silence, Delora nodding as if to himself before he could bring himself to say, "It was *mordida*, a simple bribe, a kind of 'thank you.' Do you know how the director raised that money? A bribe from the Americans so that they could legally buy other antiquities. To him it is business as always, not immoral, barely illegal; *his* money, Juanito."

"But you're supposed to have another ethic. Incorruptible old Morgan Delora, that's you."

"If this was corrupt, who are the victims? No one. You know, I could easily claim I intended to turn the money in, instead of funding my daughter's graduate work." Delora sighed.

"You could if you'd thought fast enough back in that cafe."

"I still could. But I won't. By the way, why didn't I get word of this DEA sting? It is highly irregular. In fact, I am disappointed and hurt."

"Back up, Morgan. You said you won't claim innocence. Why?"

"Not to you, Juanito. But I would hope you might let me do so to anyone else."

"Yes? And what do you offer?"

A slow headshake in moonlight. "Not money."

"Why not?"

"Because that is not your . . ." He searched for the Anglo phrase and found it. "Bottom line. You would spurn it, damn you. And we would not be able to trust one another fully, ever again."

"So what's my bottom line, Morgan? Give me one."

"Information. Something that concerns *los Estados Unidos*, which my country intends to keep hidden because it might compromise our source."

"And what source is that?" Juan asked.

"Pablo Escobar," said the Colombian, all but whispering it into the coffee-scented silence. "We have bugged his little prison castle in ways he does not dream. As he grows more careless, we learn more of use to both our countries. This just did not seem quite important enough to risk revealing our surveillance, since it would not involve harm to any yanquis."

"Listen, Morgan, I have to tell you this or I won't sleep. This little radio at my throat? It's a fake. Oh, it gets me all the salsa tunes I can handle, but there was no team, no sting, get it? I just happened to be in that cafe," he said, starting to laugh, hands out as if offering his explanation on a carven plaque. "And I haven't so much as a pigsticker on me. I played it by ear."

Morgan Delora's own laugh started softly and built into a boom to shake dust from the rafters, tapering finally to a sigh. "Very well, and I am a fool. I am even fool enough to trust your word that none of this happened tonight. Do I have it?"

"You know damned well you do. I'll have to source this, but not close enough to identify you personally."

"My thanks, Juanito. All right; you may recall a major sting that your yanquis ran a year ago, stopping a billion dollars in cash from leaving your country by air. Yes?"

"Common knowledge," said Juan. "It was in the papers."

"But you also imprisoned one Colombian named Guillermo Borges. Our Señor Escobar believes that Borges has been running his mouth so hard he needs his oil checked," Delora went on, using a phrase that represented a slender blade slipping into a man's belly. "It now appears that a foreigner has taken the contract, claiming the ability to put a hole in any man's head from many *kilómetros* distant. We were not able to discern the man's name or nationality from the tape, but the assassin was described by Escobar's attorney as an invisible demon, not human. The days of Guillermo Borges would seem to be limited, unless this was all a pack of lies. And there is more—where are you going, Juanito?"

"To my office," said the DEA man. "It's hot in there, but I want to get this down on paper."

FOURTEEN

MAY 1991

LEADING HIS LITTLE group through Customs at Tampico's Aeropuerto General Mina, Clement announced that his "Algerians" had brought equipment to gather weather data, and found to his disdain that spoken English was preferred to French. He also found Mohmed Ashraf trying to stuff French coins into a pay telephone and realized that this sturdy little Syrian was nearing panic in his anxiety to call Damascus again.

Clement motioned his assistants together and spoke softly, keeping a pleasant expression on his face. "Ashraf, a port of entry is no place for an emotional outburst by a man who may have a price on his head. I, too, need to use a telephone because we have a two-day wait before the next flight to Athens. After I call, it will be your turn. Meanwhile, you will please allow me to find an inconspicuous place for us to stay. It may require unusual tactics. You will all now marshal our equipment while I rent a suitable vehicle."

A chastened Ashraf let Mansour lead the way to their luggage, Odile Marchant following them in her travel finery at a languid pace. Her studied indifference managed to suggest that she had no connection with the men. Clement found the exchange booth where he studied rates of exchange for a long moment. His companions were not in sight. He withdrew a sheaf of bills from inside his coat and, with no show of interest, exchanged two dozen of them for a thick stack of Mexican hundred-thousand-peso bills plus a handful of coins. He knew that seven million Mexican pesos were not as much as they seemed in the year 1991, but should get them as far as the border.

At this point, Clement's mental circuits were computing at double-time. He walked quickly to a shop selling duty-free booze and paid out a pair of those *cien mil* banknotes for the privilege of using a telephone that was out of sight. The Panamanian consulate in San Antonio, Texas, took his call, and the fellow at the consulate switchboard responded correctly to the name Charlemagne. Another voice, somewhat older, confided that the diplomatic pouch with the relics of Charlemagne had arrived mere hours before. And since they were somewhat shorthanded, he would have to pick up those relics in person, at the consulate on Castle Brook, reached from San Antonio's Four-Ten Expressway. And by the way, did he need directions?

Clement rang off immediately. He had spent hours scanning maps and counted himself lucky that Panama had a consulate in Texas and a past understanding with Pablo Escobar's people. The important thing was that, with the delivery of that reactor fuel into the United States, he had closed a window of vulnerability and could now concentrate on smuggling the rest of his operation to the north.

He drifted outside and determined for himself that no available taxi would handle all their goods, then returned. He made no mention of that telephone call when he found his trio struggling with luggage. There was no option, he told them, but for Odile and Mansour to remain with their equipment while he and Ashraf went in search of a rental truck.

"I shall be content here with Selim," Odile said wickedly. Instead of slapping her, Clement motioned for Ashraf and strode out the door, silently rehearsing his next story.

It would be necessary, he told the Syrian, for them to disappear for the next two days; no hotels, no set location. It was simpler to rent a serviceable van, using Algerian papers. They would drive inland for a day, sleep as best they might, then drive back. As the man-of-all-work and a decent mechanic, Mohmed Ashraf must select a vehicle for the purpose.

He is full of questions, Clement thought as he instructed their taxi driver to find an area likely to rent vans. *They are ripping his tongue apart but he knows better than to seem too curious. Oh yes, Mohmed Ashraf thinks he is fingering a crevice in my armor.*

As entertainment, their taxi ride ranked somewhere between a roller coaster and a train wreck. After their third near-miss, Clement concluded that two objects could indeed occupy the same space simultaneously, but at least the ride gave Ashraf something more pressing than his tomorrows to think about.

Three hours later, with freshly purchased maps and Ashraf at the wheel of a Dodge van, Clement stepped briskly into the air terminal to find Odile sitting alone on a crate, surrounded by their equipment and swinging one elegant nylon-clad leg in impatience. Mansour, she said, was searching for a clean toilet.

"If my own experience is any guide, he may be gone forever," she added, dripping acid with each word. Her expression brightened a bit then. "But here he comes now," she said.

Clement pulled a bill from his pocket. "Find sweets for us, Odile, and be certain they are wrapped. No fresh fruit, unless you crave living in one of those toilets for awhile. Perhaps we can find juice concentrates; they will be safer."

Because they would not trust anything to baggage handlers, they did not leave the terminal behind them until nearly sundown. Clement directed the sullen Ashraf to Route 80, speaking only when necessary, while Odile and Mansour found uneven seating amid their equipment. Having heard much about the charms of Mexican cities, Clement had been unprepared for Tampico with its crowded arterials, its air choked with insects, its smells testaments to a Gulf port awash in petroleum and livestock. They did not leave the stink behind, nor even think of Odile's candy bars, for another half hour. They did add juice concentrates, distilled water, and tortillas to their stocks at a *supermercado* on their way through the suburbs, and then they were cruising through the Mexican countryside. Briefly, the two Syrians shared the front seats, with Ashraf driving. It was then that Clement mixed their fruit juices, urging Odile to drink with him before he capped the bottles. After an hour, Clement reclaimed the driver's seat and Mansour moved back.

Presently, as they neared the town of Manuel in twilight, Ashraf spoke. "It would seem that our effendi has forgotten his telephone call."

"I forget nothing, Ashraf. I simply have other priorities, and so do you."

"And why do our priorities lead us north?"

"Because—because we will be more comfortable away from this accursed coastal weather. Chew on your sweets, not on my decisions. In Syria, this kind of insolence would have earned you a thrashing."

Mohmed Ashraf took a draught of fruit juice and said nothing, but his sidelong glance could hardly be interpreted other than, "You may try it at your peril, Frenchman."

When darkness fell, and the jouncing prompted Odile to complain of a full bladder, Clement used her need to fulfill one of his own. "We are far from any lights. Ashraf, let us all find relief. I will drive and you can change places with Odile."

Ten minutes later, the snores of Mohmed Ashraf drummed against the hide of the Dodge. "And when do we stop for the night?" asked Odile softly, holding her purse flashlight on the map.

"We do not, until Monterrey."

A brief pause as she scanned the map. A small gasp: "But that is hundreds of—"

"Be still, *ma coquette*." Then, softly: "Is Mansour awake?"

"Asleep; a defense against Ashraf's snores, I should think."

Clement knew it was not a defense, but the result of the lightly drugged fruit juice he had prepared. "Odile, you complain of my mistrust. But in matters of wealth, of the good things life can supply, I know I can trust your intelligent self-interest. Is it not so?"

He could almost hear the shrug that accompanied her reply. *"Comme ci, comme ça."* More or less true, then. He knew it was true, but the admission was an honesty he very much needed.

He braked hard and cursed as an enormous bull appeared in his headlights, standing perfectly still, evidently asleep on its feet in the exact middle of the highway. He passed behind it, then slowly accelerated again.

"They are still asleep," Odile murmured after a moment.

She wants to hear more. And with Ashraf near open rebellion, I may need her help. Mansour, I fear, is an enigma but we can handle him with logic. "We have been offered a business proposition, Odile. We could return to Syria immediately, as captive scientists who might soon become expendable or even a deadly embarrassment to a pitiless tyrant. Or we can proceed into American territory and become very, very rich."

A thoughtful pause. "Sell the djinni?"

"No; sell its services. Selling service is the province of experts," he reminded her. "And I have already made a sale. What do you think of that?"

"I think we would find a home in an American prison, sooner or later."

"And in the Middle East? A shallow grave in the sand, rather sooner than later. Without the immediate promise of even more advanced weapons from me, what unique service could you offer them?''

"Perhaps the same services I offer you," she said slyly, and reached across to lay her hand in his lap. That hand had always seemed to have a life of its own.

"For them, you would need more hands than a Hindu idol," he teased, squirming forward slightly to give those manicured fingers better access. Odile Marchant giggled, her reply silent. But as he drove erratically on toward the city of Monterrey with Odile kneeling sideways at her chosen task, he knew that her lips had framed the right decision.

FIFTEEN

May 1991

I T WAS NOT unusual for Ben Ullmer to stump down the stairs
from his office long after most of his employees had left for the
day. Though his fingers had developed enough tremor to keep
him from the exacting work he loved, aligning and bonding panels
of the Nemesis aircraft, the phrase "hands-on management" remained perfectly apt for the old design wizard. He swept his glance
over the three winged wraiths under his hangar roof, noting the
filmy plastic sheets that covered work in progress on two of the
craft, and sighed into the stillness.

A special crew would arrive later for a night checkout flight of
the newly completed bird that seemed poised, its ninety-foot wing
drooping in repose, ready to leap from its nest the moment those
hangar doors opened. Of course a Nemesis did not leap, nor rocket
vertically upward, nor even reach Mach One, the speed of sound.
With its horizontal tail mounted canard fashion ahead of its two-
place cockpit while the twin-boom rudders canted inward at the
rear, a Nemesis had only one very special duty: it gave the United
States Coast Guard an eye that would soar on station over sixty
thousand feet high, for weeks at a time. Its crew of two literally
lived in that long, graceful bullet of fuselage during a mission, using
equipment expressly designed by Aerosystems Unlimited to keep
them comfortable, well fed and in shape ". . . until they run outa
ham sandwiches," as Ben put it. Once aloft at the fringe of the
earth's atmosphere, a Nemesis could shut down its rotary engine to
run on solar power.

He did not miss the fact that the newly completed craft had its forward cockpit bubble raised. *Even in the hangar, the air could get pretty ripe with the canopies down in my bassackwards birds*, he reminded himself. He quickened his pace, puffing as he ducked beneath the endless reach of a wing. Standing below the access ladder, he could see no one in the cockpit. Those seats, however, would both swivel and recline.

He grasped the tip of a canard fin, just beyond the solar cells that covered the upper surfaces of a Nemesis, and hauled down. The combination of flexible piezoelectric skin and ultralight carbon filament structure was what made a Nemesis so gossamer; Ben Ullmer's momentum made it nod. "Leigh; you in there?"

A faint female whoop responded first, and then the honeyed tresses of Petra Leigh bobbed into view inside the cockpit. "I'm not sure anymore. For a second there, I thought I was going for an inside loop right here in the hangar. Uh, isn't this where I was supposed to wait?"

Ullmer grunted an assent, moving up the yellow access ladder slowly, letting his arms do half the work. His friends were fond of warning him that, with his bad hip, blood pressure and gout, crawling around on his creations was going to kill him one of these days. And that, he would tell them, was how he wanted it.

Younger pilots swung their legs over the canopy sill without trouble, but Ben had to grasp his trouser cuffs to make it. "Gotta cobble up a geriatric version." He panted, lowering himself to the vacant seat.

"I'll stress it for you," Petra said brightly.

"You've stressed me enough for one lifetime, young lady," Ullmer replied, pulling a folded fax sheet from his pocket.

Her pixie eyes became serious. "Uh-huh. My uncle told me how you two were in the chase plane when that old guy kidnapped me in Black Stealth One."

Ullmer snapped the folded page on his leg as he studied her. "You mean Kyle Corbett? Yep, I s'pose he's old by your standards. By God I hope he's decrepit, he aged me ten years in a few days." He fell silent, still looking at her, now with no amusement.

"Did you—um, is that what you wanted to talk about, Mr. Ullmer?"

She's wary as hell. But not scared, and I want her scared. "No, not about then. I want to talk about later, and about now." With that, he handed her the folded fax.

Her troubled glance went from his face to the page. She

opened it; became absolutely still. Three small drawings lay spaced on the page in a neat draftsman's layout, dimensioned with exact tolerances and printed notes. The page gave every detail necessary to define a device like a twisted knife-blade—or the single blade from a small propeller. The only firms capable of producing blades like that were R & D labs that worked to aerospace standards, in government-mandated secrecy. Even if a private citizen had the money to request such stuff, it would be produced only for another firm immersed in the Official Secrets Act; a firm such as Aerosystems.

"I don't understand," she managed to say, her face gone sallow with a border of dead-white flesh around her lips.

"Put your head down if you think you're gonna faint on me," Ullmer growled. *This isn't the time to show sympathy. But I'm not sure I have any.*

Yet Petra Leigh was made of sterner stuff than that. With carefully controlled deep breathing, she said, "Why would I?" She returned the fax to him.

" 'Cause you're deeper in dookie than a sludge farmer, is why. CIA uncle or not, you're involved in the most serious breach of national security since, hell and damnation, since *ever!* I gotta spell it out?"

Maintaining a glacial calm that, he decided, was pure desperation: "Perhaps you'd better," she said. "I have no idea where you got that fax or what it—"

"I got it from the supplier who fabricated the prototype impeller blades for Black Stealth One, and the requesting facility is Aerosystems Unlimited but the requestor's name on the order is one Petra Leigh."

"Forged, I suppose," she said; but he thought her mouth too dry to say it clearly.

"Right, sure. But whoever signed the check for fifty impeller blades managed to break Marie's computer codes, and paid the company back so everything balanced, and erased every piece of the trail in my shop slicker'n a drum major's whistle." He dropped his voice a few decibels. "And as it happens, you're the number one computer nerd around here."

"I get by," she said, the pretty brow in a furrow that would have been utterly convincing, had he harbored a shred of doubt. "You know, Mr. Ullmer, maybe I could take a crack at Marie's system. People usually leave traces when—"

Ullmer hammered his fist against the cockpit sill in a fury.

"Leigh, you've already cracked our system! That's not what worries me, but lemme tell you what had better be pushin' a cold wind up *your* tailpipe." Softly, now, holding that fax up as a reminder. "You couldn't get to the supplier's system, you had to hope it'd never become an issue because they photograph checks for their records. So in March, when they sent back a smaller check for our goddamn volume discount you'd forgotten about, I didn't know whatthehell to think. All I knew was, you had taken a shipment of something in February. And I called 'em up and asked for a reminder. And got this. By the way, my shop owed you six thousand and change, and you'll get it. You gonna give it back to Kyle damn-his-eyes Corbett, or keep it for your defense shysters when I turn this whole shootin' match over to the feds?"

Petra put her hands together for a moment, as if praying, and shifted to face him directly, as though to face the issue in full. "Mr. Ullmer, please don't. I can see a vein in your forehead that looks as if it might burst. Really; it scares me."

Jesus sneezes, that should suit her fine. I haven't even told Marie about this. But the kid is right; got to calm down. "It'd pull my pressure down a few thousand notches if you'd just own up to what we both know is an open-and-shut case."

Her headshake was in slow motion, but immediate. "I was raised with some absolutes, Mr. Ullmer. You take some chances, but if it makes you sick you take your medicine too. If, I say very hypothetically, *if* I were that deeply involved with a man like Corbett, I wouldn't send him to a maximum security prison for the rest of his life. First, I'd be convinced he shouldn't be in prison before I had anything to do with him. Second, if I were taking such chances already, I'd probably take a chance on acquittal or a light sentence."

"Glad you know the stakes, Leigh. And I'm sure you know what it would do to your uncle."

"Oh shit," she whispered. "I've thought about that side of it. But it never seemed real until now."

"Even if he was CIA, maybe especially if, he might have those bozos on his backside looking for a connection."

A lone, silent tear began to slide down her cheek. "But I still can't, I mean I won't. Betray the best—betray my guy, I mean."

Ullmer had as much of an admission as he needed. "Okay, you know what I have to do: the best thing for everybody as I see it. My problem is, maybe Kyle Corbett in the jug isn't the best thing; I mean, hell, that guy could build himself a battle tank outa bedsprings. You hear what I'm sayin', Petra Leigh? We need him! Actually, what we really need is the Hellbug. And I know it's still flying because every so often a Black Stealth bird inhales a wasp or something and nicks an impeller blade. That's why he had you order enough spares for a lifetime, isn't it? Isn't it?"

Head down, she spoke to the control stick. "He didn't ask me. I did it on my own. The money wasn't a problem, and he was happy enough to get the blades, but he was furious with me."

"Kyle Corbett was *born* furious," Ullmer grated.

"No he wasn't, and you know it. He was betrayed; nearly killed. The original Hellbug was what he saw as his payment. It wasn't because of anything you did," she added. "And I'll deny all of this later. But what did you mean, you need him? You mean, still free?"

"Loose on the world." Ullmer nodded wryly. "There are a few other Black Stealth craft now, but they're dedicated to—let's just say they won't be made available, period. No point in gettin' them famous in the media when they aren't even s'posed to exist. For all anybody knows, Corbett's Hellbug was destroyed. Except for us; I've known since March, thanks to you."

"And who else did you tell?"

The grizzled old head shook firmly. "I'm askin' the questions. I better like your answers. Leigh, there are things a Hellbug can do that nothing else can even approach, and turning itself invisible with that pixel skin is one of 'em."

"I know." Her gaze suggested that she had caught a smile on its way out and swallowed it again. "But you're not making much—uh, I don't know what you have in mind."

After a long pause, Ullmer pocketed the fax and said, "You already have the need to know whatever our spook agencies learn about the Butcher Bird. Okay, here's the latest according to Bill Sheppard. He tells me a DEA source has passed the word that one of the world's richest Colombian felons, who's in a reg'lar country club of a prison down there, has put out a seven-figure contract on a man who's doing time in another prison."

"I thought they did things like that all the time." Petra shrugged.

"Not using a man who claims to control an invisible demon," Ullmer said flatly. "The hit is silent and punches a tiny hole in the victim."

Petra's face, so recently pale, flushed angrily. "You don't think Kyle—" she began.

"No! It would've been barely possible for him to get in cahoots with a foreign government, but those impeller blades were delivered before March. Corbett is too smart to fly the Hellbug with a few impeller blades ready to come apart like shrapnel. He'd pull it out of service just like I would, and fix it. But it takes a long overhaul with special fixtures to pull that engine, and a lot more tooling to replace blades. He wouldn't turn the job over to anybody else, either; I know the son of a bitch. Yeah, it's possible," he repeated, rubbing stubble at his chin. "He could've been screwing around in the Middle East. But whatever the Butcher Bird is, it was killing people ten thousand miles from here ever so often during the past few months. That'd be a logistic nightmare for Corbett unless he put himself in the hands of some very competent government." Another headshake. "He wouldn't do that either, they'd take the Hellbug away and he damn' well knows it.

"So." The old man sighed. "Kyle has the only other vehicle on earth that can do what a Butcher Bird can. I intend to ask him to help us bag the little bastard. I don't know exactly how, yet; prob'ly a surveillance pod for tracking it."

Petra mulled this over for a moment. "I'm not going to tell you why, but I don't think he'd be able to operate for very long in South America."

"Logistics again. He needs hangars, more than one of 'em. It's been almost fun, working out the problems Mr. High and Mighty Corbett has with his stolen bird," Ullmer said, and for the first time he let a grin slip out. "Well, I could ask Sheppard for money to fund that sort of thing, but only after I knew Corbett would go for it. And he won't have to go to South America, Leigh."

"A Colombian prison, you said."

"Not the victim. That one's here in the States. Whoever operates the Butcher Bird, they'll be doing it here, or from northern Mexico. We don't know whether they're here already, but we know where their Butcher Bird will be pretty soon. We just don't know when. It may already be too late."

"I don't suppose you give a damn whether Kyle survives the mission," Petra said.

"Don't you get all starched-shirty on me, young lady," Ullmer told her. "Since you mention it, I'm of two minds about that. I hope to God he can help us stop this—thing," he said, waving a hand in irritation. "But if they took each other out I don't figger I'd shed many tears."

"I would," she said softly.

"I know you would, you're young enough and dumb enough. I just hope you're smart enough to get Corbett where I can talk with him face-to-face."

"How would you set that up, Mr. Ullmer?"

"You know better'n that. I won't set it up, *he* will. It's the only way he'd ever do it," Ullmer replied, grunting as he began to ease himself up from his seat. "Oh, and Petra?" He paused, sitting on the cockpit sill. "Tell Kyle I have a good idea how much you two are risking when you could just drop outa sight with him. They might not find you, that's always in the equation. But as of now, nobody's even looking. And I swear by Almighty God, if he chooses to fight this thing with us I'll try to cover his butt. And yours." With that, he swung over the sill.

Petra's voice followed him down the ladder. "Then I'm not canned?"

"Huh; not by a long shot," the old man scoffed. "This'd be a helluva fine time to pull in another stress analyst, just when the project's making sense."

SIXTEEN

MAY 1991

ALTHOUGH THE SLUGGISH river that separates Mexico from Texas is known to Americans as the Rio Grande, to Mexicans it is known as Rio Bravo. Odile shook the sleeping Clement near dawn to resolve this mystery, having taken the wheel when they refueled on the outskirts of Monterrey.

"We seem to be near here," she told him, her finger in the flashlight beam. Evidently they were within a mile of the border.

"Excellent, *ma coquette*. Continue to Nuevo Laredo," he said. "I must use the telephone at the next Pemex station. Without waking those two, if possible." And with that, he closed his eyes again.

But sleep would not return. He could not forget the baleful glare of Mohmed Ashraf, and the insurrection it promised unless the Syrian got to make his damned telephone call. Well, that was one connection Clement had no intention of allowing any longer, and in earliest light he moved back on hands and knees between the sleepers. His personal luggage lay near the van's rear door, and for once he was glad that the old Dodge creaked so much. His little HK4 automatic pistol still lay among his toilet articles, the .22 caliber conversion barrel threaded for its silencer. Extremely light in weight for an eight-round pistol, the HK4 was bulky only when that silencer extended its length, and it was not the sort of weapon to catch easily on clothing. He thrust the silencer in one pocket and the pistol in another before making his way back to the cab.

Luck was with Clement, in the form of a Pemex station at the confluence of highways south of Nuevo Laredo. He directed Odile to park away from the pumps, stepping out as she coasted slowly to a stop near the highway. Snores from their Syrians testified that the spiked fruit juice was doing its job.

Clement walked quickly to the government-run station. Thirty seconds later he was picking up a telephone, notepad in hand. Though it was still early, the voice he heard was alert. "I need to speak with Melchior Ocampo," he told it. When asked who the caller might be: "I am one of *Los Quatro de Medellín,* the Medellín Four," he said. "Quickly, if you please."

Señor Ocampo answered in a leisurely Spanish baritone but quickly switched to English that was quite as good as Clement's own. Yes, he had expected the four Medellinistas, but not so soon; and how would he recognize them?

Clement described the van and his location. "I was told you would return our rental vehicle and provide further transportation. My maps do not have your lovely city in detail. I will need exact directions."

Ocampo's laugh was harsh and came easily. "My lovely city is no longer quite a pigsty; so why do so many *pollos* want to peck their way north of it?" The town of La Jarita was not far south of the city, he added, and at this hour the traffic would be light. Clement must drive toward it. When he found himself preceded by a black Firebird and trailed closely by a red Camaro, he must follow the black car.

Clement jotted his notes quickly; read them back and found them correct. "But what exactly is a Firebird?"

"Just follow the black car with a bird painted on its hood; very garish, bad taste, you cannot miss it," Ocampo advised.

Before hanging up Clement could not resist asking, "Is my aircraft ready?"

"Yes, but not on this side of the border, Señor Pollo. And by the way: your group must be together and ready to pay when we meet on the highway. If it seems that we are being observed by ground or air, you may drive quite a distance. Perhaps Acapulco, if you take my meaning," he finished, and then the line went dead.

Clement brought a half-dozen bottled drinks back to the car, discarded the drugged fruit juice, and took the wheel from that point, fully aware that the sleepers might be waking at any time. When he asked for Odile's purse she frowned, but offered it. He let her see him stuff the HK4 and its silencer in, then found her linen kerchief and blew his nose resoundingly. "Here. If I need this, be quick," he said with a smile.

"I don't like those things, Roland," she replied. Presently he saw her stuff the silencer tube into her brassiere. He did not see exactly where the pistol went, but no matter; he had been there before.

The main highway out of Nuevo Laredo toward La Jarita thronged with dilapidated pickups and produce trucks chugging their way to market, but at this hour few vehicles headed in their direction. It was Ashraf who awoke with a strong need to relieve himself. "It should not be long now," Clement said, truthfully, because the blunt black carapace of a sporty American coupe had bellowed past them only moments before. The stylized decoration on its hood made its resemblance to a flying beetle even stronger and very soon another car of similar shape, but painted a howling crimson, had perched off their rear bumper. *These people do not believe in understatement*, Clement said to himself.

Soon Mansour, too, was fully awake, hinting that he needed fast relief. Clement felt that the time had come to divulge more of his plans, lest his Syrians panic and go loping off across the arid gray alluvial soil of Mexico when he still needed them.

"I am sure it cannot be much farther," Clement said, "and I must caution you all to remain circumspect in every way. Until now I chose to keep a Syrian state secret—for your own good," he added, deliberately vague. "But as it happens, our success in Guiana has given us fresh targets who could otherwise reveal the djinni very soon."

At this, both of the Syrians burst out in Arabic, speaking so quickly that Clement could not follow. He did follow the black Firebird, however, as it turned onto a side road, jouncing across railroad tracks a moment later. Between the groans of the Dodge and the hubbub of Arabic, Clement found his head ringing while Odile clapped hands over her ears.

"Now, it is absolutely imperative that I reach a telephone," Ashraf cried in alarm.

"Ah, yes. I was told you would want to contact Damascus when we made contact with our Mexican travel agents," Clement lied. "We laughed about that. But in Syria they are well satisfied with your reports and in future I will make your calls for you. However, for the present I do not think these Mexicans would appreciate any of us making any calls whatever."

Ashraf, stunned by the implications, fell silent. "What Mexicans?" Mansour asked.

"The ones in the cars ahead of and behind us," Clement said.

"I do not believe it," Ashraf burst out. "I believe—"

"They do not care about your beliefs, Ashraf. They will provide us safe passage to an aircraft, for which I am to pay cash forwarded from Damascus. It is a great deal of money. Shall I show you Assad's money, then? Would that calm your fears about my allegiance?" *Money has no allegiance but it might quieten this fool for awhile,* he thought.

"Then that is what you were doing during your absence," Ashraf guessed.

"That, and more." The Firebird slowed, avoiding the biggest potholes in the road, and Clement's braking made them grab for handholds. "Find my big personal bag, Ashraf. In its smaller side pocket is a package wrapped as a gift. You may open one corner of it to inspect it, then put it back. Selim, you may help if you like."

For the next moments he was blessed with the peace to concentrate on this villainous road. Into Odile's questioning gaze he shrugged and said, "It is there. The arrangements have been made by experts."

"I hope you are right. This mad dashing about on back roads seems very like children playing dangerous games," she said.

But she took out her compact and began to rouge her face all the same. *Making yourself presentable for those dangerous children, eh? Well, who knows? It may help,* he mused.

At this point the Firebird turned onto an even worse road, little more than a track, passing a barbed wire fence. Briefly, they were not in sight of a paved road nor, Clement realized in one agonized instant, any sign of civilization. With a sudden and terrifying thought, Clement braked hard. He would have asked for the pistol, but as the car behind them stopped he saw a man leap from the passenger's side with what looked like an assault rifle. That little HK4 of his had its uses, but a show of force against a spray of rifle bullets was not one of them. Clement found his arms trembling as he said, "Put the money away and be still. Let me see what is happening here." *My God, what if this is a simple robbery? I have put myself in the hands of people I do not know or trust.* This had been an extraordinarily foolish gamble for Roland Clement, who did not even trust the people he knew best. He stepped out of the van and faced the rear.

The man with the rifle was holding it casually, but giving orders in rapid Spanish. "I must know," Clement began, without slowing the torrent of words. "I must know where—" and then in a shout, "I must speak with Melchior Ocampo!"

From behind him came a familiar voice and Clement spun to face another armed Latino, a fellow in neat slacks with gold chains showing through his half-buttoned sport shirt. "I am Ocampo, and you are a fool for stopping like this." He made a languid wave toward the man behind Clement, and stepped up beside the Frenchman. His grin was beguiling, but Clement found little satisfaction in that. Ocampo went on: "You must be the *pollo* who called." His glance went to Odile, who was trying to peek at him without being seen, and his voice rose commandingly. "Unless you have a transmitter in that oxcart and more guns than we do, either show me your federal identification or open that van. Now," he barked, and cycled the bolt of his weapon.

"Do as he says," Clement called, in a rush of something far worse than fear. His fears he could master, but embarrassment was worse. To be forced to take such orders from a Mexican *salaud* was a violation that made him dizzy with rage. "Have you forgotten who brought me here, Ocampo? Does the name, Escobar, mean nothing to you?"

As thumps and creaks came from the van, Ocampo grasped Clement by his collar and let the barrel of his weapon graze his captive's chin. "I could just as easily thrash you," he said calmly. "Never forget that the coyote is always master of the *pollo*, the chicken. But you know nothing of this, do you?" He scanned Clement's eyes, then released him. "The clever fellow who finds ways to move less clever folk across a well-guarded border is known as a coyote. Those he escorts are his chickens; his *pollos*. El Señor Escobar is a very large wolf, but a trapped wolf. And the coyote may share the wolf's spoils but the relationship is not close.

"Very well, then, Señor Pollo. I have agreed to take you and your friends across in one of our own vehicles, and even to provide you with a legally purchased aircraft for you to fly in yanqui airspace. But what if I chose to simply take your money and your lives?" He waved Clement toward the rear of the van as its door opened, walking with him. "Nothing. I simply would no longer be working with that particular group of Colombians. Believe me, there are plenty of others. But I am a businessman, Señor Pollo, and it pleases me to honor my pledges."

Ocampo waved the Syrians outside and stood by while his confederate patted all three men down. The looks his Syrians gave Clement had never been so filled with disgust. When Odile emerged at Ocampo's wave, she did it with a show of leg that, Clement judged, was precisely enough for a lady. Haggard and

SEVENTEEN

MAY 1991

RAOUL MEDINA HAD spent two *chingada* years modifying his tiny sportplane for STOL, short takeoff and landing, and *still* she would not clear a short field as well as he'd hoped. Long before he linked up with Kyle Corbett to spirit the Hellbug away, even before Medina was co-opted out of NSA's Black Hangar when Ben Ullmer ran it, Medina had quietly vowed to make his version of a Mini-Imp land like dandelion fluff. Later, as a fugitive, he had found short-field landings even more imperative. Now, on a warm ry evening in May with a welcome breeze through their shop ors near Barstow, California, he and Corbett were wondering ether to say the hell with it. He was trying to convince himself lowered her stall speed as far as it could drop when the tele- rang.

rew it, Speedy," Corbett murmured, surveying Medina's while sipping coffee beside him. "Let 'em find another e."

might be Lola," was Medina's reply as he ambled across floor.

f a dozen others." Corbett laughed. "Just remember, it's all yours."

w better than that; with the shared millions in cash e Russian attempt to buy the Hellbug, they had 's Tow Service as a cover operation and they ny jobs as they took. One thing about a tow ted you to be a bit antisocial, and sometimes rumpled a few moments before, she looked ravishing as she stepped daintily to the dirt with the air of a duchess. *How do they do it?* Clement asked himself.

Ocampo seemed impressed, so much so that he did not seem to entertain the notion that this French bonbon might carry anything more lethal than her killing smile. "My apologies," he said. "This little charade might have waited a few more minutes. But we are already on my ranch, so no harm done." Turning to Clement he added, "In my country a stranger does not brace a man on his own land. It seemed a point worth making. Now, if you will follow me." And with that, he strode back to the black Firebird.

Clement followed with two thoughts vying for supremacy. One: it looked as if they were in the right hands, after all. And two: in running a business of such a nature, this posturing coyote had probably found it necessary to make a show of his mastery to all of his clients. But it was particularly galling to be addressed as Mr. Chicken. . . .

that suited both men perfectly. Also, nobody thought twice when you towed trailers with tarp-covered objects of weird dimensions around in the California badlands because, after all, the weird shit probably belonged to somebody else. Usually it did. But sometimes it was a set of laminated beams brought in to permit a false ceiling in their sheet metal building, or the useable remains of a wrecked helicopter they'd picked up for practically nothing. If anybody ever walked in to the shop they'd see a thicket of high-tech junk all but hiding the Imp, a high-wing, streamlined little screamer pushed, not pulled, by its propeller. And they wouldn't see the Hellbug at all because any time the doors were open, that prodigious machine was winched into the attic with inches to spare, hanging like a great insect between roof and ceiling. That's what laminated roof beams were for. Their second haven, leased on Reservation land near Port Angeles, Washington, included a refurbished crop-duster's hangar.

For a special few with consuming interests and all the money they needed, this sort of stealthy life was no physical hardship. No one told them what bizarre devices they must or must not develop for the sheer hell of it, and when the elk or salmon beckoned they asked no man's permission for time off. That was fine as far as it went, Medina concluded, but it could play hell with a man's social life.

Take, for example, something as basic as EAA. Medina could never understand how the Experimental Aircraft Association, with one of the world's finest air museums and upwards of 200,000 members spanning the globe, could remain completely unknown to most groundhogs. Pity the aircraft nut who could not get to the Oshkosh Fly-in every summer to brush against twelve *thousand* private aircraft, some of them revolutionary, and to swap ideas with others of that flying fraternity. These days, Medina could pity himself. At any major fly-in, he would have been recognized instantly by too many people. No, a man supposedly dead in a balls-up CIA operation could no longer hope for that kind of fellowship. Corbett never seemed to mind, but hell, he'd always been a solitary bozo and besides, he had Petra. Raoul Medina, basically a friendly macho who enjoyed a dance or a card game, missed the social whirl. Nobody had warned him that the life-style of a dead man had its drawbacks.

Medina reached the phone on its fifth ring and put on his slovenly singsong, "Speedy's Tow Serveess," accented so that the dullest Anglo would obtain a clear and spurious mental picture. That all changed the instant he recognized the voice of Petra Leigh, and

"Speedy Gonzales" became the alert ex-military pilot Petra knew he was. "Hello there, high-pockets," he said, his finger-snap and wave alerting Corbett. "Oh, not too bad when the air conditioner's cranked up. It's the damned boundary-layer flow on the Imp; driving us nuts. But you didn't call about that, or did you? —Sure, he's on his way. Pat your fanny for me," he finished, and put the earpiece down. "Your other copilot," he confided to the approaching Corbett, and wandered back to the drafting board.

In some ways, Medina's relationship with Petra Leigh was more easily maintained than any he had ever known. They shared warm regard without the infection of romance to fever their times together. Raoul Medina cut as wide a swath as he dared among the casually available, and some not officially available, women around Barstow and Daggett. He'd told himself a hundred times they ought to count; yet for him, they didn't. Meanwhile, Petra Leigh and Kyle Corbett slaked one another's thirsts from time to time; lovers, but more than lovers. Together, the three of them could spend half a night pondering the vagaries of airflow over a control surface, or the best way to build a structural support. Medina had never expected to meet a woman like that, and when he did, go to hell if she wasn't Kyle's lady!

But you don't romance your fellow outlaw's woman, he thought, ignoring the muted gravelly buzz of Corbett's voice across the big room. None of that share-the-wealth, Butch and Sundance bullshit was in the cards where Petra Leigh was concerned. Corbett, the loner, had stumbled on a treasure in Petra. Medina, the womanizer, now found himself over forty and had to admit it, he was still tap-dancing around a bevy of small-change bimbos. *Hell, Kyle's in his fifties, maybe I just wait. Might find another Petra if I hung around engineering schools a bit*, he told himself wryly. A tiny corner of his mind noted that, in good time, Kyle and Petra might grow apart. He shook his head to chase the thought into shadow. *Your problem is here with your Imp*, he reminded himself, *not with Kyle's blonde imp.*

Though he was not deliberately listening to Corbett, he found himself troubled by something in that voice. It wasn't the usual banter with occasional chuckles, not this time. And come to think of it, Petra's greeting had not contained its usual bounce. Corbett stood up, scratching his scalp, pacing as far as the phone cord would allow as he listened for a time; a very long time, with only a few muttered responses. *None of your business*, Medina told himself, and took his empty coffee mug for a refill.

When he returned, Corbett was sitting on his stool next to the blueprint, swinging one leg as if anxious for action. Medina thought the man looked ten years older.

Medina tried to make light of it. "Somebody walk over your grave, 'migo?"

Corbett looked up quickly, his eyes haunted. "Worse. Somebody's dug it up. Not yours, Speedy; just mine. Well," he went on, rambling as if to himself, "at worst you've still got the Reservation hangar. You might even keep this one unless—yeah, but if they come down on Petra, who could blame her for turning state's evidence? God*damn* that old man, give him a micron and he'll measure your world!"

"Whoa, hang on, you're scaring the shit outa me," Medina protested, hands splayed and waving as if to dry them. "What old man, and who's coming down on Petra? Talk to me."

Corbett's sigh was explosive. "Christ, I believe I'm about to hyperventilate. No, I am not," he answered himself with slow deliberation. He looked into Medina's frown and fashioned a grin for himself; not a very convincing one. "I am about to work it out somehow."

I hate it when he does that, Medina thought. *He's more afraid of panic than he is of dying. Yeah, but it's panic that kills you.* So Raoul Medina waited patiently.

After a moment Corbett sat up on his stool, hands on his knees. His voice was remarkably steady, considering the bombshell he proceeded to drop. "Ever since Petra got us those blades for the Hellbug, Ben Ullmer has had it all pegged. *He knows*, Raoul! He doesn't know the details, but that doesn't matter. An hour ago, he braced Petra about me and the Hellbug and of course, her connection with it. Not about you, though, Petra thinks you're still running clear. And if you aren't, you can still use your spooker kit and start over. Shit, you've got all of Latin America to hide in."

Medina placed his narrow, chino-clad butt carefully on his own stool so he wouldn't collapse. "*Chinga-cabroncito,*" he swore softly, "do I have time to button up the Imp? But wait, why isn't this place surrounded already? You've gotta give me some details, man, all I'm getting from this is nicotine stains in my shorts!"

Corbett's grin returned briefly, this time carrying more confidence. "Nobody knows where we are, Speedy, it's not like that. But here's what I gather." With that preamble, he sketched the facts to Medina.

Then they argued their options through two more mugs of coffee. Curiously for Medina, it was he and not Corbett who shrugged off the notion of Petra's defection. "Because she's got a spine of chrome-moly steel is why; Jesumaria, even I know that much," he insisted with some heat. "And old Ullmer's holding a carrot as well as a stick. He *wants* you running loose, 'migo. He needs what you can do that nobody else can." He looked across the shop, not seeing it, chewing his lip as a lopsided smile grew on his face. "We could come out of this with brownie points, a, uh, quid-whatchacallit."

"Quid pro quo? I hire out for this search-and-destroy thing and they leave me alone?" Corbett shook his head. "Bloody likely. And what's this 'we' shit, Speedy? This needn't concern you. You're dead. Stay dead."

"Yeah? If I let you have all the fun it'd kill me," Medina replied. He wanted to say, *I'll do it for the three of us,* but knew it would sound smarmy; worse, it would sound naive. "Besides, if there's brownie points to be had, I could collect a few." That had a nice selfish ring to it, and it might even be true.

"And you don't think Ullmer's pals would cross him up and collar us anyway?"

"Depends. They might not even look for me if you don't tell 'em who to look for. You've got a partner; could be lots of people. I wouldn't have to be named unless they nailed me somehow."

"They'd insist on knowing. You know what control freaks those desk jockeys are," Corbett argued.

"Yeah, but they can be torqued when they're up against deadlines. You say Ullmer wants a face-to-face with you fast, to figure out your tactics, 'cause he thinks there isn't much time. That gives us some power to negotiate. I trust Ben Ullmer, he sounds like a Georgia cracker but he knows how to play the NSA's games and he's straight as a surface plate. Same goes for Doc Sheppard. But that slick-as-snot second banana of Sheppard's, I wouldn't trust with my warm Dr. Pepper."

"Aldrich? That's true, I suppose I could make that a condition. Ahh, shit." Corbett wiped his face with dry hands; shook his head. "You realize we're already talking about both of us risking everything—*every*thing—on nailing some kind of murder machine that may just punch our lights out."

"Yeah. We're also talking about pulling out, maybe to Argentina, taking Petra along if she'll go."

"She'd go," Corbett snorted, "and I'd have to take her to keep her out of prison, which would fuckin' kill her family, by the way; and one day she'd learn to hate me for it. I wouldn't blame her, either." The men fell silent for a moment. Then: "Raoul, do you ever wake up in the middle of the night worrying that we were too selfish?"

"You mean, am I jumpin' into this out of guilt? No. Some people draped us in flags and hung us out to dry a long time back, 'migo. Is that your real reason for letting Ullmer co-opt you?"

"Maybe a little but I've uh, well, beside my other reasons, nobody lives forever. You know how I hate the idea of becoming a boring old fart, Speedy, and I might not get another chance like this."

Medina's frown had a touch of horrified fascination in it. "To show off? Push the envelope? Be a *chingada* hero to people you wouldn't invite to a rat race?"

"You put it so well," Corbett said, with bogus awe. "Okay, call it that. How about you? Any hidden motives?"

"If I've got one—I guess it's wanting a chance to settle down, not run around waiting for some fed's paw on my shoulder for the rest of my life. A brownie point might do that."

"Plus, you're secretly in love with me," Corbett said, straight-faced.

"There's always that." Medina grinned. "So: it's decided, you know it and I know it. When do you sit down with Ullmer?"

EIGHTEEN

May 1991

CALE HURST HAD been a U.S. Customs inspector long enough to know how a Company ringer might be spotted. Customs was a branch of Treasury, not of the CIA, though both hired seasoned people as well as young guys. The basic difference you got from seasoning showed up first in the eyes. It took years to dim that young-buck sparkle in a man's eyes that, veterans claimed, was really just the sun shining through the back of your head. Of course, most of the new-hires with tired eyes had a lot of by-the-book ways you developed soonest on a metro police force. But if you noticed some new Customs inspector in his thirties who didn't spend much of his time checking procedures and didn't give a shit about the peculiarities of previous cases, maybe he wasn't only Customs. Maybe he was CIA as well, which was not by the Treasury book at all, in fact definitely against it. And if a guy was drawing two salaries, he probably had more than one agenda, which could raise a few suspicions among guys with only one. Bad karma all around.

Because Cale knew all this, he concluded that others could figure it out too. That is why he tinted his graying sideburns and read up on procedures a lot and prodded the older hands to yarn about the nuances of cute stuff they'd seen people try to pull on Customs. Cale Hurst was drawing two salaries from Uncle Whiskers, only one of them to prevent crossings of illegal elements into CONUS, the continental U.S., at Laredo.

On this particular morning, Cale was feeling his oats a little

because he had already made the kind of bust that brought com-
mendations: a Datsun spare tire containing not enough air but
plenty of rock cocaine, close to a full kilo of it, heat-sealed into a
long thin polyethylene tube. It wasn't the extra weight of the tire,
Cale had explained to plainclothes agents; two extra pounds wasn't
much. The only reason he was interested in the spare was the fact
that the Datsun's other tires were all threadbare, but that spare
looked brand-new. Dumb bastards were obviously small-time
mules, maybe even ignorant of what they carried. Cale could care
less about that part of it but he'd seen friends strung out on drugs
and truly enjoyed stopping more of that shit from entering CONUS.
Job One, for him, was making the bust. Agents would take it from
there.

Job Two arrived shortly after his break, in a creaky old panel
truck with Mexican plates crossing over the bridge from Mexico
with five people and something less than six plugs firing. Cale was
checking IDs on a couple with identical sunburns and Kansas plates
when he saw the clunker pull to one side, losing its place in line just
before its engine died. The driver, with a Latino haircut and a lithe
step, hopped out and lifted the hood. That's when Cale saw the
yellow paint sprayed on the hood's underside.

Cale, one of four uniformed inspectors on duty, did what anyone might do: he called for a replacement and strolled back to the
panel truck, idly swinging his big long-handled mirror like a golf
club. He said nothing to the Latino, who was fiddling with ignition
wires, until after he ran the mirror on its roller wheels under the
chassis, just doing his job, twisting his wrist this way and that. He
didn't fail to notice the woman in the front passenger seat, he simply pretended to. The Latino latched his hood and restarted his engine, waiting patiently until Cale had made a circuit around the
vehicle, which was now thrumming without a skip. If anything, it
sounded a hell of a lot healthier than most.

Cale asked the usual questions and accepted a set of papers.
The Latino had a good strong baritone and better English; a shopping spree north of the border for his friends, he said, a day-trip
only. "You will be Hurst," he added.

"Unless my tag lies." Cale nodded, studying the IDs as always.
"And you're Ocampo?"

The Latino was waiting for something; seemed uncertain
whether he had the right man. That's why Cale had waffled about
his name, to make it interesting for the guy. At the Latino's nod,
Cale took the edge off. "Nice color scheme," he said.

"It is best under the hood," said Ocampo, starting to relax.

All correct and to formula, but, "You should've come through when I'm on nights," Cale said. "Now I gotta make a production of it, look you over."

"They could not wait." Ocampo shrugged. "And we had your duty schedule."

Cale held up the traffic flow to let the van in, gesturing to show Ocampo where to stop again. As he opened the cargo door wide, he saw the three men staring back at him from perches on luggage and well-built crates with locks. One was cue-ball bald, built like a wrestler; one slender, dark, hook-nosed; one older and chunky, blondish, light-skinned. The smell wasn't too bad, spiced with chocolate and orange soda pop. The men were not staring at Cale Hurst, but at the papers he still held. "This is fucking crazy, Ocampo, all these crates and shit."

"They would not wait," Ocampo insisted.

"Do they speak English?" He looked at the men. *"Habla inglés?"*

"They were warned not to try," said Ocampo. No one else spoke.

Now genuinely interested, Cale could not resist the question. "What *is* all this crap?" He toed the nearest crate. By God, if all that stuff was heroin, it could zonk a million people. Cale's Job Two was to pass special people, not special chemicals. There were limits to what a man was expected to do when making accomodations in the national interest.

No one spoke. "Open this one," Cale said, nudging the crate again, then stepping back, bent over to avoid the van's roof.

"Environmental study equipment," said the chunky blond, his pronunciation very crisp but nasal. Maybe French, possibly Brazilian, but his English was good.

Cale saw Ocampo's frown, and smiled back, letting his hand rest idly on his side arm. "Better," he said to the chunky guy. "Show me."

"This is against protocol," Ocampo hissed, as the man got down on his knees to twist a combination lock. "Accomodated entry includes personal effects."

Cale leveled a forefinger to point at Ocampo. "Scientific equipment? What'd it be next time, a fucking eighteen-wheeler with a pipe organ fulla nose candy? If you people want accomodated entries, don't start broadening your charter. No contraband. No drugs."

"I could name some of your people who thought differently," Ocampo said slyly.

"Before my time," Cale said, watching El Chunko open a case. "It's my name you want to remember."

"And if they are bringing anything in, I have no knowledge of it," Ocampo went on.

"We'll see. Ah," said Cale, as the casing opened. Inside, packed in molded foam rubber, lay what might have been a computer screen with extra dials and switches on a console. "What kind of environmental study?"

"Air and water quality," said the blond guy. "To verify the figures we are given."

Now Cale began to smile. "You don't trust us to be the world's quality cop, is that it?"

The guy's shrug said, *You got it.*

"So somebody's letting you see for yourself," Cale said, mostly to himself. "Makes sense. That what's in the other cases too?"

"Gas analyzer, spectral scanning equipment," the guy said. "Atmospheric sampling devices as well."

Cale nodded and backed out of the panel truck, unkinking his back as he closed the door. He walked to the driver's window and handed Ocampo the sheaf of papers, noticing the dark-haired dolly in the other seat again. Man, if that was an environmental scientist, Cale Hurst had chosen the wrong line of business. Whatthehell . . . "See, that wasn't so bad," he said. "Have a good day."

Ocampo started up the engine again, jaw set, obviously pissed at Cale's way of doing business.

But before he moved away, Cale said, "Oh yeah, one more thing, just for my curiosity. You're the third Melchior Ocampo I've met. How many Melchior Ocampos are there?"

Cale thought for a moment that he wasn't going to get an answer. "As many," said Melchior Ocampo, "as we need," and then Cale was standing in exhaust fumes, watching the panel truck weave itself into Laredo traffic.

NINETEEN

MAY 1991

CLEMENT DID NOT speak to the Mexican until they had left Laredo far behind them, and scarcely noticed when the panel truck aimed its nose up a broad thoroughfare proclaiming itself U.S. Route 35. What would have happened had he not disobeyed Ocampo, not spoken to the uniformed American at all? The man had been armed, watchful, probably intelligent, and certainly a federal employee. Had he ordered a body search, Clement would have had some hard choices. It was perfectly obvious to Clement that they were crossing an international border, but he had expected an easy crossing. Ocampo's instructions had not prepared him for such close scrutiny, and Clement's first impulse had been to keep an obedient silence. Only when he saw Mohmed Ashraf's eyes start to flutter, pupils rolling up in what might have been the start of a faint or a seizure, did Clement take the matter in hand. The master control panel he showed the American might have actually been used for environmental sampling; the djinni itself might even have passed as an upper atmosphere sampling device.

On the other hand, nothing might have passed. In a universe equally likely to this one, they might all be under guard at this very moment, and it would be the fault of this arrogant pig driving the panel truck. This was the kind of event that could erode the team's confidence in their leader, and no doubt the others were equally full of misgivings as their silence extended. To assert himself more than anything else Clement leaned forward, keeping his tone civil because he still needed the aircraft Ocampo had promised. "That was a very near thing at the bridge."

"Not as near as you think," Ocampo replied, slowing as they skirted the verge of the weatherbeaten Texas town of Encinal. "That officious *pícaro* has his orders, and they are not to be violated merely because he chooses to dislike my face, or yours. Unless those orders include a special alert for you, Señor Pollo." He turned to give Clement a sidelong glance. "Could that be the problem?"

Clement, who had regained his little silenced automatic from Odile before their crossing, restrained an impulse to use it then and there. "I cannot imagine why," he said evenly.

"Perhaps your imagination is less active than mine. I am always imagining things. I can imagine a team of scientists bringing in a nuclear bomb, or chemists with equipment for refining very expensive products sent by your friends in Colombia. I can even imagine . . ."

"But have you imagined the size of the organization I represent?" Clement cut into the man's soliloquy with his own imagination rampant. "Did you imagine that this was the only way we could cross the border? Try and imagine what could happen the next time you try, if certain of my colleagues should learn of the cavalier treatment you seem to enjoy so much."

For a moment, Ocampo held his tongue. Then, with a bit less of that bantering tone: "I doubt that sovereign nations would stop accomodating one another's special needs merely because of a trivial clash of personalities," he said.

But Clement had heard the interchanges between Ocampo and Hurst, and he knew from the beginning that his entire team had been inserted into a kind of pipeline, an occasional conduit to assure safe passage of a few illegals across national borders. And from Hurst's sudden outburst he realized that the rules prohibited some things: drugs, for example. Why, then, had Ocampo's thugs failed to inspect his equipment for illegal substances? Doubtless because Ocampo, or his superiors, had been well informed by the Colombians. Perhaps too well informed. If all this was so, Ocampo was merely one of the minnows among bigger fish, and killing the swaggering fool would gain nothing.

"You are correct," Clement told the Mexican, "about the needs of nations. But I feel certain that all nations could pursue their needs very well with one less Melchior Ocampo, when so many can be had so cheaply. You do enjoy your pay, and your work," he persisted.

Ocampo's shrug was almost French.

"Just try to enjoy it a little less, and you may keep it longer," Clement said loftily, and gave Ocampo a patronizing pat on the shoulder. He could see Odile in profile, and knew that she was enjoying his sport with Ocampo. His victory was purely verbal, intellectual, but the strutting hoodlum Ocampo no longer called him Mr. Chicken, and now drove as if someone had let the air out of him.

When Ocampo turned off the main highway at Cotulla, Clement saw a highway sign and suffered a kind of vertigo. "This is madness," he exclaimed. "We cannot be within two thousand kilometers of Los Angeles!"

"Directly ahead, fifteen yanqui miles," Ocampo told him, virtually wriggling with pleasure at his passenger's concern.

For the first time in an hour, Odile spoke. "There could be many towns by that name."

"Of course," Clement said, subsiding. "How—provincial of them."

He never got to see whether Los Angeles, Texas, had multiple freeways for its handful of citizens because Ocampo turned off again near a creekbed that ambled through the arid plain. Though the loamy soil did not seem to rise enough to hide anything as large as an aircraft, the road presently revealed a natural brush-dotted rise and, behind it, a solitary single-engined craft baking in the sun.

Clement emerged from the panel truck almost running, lustful as a youth facing a Ferrari. The aircraft was basically an aluminum Cessna, with a tan-over-cream paint job designed to blend into the South Texas soil without being too obvious about it. He walked around the craft, his gaze alert to detail, admiring the stretched fuselage with its turbocharged Continental engine and the right-hand rear door that would easily accept his largest container. The main landing gear splayed in a comically wide stance, flanking an external fiberglass container that fitted the underside of the fuselage and should hold still more cargo. It gave the plane a pregnant guppy look. Even an untrained eye could tell that this was not your basic transportation.

Clement, who had piloted light aircraft for many years, had flown planes somewhat similar to the Cessna 207 and knew that he could not have picked a better one for his purposes. Its tail fin proclaimed that the Cessna was a Robertson conversion, and the letters *STOL* had been printed high on the fin. "I will need to try it," Clement called to Ocampo, "but it may be marginally acceptable."

While his team unloaded their equipment, Clement checked the Cessna's papers and fired up the big air-cooled Continental I0-540. Ocampo sat beside him to enjoy the cockpit airflow behind a whopping three-bladed propeller in what, by now, had become stifling heat. According to the operation manual, the Robertson 207 conversion could enable the Cessna to take off from a soccer field and land across three of them, if not too heavily loaded. It was hard, Clement found, to keep his elation from showing as he checked his instruments and failed to locate any basis for complaint. "I must take it up for a few minutes," he said at last. "Do you know how to fasten your harness?"

"No. Nor need to," said Ocampo, exiting the plane. "One warning for you: I am told that the mere sight of this thing is enough to draw federal agents, near the border. It looks exactly like what it is, a perfect vehicle for hauling illegal merchandise."

"So I must not fly south for any appreciable distance." Clement nodded. Yes, with all its navigation gear and external antennas the damned thing looked like a streamlined pincushion. No doubt it was affordable only because it had outworn its welcome on the border.

"So I am told. Enjoy your toy, Señor Pollo," said Ocampo, and latched the door.

Clement did not firewall the engine by mistake; he did it to flatten the man who had this penchant for pet names, and very nearly succeeded, missing Ocampo with the horizontal tail by no more than an armspan. The local brush twanged like steel cable against his landing gear, but three hundred turbocharged horses hurled Clement forward so powerfully that, within moments, the craft had lifted itself off and was clawing for altitude at an astonishing rate. Clement found the controls familiar and busied himself for the next few minutes in seeking his own feel for the plane's limits when virtually empty: its stall speed, cruise speed, lateral stability.

Not until he turned and headed back did he notice the blunt toylike mass far below trailing the roostertail of dust. It was Ocampo, of course, leaving at high speed. That could have meant anything, but any properly suspicious man might quickly hypothesize about Ocampo's haste. One, he had kidnapped Odile; everyone knew about Latinos and women. Two, he expected federal agents on the scene at any moment, perhaps having alerted them himself. Three, he feared that Roland Clement might kill him now, having no further use for him.

Pleased with this third scenario, fearing the second, Clement quickly laid the first to rest when he saw all three of his team below, Odile standing with fists on her hips as she stared up at him. Clement landed immediately, realizing that if Odile was sweltering in the sun, some of their equipment might be nearing its temperature limit as well.

Now Roland Clement was in another of his favorite elements, an excellent light aircraft, and after landing he cut the ignition in time to swing the Cessna around smartly near his team; propeller stilled, nothing but momentum to complete his turn. He stepped to the hard-packed soil within a few paces of their equipment.

His helpers did not need Clement's urging to work fast. Ashraf had only the vaguest concept of an airplane's balance, but Selim Mansour, of course, understood. Although the Cessna had seven seats, they would need only four. It was the work of minutes to remove the rearmost seats, using nylon stowage belts to secure their cargo. A small door on the right side of the fuselage, between engine and cockpit, proved capable of swallowing much of their luggage. Working at top speed, the men placed their equipment inside the fuselage with the objective of making it all balance well ahead of those wide-splayed wheels.

Finally: "You sit back here, Mohmed; and you here near him, Selim," Clement said, slapping seats that were reminiscent of extremely rugged lawn chairs. "Odile, take the right-hand front seat. The safety harness is self-explanatory." With that, he trotted around the aircraft and claimed the left front seat. The engine started instantly.

Clement fed the metal tongue of his seat belt through metal holes at the ends of his twin shoulder straps, then latched the seat belt halves together in a standard single-point release, meanwhile twisting about to search for signs of the federal agents his paranoia had created. He was already urging the Cessna across rocklike soil when he saw that Odile was still struggling to make sense of her harness. A quick look in his inside rearview told him that all three of the idiots were still unsecured. *If all goes well, they will come to no harm*, he told himself in a perfect truism, and set the wing flaps for maximum lift. Owing to the uneven character of the Texas plain, and this gargantuan load for such a small vehicle, the Cessna seemed to wallow a bit until, after two hundred yards or so, it lifted its nose and snarled upward, the noise sufficient to drown out all normal conversation. He set a course to the northwest while watching closely for any sign of pursuit, both on the prairie and in the air. After ten minutes or so he had to admit that his fears seemed unfounded. The tethered Aerostat surveillance blimps that formed a radar picket line against smugglers were, according to Ocampo, suffering another in a long line of "downtime interludes," but they might go into operation again without notice. Ocampo had guffawed at the Aerostats, which, he said, could not see past hills or rocks and were operational only forty percent of the time.

Presently Clement reduced power, the many sympathetic buzzes in the airplane quieter now, and called to Odile. "Study my harness. It is a very simple thing. Then turn around and show the others." If he hit a downdraft with passengers unsecured, those flying bodies could seriously damage the aircraft and might deprive Clement of the help he needed. He did not bother to explain that aircraft safety harnesses can be linked up in a dozen wrong ways as easily as the right one but when Odile finally got it right, he nodded and gestured for her to help the others. Roland Clement had never been the sort of man who spent unnecessary time helping those less adroit than himself.

The Cessna had big fuel tanks, and they registered full. Clement began to make himself at home in the cockpit, locating mini-tel headsets, searching map pockets, checking stowage compartments. This airplane had one thing in common with virtually all private aircraft in Christendom: the location of its maps and charts. They were everywhere. The one he wanted was wedged into his seat's slide mechanism before he unfolded the big paper accordion in his lap. The Americans made and frequently updated the world's finest aircraft charts, he reflected, then handled them like yesterday's newspapers.

Fully fueled, the craft would take them something over nine hundred miles while cruising at upwards of a hundred and seventy miles an hour. Clement judged he would still have half his fuel left when he landed, and consulted his compass to begin a vast arc that would take him nearer El Paso without straying near the border of Mexico, which followed the Rio Grande in a great bow known to most Americans as the Big Bend. He knew United States geography as well as most educated Europeans, which was rather better than most American college graduates, and his several trips to American technical colloquia gave him an added advantage. He was now climbing steadily, gradually, from low Gulf Coast prairieland toward the Llano Estacado, or high Staked Plain, of Texas and New Mexico. He was looking for a particular airport where he had once landed; not a large one, nor one so little-used as to excite comment. He was looking for Whites City, New Mexico, a hamlet long accustomed to foreigners and their accents. For it is Whites City, not Carlsbad, that lies only a few miles from world-famed Carlsbad Caverns.

One could blend in among other tourists, leave the Cessna for a few days, find decent lodging where Arabs could cool their heels without drawing suspicious glances, even leave and return by commercial bus among an international grab-bag of strangers. It was important that he make good his boast with haste, yet he must find or make a base first. His was the kind of haste one must make carefully.

Three hours later, Clement identified Monahans, Texas, by a water tower and, soon afterward, passed into New Mexico. By the time he found Runway 7 at Whites City he still had plenty of fuel; but the bellies of his passengers were running on empty.

TWENTY

—

June 1991

THEY HAD DEBATED whether Corbett should fly the Hellbug or the Mini-Imp to Oregon, and Medina finally tipped the scales of decision. "Ullmer would love to get that billion-dollar gadget back again, and you trust him. Petra trusts him, I trust him. Too much trust, too much consensus. That always makes me nervous, 'migo."

So Corbett had flown the Imp, a tiny unconventional single-seater with a bullet nose and mostly metal skin, not nearly as fast as it looked, but it could slip through the air with almost unbelievable efficiency. Though not common, a few examples of the basic type existed. As modified by Medina, with its predatory lines and its landing gear retracted, it used no more fuel than a compact car when cruising and, firewalled, could achieve nearly two hundred miles an hour. It looked like something the Germans might have built, if World War Two had lasted another year.

In the false light of predawn, three hours after takeoff, Corbett entered Oregon airspace. Some hamlet below lay within a corrugation of earth, lights glowing through a macramé woven of coastal fog. From above it seemed a faerie kingdom. Down there, Corbett thought, the manager of the Exxon would be brushing bad teeth; the cafe's waitress was already brewing a carafe of strong coffee. Maybe, if they saw his running lights, they too would think of faerie. *Exotic is whatever you're not*, he decided.

When the sun showed above the Coast Range, its reflection danced across farm ponds, pacing him perfectly, a pour of molten gold so real he half-expected it to leave a trail of steam. Then he was noting familiar landmarks near the Siamese-twin towns of Coos Bay and North Bend, reducing power, skating along above fogwisp that seemed to dissolve big trees. Clear-cutting had dissolved more of the forest down there, vast scars on the earth's patient hide with not enough newly planted seedlings to replace the big conifers. *And one of these days,* he thought, *the planet is going to wipe us off it like mildew, if we keep up that kind of insanity.*

He found the dark strip of Ullmer's surfaced runway shortly after six in the morning, as promised; and in circling the acreage of Aerosystems Unlimited he saw something that twisted, not altogether unpleasantly, in his guts: Ullmer's ancient tan '49 Cadillac coupe, still evidently roadworthy after all these years, parked outside a utility building that might be used as a garage. He had sat in that stylish tub many a time while Ben Ullmer drove it, the old man never allowing anyone else to take the wheel. The idea, Ben had said, was to make it last as long as he did. So far, so good . . .

Corbett quickly flared out for his landing, the special slotted flaps deployed, gear indicators showing down and locked. The Imp's engine was no larger, and therefore no louder, than necessary and Corbett guided the craft whispering to the Caddie before he shut Medina's little beast down near the sheet metal outbuilding. He levered his canopy up and smiled ruefully. Ullmer was sitting in the car, a stained yellow baseball cap perched on his head with its bill slightly askew. It said, CAT, a reference to heavy earthmoving equipment and an ancient in-joke because, while some engineers developed flying sashweights, Ben Ullmer built feathers. At the moment he was wrapped and tied in cigar smoke.

"I thought you weren't supposed to light any of those things ever again," Corbett said, stripping off his gloves as he strolled the few steps to the Caddie. He hoped his darting gaze toward the perimeter fence wasn't too obvious.

It was, though. "I'm not s'posed to," Ullmer grunted, and got out of the car. "You keep lookin' around like that, your eyeballs are gonna fall out. If you see my wife, warn me." The old man made no move to shake hands. Small wonder. He looked down at the cigar; tossed it aside. "First one of those things I've lit in years, Kyle. I needed it more'n I need longevity this morning."

At Ullmer's suggestion, they pushed the Imp backward into the shed and swung the doors shut. "I'd rather you didn't lock it," Corbett murmured when Ullmer fingered the hasp.

The old man shrugged; left it unlocked; waved Corbett to the

Caddie and harrumphed himself behind the wheel. He did not volunteer their destination, and Corbett did not ask. After a brief silence, driving outside new cyclone fencing to leave the site behind, Ullmer spoke. "I think the only way you and me can do this right, is pretend we're two other guys. You didn't do what you did, I didn't try to catch you, and a more decent man than you didn't die in the process."

He means Medina! I wish I could tell him. "You think I had anything to do with that part of it, Ben?"

"That's what I mean, we're about to get tripped up by our old dirty laundry," said Ullmer. "We're two other guys now, okay?"

Corbett nodded. "In some ways I suppose we are. I sure am, or I wouldn't be here now."

Ullmer said that was a roger, and then began to explain certain rules that must be observed. The upshot, he said, was this: he, Ullmer, had been empowered to hire a private subcontractor and no federal employee had to know what aircraft, or pilot, he was using. "That includes Bill Sheppard," Ullmer added. "He'll probably guess, but he won't ask. Rules of the game," he said.

"And you believe him," Corbett suggested quietly.

"During the operation, I do. This thing is more important than settling old scores. Gummint is scared straight and I can see why. But at debriefing time, you may wanta watch your ass," Ullmer said, with a quick glance at his passenger.

That's a piece of honesty he didn't have to share, Corbett thought. "If I'm still firing on all cylinders," he said. "I still don't know exactly what I'll be chasing, or where or when, or what I'm supposed to do if I catch it."

For some minutes, Corbett had caught whiffs of tidal wetland and now, as the road straightened along the verge of an estuary, he saw an ordinary street sign: BAY DRIVE. Ullmer gestured across a narrow arm of salt water. "Golf course up Kentuck Slough here a ways. Coffee's fair and walnut waffles are worth the trip. We can sit outside. Problem with that?"

"No problem. My problem is with the job, Ben. You act as if I've already been briefed."

"Haven't you?"

Corbett sighed heavily. "You think Petra and I haven't got better things to do than discuss classified shit I have no interest in? No, goddammit, she hasn't briefed me! That's why I'm here."

Ullmer crossed a bridge and navigated a serpentine drive in the old Caddie. "Gotta tighten those tie-rods," he said and, in the same casual way, added: "Then you didn't know you'll be up against a very smart little UAV firing a laser cannon?"

Corbett's brows went up, mouth pursed in a silent whistle. "Jesumaria."

Ullmer parked, got out, waited for Corbett to join him. "Medina used to say that a lot," he growled.

Shit, shit, shit! "Did he? Sorry," Corbett replied, wishing that old Ben's glance were less sharp, less speculative.

They were seated outside in bright sun, elbow-to-elbow by choice so that neither of them had to squint. Ullmer ordered sensibly and then chuckled as he heard Corbett's order. "I s'pose you know what your cholesterol count is," he said to the younger man.

Corbett thrust a thumb upward. "Pushing the envelope," he said.

"With all that bacon and butter you asked for, it's gonna be in orbit," Ullmer rejoined.

"Doesn't matter," Corbett said. "I've got a secret weapon. Speaking of which: don't tell me there aren't a few more Black Stealth One aircraft by now; I wouldn't buy it. There's *got* to be others. So why not use 'em?"

"I'm not saying there are. But if they exist, there's only a few of 'em. And there's—there *would* be," he corrected himself quickly, "a prohibition on using 'em for any iffy purpose whatsoever. Can you imagine the political fallout if a second Black Stealth airchine made headlines of the wrong kind? They had enough trouble with the F-117. They had too much with you. No-o, they won't lift the prohibition. They should, but they won't. It was the first thing I asked Sheppard."

"Why is it that you can predict what the government's going to do," Corbett said with some heat, "if you figure out the action that combines the best short-term outcome with the very worst possible long-term outcome?"

" 'Cause expedience is more important to a politician than his grandchildren are," said old Ben. "Our politicians, I mean. Foreigners take a longer view."

Corbett glared at the older man, accepting what he had said, loathing it too. Then he looked away, refocusing on the present circumstance. "Okay, let's say I agree to hire myself out with the Hellbug. What do I have to do, so that Petra doesn't take a fall she doesn't deserve?"

Ben told him then: the killings on both sides of the world, his team's developing profile of the Butcher Bird, the warning passed on from a DEA man in Santa Marta, the man to be targeted. He switched to a catalog of the Caddie's ailments as the waiter served them: headliner, body rattles, brakes that made a man wish for a boat anchor and a short chain. Then, the waiter retreating, he switched again with: "This guy Borges may spend the rest of his life at a facility near El Paso; I'll get a chart for you."

"And it may be a shorter life than he thinks, huh? Does he know?"

"Can't say, but I tend to doubt it," Ullmer replied. "Gummint boys prob'ly aren't scared *that* straight. And your charter is to bore holes in the sky around this La Tuna place, pretending you're not, so you can get photos of the Butcher Bird, maybe trace it back to wherever it's based. Other people will take it from there. You'll get a little equipment pod to mount under the Hellbug's wing. Camera, scintillator trace in case it has a radiation signature, stuff like that."

"Better make it two. I'll need one for the Imp as well."

"No can do. You can't make that little mixmaster invisible," Ullmer replied.

Corbett attacked his bacon with gusto, his waffle with slathers of butter and syrup. Around a mouthful of it he said, "I do know a little about those solar-winged airchines of yours, Ben. Seems like they'd be better surveillance ships than, uh, mine."

"You mean *mine*, you son of a bitch," Ullmer responded, and softened that with a demi-smile. "I always had half a mind to steal it for myself. Well, we're installing some special gear in a Nemesis now, because in some ways you're right. You can't stay up there by yourself, bored out of your gourd while your fuel runs out, for days. A Nemesis can, but it'll be flying very high cover above you, sixty thousand or so. Your job is close cover, down where the Butcher Bird is. We don't know just how smart it is, but I figure you can put the Hellbug in her buzzard plumage and fool it. The pixel program's still working, I take it."

"Yep. And if I don't fool the robot, what then?"

"It could kill you a whole lot faster than cholesterol," Ben rejoined, with a judgmental glance at Corbett's plate. "A laser beam doesn't fuck around, you know. Speed of light, a hearty hi-yo, Silver, and you get a hole burned through your brain before you know you're in trouble. I think maybe we could supply you with some protective blankets for the cockpit, it might stop most of the beam energy. But that might not be enough. If the energy level's high enough, just a grazing reflection can blind a man."

"Then again, if it did shoot, it might hit the Hellbug without hitting me," Corbett offered.

"Maybe. Or maybe it can scatter shots like shit through a tin horn; we don't know." The old man clenched a fist; brought it down softly on the table, twice. As if to himself: "We just don't—fucking—know." An admission with some guilt in it now: "If we knew who developed it, we could make better guesses. We're in that phase now, but all of a sudden here's a hot flash from DEA telling us we don't have the luxury of time to pursue that phase much longer.

"Look, Kyle, I need to know a few things so we can support you better. Like, can you operate from around El Paso?"

"Given a base, sure. Only I don't have one near there."

"So I can get you one," the old man said.

"Not a chance, Ben. Give me cash and don't worry about it. That could keep you clean later, when they're looking for innocents to blame."

"I can do that, and it makes sense for both of us. Fifty kay enough?"

"Plenty. I won't need much; something to serve as a short runway for the Mini-Imp, something for a hangar—maybe a small four-wheel-drive vehicle I can use for a fuel truck, stuff like that." Corbett, always with a plan, had saved one hunk of waffle to mop the last of the syrup. He inhaled it now, getting butter on his chin, grinning like a truant schoolboy.

"You eat like there's no tomorrow" was Ullmer's comment, amused in spite of himself. "But listen, you can't do it all as a singleton. You'll need support people. I mean, won't you?"

"I was figuring Petra Leigh. She knows the Hellbug—"

"I bet she does," Ullmer said, eyes narrowed, then snapping wide in sudden surmise. "I bet she flies it."

"For a long time now," Corbett said. "You need a light touch, but she's got one."

"I hope you don't expect her to fly with you against the Butcher Bird."

"No way. That's a combat mission, pal."

"My thought exactly," Ullmer said. "It's not just that she's a woman."

"It's that she's *my* woman," Corbett said. "She's not the cautious type; hasn't lived long enough to see how many ways you can buy the farm."

"We're agreed, then. I'm guessing she'll fly that little gadget

Molt Taylor designed," Ullmer hazarded, referring to the Mini-Imp. The design was highly regarded, its designer a legend.

"Guess all you want. One thing we won't need is a lot of air traffic around, trying to keep an eye on us. That would piss me off, and it might just give our game away. Give us a dedicated radio channel so we can keep in touch with your people, and stay the hell out of our way until I've found its base. Can you arrange that?"

"If I can't, I'll say so." The old man regarded Corbett soberly over his coffee cup. "You absolutely sure you won't need more help? Black Stealth One isn't exactly a low-maintenance aircraft. I could prob'ly get you somebody."

"You're pushing, Ben," Corbett said. "I can hear a lot of questions you're too smart to ask, and I'm not dumb enough to answer. Put it this way: if you want to have someone from the old Black Hangar ready to help, go ahead. If I need him, I'll holler, but don't hold your breath. Meanwhile, I suppose you want me loitering over La Tuna by noon yesterday."

"No telling how soon it's gonna happen," Ullmer said, endorsing the notion of instant response. "NSA will have a dedicated comm link for you around El Paso before you can be on station. I just need you to say when you'll be there."

Corbett nodded, feeling a tingle of adrenaline as he prepared to undertake this mission; enter the throat of the beast, as it were. "How 'bout sixty hours from now?"

If Ullmer was surprised at the promise, he avoided showing it. He paid their bill and soon they were touring the bay's edge in the Caddie, arguing the kinds of detail that always surfaced when readying modifications to an aircraft. Petra would take charge of the surveillance pod and other hardware, including an attaché case with unmarked cash. After that, Corbett's next contact with any arm of government would be by way of that surveillance pod and its radio's special frequencies.

Though they saw not a living soul, the parking lot of Aerosystems Unlimited was well stocked by the time Ullmer arrived at his little outbuilding, a quarter mile from the plant. Corbett got out and turned back toward the old man. "Any clearances for me to make, Ben?"

"Nope. Can you push that little trike out by yourself?"

"Yep." Corbett turned away.

Lingering, with a tone that might have been wistful in another man, Ullmer watched him open the doors. "You really fooled me, Kyle. I'd have bet my gout pills against your doing this."

Corbett positioned a door. "You'd have been right, two months ago," he admitted.

"I've gotta—well, I'd give a lot to understand it," Ullmer persisted.

Corbett stopped; thrust hands into his old leather jacket. Looked down at his feet. "And you'll see that Petra's taken care of, we both know that," he said, weighing it in his mind, then looking up. "This is just between us, Ben. You'll be the third person who knows, and I want it kept that way. Agreed?"

"Agreed." Something hopeful sprang into the old man's face. "Who's the second person?"

"I am. My doctor was the first." Corbett saw that hope dashed from Ullmer's face as he went on: "Now you'll know. I've been losing weight, off my feed, and feeling like shit for a while now. Turns out it's primary brain cancer, probably something called astrocytoma. When the tumor isn't swollen I feel okay. Inoperable; the doc talked a lot of crap about chemotherapy, but I'd probably just wind up dying a little later, and dying bald at that. This way I should still have a few months. There's a cortisone-type drug that helps: Dexamethasone.

"That's my secret weapon, Ben. I know I'm going to cash in, and I can decide what kind of fun I want to have while I'm waiting. I don't want Petra trying to affect my decision. Anyway," he grinned, "I figured this is the best present I could give you."

Ben Ullmer's jaw twitched in a pale countenance. "You know," he said in wonderment, "I used to think you knew a good bit about everything. Now I think you don't know nothin' from nothin'." And with that, he drove away.

TWENTY-ONE

JUNE 1991

C LEMENT REASONED THAT a pair of camels traveling together might draw an occasional glance, and the same might
be true for a pair of French poodles. But in the eyes of locals, a
quartet of camels and poodles would draw entirely too much attention. Even the crestfallen Ashraf agreed that, split into pairs, Clement's crew was far less motley. While the Syrians stayed in a Whites
City motel room, Odile Marchant accompanied Clement on his
search for a site. They found El Paso confusing, its tendrils reaching
along highways virtually to the gates of La Tuna.

Las Cruces, New Mexico, lay less than an hour's bus ride to the
north of El Paso, however, a college town that managed to retain a
certain high desert panache. It was here that Odile charmed her
way into an Avis rental minivan, and Clement breathed a prayer of
thanks to the Syrians who had made up their false Algerian identification. Her one credit card, somewhat to her own astonishment,
was American Express. Clement had to explain to her that the
Amexcard's one real advantage lay in its being truly global; while
many vendors chose not to honor it, plenty of them did. That, and
her forged Algiers driver's license, was enough to put her in a gray
Chevrolet Lumina APV, a vehicle with spaceship aspirations and an
upper dashboard surface deep enough to sleep on.

Clement called Mansour twice a day between forays into the
countryside, using his men as his usual tripwires. If anyone was
watching them, they were doing so too subtly for Selim Mansour to
detect it. On the second day, Clement realized how near Las Cruces

lay to White Sands, the site of the still-active missile range. Americans had spent a lot of money on secrecy and surveillance over the past forty years, and some of it had gone into small airstrips in the vicinity of Las Cruces. Some of those strips, including the Army's Condron strip that had long served White Sands, were still useable but, he suspected, by now others might be only faint scars on the landscape. Here the earth lay like a rumpled quilt, alkali dirt baked hard between jagged peaks that rarely saw rain. Those old strips might still be serviceable for a Cessna STOL.

Without a word to his Syrians, at dawn on the third morning Clement drove the Lumina back to the Whites City airstrip and marked a spot on Odile's map before sending her off again in the Lumina. In less than an hour, he was flying past Las Cruces on his way west. To the east of the town were too many roads, too many people, too much surveillance equipment designed to watch robots in flight. To the west he found only one major highway, and dry washes, and the occasional ranch structure. And finally, in midafternoon near a natural feature marked on his chart as a crater, the location he sought.

To make certain, he landed the Cessna, switching the ignition off and on a few times as he taxied toward the single sheet-metal building that sprawled like a huge barrel on its side, half-submerged in the hardpan soil. He found that he had faked ignition trouble for the sole benefit of bugs and lizards. To judge from broken windowpanes in the Quonset structure and the pall of dust over abandoned benches inside, no one had stepped into the building for years.

The single door set into one side of the building was padlocked, and no one could miss the sign proclaiming the premises as U.S. Government Property, entry prohibited. The big corrugated sliding doors that faced the old airstrip, however, had no lock of any kind. Clement hauled mightily to push one door open enough to squeeze inside, ignoring the squall of bearings unoiled for years, and stood beneath that staunch old steel roof for a long moment while gooseflesh surged across his torso. *Abandoned and off-limits,* he mused. *We might stay here for months without arousing suspicions, if we are careful with lights.*

He found overhead light switches but knew better than to try them; if the power lines stretching away from the building were still connected, they would be metered somewhere. He was not sure how often that metering would be done, but a small electric generator of his own would render the problem academic.

Grit on the concrete floor crackled and sizzled like snow under his shoes. In the breeze outside, a tumbleweed scratched for admittance against the Quonset's armor. Some sixty kilometers to the east, roughly forty American miles, a Colombian was shuffling around in a prison exercise yard, unaware that he was awaiting his own execution. All in all the site was so perfect, Clement considered trying to unload the Cessna himself. But getting those hangar doors open was donkeywork, and his donkey was waiting in Whites City. Clement managed to trundle the door closed before firing up the Cessna.

While he was refueling at Las Cruces Municipal, a gray Lumina minivan drove into its parking lot. Because the filing of flight plans is optional, certainly not an option on Clement's agenda, he paid for the fuel and then walked straight to the commercial terminal. He found Odile waiting at a corner table in the lounge.

Though cranky after her long drive, Odile soon brightened at the news. She did not even pout when advised to change out of those stylish clothes, because with his instructions he handed her a very large fistful of U.S. currency. Odile could always be counted on to enjoy spending money.

"The longest ladder that will fit in the car," she recited back to him, consulting the notes she had scribbled on her road map. "Four kilowatt alternator unit, cots, sleeping bags, insect netting, lubricant spray, brooms. Brooms?" Her raised eyebrow suggested an expectation of more dirty work as she continued down the list: rolls of tape, large bolt cutters, rolls of thick opaque plastic sheeting, big water containers and canned food for a week, et cetera. The final item, a portable chemical toilet, actually provoked a smile from her. "No bidet, *mon chéri?*"

"No running water," he admitted. "But we will have some amenities. A decent French wine, if such is to be found. Now hand me that map for a moment. You may need to cut your way past a locked gate, but you will have bolt cutters. I expect we will be there before you. The main thing is to maintain the illusion that the place is still abandoned."

Ten minutes later, a call from the terminal lobby found Mansour in fair spirits. He seemed pleased to hear that he would be met at the Whites City airstrip in an hour or so. "Ashraf, of course, will have questions," he added in tones too noncommittal to be natural.

Soon afterward, Clement pointed the Cessna's nose eastward and busied himself with a mental rundown of his agenda, in detail. Aware of the radars that kept track of light aircraft, he flew a cir-

cumspect pattern and arrived at Whites City as shadows length-
ened across the single asphalt runway.

Though Mohmed Ashraf clearly intended to take the seat next
to Clement, he did as he was told, taking a rear seat while Mansour
sat in front. After he paid the landing fee, Clement returned and
moments later they were aloft again.

Mini-tel headsets, wired like intercoms, lay here and there in
the cabin, and Clement wore his as much to muffle the engine
noise as anything else. He studied Ashraf in his rearview; jaw set,
glowering at the terrain below, lips moving now and then in some
private monologue, the Syrian had not noticed the headsets near
him.

Clement's gesture toward Selim Mansour was subtle, but sufficient. Now both front-seat occupants wore headsets and Clement
spoke softly into the tiny mouthpiece extension. "Selim, what sort
of questions may I expect from our spy?"

"Why, the same sort he asked of me," Mansour murmured.
"You know he is a security spy, surely you would expect him to
take any measures he thinks necessary. I convinced him it would be
foolish to call his mother from the motel room, but he found a
public telephone. He was not happy with his discoveries after using
it," Mansour went on.

In the regime of cursing, Arabic beats French. Clement employed a few choice phrases. Then: "And what does he think he has
discovered?"

"He wonders whether we have abandoned Syria. He wants to
know whether you intend us to return, and how soon."

"Stupid Bedouin," Clement said.

"And yet," Mansour replied, "an intelligent man might ask
the same questions."

Clement thought about that for a moment. "A man like yourself, for example." Not really a question.

Mansour appeared to be gazing innocently out the windshield
as he said, "Would you prefer that I lie to you, my friend?"

"Selim, we will return when I have decimated the ranks of
men who lead the West in advanced weaponry. Assad will be deliri-
ous with joy. It should not take us very long." *No longer than, say, the
rest of my life,* he added to himself.

"You put me in an awkward position, Roland. I believe in
Syria's future as much as in her past. My countrymen will think me
a turncoat."

"Not when we return triumphant, Selim. And meanwhile,

you are only obeying my orders. How could Assad fault you for that?''

Mansour said nothing, but his slow gaze, turned on the pilot, as much as replied, *With red-hot pincers and cattle prods. How else would you think?*

Barren peaks reached dark fingers of shadow across the desert as Clement crossed Interstate Ten and found his landmark crater. In minutes he had lined up for his approach; saw no sign of Odile; ghosted the Cessna to a touchdown and taxied to the sandblasted half-cylinder of sheet metal that would be their new base.

The Syrians, perhaps from a sense of vulnerability in this open country, lunged and cursed against the hangar doors in their efforts to push them wide. Finally, with Clement adding his weight, the overhead bearings uttered a final penetrating screech. Clement earned a blood blister on his thumb while adjusting the Cessna's nosewheel, but at last they pushed the aircraft inside and pierced the desert silence again with the music of dry ball bearings.

The three of them had their equipment ranged in neat piles beside the Cessna when Ashraf ran to the multipaned window. ''A strange vehicle,'' he cried. ''I knew it! You have trapped us all, you lying Christian fool!''

Clement hurried to the window and smiled, seeing the gray Lumina advance in gray twilight. ''We are trapped by Odile bringing food and comfort,'' he replied, and the lack of malice in his voice should have told Ashraf something.

TWENTY-TWO

JUNE 1991

SHE'S ON TEMPORARY assignment," Ullmer told his remaining three study team members. "All I can tell you is, Petra will be working on the same problem but from another angle. I gather you've got something to tell *me*."

"Computer nerds," Colleen Morrison sniped. "Takes a machine to catch a machine, I suppose."

Jared Cutter, who had long since cured himself of lusting after Morrison, only muttered, "Catwoman strikes again."

Ullmer made no reply, but his aspect was not benign. To keep the peace, Wes Hardin stepped into the breach. "We've got some conclusions for you, Ben. You were worried that some third-worlders might have the technology as well as a motive. China, Indonesia, Singapore, all those." He handed the old man two sheets of paper.

Ullmer scanned them, grunting to himself. The Chinese, it seemed, were still developing their versions of Russian versions of American hardware. Indonesia's Nusantara Industries and Singapore's Aerospace Group had vastly more skill than previously thought, but had yet to turn their energies away from commercial aircraft. South Africa, Brazil, Argentina: all were comers in military aerospace but for various reasons each of them lacked the ability to field a Butcher Bird.

"Good reasoning here, team," Ullmer said at last. "Sheppard will be glad of the China verdict, it was bothering his people. In any case, he's sent new data this morning." He began to tap with a forefinger against the digits of his other hand. "Israel. France. Iraq and, God help us, Syria. I know," he said into the silent scowls of protest, "the last two have their own iron curtains and the first two are s'posed to be helping us find the bad guys. But just about everybody else has been ruled out. The ex-Sovs have the best excuse: two victims of the Butcher Bird were on their payroll. We'd have ruled out France, but they probably do have the technology and they're a subtle bunch politically. In the region where the bird first showed up, they've got links of interest that are older than bronze."

"Yeah," Hardin said. "But we're looking for the technology. Iraq? Syria?"

"A few years back, the Iraqis bought a guy who gave 'em the longest-range siege gun on earth," Cutter reminded him, after a thoughtful pause. "He got killed for his trouble before it was ready, but the point's made. If you buy the right guy, maybe you don't need a big program."

Morrison sighed her exasperation. "Well, hell, then we're looking at China or Indonesia again!"

"No we're not," Ullmer shot back. "Those four sources I listed are those that have hired top-of-the-line designers they wouldn't need for peaceful development. Very special people with heavy track records in weapon systems. They tend to be expensive, though Israel ain't known for her pay scale. Sheppard tells me they still want their hotshots cheap and committed, or not at all. Still— they're one of the finalists. So: what does that tell us about those designs you've been playing with?"

"I'm a blank," Hardin said, then quickly cocked a thumb and forefinger at Morrison. "And don't say it," he warned.

"Goddamned grown children," Ullmer muttered. "It tells us to check on those hired guns! Who are they, what are their personal design signatures? Never mind, it's been done," he went on. "Turns out Saddam Hussein has hired two Israelis—who may be playing double games, but at least we know what kind of bird they'd most likely build."

"Hell, that collapses several categories," Cutter exclaimed. "We look only at French and Israeli stuff, and we've already got those worked up. That leaves—"

"Syria," Ullmer finished for him. "And there's reason to believe they've installed a very secret R & D site under an ancient ruin in the desert. Satellite coverage says nothing much is happening there lately in the way of heat and trace emissions. There was, and now there's not."

"Cut to the chase," Morrison cut in. "Do they know who might be behind it?"

"Frenchman," Ullmer replied.

"Body of revolution," Hardin said instantly, "or a small helo. Unless the guy is one of the oddballs."

"He is, if it's the guy DGSE's computers coughed up in France. But he's always had a special twitch for bodies of revolution." Ullmer nodded.

"You mean a flying saucer freak," Cutter put in. "The French gave us a profile?"

"Yep. Not that I needed one, once I saw the name. A hardnose named Roland Clement; I met him a few times, 'way back when. One of those snotty toads who thinks his stuff can't fail. Turns out his design philosophy got more risky than the French could stand. More vicious, too. The froggy word was 'sanguine,' I understand."

Morrison: "So they fired him?"

"Not exactly," Ullmer replied. "Shuttled him off to one side though. As I recall, Clement wasn't the sort to stand for that. The guy had a long memory, too; never forgot a slight or an argument, took it all very personally. In any case, he dropped from sight two years ago. I've asked Sheppard to check on what was in his classified files in France; stuff he had to leave behind, computer records, requests he'd made for tech papers. Even if he cleared out his files, some of that would be available."

"Meanwhile, we twiddle our thumbs," Cutter complained.

"Maybe not," Ullmer hedged. "DGSE says this guy had a girlfriend who was a fair hacker, and she's missing as well. When Sheppard got all this, it took him about a microsecond to alert our border control agents. That was this morning."

"And he might not even be our guy," Hardin mused.

Ullmer shrugged. "You're right, but the word is out on Roland Clement." Pause, with his gaze fixed on nothing. Then: "I don't want it to be him."

Cutter: "But it narrows the problem down, Mr. Ullmer."

"To one smart, bloody-minded sonofabitch," said the old man.

"I'll need to look at Clement's records as soon as the data comes in," Cutter said.

"Go tell Marie," Ullmer advised him. "Right now." He waited until Jared Cutter had closed the door behind him before turning to Hardin and Morrison again. "All right, you two. The Butcher Bird is expected near El Paso at any time. We'll have someone flying daylight surveillance at low altitude and we need a Nemesis for high cover. The Coast Guard could do it, but for reasons I can't go into yet, you're a better option. You have a track record as civilian deniables in a Nemesis. Cutter won't have the need to know, according to Sheppard. So whatever you decide, it stays among the three of us."

Colleen Morrison's surprise carried a hint of amusement as she glanced at Wes Hardin. "Not beyond CONUS borders this time, I hope."

On a previous Nemesis mission together, they had made a forced landing in jungle highlands within sight of Guatemala. Whatever her misgivings, Morrison's reaction suggested that she was willing at least to consider the idea. Hearing this optimistic note, Hardin voiced a caveat with, "A laser beam has a long reach, Colleen. We don't know whether the Butcher Bird is limited to close range, so this may not be a milk run." He turned to Ullmer. "When do we have to decide?"

"Yes or no by tonight," Ullmer told him. "And you're to stay out of Mexico. Let your sensor pod do the work. If anybody takes a laser hit—well, you're at some risk, but if we get a casualty it'll prob'ly be somebody a whole lot nearer the ground than you are."

"Why do I get the feeling that Petra Leigh—" Morrison was saying as the office door burst open, stirring papers on the desks.

Cutter kept his hand on the knob, only his upper body protruding into the room. "Incoming fax from NSA," he announced. "Looks like the stuff we want." Then he was gone again, the door fanning them a second time.

"It's no one you know flying close surveillance," Ullmer told Morrison. "But you'll be told what's essential, if and when." Without another word, the old man hurried out in his haste to read that fax message.

Morrison leaned back in her chair and clasped hands behind her head, eyes narrowed as she gazed at Hardin. "No foreign airspace, we won't be the nearest target, and we get to follow up on this little killer bird firsthand. I say we go for it. What do you think, Tex?"

"I think you sound like Pandora with her hand on the lid," Hardin replied. "I also think, whoever's flying that close cover mission, Ben Ullmer doesn't want to share the details with the military." He fell silent, trading eye contact with Morrison for a long moment. Then, bursting out: "Ahh, shit, Colleen, Ben's caught my tail in a curiosity crack. Besides, last time we drew a very nice salary as deniable civilians. A little hazard pay would come in handy. We'll be back in, what, a week? Ten days?''

"One way to find out," she said, with a wink that managed to be lascivious.

"Why does risk always make you horny?" he asked, grinning.

"Ask me again tonight," she replied. "Right now, you may as well tell Ullmer we'll fly the mission."

TWENTY-THREE

JUNE 1991

THE SURVEILLANCE POD needed little more than a trim to its fairing before it cupped, a modest blister, beneath the port wing of Black Stealth One. Corbett wriggled up from his labors on the hangar floor, grunting. "It's secure as it's going to get, Raoul. Where's Petra?"

"In the ready room, trying to sleep," Medina replied, inspecting the pod. "She's got a six-hundred-mile drive ahead of her, remember."

Corbett wiped sweat from his face; shook his head. "Man, this is shaping into a real logistic hairball. You get that radio rig of Ullmer's wired in her Cherokee?"

"Done. You two can talk on a dedicated and scrambled channel. I wish we had one for me. Supposedly all yours and Ullmer's, is it?"

"Yeah, and they're really NSA units with satellite links; so if you believe nobody but Ben Ullmer will be monitoring—"

"I said supposedly," Medina interrupted. "Just don't forget who you are, Yucca One."

Corbett snorted. "Keep it up, Speedy. I'm not too senile to fly rings around you."

Together, they put away their tools before raiding the refrigerator; chicken salad slathered on rye bread washed down with mint tea. Neither of them chose to touch cold beer because they would soon be airborne, each alone, while Petra Leigh drove her Cherokee toward the state of Chihuahua.

The logistics had become a small nightmare because they needed the Cherokee's cargo capacity for inconspicuous ground travel. Petra had never soloed in Black Stealth One and could not fly the Imp at all; Medina's initial flight to the El Paso region had turned up only one known landing site, that one temporary and in the desert of Northern Mexico. The chief advantage of that site was that all three of them had used it, camping and fishing near Laguna Santa Maria. The road from Guzman to their site was little more than a miner's trail, and Medina's morning overflight had shown no sign of cattle or men around the dry bed, which had once held a small lake. Though the Hellbug could land in a melon field—and had proven it—the Imp needed a few hundred yards of decent surface.

The main disadvantages were that they always took a chance, camping in the open with such aircraft on a Mexican rancho, and the Imp was not immune to border radar. Some bear in the air without a need to know the Imp's mission might well decide to follow it, and that would vastly complicate their problems. The Aerostats, when functioning, could see a long way. The sooner Medina found a suitable location on U.S. soil, the better.

Meanwhile, from that lakebed Corbett could fly to La Tuna in a half hour and loiter there during the hours when, according to new information from Ullmer, inmates strolled or sunned themselves in a fenced compound. For two hours in midmorning and two more each afternoon, Guillermo Borges would be among the strollers. To save fuel, Corbett had chosen to use the Hellbug as a sailplane much of the time. Engine off, searching for thermal updrafts, he could cut his fuel consumption in half but would have to refuel after each flight. And this involved another special problem.

If armies march on their stomachs, high-tech aircraft fly on prescription medicine. Untreated auto gasoline, especially most Pemex fuel, will not power an engine that demands avgas. Petra could shuttle back and forth with more fuel from a Pemex station in Guzman, but below the tent packed in the Cherokee lay two full cases of octane additives. Once common, the stuff was now hard to find and pricey as liquid gold. Fuel bladders and tools shared space with hardware for minor repairs. Both aircraft carried extra fuel as well. After a few years of the fugitive life, these men did not trust luck.

Eventually Corbett waked Petra Leigh, though reluctantly. "You looked so damned young and vulnerable," he apologized, sitting on his bed, stroking her hair as she completed a yawn. "But you won't want to be on that Chihuahua wagon track after dark.''

Petra gave him a heartbreakingly tender smile; sat up; kissed him. ''My Cherokee ready?''

''Topped off and packed,'' he agreed.

''I hope you'll keep my place here for a few hours,'' she said, patting the bed, rising. ''You look exhausted. Worked all night, didn't you?'' Into his shrug, she persisted: ''What time is it?''

''Oh-nine-hundred or so. I may catch a few zees after you leave. So leave already.'' He grinned, with a gentle slap for her rump.

Medina, efficient as always, had turned a pound of chicken salad into a half-dozen sandwiches for Petra, who gave him a hug before she made them both happy as doting uncles. That is to say, she studied her oil dipstick herself, checked her tire pressures, noted the fuel gauge and tested the cargo tiedowns before sliding into the Cherokee. ''Can't depend on the help these days,'' she teased, watching her oil pressure rise.

''You'll make a pilot yet,'' Medina said.

''One, at least,'' she retorted, with a wink toward Corbett, and then drove out of the hangar, waving.

The two men watched her turn on to the highway, then faced each other smiling. Medina: ''You gonna idle along overhead and talk to her?''

Corbett: ''Thought I'd catch up to her later. Right now I'm heading for my bed, amigo. Graveyard shift isn't what it used to be.''

''That's good,'' said his friend, with a light touch on his shoulder. '' 'Cause you look like shit warmed over. When all this is finished, do yourself a favor; get a checkup.''

''Might do that,'' Corbett said, pressing the button that closed the big doors. ''Do I set my clock, or can you wake me at noon?''

''Set your clock,'' said Medina. ''I'll be nosin' around over New Mexico by noon, so you'll have to close the place up yourself. Kind of a shame I can't stick around and wake you, though; you're ugly as hell then.'' Pause. ''I love it.''

Corbett did not lift off until nearly one o'clock, setting the Hellbug's pixel skin in its buzzard plumage. Because his sectional charts told him that he would overtake Petra in the vicinity of Phoenix he lazed along, conserving fuel while staying aloof from aerial traffic patterns. He spotted the *X* of duct tape across the Cherokee's top in midafternoon as Petra sped along Interstate Ten, not far from Tucson.

"Yucca One to Yucca Two, and my but aren't we making knots," he said. Then he said it again. His curse was ready for utterance when she made him smile.

"Yucca Two, klutzy with an unfamiliar mike button," she replied, the comm set wonderfully free of static. "Get your beauty sleep?"

"For all the good it did me. A friend says he loves waking me up; the way I look makes him feel superior," he replied.

She laughed at that. Then: "Could I see you from here?"

"Get real, kid, sure you could, if I were an idiot. Pay attention to the freeway. And slow down, you're looking for a ticket."

"I don't take criticism from buzzards," she said calmly.

There's such a thing as too much instruction, he reflected. *She got this far, this fast, without my help.* "Ouch. Just trying to help. Why don't I mosey down and see how the campsite looks?"

"Good. Ah, you running in the green?"

"Everything nominal, Yucca Two. Didn't know you cared, honeybunch." He was cozening up to her, and he knew it, hoping for a more civil tone.

Evidently she knew it too. "Sorry, I'm not good company this afternoon."

"Papa Mike Sierra?"

"No, not PMS, dammit. *Tee* emm ess. Too Much Supervision."

"Pardon the hell out of me, ma'am. And if I'm not mistaken, there's a patrol car parked a couple of miles ahead. We buzzards have our uses," he insisted.

"Oh, go scarf a roadkill," she said crossly. "Yucca Two out."

Whatever's eating her, I'm no help, he decided, and eased his throttle lever ahead. Black Stealth One's forward surge was gentle but it soon left Petra behind. At two-mile altitude he passed level with the top of the dessicated lump that was Chiricahua Peak; found a whopping thermal near Animas Peak, just inside New Mexico, and let it lift him above twelve thousand feet. He crossed the border that way, resolutely holding his course between the Scylla of oxygen starvation and the Charybdis of squandered fuel, and found his landing site by its direction from the gleaming surface of Laguna Santa Maria. As Medina had reported, the place was as untenanted as the backside of the moon.

It struck him suddenly that he was only a few minutes south of the border. With hours of daylight left, and no compelling reason to land, he lifted one wing to bank the Hellbug lazily toward the jutting jaw of West Texas formed by the Rio Grande. During the past fifty years, here in what Texans called the Pecos region, mineral shortages had given rise to several waves of mining: asbestos, talc, mercury, gypsum. Corbett had known men who had flown mercury's bright cinnabar ore from improvised airstrips in that area. *At least I can tell Speedy whether or not to bother with it,* he thought, letting his great bird wheel above mountains innocent of water, basins just as dry, bisected here and there by broad ribbons of highway. Texans might wear funny hats, but their roads were absolutely first-class.

In some places the pale land bore great splotches of color; the green patch of an irrigated field, the sparkle of gyp embedded in a cliff, the orange of cinnabar angled across a hillside as though slashed by an enormous paintbrush. Here, most forms of life were overmatched, unequal to the challenge of a hostile earth. The region had a kind of sterile purity for Corbett, but it was no place for a morning stroll.

Sailing while his engine idled he found long-forgotten airstrips, but none with a building that might hide an aircraft and, at last, he turned and chased the sun to the western horizon. His path took him north of El Paso where he identified the La Tuna facility without trouble, imagining for a moment that he was inside the sprawl of barracklike buildings. Men were eating dessert down there, or perhaps writing memoirs or playing solitaire. Or simply lying on a Spartan's bed, staring at a ceiling, caged animals awaiting freedom—or slaughter—perhaps without much curiosity as to which it might be.

Okay, bear in mind this Borges guy was a major drugrunner who's poisoned too many lives, he told himself. *For that matter, he may outlive me by thirty years.* Put in that context, the plight of Guillermo Borges could be shrugged off. At Corbett's urging, the Hellbug banked toward the left, and the lights of El Paso, multiplying like yeast under a crimson sunset, soon became lost from his rearview.

When he did not find Petra's Cherokee on the ancient lakebed, Corbett broke radio silence again. This time he did not have to await her reply.

"I'm on the damn' goat track, Yucca One," she said. "Save your fuel, I'll be there soon."

"I don't see your lights," he complained.

"That's because I'm not using them," she replied. "I'm doing fine, if I need lights you'll see them, and so will anyone else within twenty miles."

"Understand, Yucca Two. I'll shut up and let you deal." He had caught a hint of *let me alone* in her voice and decided to obey it. This was not the side of Petra Leigh he enjoyed, or often encountered. He still had enough sunset to land without lights and brought Black Stealth One down, hovering with a brief burst of power, in a vertical landing.

He stamped the pins and needles from his feet as he walked around the Hellbug in a postflight inspection, studying those impeller blades carefully with his pocket Maglite before he was satisfied. Five minutes later he looked up from his chores and smiled to hear the Cherokee growling its way down to flat alkali dirt.

Oddly, Petra seemed almost grateful to see him as she parked near the Hellbug. Her hail was friendly, and her exhaustion was plain as she leaned back on her headrest. "Mister, that was one long drive," she breathed softly.

He leaned past the window ledge to kiss her, then stopped, sniffing carefully. "You're sick," he accused.

"No I'm not. Just bushed."

"Somebody's been using a barf bag in here," he insisted.

"Didn't have one. I used sandwich wrappers," she explained.

"And you didn't want to tell me," he said, opening the door for her.

But Petra was not ready to step out yet. Her gaze, through a wan smile, was pathetic. "This is home on the range, isn't it? Well listen, Kyle, 'seldom is heard a discouraging word' is not enough tonight. If I hear one teeny syllable of criticism out of you I fully intend to burst into tears. Count on it," she finished.

He patted her shoulder, told her to relax, and erected their tent by himself. When her sleeping bag lay in readiness he carried her to it, murmuring things she loved to hear, promising hot soup from his thermos.

Eventually she downed the soup and kept it down, and she fell asleep an hour after the last vestige of sunset had fled the sky. The night breeze cooled the desert, dependably, and Corbett took his little monster of a shotgun from the cockpit of Black Stealth One before spreading his sleeping bag next to Petra's.

Then he monitored certain channels of the Hellbug's normal radio set for a time before giving it up. Finally, he lay awake beside Petra for a long while. He was not too worried about her upset stomach; eyestrain, a hot day, a swaying vehicle, all could have contributed, and her brow was cool to his touch. In a way, he was relieved that Petra was too tired to lie awake. She would have worried, even more than he, because Raoul Medina was long overdue.

TWENTY-FOUR

JUNE 1991

MOHMED ASHRAF, PERHAPS embarrassed at his own outburst on seeing Odile's return, helped unload her vehicle and even consented to help oil those bearings on the hangar doors before taking up his refrain once more. "You must talk to me, Frenchman," he said for the third time, as the others spread a huge sheet of black plastic like a lean-to. "If not to me alone, then in front of the others. You have much to answer for."

Clement straightened from his labors with a show of impatience, glanced at his watch, then nodded. Ashraf no longer accorded him the slightest respect. From an Arab this was the worst of signs. "Very well. I take it you have learned about the Israeli general, then."

"I have learned that you are a traitor to Syria. No one said anything about—"

"Ashraf, Ashraf," said the scientist, with the saddest of smiles, "have you read nothing about the Israeli attempts to buy the new American antitank weapon? No? I suppose you did not know the Americans will be demonstrating it, only minutes from here by air, for Syria's most implacable enemy. The Jewish arms expert is already near; temptingly near. If that general should die on American soil—well, I expect we shall all be heroes in Damascus."

Ashraf's hands hung straight down, gripping, releasing, the forearm muscles a study in ligature. "I do not believe a word of it. As for the woman, she may believe what she likes, but I have told

Mansour my real mission here and it is time you learned my connections with Mukhabarat."

Roland Clement allowed his mouth to sag open for an instant and saw the lamps of vast satisfaction lit in Ashraf's eyes. "But," he said, modifying his bogus astonishment into a smile, "this is wonderful. You will certainly be a credible witness to a great Syrian triumph when we kill the Jew."

"It is a lie," Ashraf said, but with less conviction.

"You will see. I could even fly you there in a day or so."

"Fly me now," Ashraf demanded.

"It will be dark in an hour," Clement protested. "I am not sure there will be time."

"Only minutes, you said. Show me *now,*" Ashraf challenged.

Clement checked his watch again, gave the Syrian a heavy glance, then sighed. "Help me move the Cessna outside," he grumbled, and together they opened the hangar doors.

This time, when the Syrian entered the copilot's door, Clement only opened and then shut his mouth, shrugging, as if dismayed to share the front seats with Ashraf. The announcement of his Mukhabarat ties had given Ashraf confidence to burn; so much that he enjoyed himself by giving fatuous orders, testing his power. "Be quick," he said, a split second after Clement advanced the Cessna's throttle, and, "Look out for that stone," which Clement was already doing. With no cargo and only its crew of two, the craft soared upward with breathtaking ease. Clement kept the engine at maximum power and arrowed away, still climbing, toward a group of hills to the south.

A thousand feet above the plain, Clement flew past the largest of those weathered lumps of stone. "You will note the trails below," he called over the engine's drone, pointing below where cactus and ironwood eked out a precarious living. He then throttled back quickly as Ashraf stared downward. "The vehicle tracks are faint, but you can see them if you look carefully."

"Tracks are nothing," Ashraf called back after a moment, as the Cessna slowed, and slowed, and slowed still more. "And I see no sign of any vehicle track," the Syrian went on as the wing began to shake ever so slightly.

A Cessna STOL is capable of flying very slowly if its big flaps are employed. If not, and flying level with its engine idling, it will eventually reach a speed so low that airflow over its wing can no longer support it. A modest buffeting from the wing is the first warning sign that it has approached its stall speed. If the pilot does not apply power and drop the nose a bit, the airplane will simply fall, nose-down, and may drop one wing in what can become a spin.

"Something is wrong," Clement called out, perfectly aware of the problem, as the Cessna suddenly bowed its head and began its dizzy descent. He applied full power then, slipping the aircraft into a bank to the right, avoiding the spin but continuing to turn, the right wing low in a descending spiral. It was a masterful display of control and had its planned effect as Mohmed Ashraf found himself sliding sideways, the victim of gravity. That was when his dagger flashed into view.

"I thought you might—" Ashraf began the sentence he would not complete, flicking his right arm across his torso, thrusting toward the pilot's arm. His ploy may have been merely a threat but, as the wicked little blade slipped past cloth and tasted flesh, the Syrian glanced from Clement's icy gaze to his right hand, which was controlling the aircraft. He saw, propped above the forearm, the tiny dark pit that was the business end of a .22 caliber pistol, and realized that he was gazing directly into it. He may even have seen the first flash from the muzzle.

Roland Clement had chosen his weapon, the same caliber used by Israeli hit teams, for just such use at point-blank range. Its staccato reports, even without a silencer, were no louder than small firecrackers and its light recoil did not impair his aim. Of the five rounds he fired in quick succession, all remained in Ashraf's head and upper torso. The Syrian, eyes wide in astonishment, began to slump sidelong until he lay twitching against the doorframe.

Clement quickly leveled the aircraft, breathing hard not because he had just murdered a man but because he had come within two hundred feet of running out of airspace. In moments he was regaining most of his altitude.

A thin runnel of crimson had begun to issue from the blue puncture in Ashraf's cheek; doubtless he would be bleeding from some of those other holes. Clement loosened his own harness, reached across the dying man to unlatch the right-hand door, and cursed because the slipstream would not let it swing open. He managed finally by releasing Ashraf's harness, putting the Cessna into a steep bank again so that the man's body fell against the door. Mohmed Ashraf hung there for an instant, feet tangled crazily, until Clement steepened his turn. Then the Mukhabarat spy was tumbling with the indolence of a rag doll, plunging down through nearly a thousand feet of space, one arm waving as though in protest. A human body reaches its terminal velocity, roughly one hundred and twenty miles an hour, in less distance than that. Clement, pleased to note that the sting along his upper arm was tolerable, grunted his satisfaction as he saw the faint explosion of dust on the plain below, latched the right-hand door, and flew back to his hangar thinking ahead. Momentarily he worried about the warm, sticky sensation at the elbow of his right sleeve. Chiefly, he worried that he and Mansour would now be forced to do all the heavy labor.

The long twilight had just begun as Clement flared out for his landing, then cursed aloud at the sleek shape sitting near the hangar. He pulled up and made one slow pass overhead, studying what he saw below.

Hardly an aircraft designer lives who would not recognize and admire the lines of a Taylor Mini-Imp, and when he spied the little aircraft near his hangar Clement's first thought was that some official had stumbled upon his own death warrant. His second thought was relief, for it was plain from Mansour's wave and the stubby weapon he carried that he was holding a slender dark man at bay. Clement brought the Cessna down cleanly, though the triceps of his upper right arm had begun to throb by now. As he taxied near he saw Odile running toward him.

Her first words lacked coherence as she watched Clement deplane. "He simply appeared from—but where is—my God, Roland, your hand," she stammered, trying to look in three directions at once.

"That can wait," Clement muttered, holding his right forearm up to prevent more blood from dripping on his trousers. As he strode toward Mansour and the stranger, his mood darkened. That damned cut on his arm was beginning to throb badly. Odile had begun to pick gingerly at the fabric the dagger had razored apart as Clement barked in English: "And who authorized this landing on government property?"

He had hoped for immediate clarity, but Clement found disappointment. The swarthy fellow only gave him a blank look, and his reply was a torrent of Spanish.

TWENTY-FIVE

JUNE 1991

ON HIS SURFACE, Raoul Medina remained impassive but inwardly, he raged at himself. The abandoned hangar had looked so goddamned perfect from the air, worthy of a surge of optimism during one last look around before his rendezvous with Corbett. On closer inspection that place had pay dirt written all over it. Trouble was, it was paying off for the wrong guys. The irony was the worst of it: this great howling fuckup wasn't entirely a matter of chance. He'd been looking for the same thing these people needed, but they'd found it first.

They'd also been clever enough to keep it looking innocently abandoned, too, until the very moment when he trotted up to those old hangar doors only to be surprised by some foreigner with a burp gun. Within moments Medina realized what he'd walked into. He needed only a glance inside to spot fresh tire tracks of a light aircraft in the dust and one hell of a pile of high-tech equipment, not drugrunning stuff but heavy on the electronics, judging from what they'd unpacked. Both the gun-toter and the woman, a spiffy brunette, spent a lot of time talking through their noses, evidently at two hundred and fifty words a minute—with gusts, he decided, up to three hundred. He knew French when he heard it, and he was hearing it now.

Trying to pass himself off as a Mexican with a bum engine was the first thing that had come to mind, and Medina hoped to stick with it. Now that this hefty pilot had landed in a very nice Cessna STOL to take over, the imposture wasn't working worth a shit.

Medina kept it up, though, until the two men took him over to his Imp. Even though the registration number stenciled on his fuselage was a fake, the *N* prefix made it obviously American. The Cessna pilot wasted little time going through the Imp's flight log, a record Medina kept religiously for his own good. "Since you write in English, you must speak it," the man demanded, tossing the log back into the Imp. "It is the common language of control towers everywhere, m'sieur, as you must know. If you do not, we will dispose of you as a common criminal."

If they know I even suspect, Medina told himself, *I'm dead meat.* And "dispose of" had a resoundingly final ring to it. "Okay. Sure, I speak English. I don't know whether your cargoes are cigarettes or hard stuff," he said. "None of my business. I've been known to fly a little contraband myself." The lopsided grin he gave them was full of complicity. *No big deal, just between us shitrunners,* it said.

More rapid French from the men, now with the woman chiming in as well. The topic seemed mixed, with a lot of hand-waving toward the south and maybe some defensiveness from the leader with repeated shrugs and dismissive gestures. The slender hooknosed guy with the burp gun finally gave up his questions, but any damn' fool could see he wasn't happy with the answers. The woman seemed unhappy too, but more disappointed than angry. Whatever she said then, it made the two men face Medina again.

The leader drew a stubby little automatic from his jacket, seemed to weigh it in his hand. He couldn't have seen what Medina saw then: a quick narrowing of the other guy's eyes, a twitch of his jaw, that said he'd settled something in his mind. Another murmured phrase, almost pleading, from the brunette hotsy, and then the pistol went into the jacket.

"She is correct, we must get these aircraft inside," said the pilot in English, and pointed a forefinger at Medina. "There is much heavy work to be done. You will do most of it. The first time I believe you are doing less than your best, you will be shot, m'sieur— ah, your name?"

"Call me Speedy."

"That is a *nom de*—a nickname. Name," he prodded.

"Juan Gonzales." Shit, that was on his false ID anyhow, the nearest you could get to John Smith in Spanish. "They call me Speedy," he added.

"Speedy," the woman murmured; and something in Raoul Medina went belly-up, paws folded, tail wagging.

First, they pushed the Imp into the hangar, now deep in evening shadow. Despite his bleeding arm Frenchy seemed to be ogling the little single-seater with more than ordinary curiosity, lingering to inspect its boundary-layer wing slats as Medina followed Hooknose back to help trundle the bigger Cessna inside. That was when Medina considered his big break, angling off so that he would pass on one side of the Cessna while Hooknose took the other. Those short-barreled little stutterguns weren't all that accurate beyond fifty yards. Maybe, if he had the fuselage between them, it would take Hooknose a few seconds to get the weapon unslung and another few to draw a bead. With luck, Medina would then be loose on the prairie in gathering darkness.

Only it didn't happen that way. Hooknose started around the opposite side, all right, but then dropped to his haunches and unlimbered his weapon very fast, and his first words in English were, ''That is what I would try, M'sieur Gonzales. I would be killed instantly.'' His smile appeared genuine, even a bit sad, but with no softness in it. After that, Medina decided to bide his time. A man could learn a lot that way; for example, when speaking English, Hooknose didn't have much of a French accent. And just maybe that meant they weren't on a French payroll.

It took all four of them to get the Cessna parked, and Medina noticed the fresh bloodsmears near the front right-hand door. Hadn't Frenchy exited from the left side? Well, no matter. He couldn't be hurt too badly the way he was working.

Or maybe, Medina reflected, he could at that. Frenchy gave up tugging at the hangar doors and sat down on a big carton, head lowered, massaging his right arm with care. The woman rushed to his side, murmuring more French, helping draw the man's jacket off, and when she called out for assistance she broke off, switching to English. She wanted more light.

Medina thought he saw another chance coming when Hooknose began rummaging for a flashlight, but Frenchy said something to her and damned if the woman didn't haul that little peashooter from the jacket and train it on him. She handled it as if reluctant, but it was steady enough in her hand. ''It is not too dark to see you,'' she said, very softly. Then Frenchy muttered something abrupt and she replied in English with, ''No, not as long as he remains an asset,'' and Medina knew that, at the moment, Frenchy would sooner shoot him than not.

''Look, I have a work light with a twenty-foot extension in my cockpit,'' he said. ''Won't take a minute.''

With the hotsy right behind him and Frenchy following,

Medina found his little work light, plugging it in to one of the three receptacles he'd installed flush against the Imp's skin. At the woman's order, he sat down before them, hands in view.

Frenchy didn't fail to notice the receptacle. "Why did you install so much special equipment?" he husked, the first halfway conversational tones he'd used with his captive.

"So I wouldn't get stuck in the dark like you guys," Medina replied.

"But the boundary-layer devices," Frenchy went on as he held the light for the woman. "Do they improve your short-field performance that much?"

"Not as much as it looked like on paper. I've wasted lots of hardware—" he began, then stopped, wishing he hadn't said so much already.

"EAA," Frenchy said, then hissed as the woman peeled his shirt away from a drying slit of gore. She called something to Hooknose, who answered curtly, and then Frenchy went on. "Some men buy such aircraft, but not you, m'sieur. You are a builder. You will be a member of the Experimental Aircraft Association, there is no point in denying it."

And I'm not, these days, but that's the first mistake he's made. Let him make a million more. "Like the man says: no point," Medina said. "Don't tell me EAA has members in the contraband business."

"I will not tell you anything that you do not need to know," said Frenchy as Hooknose hurried up with a small medkit.

Now and then, as the woman cleaned the wound, Frenchy would say something and she would flash the light in Medina's face, then resume. After the third time, Medina realized they were keeping him effectively blind to night vision. He also realized that he was dealing with one very, very cagy Frenchman who obviously knew his way around aircraft. Not many men would have noticed the wing mods, nor recognize instantly what they did. *So what else would you expect from a man capable of developing a flying killer robot? He may be the biggest unwiped asshole in creation, but he's probably forgotten more about aircraft than I'll ever learn,* Medina reminded himself.

Frenchy seemed in better spirits, once he'd been patched up. After brief squirts of French with Hooknose, he ordered his captive to submit to bonds of duct tape. Medina's, "If I don't get outside pretty soon, you won't like the smell in here," earned him relief in a night breeze with a billion starry pinpoints and a burp gun muzzle against his backbone—which did not help unstopper his bladder one bit.

With hands bound behind him, hobbled so that he could only inch around on his feet, Medina was led to a cheap bedroll so new it smelled of cotton batting. While they busied themselves with a flashlight and forays into their equipment he tested the tape a number of ways, knowing damned well the stuff would defeat a grizzly. Then he lay quietly, thankful that the desert heat bled away so quickly at night, and thought about things that did not add up.

They had four bedrolls. How could they have known he would stumble upon their operation? By God, they couldn't. Was there another member of this bunch? And how had Frenchy managed to get such a clean little slice taken out of him? It looked like a swipe from a straight razor and it had leaked maybe a pint of Frenchy into his sleeve, and whoever had used the razor, more power to him.

Then he heard the brunette's voice, velvety in its echo, and his reflections took a new tack. He wondered what she looked like in a skirt. She had great arms, well-muscled like a swimmer's but slender, and women's legs were usually fleshed the way their arms were. Hot damn, a real French bonbon, not too far past thirty, who called him "Speedy"!

In Raoul Medina's scale of values, women were not dismissed as merely fives or eight-and-a-halfs. A dedicated techie, Medina used the decimal system; his current Barstow flame, Lola, was a seven-point-nine. Without her technical expertise, Petra Leigh would've been an even nine; with it, a nine-point-five, the highest rating Raoul Medina had ever accorded a real live human being.

The perfect ten was the unreachable ideal, the girl of your dreams, the perfect personality in the perfect body. He had never seen a ten; had never expected to see one. But now he wasn't so sure of that "unreachable" business, after an hour or so around the bonbon. On further acquaintance he would determine whether she rated only an eight-point-six, or a rousing nine. But already he knew one thing that he'd never realized in over forty years: a ten was a nine-point-five who could murmur in French.

TWENTY-SIX

JUNE 1991

CORBETT DID NOT consider himself much of a worrier. Worrying, by his definition, was the effort you wasted in deep concern while doing nothing about it. When Raoul Medina failed to show for breakfast, Petra worried enough for both of them. She even took a walk alone while Corbett made his preflight inspection but she returned soon looking, if possible, even more downcast.

"Oh, Speedy will turn up," Corbett assured her as he placed his ugly shotgun in their tent. "Can't worry about it, we can use this site for a few days and you can raise me by radio if you need to. By the way, if you have to use this, remember it works like a semiauto. Better unfold the stock, let your shoulder take the recoil." His gaze softened into what anyone else would call simple worry. "Sorry I've got to leave you, Pets. But I should be back by noon unless I get lucky with that Butcher Bird gadget."

Petra did her best to surrogate good spirits. "Good hunting, Kyle. I'll be okay; plenty of books to read. I may monitor the radio. On the study team, we pretty much concluded that machine won't be able to fly for more than a few hours without refueling. And unless its controllers are stupider than I think, it won't take them long to figure out the daily routines at La Tuna."

"I hope you're right," he replied, and knelt to kiss her. "Be back before you know it."

He climbed into his great sweptwing creature and watched Petra disappear into the tent to avoid vagrant dust from the plane's downwash. He started the rotary engine and, after watching his gauges briefly, he advanced the throttle. The three air diverters of Black Stealth One began to moan softly, then to sing in muted, hackle-raising three-part harmony, hurling sandy debris in all directions for a moment, and then the craft was skating forward as it levitated from the Mexican desert. Having helped develop the gossamer brute, Corbett could identify specific thunks and whooshes as its wastegates diverted air back to the tailpipe, a huge invisible stream of cool air that characterized ducted fans.

In thirty seconds the Hellbug had borne him well aloft, slipping easily upward toward cooler air. He set the pixel skin for its plumage and noted that he could cruise at a fuel-hoarding pace while arriving over La Tuna before nine-thirty. Even if the Butcher Bird were already in the area, its target would not come into view before then. Corbett wondered, however, whether the damned robot would react to aircraft in the area as targets of opportunity. El Paso International lay near enough to La Tuna that its traffic patterns might bring aircraft dangerously near.

Numerous times, the Hellbug's infrared sensors warned of aircraft. Black Stealth One's exhaust was cool, its radar signature nearing the invisible. Corbett knew that this was the stuff of midair collisions, and kept a heightened awareness that he flew in crowded skies. Even the turbulence of a near-miss by a commercial jet could spell disaster for a craft as light, as tenderly constructed, as the Hellbug. He could not tell whether the headache he began to nurse was a symptom of his cancer, or merely the result of tension and eyestrain. He'd been told the Butcher Bird would probably resemble a disk, or possibly a tiny helicopter. He suspected, in fact, that it could be an exact replica of a common aircraft scaled down to ten-foot span. That particular little nightmare kept Corbett scanning each interloper for evidence of scale: passengers in the cockpit, registration numbers, a smoky exhaust that might suggest a small two-stroke engine. At times like this, he was glad that his distance vision was still that of a fighter pilot.

His special channel clicked to life shortly before ten o'clock, and Ben Ullmer seemed to be perched between Corbett's ears. "Yucca One on station," Corbett replied. "Gobs of air traffic around, but nothing I want to see."

"I will admit you got in gear sooner'n I figured," Ullmer said. "It's still early here in Oregon. I'll keep a voice-activated tape ready for you, but I may not be monitoring all the time."

"You mean you're the only control we'll have?"

"Me or Bill Sheppard," Ullmer said. "I've got a business to run but I'll be near my comm set during daylight hours."

Corbett loosed his gravelly laugh. "This is—wait one, Control—nope, just a Lancair entering the pattern. This is a real shirttail operation we've got, isn't it? I mean, if the feds are so worried about this thing, why don't they curtail some of the air traffic around here?"

"Unusual amount?"

"Hell, I don't know but it's like oh-eight-hundred-on-the-freeway this morning." He spotted another light aircraft from its IR signature and changed course a bit. "If your Butcher Bird doesn't have a good IR emission, I might whomp into the effing thing—but maybe it's smarter than I am."

"About that traffic," Ullmer said. "I've already taken it up with NSA. That's the charter we're operating under. They say it's business as usual for everybody but us. Reading between the lines I know the Company, not my company but Uncle's, has got its fingers burnt recently for operating on U.S. soil."

"Old news," Corbett grunted. "But that puts it right in the FBI's lap."

"Only they don't want it," Ullmer told him. "They suggested to NSA that this would be better as a military operation, 'cause they lack the assets to pursue it at this stage."

"Oh yeah, buncha helos crisscrossing the sky and everybody's headset full of jargon," Corbett replied. "Nothing like tipping your hand to the bad guys, hm? By the way, this is a great comm set. My compliments to somebody."

"You know who. By the way, once you've done all you can, this just might get, uh, militarized. There's already a couple of my people over you in a Nemesis, which is a military surveillance bird, but officially it's on a long-range acceptance trial with a civilian crew."

"Great; don't tell me they can monitor this," Corbett warned.

"I won't; they can't. Partly a matter of recognition. Yucca Two would sound too familiar."

"Hold on," Corbett muttered. "I'm eyeballing a light plane, little taildragger, that's trailing too much smoke. Could be of interest, I think."

"Not according to a Customs inspector who's been debriefed with, I kid you not, a hypnotist. Our man is almost certainly Roland Clement with a team of three flunkies. Whatever came through with him, it wasn't in crates that would likely fit a disassembled airchine big enough to carry a payload."

"Well, this one I'm watching is damn' near disassembled, with carburetor problems. But he's legit," Corbett reported. "Now let me ask you: how do we know this Clement didn't just *fly* his Butcher Bird over the border?"

The silence lasted two beats. "Aw hell, man, nobody knows that. Nobody knows *any*thing, we're just playin' odds. Could be exactly like you said."

Corbett put the Hellbug into a gentle bank to improve his view as he studied the La Tuna facility. "Wup. I think, ah, yeah, there's the target, I suppose. Can't make out—"

"What? You sure?" Ullmer's voice went flat, almost breathless.

"The Colombian, I meant," said Corbett. "Like you, I was only playing the odds. A bunch of dots just started spreading out in what my map says is an exercise yard down there. One of 'em is probably the Butcher Bird's target."

"All of those guys are targets, that's why they're there," Ullmer retorted.

"Can't argue that. Look, what passes for my brain has turned up the wick, Control. I'll get back to you; Yucca One out."

Corbett's altitude, roughly a mile above ground level, had been mandated by guesswork, some of it Petra's, at the last minute. Once the consensus had settled on French technology, she had studied the current limit of visual pattern recognition that France could achieve. It was awfully good, according to NSA, perhaps as good as ours. It might be good enough to let a killer robot identify a particular human face from a quarter of a mile.

Argument had swirled over the question of the robot's next move. Petra had thought it might fire at the instant of recognition. Dr. William Sheppard's decades of expertise told him otherwise: the Butcher Bird had never been seen in flight, which suggested that it would need to gain altitude while keeping aim on the identified victim, stop dead in the air, and then shoot from afar—between a half mile and a mile above. It is far easier to aim at the top of a man's head than, say, to gauge the distance across the bridge of his nose or the height of his lower lip.

In the end, Petra had agreed. It would have made little difference had she not; Corbett believed in experts, and if NSA's top technical wizard said to expect a flying pancake hovering at a thousand meters, that was his expectation.

For two hours and more, Corbett lazed the Hellbug through corridors of cloudwisp and clear, occasionally bumpy, air. Every maneuver he made became a weighted decision involving nearness to the La Tuna facility, distance from El Paso International's traffic patterns, the view between cloudlets that moved eastward while changing their shapes, and fuel consumption, among many lesser factors. An old aircraft designer's dictum ran, *If you watch the ounces, the pounds will take care of themselves.* That was just as true for fuel as it was for hardware, especially if every blessed gallon had to be transported in Mexico by an automobile.

Corbett found himself fluctuating between terminal boredom and brief moments of gut-churning tension until a half hour before noon, when the dots began to migrate back under La Tuna roofs like so many BBs from the surface of a small game board. He waited until the dots had disappeared before banking toward the west, facing a modest headwind and gaining altitude in an economical cruise. More altitude brought safety, in some ways; he was less likely to be noticed, even as a buzzard, and if that jazzy little rotary engine ever quit, the higher he was, the farther he could stretch a glide.

Soaring home with his engine off might have taken hours, and was not an option he entertained today. "Yucca One to Yucca Two, I'm heading for the barn," he said to the headset. "Please acknowledge, over."

Silence. He realized that the Cherokee would be a roaster by this time of day, and fifty yards from the tent. After waiting a minute he tried again. Silence. He shrugged and set a new heading that took him across the Rio Grande, now only a twisted thread of silver against earth's scraped hide. And wondered if Petra had thrown off her malaise of the previous day, or had managed to step on a rattler this morning, and wished he were on the ground with her at this very instant, and told himself he was not a worrying man.

TWENTY-SEVEN

JUNE 1991

T TOOK MEDINA a full day to understand, chiefly by innuendo, that his life had been spared through the defection of one of the Frenchman's team. He learned their names sooner than that. Judging entirely from a few nonverbals, Medina thought the hook-nosed Arab, Mansour, had his own reservations about Clement's version, but the cut on the Frenchy's arm was strong evidence. If one of that team had forced Clement into a desert landing before taking off on foot across an arid landscape, maybe he would survive to tell someone about it. That was the good news.

The bad news was, this Clement hotshot wasn't wasting any time getting his operation under way and, from the way the men employed him, Medina figured they didn't much care what he saw. That meant they never intended him to live long enough to talk about it. Clement and the woman went their separate ways after breakfast, she in their van, he in the Cessna. Medina heard a little lecture before Clement left; his wrists would be freed and the hobbles would be replaced with looser ones for work, but if he tried anything that so much as hinted at escape, even fooling with his hobbles, Mansour was to empty a full magazine into him.

The woman—she told him to call her Mamzelle—brought a load of concrete blocks back in midmorning. Sweating his butt off, Medina helped the Arab erect a low retaining wall in one corner of the hangar and lugged dirt inside to fill the voids in those blocks. Blessed with an absence of fat and a good ropy musculature, Medina soon took his shirt off, first because he did not want it to get filthy in this heat. But second, and more importantly, he knew Mamzelle was covertly watching him and he hoped to make it a pleasant experience for her.

It was the only thing he could think of that might improve international relations in this monumental fuckup. Medina's mama hadn't raised any stupid kids; just as women knew how to take advantage of their best features, Raoul Medina had learned that his own flashing eyes, flamenco dancer's rump and slim thighs could often be parlayed into friendly overtures. Not that he intended to hit on her, not yet at least: too obvious. After so many years of womanizing he had learned women's strategies so well that he could use them himself, but he knew a woman was highly perceptive in such matters. In the past, his personal fairness doctrine had often intervened, but when his life lay in the balance he would focus on tactics, and ethics be damned.

His best tactic had always been a waiting game. In a honky-tonk he might wait twenty minutes. With an Arab's burp gun at his back, he might wait twenty days. Somehow, Medina reflected, he didn't think he had twenty days.

Mansour's English was pretty good. He made sure Medina understood that the blocks were staggered so that no light could possibly pass all the way through the wall. Mansour could've saved his breath. Medina knew the international symbol for radiation hazard as well as anybody, and by noon it was obvious that something really nasty was going to go behind that little wall. No telling, and no point in asking, whether the nasty stuff was already in their equipment. Besides, the dumber he acted, the longer he might avoid the muzzle of that burp gun.

Lunch was late, an assortment of cold cuts, bread, and cheese washed down with a red wine that Mamzelle diluted to two-thirds strength. Medina took it neat, wondering why anybody would drink dago red that was a third water. Mansour pointedly avoided the wine. Since the guy had already knelt once that day, facing east while Mamzelle took the stuttergun—she held it as if it might bite her—Medina decided the man took his religion seriously.

Though he wasn't all that tired, Medina let his head droop as he sat, legs folded sideways to accomodate the hobbles, before the cold cuts. Not once did he make eye contact with Mamzelle, letting his arms drop as though nerveless, taking long breaths, keeping his face impassive. Nor did he indicate awareness when Mansour went to raid their food cooler.

"We work you too hard, Speedy," she said softly.

He couldn't tell whether it was a statement or a question, and gave no sign that he had heard. He simply closed his eyes, and waited.

"Husband your energy," she advised. "If you cannot work, you will not live."

Medina had extravagant Latin eyelashes, and studied her through them with just the right amount of sadness. Then he nodded, making it look like a herculean effort, and waited some more.

Mansour spoiled the moment with his return, bearing a can of orange soda. "Empty your cup and I will share this," he said, with a gesture toward Medina's paper cup.

Medina's head shook ever so faintly. "But thanks anyway," he muttered, and the glance he turned on Mansour overflowed with bogus gratitude.

At this point, Mamzelle began to speak in rapid French, to which Mansour replied, and so on and on while Medina strained every bone in his head to make sense of it. He'd heard it said that French was like Spanish with sprained adenoids, but Medina did not understand one word in five of this palaver and felt like jumping up and shouting at both of them. Instead, he sat in a boneless slump and waited.

Finally, with evident disgust, the Arab stood up and said, "You will assist the woman. Some of her work is heavy," and then strode away to finish the retaining wall alone.

If Raoul Medina had smiled at Mamzelle then, she would've known. Instead, still stripped to the waist, he made a production of stretching his back and arms, then a one-act play of getting up. Together they repacked the food in the cooler and then she told him where she wanted the remaining crates to be moved.

Throughout the afternoon, Medina tried to find the best order for his priorities. Foremost, without question, was escape. He argued with himself over what should rank next, given the chance: trashing their equipment or getting the Imp safely outside. Eventually he admitted that the Imp was only a goddamn machine, whereas trashing this Frenchman's operation could save some lives, and it just might be his ticket to a new legitimacy someday; another chance, another life.

Surveying all the high-tech hardware he unpacked, Medina grew bewildered at first because, for the life of him, he could see nothing that looked like a flying machine. Maybe, he thought, that was what Clement had gone to get. His suspicion settled finally on one big, flat plastic case less than four feet square and roughly two feet thick, that he and Mamzelle trundled around on rollers recessed into its corners. The equipment that he saw looked well crafted, not commercial stuff but shock-protected in its cases and built so that some of it could be mounted atop the same empty casings. Somebody, probably Clement himself, had spent a lot of brainwork designing his hardware to be portable.

Mamzelle proved a whiz at matching cables to the appropriate hardware, though she managed to break a painted fingernail on a coaxial terminal and uttered a charming, *"Merde, merde, merde,"* as she bit the nail off. This was close enough to *mierda* for understanding; no one could say Raoul Medina didn't know shit when he heard it.

"My fault, I must have moved it," he lied.

"Certainly my own," she said, kneeling two feet from him, and then the rosebud mouth smiled at him for the first time, and for the briefest, devastating instant he was looking into her eyes before he gave her the merest fraction of a smile, erasing it quickly, looking away with the shy guilt of a schoolboy. She turned away too quickly and made her next orders too peremptory.

Six points, Medina thought.

Mansour heard the Cessna's muscular turbo first, as the first breezes of evening wafted through the hangar. The woman, herself sweat-streaked and smudged with dust by now, went outside to wave the man in. Medina knew better than to play games with Mansour and approached him with, "I guess the woman is finished. What can I do?"

Mansour grunted, a pissed-off noise in any language, and then said, "Roll that case over here, if it does not tire you too much," and Medina complied with such energy that it almost tipped before he steadied it. The event took only an instant, but Mansour blanched as he helped lay the casing flat. "That would have cost you your life," he said. "You must be very, very careful." That was when Medina knew, absolutely, about the plastic case.

They pushed the Cessna inside and secured the doors before Clement, with a broad smile, lifted a case from tiedown straps and placed it in Mansour's arms. It had no warning decals, but from the way Mansour carried it and did not ask for help, Medina inferred that it was both precious and supernaturally heavy.

"And how has our new member performed today?" Clement asked, doubtless so that Medina would know he was on probation.

"Well enough," Mansour admitted. "But I believe he is looking for sharp objects."

A nod from Clement. "I gave that some thought en route to San Antonio," he said, and pulled a little sack with an Ace Hardware logo from his pocket. It proved to contain a length of wire rope and small U-bolt fixtures. Medina's heart fell when he saw them because, while he could have severed duct tape with a piece of broken glass, that multiple-strand cable would defy a knife or, for many minutes, a file.

It evidently pleased Clement to do precision handwork. While Mamzelle sat nearby holding the handgun as though reconciled to it, the Frenchman measured his wire carefully. Once he had cut the duct tape away he secured the cable by making loops at its ends with U-bolts, securing them with a finger's width of extra space around Medina's ankles. When he had done the same to his captive's wrists, he told Medina to try walking.

Medina found that he could spread his wrists a foot and a half now and could take normal steps, though running was out of the question. "That's going to chafe," Medina said. "You might let me put some of that tape between the cable and me."

"I might, but I will not. Whatever you really want it for, I am sure it is not in my best interests." And with that, Clement put away his adjustable wrench and diagonal cutters.

From then until dark, Medina shuffled around and did as he was told while the experts rigged up a remote-handling fixture across the low retaining wall. Mamzelle busied herself at a distance, making a hot dinner on their new Coleman stove.

It suited Medina perfectly that she did not ask for his help in making dinner. While Clement was making the new hobbles, she had studiously avoided taking part in the process; treated Medina, in fact, as though he were a farm animal. That was the best of signs, he thought. With Clement out of the loop, she was becoming friendly. When he was in sight, she wasn't. *I'd bet my ass Clement's in the saddle*, he told himself. *And I'm betting my ass on a change in rides.*

If Medina had entertained any doubts that the Frenchman would kill him sooner or later, they seeped away with every glimpse he got of the Butcher Bird operation. He knew the fact that Mamzelle's given name seemed to be Irish, something like O'Deal; he knew that the men had set up something as precise as a surgical operation behind that low wall; and he knew when they opened that big casing that the Butcher Bird itself was a sure 'nough little UFO, a flying saucer right out of the *National Enquirer*.

TWENTY-EIGHT

JUNE 1991

G O HOME, CONTROL," said Wes Hardin, his grin an inch from his tiny headset speaker. "We haven't got zip to report from here and it's gotta be past quitting time back there." The time in southern New Mexico was a few minutes past nineteen hundred hours, seven P.M., and from the canopy of his Nemesis craft the view, at sixty-three thousand feet, was simply breathtaking. Hardin could see cloud tops far below, their shadows slanted across a patchwork of broken plain.

"I got a little rocket from the guy who's paying our bills," said the voice of Ben Ullmer with near-perfect fidelity. "Military radar says you nicked the Mexican border on one circuit. He doesn't like it when they bug him so be nice, okay? See if you can fly a decent pattern for a change."

"Wilco. Ah, is our close cover in place down there?"

"Not anymore. Says he was," Ullmer replied.

"Couldn't prove it by us. There's been lots of air traffic but nobody who looks like he's on station over La Tuna," Hardin admitted. "I reckon that's the way it should be, hm?" An inch beyond his climate-controlled cockpit, the air was cold enough to freeze alcohol, thin enough that blood would boil as it froze. Supported by ninety feet of slender airfoil, the Nemesis continued its endless circling, the electric engine absorbing much of the output of the craft's solar array. The remainder went into storage cells that, at sundown, would begin to feed energy to the engine. And when you are twelve miles up, sundown comes late. *You wouldn't think a man could get bored while he can see the earth's curvature,* Hardin mused. *But here I am, starved for small talk. . . .* "So tell me what's new in Oregon."

"Spookships are still on schedule and my wife's making blackened redfish for dinner," Ullmer replied.

"And you're gonna be late for it," Hardin reminded him.

"It's *supposed* to be burnt, dammit," said Ullmer. "Jesus Christ, you sound like Marie! Why don't you nag your copilot?"

"She went for a walk," Hardin joked. Ullmer would know that Colleen was in the "pipe," the cramped living quarters behind the cockpit area. "By the way: this new bird isn't quite ready for acceptance. Cabin climate control tends to throw little snowballs at us now and then. No major squawks, though. How's it going on your other channel?"

"I talked to him before I raised you. He made two sorties today, bitched about all the traffic like you did but no sighting of anything suspicious. He was buttoning down for the day."

"Do we know whether this poor bastard at La Tuna was wandering around outside as usual?"

"We do, and he was," Ullmer growled. "That's the one part of this I hate the worst. Truth is, it hadn't fully struck me until today."

Wes Hardin fell silent for a few moments. Then: "Correct me if I'm wrong," he said. "You're holed up after hours in an office you don't even like, talking to a captive audience of one halfway across the country, while your wife is waiting dinner, all because you feel guilty over some schmuck who may or may not be about to get what he's had coming to him for years. Have I left out anything?"

Ullmer's rusty-pump chuckle came through perfectly. "Thanks, Doctor Feelgood, now I can slit my wrists. Look, I really hadn't thought about the guy as a person until late this afternoon. I mean—Wes, the sonofabitch is just a tethered goat."

Poor old Ben, he can't talk to anybody else about it so he's elected me. "Okay, you're right. And you didn't tether this particular goat and neither did I, it wasn't our decision. Plus, in a well-run world the tiger would've eaten him a long time ago. Only it's a butcherbird."

"In the last few hours I've grown to hate that word," Ullmer confided.

"Focus on what it does," the little Texan suggested, realizing that he had stumbled on a tactic that might keep guilt at bay. "It pulls a trigger for somebody; not for you or me but for somebody we're trying to stop. Without us, that Colombian wouldn't have any chance at all. With us, who knows? We just might spot the damned gadget before it can zap another guy. It could happen.''

"Good point," Ullmer agreed in slightly more cheerful tones. "Well, I've bent your ear long enough, Doc. Thanks for the use of your couch."

"You'll sing another tune when you get my bill," Hardin riposted, then signed off.

The sun lay behind his left shoulder now, fading the digital readouts on his console to faint golden runes against black velvet. He twisted to peer between the twin seats and saw that Colleen had darkened the tiny living space for a nap. In another few hours it would be her turn to pilot, his to snore.

He moved his gaze back to the earth, twelve miles down; considered bringing up the magnified cockpit display that could actually pick out guards at the La Tuna periphery; decided against it. *Who needs to get any closer than I am to that sorry slob down there?* he asked himself. *One thing I won't do is talk it out with Colleen the way Ullmer did with me. Oh yeah, we might possibly screw up that damned thing's aim; it could happen. I hope that makes old Ben feel better, it doesn't do shit for me.*

TWENTY-NINE

JUNE 1991

O DILE KNEW WITHIN moments of waking that Roland Clement would be a monster that day. He jerked on the wire that connected the captive's manacles to Mansour's wrist, in order to wake them; he wolfed his fruit and cereal; he begrudged Mansour the time he spent on morning prayer; he made every order to the American a threatening snarl; he was, in short, a walking nervous breakdown in his anxiety to fly the djinni.

"Stay close to the American while he opens a hangar door," Clement told her, preparing to help Mansour lift their murderous little craft by hand. "And let him see the pistol."

"He smells," she objected. She knew Roland would enjoy that.

"Douse him with your cologne," Clement snapped, "but not now. Will you get your backside in motion?"

She did, wiggling it in deliberate impudence as she hurried to give Speedy Gonzales his orders. She found him trying to flick a small bolt out of a crease in the concrete floor and, waving him away, did it herself with a tapered fingernail. "Tempered steel," she commented softly, pocketing the little bolt. "Naughty Speedy. If you are not very nice I shall show this to m'sieur. Now open one of the doors by three meters and be quick about it."

The American obeyed as quickly as possible, though those nice athletic legs of his were rendered clumsy by the hobbles. Unable to remove his shirt because of the manacles, he wore it without complaint, a great pity in Odile's view, but the sight of that slender waist tapering to delightful sloping shoulders would have put Roland in a fury. And why should such a splendid animal be destroyed when watching him was one of her few current pleasures?

As the men approached carrying the djinni, Odile waved their captive aside with the pistol and hardened her voice. "Stand well away," she told Speedy, so the others would hear. "This is work for experts."

He put his hands up at breastbone height, stumbling back, nearly falling. Moments later the djinni sat on its landing pads in early sunlight and Clement devoted five seconds to studying the captive. "What did he do?"

"Stumbled," Odile said, and lifted her lip delicately. In English, then: "He is merely *gauche*, clumsy."

Satisfied, Clement hurried away, calling over his shoulder, "Bring him to help move the launch modules. He can pull those on their casters."

When the launch equipment lay just inside the hangar doors with umbilical cabling mated to the djinni outside, Odile made the captive sit down, facing away from them. His was a perfectly natural question: "What the hell are you people doing?"

"This sequence is not your business," she said sharply. "You may prosper longer in ignorance." Then, with an occasional hard glance toward Speedy that she knew Roland would appreciate, she set about calibrating her dials.

The launch sequence proceeded quickly, in part because the little reactor was not installed. This was merely the surveillance flight with extra fuel replacing the heavy reactor to permit wider ranging, more loiter time. The djinni's blades engaged, adding their hiss to the turbine's soft keening, and at Clement's order the umbilical dropped onto concrete. The djinni blew dust into the open door as it levitated, then sizzled upward, its shark-fin rudders adjusting for a course almost due east.

As it dwindled to a spot and disappeared, Odile felt an old excitement, almost sexual in its intensity. Not the familiar sense of sweet control she felt with men—most men, at least—but a thrilling tension that implied uncertainty, awe, and yes, danger, even for those who groomed it. Roland Clement had truly created a wondrous thing in the djinni, one with its own perceptions and, though the idea was scorned by Clement himself, with some elements of subtle intelligence. It knew when unstable air created too much buffeting to fire its laser. It was programmed to avoid other flying objects. It even knew, given circumstances that had never arisen yet, when to defend itself. *It is not alive, yet it lives,* she thought. She found it much easier to simulate passion with Roland Clement when reminding herself that he was the creator and master of this deadly creature.

While waiting out this mission, the little group busied itself with two tasks: a tentlike enclosure of opaque plastic so that night-lights would not gleam from high hangar windows, and final preparations for the laser weapon.

Odile found herself teamed with Speedy again, rigging the plastic film some distance from the others. With Clement occupied elsewhere she found herself making eye contact with the American, more relaxed, sharing a smile on occasion. His shyness, she discovered, was becoming a kind of provocation. How, she wondered, could she break through this reserve? Did he not find her attractive? Was he, perhaps, homosexual?

"It must be irksome to be forced to work with a woman," she said finally.

He shook his head. "I do what I'm told. Dying isn't in my plans, Mamzelle."

"But you would rather work with men," she persisted, pulling a corner tight, securing it with tape.

"Not those two." He smoothed out a wrinkle, made clumsy by the manacles. "I guess I'd rather work alone."

"Preferable to working with me," she interpreted with a sigh.

He paused, motionless, regarding her through those long lashes of his, and made his reply impassive, as if discussing something of no personal importance. "Trying to get me killed, Mamzelle? Being around you with those guys watching is like a stroll in a diamond mine with armed guards. You must know how you look, how female you sound. Do you enjoy torturing men?" Then he was working again, with an unspeakable sadness on his features.

She said nothing more for long minutes, completing one end of the plastic tent with him, but she found that her fingers shook. When he was engrossed with the duct tape she moved nearer, near enough to smell the sweaty musk of him, liking it. "Have you been hurt so much by women?" she asked softly.

"None of your business," he muttered, and looked away.

He has been wounded by sex, she decided. Though her experience was considerable, it had all been with men who met her at least halfway. She found it a heady vision to contemplate dalliance with such a reluctant, lovely animal as this American. *American women probably think his swarthy coloring makes him déclassé.* "Poor Speedy," she said, and saw something flash in the glance he gave her, a compound of longing, anger and restraint. It made her dizzy with desire.

For Odile, this sensation was unique. *In another moment I shall fling myself on this poor fool, and he is perfectly right, it would mean his execution.* She tried to make her command harsh with, "Try not to be so *gauche* with the plastic," as they moved to complete the job. She thought that it might at least fool Clement.

The djinni returned as she was preparing lunch, its whirling vanes producing their audible hiss as the tiny craft settled within centimeters of its launch point. The American again wrestled a door open, this time without being told, and seemed willing to face away from the other men as they carried the djinni inside.

Clement and Mansour wasted no time in their postflight efforts. Though she wanted very much to watch the videotape, Odile directed Speedy in setting out their food and pretended to ignore the small exclamations that echoed through the hangar from Clement as he sat at his console. She and the American had eaten before Clement, in the best of spirits, brought Mansour to their meal.

Of course he would not talk about it until she asked. "One of the avoidance programs kicked in for the first time," he told her in rapid French, eating like a starved pig. "The sky is full of airplanes, chiefly light aircraft. It was an excellent test, excellent," he crowed.

"And the target area," she prompted.

"In visual memory," he said. "But the exercise yard was empty during that pass. Perhaps our man does not take the sun every day. Or perhaps he does it for brief periods only. In any case, we will know more this afternoon."

"It would be a pity to wear out the turbine waiting for this man to appear," she said.

Clement's gaze burned. "We have spare impellers. Have you any idea how much . . ." he began, and paused. Odile thought his next word would have been "money" if Mansour were not near. ". . . importance this scientist represents to the West?"

"But surely," said Mansour, a slice of beef held gingerly in his fingers, "the place you identified on the scan was a prison of some sort. Why would the West imprison its best minds?"

"Not a prison, a place of relocation," Clement said, happy to weave a tiny thread of truth into his tapestry. "The man is a defector in hiding, Selim. When the Americans have his false identity complete, he will walk out of there, and our window of opportunity will close."

Mansour chewed on that for a moment. "Then the place is intended to keep undesirables out, not in."

"Yes, but," Clement went on, choosing another thread of accuracy, "some of those people are themselves undesirables, I am told. The Americans keep a very mixed bag in there."

"Then our target may have the freedom to stay indoors," Mansour said. He watched Clement eat, distaste obvious in his gaze.

"That is possible," Clement replied. "As it happens, we have an excellent way to find out." With that, he crammed another hunk of pork sausage into his face, drained his cup, and waved Mansour after him. He paused for a moment; studied the tentlike arrangement Odile had contrived; called back to Odile. "Is your ugly American worth the food he eats?"

"My American? *Your* American," she called back. "He is a clumsy bear, but works hard. If you need him, take him."

"I am thinking none of us need him much longer," was his reply.

Odile, acutely aware that anything she might say could be twisted into a death notice for the charming Speedy, made no reply. The reprieve came from another quarter, with Mansour's, "Not at the moment, perhaps. Will we continue to operate from this place indefinitely?"

Clement turned, started to speak, thought better of it and nodded to himself. Then he walked quickly back to the retaining wall and was soon engaged, with Mansour, in the laser installation.

When the food had been put away, Odile caught the captive glancing across toward the hangar. "We have our own work," she said sharply. "I will not tell you again, Speedy: do not, for your life, show any interest in what they are doing."

"Yeah, but what was all that stuff about the American? You were talking about me, right?"

"Nothing very important," she told him. "Merely saving your life for the moment." She did not add that Selim Mansour, bless his Moslem bones, had been the savior.

They were testing their little gasoline-powered lighting system when the call came again for donkeywork on the big door. Speedy rushed to comply, then sat down facing a hangar wall as the djinni made its exit in the hands of its operators. This freed Odile to help with the cabling and made quicker work of the launch procedure.

The djinni hissed away more slowly this time, rising with a

heavier payload. Odile savored its climb until she glanced at Roland Clement and saw the sudden ferocity on his face as he looked about the hangar.

Speedy Gonzales, true to his name, had speedily disappeared.

THIRTY

June 1991

W HEN MEDINA HURRIED to open the hangar door, he left
that little metric wrench next to the generator only because
Mamzelle was watching him so closely. Metric sizes didn't
match American hardware exactly, but hardware store crap wasn't
exact either and a European metric wrench worked on a lot of half-
inch bolts, including those on the generator. He needed only one
tool to loosen the U-bolts that hobbled him so thoroughly, though
it might take a minute or two. The best time for that would be while
the others slept but it was beginning to look as though he might not
live that long. If Mamzelle had saved him for the moment, that said
nothing about all the other moments; and if Medina was any judge,
that fuckin' Frenchman was just aching for an excuse.

He had counted the seconds, *one thousand, two thousand,* on and
on, during the morning's launch procedure, and found that it had
taken them over four minutes of solid concentration before the
gadget lifted off with a howling hiss that unnerved him. Four minutes might not be enough, but it might be the longest chance he
was going to get. That was why he rushed to perform his tasks to
perfection, hoping they'd all focus on the damned launch again
while forgetting him for that crucial period.

And it had worked, and then again, it hadn't. When Mamzelle
ignored him, stepping in to monitor some of the meters, he began
to inch his way into shadows toward the generator. They'd forced
the small locked personnel door during the previous hour to direct

the generator's engine exhaust outdoors. All he needed was a wrench and maybe two more minutes.

And when he got his hands on that little wrench, he found it failed to fit by a hair's width. *Settle down; the wrench is harder than the bolt, I can force it on one of these goddamn things.* Right; if he had the time. If they spotted him right now it was all over, and that is why Raoul Medina eased himself out that little door to shuffle at double time toward the scrub of ironwood and tumbleweed that dotted the area. Hunkered down behind some of that stuff, he might get lucky.

But he heard the soprano howl and hiss of the launch much too soon—*I forgot, with Mamzelle helping they speeded it up*—and knew, without any doubt, they'd be after him with guns in the next few seconds. Running was out of the question. Some men would have soiled their shorts at that moment, and Medina actually felt the urge. *Why not?* He could think of nothing else that might play to the bastards, if they caught him before he could make the wrench fit.

Squatting, he loosened his belt; shucked his trousers and shorts down; took the wrench in hand again even as he heard shouts from the hangar. *Come on, damn you,* he urged the wrench; *chew on that cheesy mild steel.* Forehead beading with sweat, he tried to force a fit until his sinews cracked.

The Arab spotted him at the exact moment when he realized he wasn't going to make it fit. Medina saw the burp gun come up; thrust the little wrench down between his left shoe and instep; raised his hands. "What's the problem?" he called. "Can't I even take a dump out here?"

Mansour trotted up to him without expression, calling out in French, then switching to English. "Stand up."

"Like this?"

"Exactly that way. It is the only evidence he might accept," said Mansour, with a stern face but a twitch at the corner of his mouth that might have been hidden amusement.

As Medina stood up, hands in the air, he knew he must make one hell of a sight, with his naked butt in view, his dingus no doubt shrunk with fear and maybe hidden by his shirttail, or maybe not. Frenchy was trotting toward them now, slowing to a walk, and when he saw past the tumbleweeds to Medina's predicament the sonofabitch stopped, put his hands on his hips and laughed outright.

Medina, growling it: "Can I finish before you shoot me?"

The laugh faded as the Frenchman studied him. "You could have used the portable *pissoir* inside," he accused.

"Pissing is quiet. I expected to make some noise," Medina explained. "Goddammit, I needed some privacy!"

"You were escaping," said Clement in an insinuating purr.

"With my pants down? Hey, the woman is looking, whatever you're going to do, get it over with." Medina squatted down again, hands on his knees. And managed one pathetic fart.

Now both of the men laughed, and the Arab said something unintelligible. Clement: "What were you going to do for hygiene?"

Medina realized that this ridiculous little question had suddenly become all-important if his story were to have any credibility. He hadn't even brought a Kleenex and, with sudden clarity, he recalled the tag line of a joke that must have been forty years old: *Got change for a twenty?* "Money in my billfold," he muttered, fishing in his hip pocket. "From the threats you've made, I didn't think I'd need it for anything else."

Clement nodded, and then spoke with the Arab again, and as he turned his back on them Mansour said, "Finish what you came to do, M'sieur Gonzales."

"Before you shoot me?" Medina thought wildly of a sudden lunge that might let him grasp the weapon.

"I am not so anxious as some, to destroy a pair of willing hands. And I am curious to see how Americans use their money," he added. His smile was faint, but genuine.

Medina returned a few minutes later, minus a fiver and two singletons, with Mansour walking behind him. En route, the Arab spoke to him softly. "Do not imagine that I believe your explanation, m'sieur. I neither believe nor disbelieve. What I do believe is that you are capable of dangerous games. We need your strength, but not if you become ill or troublesome. Do we understand one another?"

"Yeah. Thanks for the tip," Medina said, and knew that as she worked, Mamzelle was hiding a fit of giggles.

Within minutes, Medina had busied himself at the generator again. He managed to retrieve the wrench from his shoe while the men were stringing extension cords and noted later that Mamzelle put it in the pocket of her smock. *No loss there*, he decided. *It sure wasn't much use to me. I need an adjustable wrench.* Even pliers might do the job. During the next few hours, the four of them finished rigging all their lights. It seemed to Medina that every time the bimbo met his glance she broke into a smile. *I was doing all right with her for a while, but now I'm chopped liver,* he thought dolefully. The Frenchman's arm was giving him trouble; whenever he checked his wristwatch he winced, and he checked it often.

And when the deadly little robot came whirring back in late afternoon, Medina was helping add two quarts to the Cessna's oil so the Frenchman rushed to open the hangar door himself in his anxiety, Mansour following, and Mamzelle planted herself in front of Medina. "Naughty, *naughty* Speedy," she said, her smile teasing him. "Do not bother looking for this. I will be watching you more carefully now." And she pulled the little metric wrench from her pocket, then dropped it back.

"I'm through with it," he said, noncommittal.

"You surely are. I saw you pull it from your shoe, you know. Now you must be on your very best behavior, so that I do not tell."

He sighed; gave her another of those long sad looks that seemed to work so well; continued adding oil without a word. He could not very well dump a palmful of sand into the oil with her watching so closely, but he now had something else working for him. *She's caught me twice now, and wanted me to know it. Well, let me tell you something, lady, that means I've caught you, too. The last thing you want to do is tell that hotshot you've been hiding my tactics from him.*

When the Frenchman sent up a shout from outside, Medina caught only the word *laser.* Medina tarried at the Cessna with Mamzelle, buttoning an engine access panel, but he noticed a fresh bloodstain on Clement's sleeve as he and Mansour hurried inside with their tiny craft.

It was another ten minutes before Clement got the information he wanted, enraptured with the video on his console. Mamzelle turned at the exultant shout, marched Medina near the others, and made him sit facing away while she stood at the Frenchman's shoulder and murmured French at him while Mansour chattered with enthusiasm. Medina could not be certain, but it sounded very much like a celebration.

THIRTY-ONE

JUNE 1991

CORBETT HAD GROWN accustomed to the air traffic by mid-morning, even admitting to himself that it wasn't all that hectic by the standards of a major sunbelt city. He'd been avoiding such places so long that it had seemed, on that first day, as if the skies had been crammed with wings just to plague him. He had already switched a segment of his mind to Petra Leigh and her nagging illness, toying with an updraft as the Hellbug soared over bluff hills north of La Tuna, when his new NSA gear alerted him again.

More delicately, narrowly tuned than his old infrared sensors, it beeped his scope for small intense sources of heat. An eagle, or a commercial transport, would not interest it, but a child's bottle rocket would; and ultralight aircraft, clawing bravely through the sky on hot little engines, invariably did.

He thought at first that this was another ultralight, droning below him at roughly fifty knots, half a mile above the ground. He banked to get a better view, searching for the fabric-covered wing of brilliant hues so common among ultralights, a "don't come near me, I'll crumple like a moth" signal for more robust aircraft.

Not a glimmer. His radar said something was down there, something with the minuscule signature of a bird—or a Lockheed F-117, which it couldn't possibly be because military stealth aircraft stalled right out of the sky at speeds higher than that. *Hold it; that coastie Nemesis can do it at low altitude, and it's stealthy,* he thought, knowing one was supposed to be in the area, wondering why the hell it would be so low, and moreover, why he couldn't eyeball a ninety-foot bird so near.

When his scope said the ghost was passing almost below, Corbett pushed his throttle forward and gave up some altitude, swinging to one side as he plummeted. Abruptly, the trace showed that, whatever it was, the blip changed course by darting away, then back to its original course. That course change was when Corbett saw, tiny as a dust mote on the surface of his eye—*something*. He overshot it, and employed his wastegates until the Hellbug hovered absolutely motionless. He watched the trace continue but Black Stealth One had its own inertia to fight and, cursing, blinking, Corbett courted a neck ache trying to see it again as he twisted his head from scope to sky to scope again. Fruitlessly. One problem with coming very near was that any mismatch of speed could make your own aircraft mask the interloper from visual sighting.

The NSA gear was wonderful, but before Corbett could place the Hellbug where he wanted it, the IR and radar traces faded into nothingness. With that sudden approach of his, Corbett had lost his advantage. "Yucca One to Yucca Control, I just got a bogey on scope," he began. The local time was nine twenty-seven. He knew the equipment should record this close encounter but continued to report the event, verifying it as he was supposed to: time, altitude, vector, behavior. And with gooseflesh moving like a spill of liquid down his arms, he took up his station directly over La Tuna, spiraling like the buzzard the Hellbug's pixel skin said it was.

Ullmer did not reply to his message. *Probably out of his office,* Corbett thought. *One hell of a way to run a national security operation, but I've seen it happen before when the bigshots want to avoid a responsibility.* "Yucca One to Yucca Two, let me hear it," he said. No answer.

He saw a dot move into the exercise yard below, then another, then several, before his comm set filled with Petra's voice. "Yucca Two to Yucca One, I was fixing your lunch. Got the volume cranked up, though."

"You heard my report?"

"At ninety dB, every bug in the desert heard it. You be careful up there. I'm not slaving over a hot stove for a second man who won't come back. Am I?"

"Ah, roger that, I'm afraid you are, but save it for dinner," he said with some reluctance. "If this is what it might be, it should be back. It didn't have a target that I could see, but right now it might.

And since I'm only guessing at everything, I'd better hang around through this afternoon. Unless something breaks before then."

"You reported that you glimpsed the Butcher Bird, but you didn't give any description. Any detail at all could help tremendously, that's what we were—oh, never mind, you understand that better than I do," she said.

"I saw what I see when I'm sick. I saw a dot in my eye, barely big enough to convince me I saw something. No detail; no wing, no tail, no nothing. Well, yes, one thing."

"I have to ask? Well, I'm asking," she said.

"The way it changed course and back again, it didn't like me," he told her.

Silence for a moment. Then: "That big stick you loaned me for snakes?"

"What about it?" he said, readying himself for his stomach to become a knot.

"I wish you had it right now," she told him.

"Lot of good it'd do me. But you know something? Me, too," he said, making it a chuckle to allay her worries. He might open the small sliding hatch of his canopy and poke that limited-issue shotgun out, but with the wind buffeting the Hellbug while he tried to fly it, he'd be demanding a miracle to hit anything smaller than a cloud.

He promised to be ravenous on his return and signed off, pleased that she seemed to be in good spirits. The longer he lazed Black Stealth One around that government facility, the more he wondered if he'd been fooled by some natural occurrence, what some techies called a spook anomaly. You might see it on meters, eyeball it briefly, chase it, even sell a few million tabloids by giving it a legend. What you couldn't do was rassle the little bastard down and cage it in a building at Wright-Patterson Air Force Base. A spook anomaly, in short, was just an acceptable way of saying UFO.

He realized with a start, and a snort of disdain, that he was at that moment engaged in seeking out exactly that: a flying object that was, until now, unidentified. But some UFOs turned out to be real aircraft, occasionally an experimental type of unconventional shape. His eyes were still good at long range; still great, in fact. If what he'd seen had a wing or a tail, wouldn't he have seen some hint?

He created another of those patented headaches scanning and circling until the tiny dots moved out of sight in the yard far below. It was a few minutes before noon. Kyle Corbett knew that his logic could be faulty, but decided that he had spent enough time in the immediate area. He let the prevailing wind carry him northeast a bit, then settled back to watch his scope and give his neck a rest.

Shortly after one p.m., Ullmer popped into his headset, sounding animated but cautious. When he'd rapid-fired his first volley of questions, Corbett calmed him down. "Like I said, no details I could see. It may have been just a mote in my eye."

"But it changed course," Ullmer insisted.

"Motes do that when you move your eye. You know that, Yucca Control."

"Yup. Hostile aircraft do it too. Goddammit, what was on your scope was also on another scope at the same time. Our Nemesis is so high it doesn't have your sensitivity, and the bogey trace kept popping in and out. But what they got adds up to a dotted line, making passes a couple of klicks apart. They began—ah, you have a chart handy? Traces began roughly at the New Mexico border and ranged up past Canutillo, back down southwest on a parallel course, and so on for three hours, with a definite pattern gradually moving east. It covered all of El Paso, for that matter. Then it suddenly took off toward the west while our people were headed east. They lost it before they could come around. At high altitude, even my birds can't fly below two hundred knots."

Corbett had risked his hide as a military reconnaissance pilot, years before. "Sounds almost like a photorecon flight, doesn't it?"

"Doesn't it," Ullmer echoed. "Maybe it was."

"Did they get its speed?"

"Does a cat lick its—aah, roger, mean airspeed fifty-two knots during the pattern," Ullmer said. "But seventy-five or so when it broke off the pattern and scooted. Buckin' a headwind, at that. For the size we think it is, it can haul. It's prob'ly a body of revolution, you know."

"Say it, Control, it's a friggin' flying saucer," Corbett responded. "No wonder I couldn't see flight surfaces."

"That's still a guess. I don't wanta influence you unduly."

"Listen to you; like a bloody bureaucrat."

"Listen to *you*, like a UFO freak. By the way, your transmissions to Yucca Two are on tape and I agree with your tactics. Unless you have fuel problems."

He'd love to know how much I've increased the Hellbug's fuel capacity, Corbett realized. "Some good updrafts here," he said. "I can shut down the engine now and then. No sweat. I suppose you'd tell me if our bait has already been sampled." Somehow it was easier to discuss that unsuspecting Colombian in impersonal terms.

"Affirmative. The bait was there this morning and ought to be there again this afternoon," Ullmer replied.

"You sound like you don't know which side to root for."

"My sympathies waver, but I know which side I'm on. There's a difference."

"I couldn't have said it better," Corbett admitted. "Let's break it off, Control, I'm going to concentrate on the job. Yucca One out."

As he heard Ullmer's signoff he was already banking to resume his station above La Tuna. One thing about this particular UFO, it wasn't some Godlike critter crafted by omniscient little green men. It might not know when its target was available; it might make mistakes. It might even have a mechanical breakdown. *And so could I*, he reminded himself, circling a bit higher.

Corbett recalled later that the time was two forty-two when the scope beeped him. He traced a small intense heat source that aimed, lance-straight, for La Tuna, and the radar told him it dropped sharply as it neared the exercise yard. The Hellbug was too high and out of position, but Corbett remedied that with an abrupt noseover and swept down in a maneuver that birds of prey might envy.

The blip circled once, twice, a few hundred feet above the buildings as Corbett narrowed the distance to less than a mile; and then it seemed to be fleeing in a climb that was almost a vertical corkscrew. By the time it stopped in midair, the Hellbug was boring in at almost the same altitude, and then Corbett saw it clearly, a disc with trailing fins and a blur around its circumference.

Between those fins, something bulky had pivoted up into the airstream. His job was to identify it, not collide with it, and mindful of its evasive ability he dropped one wing, passing it a hundred yards distant, getting a decent perspective on its underside before he employed the wastegates in an effort to hover.

Bleeding off velocity from a dive takes precious seconds. Corbett kept the Butcher Bird in sight, though well to one side; saw that a blunt probe of some sort was poking out the bottom of the carapace as well. And then his radiation Klaxon hooted.

For all he knew the thing was shooting at him and Corbett did not wait for anything else, canceling his wastegate maneuver as he firewalled his throttle. In the most ferocious climb he could manage, he transmitted his bulletin.

"Yucca One to Yucca Control: it's a body of revolution, all

right! Canted twin fins curving back, blades spinning on its periphery, enclosed pod that pivots down, single exhaust port below. It's on the run now, hugging the terrain and I'm out of position like a pimp in church. But I'm following a radiation plume, ah, heading about two-seventy degrees true. As long as I can follow that, I will. Over," he finished,

The Hellbug was a faster machine, but before he could put its nose on the same course, his quarry was so far ahead and so near to the ground that its IR signature became one of many; industrial emissions that did not move, diesel truck stack exhausts that did. He set his scope to follow the hard radiation trail and found that, in little more than a minute, the trace was diminishing. Soon that telltale ribbon, shown in video as a yellow false-color image, faded entirely and again he tried to find its infrared trace.

He was reporting to Ullmer again now, describing the sudden plume of radiation and its gradual fading. He focused on several IR traces only to abandon them. *It took off in a straight line. I'm betting it's still on that course,* he concluded, hoping that he could catch it without overshooting. He snatched up his air chart and drew a line that represented the fleeing Butcher Bird's course as closely as he could, but soon had to admit he had lost his bogey.

Corbett flew west along that line for sixty miles, then retraced, scanning parked vehicles and buildings closely until he neared the suburbs. He circled one structure in the arid scrubland, evidently an old hangar with high broken windows, but saw no radiation trace or sign of habitation. *By God, that's a likely spot. Maybe I should look into it for future reference,* he thought. But he had more pressing business; the damned Butcher Bird had shown up twice over La Tuna that day, and for all he knew it might already be there again while he was noodling around forty miles distant. Because he could not be sure he had followed his quarry's path precisely, he chose to go south a few miles and return to his La Tuna sentry duty, still watching for the little killer craft.

He was almost on station when Ullmer invaded his headset again. There would be no point in holding that station any longer, the old man told him. Guillermo "Billy" Borges, playing a game of horseshoes with a staff member, had staggered and fallen dead at approximately fifteen minutes before three o'clock in the afternoon. It had been several minutes before anyone noticed the oozing puncture high on his balding head. Ullmer apologized for not being on-line at the crucial moment.

"That burst of radiation was probably to flush the excess heat out of a reactor," Ullmer said. "If you don't give a shit about the locals, you can build a lightweight nuclear energy source and use the air as your heat sink."

At a time like this, the old fart is working out all the details, Corbett thought admiringly. "Roger—I think," he replied. "But how 'bout the team flying high cover? Did they get a fix on where that murderous little fucker came down?"

A sigh, clearly audible. "Negative, Yucca One. Go eat your lunch or something, we had our chance and blew it."

"Come on, debrief me! Why didn't they follow it?"

"That dotted line they had to deal with? It wasn't what we thought, it was evidently an intermittent short in the power supply plug. They recorded the radiation plume, but the unit cut out on them completely when they pulled a few g's to orient themselves. Wasn't their fault," he added lamely.

After a few choice phrases for the NSA's vaunted hardware, Corbett signed off and set his course for Petra Leigh. He saw no point in hoarding fuel now, with the operation scratched, and brought Black Stealth One down near her a half hour later.

Petra ran to him as soon as the dust pall settled, looking young and healthy and ready for a hug, and for a time their mutual greetings were as carefree as many another. The unsettling realities pressed down on them as Corbett was spooning a lumpy soup of potatoes, canned beef, canned tomatoes and capers—which Petra herself had labeled "yuppie slumgullion." With the Colombian dead and no accurate trace of his killer, they did not expect further missions; certainly none from this primitive site.

"But thanks to you, we know what we're after," Petra insisted. "Size, shape, even something about its weapon and the idiot-savant way it operates. You managed what our whole study team couldn't do."

"Yeah, and now the question is whether it cost us one man or two."

"I'm sorry about that filthy drug wholesaler, but—" Her eyes became round with shock. "Oh, God, you can't mean Raoul?"

"Pets, ol' Speedy has fuckin' *disappeared* somewhere out here. You know him, if he saw a little spook anomaly he'd damn' well try to put it in his cockpit."

"Like someone else I know," she accused.

"So I was lucky. We know he wasn't. Whatever's happened to him, it wasn't anything good. He knows where we are, if he made a forced landing he could've found his way here by now. That's assuming he could walk away from it. I hate to hand it to you like this, but there it is.''

She nodded, staring at her feet, hands cupping her cheeks. ''And you can't call for a search and rescue operation.''

Along with his headshake: ''No. He made me swear I wouldn't, just like I made him swear.''

''Kyle Corbett, that was a goddamned suicide pact,'' she stormed.

''Not really. We'd just rather take our own chances than walk under Uncle's thumb. That's why I've got a little SAR operation to run all by myself. Speedy knows there's one sixty-foot buzzard that doesn't eat meat, and he has flares. In fact, I've been watching for that. So far, no joy.''

She straightened her shoulders, a tendon bunching in her jaw. ''All right, what do I do?''

''You drive to El Paso and check on air accidents; FAA, reporters, hospitals—especially clinics catering to Latinos, that's where Speedy would wind up if he had a choice.''

''Why not Juarez?''

''Shit! Absolutely right, honey, he's not a wanted man there. Not that I know of anyway,'' he amended with a wry grin. ''With Speedy you never know. So you've got a job to do. You might even use your official clout: what if the Butcher Bird crashed? Hell, that'd even play to *me*.''

''It doesn't have a passenger,'' she objected, as if to a child.

''But it might've landed on somebody. That's involvement in an air crash, smartass. Here, give me some more of that stuff,'' he said, handing her his bowl.

''I'll pour it on your head,'' she said, with a comic show of gritted teeth. Transferring more of the soup: ''So what will you be doing, and where do we meet?''

''We've still got our NSA comm sets so we can make a channel check at even hours on the dot. Nights, we come back here.''

''Okay.'' She handed him the bowl. ''But I asked what you're going to be doing. Don't give me any of that macho 'hush little girl, this is man's work' horseplop either.''

''A real pistol,'' he said to his bowl, cramming his face again. ''I'm going to follow the route Medina flew, and I intend to fly it pretty low. That takes in a whopping piece of West Texas and a little of New Mexico. But there's a place I saw that interested me, and the more I think about it the more I believe it would've drawn Speedy to check it out. Won't take long, but I'm gonna land and look it over. Now, that's not so scary, is it, mommy dearest?"

She backhanded him lightly, laughing. "Knock it off. Just remember, one of my two guys has already dropped out of sight doing that. Before you do it, I want map coordinates of everything."

"So you can tell the damn' government? No, thanks."

"So I can follow if I have to, on my own. Who'd believe I was any danger?" she asked, with a smile and an airhead's flutter of lashes. "And more important, who would ever believe that, in a pinch, I could fly Black Stealth One?"

THIRTY-TWO

JUNE 1991

IF NOT FOR *this damned cut on my arm,* Clement mused as he sipped barely drinkable coffee and directed his team in packing, *I could rid myself of the American now.* He could not deny that the Gonzales fellow made himself useful, however. At least until the arm healed, he would need Gonzales every time they changed locations.

Odile tucked a stray wisp of hair back under the scarf on her head and glanced in Clement's direction. "Shall we pack the console now?"

"Not just yet." He smiled, still mentally replaying the videotape of the djinni's most recent execution. "Keep the generator running until I have finished here. You may oversee Gonzales while he distributes those cement blocks outside. I want none of that wall left in here; it could say too much to some suspicious American, one day." She returned the smile and turned away, calling sharply to the American.

Clement placed a blank tape in the console and began making his copy; rather, M'sieur Escobar's copy, which he would mail to the Panamanians in San Antonio to be forwarded. The Americans might very well choose to keep the news to themselves, but the djinni's video record could hardly be denied. He reviewed the original tape at high speed, enjoying the hysterical pace as the djinni flashed across vacant scrubland at what would have been mach two. *Perhaps someday,* he thought, *one of my advanced versions can actually fly this fast.* He smiled again at the prospect.

Presently his monitor viewpoint hurtled past a set of railroad tracks, a visual marker that told him the Rio Grande's shallow channel was seconds away, and he began to copy the tape in real time as his monitor recorded that inexorable approach to the La Tuna facility. An event of this kind could be faked, he knew, given the resources of a major film studio. But Escobar's own resources must be good enough to spot any inconsistency, and of course there could be no inconsistency. The sudden, vertiginous drop toward that exercise yard had been real; the dizzying circular sweep of the djinni during its verification program, equally real.

Clement ahh'ed as the video zoomed in to full magnification to study a dozen faces, chuckled as a red dot appeared on the features of a big fattish fellow who stood near another man, sighting along a curved object he held in one hand. The dot wavered slightly off center as the view pulled back, the djinni's suspicions verified before it climbed faithfully to firing altitude.

Then the view stabilized, the video focused tightly, so tightly that it would not have shown anything even a few degrees to one side. The red dot centered again and then a faint shudder seemed to make the djinni vibrate. *Almost like a sexual climax,* Clement decided, teasing himself by giving his brainchild emotions it could not enjoy. Below, the big man dropped the object from his hand and slumped as if his spine had suddenly dissolved, forehead striking the ground in a puff of dust. Clement sighed as the body rolled to one side, yielding a perfect profile that was undeniably that of Guillermo Borges, erstwhile friend and presumable traitor to Pablo Escobar. "Friend no more, traitor no more," said Roland Clement with a sigh of pure contentment. Escobar would love that videotape and, if he wanted more such executions, he would send another large infusion of cash by way of the San Antonio consulate. *And because I have already proven that I can do what his own people cannot, no doubt he will be quick to remain on good terms with me.* It was heady stuff to think that even a billionaire druglord might pay you because he feared not to. And to underline his independence, Clement decided against seeking that second million in cash too soon. *Let them wonder. . . .*

Clement withdrew the videotape copy from his console, printed BORGES in precise looping capitals on the cassette, then stuck the cassette into a file pocket. He had mailing envelopes but they were the French variety and, when using the American postal system, he preferred the anonymity of American materiel. Odile could make the purchase. Roland Clement knew that genius, if not God, lay in the details. And no one, he assured himself, had a better mind for details than Roland Clement.

For example, he knew that Mansour's trust had been sorely tried, perhaps strained. Well, the djinni's next victim would be so obviously in line with Syrian policy that, whether or not Assad realized who had done the job, he would celebrate the fact. Clement would allow Mansour to take part in this one to a greater extent, the better to assure his Syrian teammate that the djinni was still, and increasingly, Syria's demon.

After that, a still more brilliant operation, one that he had been considering for a long time. Unlike most of the others, it could not be brought off during fifty-one weeks of any given year. In some ways it would be The Big One; in other ways, it might be the simplest job to date. Its success would be far-reaching, a *fait accompli* beyond the dreams of any of those cipher-faced fools he had known in France. Some of them would have the wit to realize the world was now faced with a surpassing technical mind. Perhaps a few of them, reflecting on Claude Didier's death, would begin to sweat. How droll, if all recognized aerospace experts went into lifelong hiding like so many Salman Rushdies; how delicious a revenge!

For decades, since his first days in Paris in the competitive barracks atmosphere of the *Ecole Polytechnique*, Roland Clement had promised himself that he would far surpass any other scholar. Unlike most universities in America and Europe—rather like the University of Moscow, in fact—some of the more severe hazing of students was done by the faculty itself. With care and deliberation, examiners probed candidates face-to-face with trick questions, voiced doubts and insinuations, left youths faint and trembling in their wake. Already burning with awareness that his father had once been imprisoned in French Guiana, teased by his peers for his provincial accent, young Roland Clement had managed to survive these repeated assaults through unwavering self-confidence. *Someday*, he would promise himself, *they will turn those sneers inward.*

Graduating near the top of his class, he had put this academic hell behind him; had authored enough papers and patents to label him as a first-rate talent. It was Claude Didier who first explained to Clement that, in the opinions of men at the top, first-rate talent could be overshadowed by fifth-rate philosophy. In short, they believed that Roland Clement cared nothing for the long-term hazards his work created for others.

Clement knew that the charge was true; knew that he had

been branded with the label of sociopath more than once. And after a series of talks with Didier, he knew that he would find his way to the top only among men who thought like himself; who would, for example, grind a city like Hama, with all the dissenters in it, into a paste of blood and masonry.

Clement snapped off the power to his console as darkness neared and selected a file from his private sheaf of personnel dossiers. The photographs were fairly recent, taken during a classified symposium near Paris. The other crucial datum was older, part of a human interest profile from *Byte* magazine. Despite a crowded schedule, said *Byte*, the man invariably returned to his Colorado home for an oldtime family gathering on his birthday.

Clement also had that date: 3 July. He leafed through his air charts until he found the one he wanted. Though it was labeled "Denver," it needed both sides of the paper to cover virtually the entire state of Colorado. In some places, the tan representing mile-high plains shaded past flesh-pink to the brown of peaks over fourteen thousand feet above sea level. Clement worried about that for a few moments, uncertain exactly where his destination lay on that chart.

In fading light, he found it: a little city sprawling at the eastern edge of the mighty Rockies, overlooking plains that stretched into Kansas. Contour lines on the chart warned the cautious airman about local waterworn creases in the land, and Clement smiled; it would be easy to find a site there. The place was less than five hundred miles from him, nearest of the dozen or so locations he had underlined on his enemies list. Like The Big One, this operation would be mounted on an exact schedule. The djinni must be on station a day before the birthday; *the deathday*, Clement corrected himself with a smile. Americans normally spent their family gatherings outdoors. Surely his victim would emerge as a target outside the family home sometime between the second and the fourth of July. When he did, with any luck at all, the djinni would be waiting.

But a few days of subtle research could make luck unnecessary. Practiced by now in various media roles, attractive enough to divert media-mad Americans from their normal suspicions, a be-wigged and camera-carrying Odile Marchant could do much of that research in a short time. In her guise as a reporter for *Dimanche*, she could pinpoint the site in advance, perhaps learn something about the schedule of that family gathering. Many such details needed consideration in the next week or so.

Another of those details occurred to Clement. He put away his files, blinking in the dusk, and called out. "Odile, you must return your vehicle to the airport tomorrow morning. You may hire another, I am sure, in Pueblo, Colorado."

THIRTY-THREE

JUNE 1991

AFTER A LIGHT breakfast on the following morning, Corbett kissed the peevish Petra and took his coffee to the Cherokee. He saw no point in running the Hellbug's battery down when Petra's comm set worked equally well. Ullmer, as he had suspected, was already at work.

"Nobody expected you to graunch the damned thing in mid-air," said Ullmer, his way of accepting Corbett's apology. "What you saw, plus the data from that NSA gear you're carrying, gave us what we didn't have before."

"All it gave me was nightmares. You're welcome to 'em," Corbett muttered. "In any case, I propose to hang out west of El Paso today, in case your Butcher Bird is aloft again."

"Why should it?"

"I don't know that; *nobody* on our side knows, unless you're holding out on me. But that's the last place I saw it." *Besides, I want a stamp of approval just in case I get in trouble while looking for Medina,* he added silently. "By the way, Yucca Two may drive around the area and ask some questions."

"Like what?"

"Like, 'Anybody see a flying saucer?' Hell, I don't know what. Give her some credit—and some leeway."

After a thoughtful pause: "Roger that, Yucca One. Makes sense if anything does. Sure as hell the Butcher Bird will turn up again, so why not today? This may help: its max airspeed is probably under a hundred knots and it can't be over two meters wide. Stick a small reactor, a pop-up internal laser enclosure and one of those little Turbomeca power plants inside and there can't be room for more than four or five hours of fuel in it at cruise velocity. But if you *do* manage a close approach again, you'll want your radiation blankets in place. You listening to me?''

Corbett: "It's a pain in the ass to deploy in the cockpit, but okay, I hear you. The truth is, I plain lost my cool when I heard that radiation warning. You're saying it's smart enough to take potshots at buzzards?''

Ullmer: "I'm saying it's smart. We don't know how smart and next time it shows up, I'd like to have you still in the loop.''

Corbett could hear an almost silent, shaky undertone in the old man's words. He knew it well. "Goddammit, what's so funny?''

"You got spooked because of the Klaxon," Ullmer explained. "Reminds me of the guy who landed wheels up, and complained he forgot to lower his gear because the gear-warning horn spooked him. My God, you're a classic.''

"Oh, I'm a scream, and screw you very much, I'm sure. It won't happen again," Corbett promised.

"Oh; you'll be without high cover until further notice. The Nemesis is already here at the shop for troubleshooting.''

Corbett acknowledged that and promised to have Petra put in a call later, then signed off.

He trudged back to their campsite where Petra squatted, stuffing their tent into a nylon sack. "Hey, I told you let me do that," he said.

"I can manage," she said, offended. "I'll be ready to roll in fifteen minutes. Oh damn, forgive me, Kyle, I'm just not a hundred percent yet.''

He went to his knees before her; enfolded her small body with his arms. "No problem." Almost whispering now: "You were a hundred and ten percent last night—or was it this morning?''

"I wasn't watching a clock," she said, and giggled, "so I can't tell you whether you're still a sixty-minute man. But for someone waked up and ravished in the middle of the night, you were wonderfully tender.''

"Galahad lives," he said.

"I love you," she answered. "You're a sarcastic son of a bitch, but I love you.''

"Especially when I'm half asleep," he reminded her.

"Especially then," she agreed. "So you better love me too.''

"I do. I love you very much. And if you don't hurry up and

give me a kiss, my knees will lock in this position and I won't be able to fly, let alone find where Speedy has put down."

She kissed him soundly and watched him rise, his knee joints crackling. "I've been thinking: he could be back at Barstow and we wouldn't know unless we called him."

"Do that the first thing, by phone, before you start checking around El Paso and Juarez," he called back, walking around the Hellbug, checking control hinges. "Let me know if you raise him but don't forget who'll be monitoring us. And give Ullmer a call before noon, Pets. I told him you'd be poking around west of El Paso, asking dumb government-type questions of the locals."

"That really is dumb," she called back. "Why would I do that?"

"For the record? To see if any flying saucer rumors have popped up in the last day or so."

"Got it," she said. "And to give me an excuse for sticking around awhile longer."

He finished his preflight check and helped her finish packing the Cherokee, with a final chaste kiss modified by a light grasp on her rump. "See you in Barstow, if not sooner," he murmured, and admired the flash of leg as she entered the Cherokee. She started the engine immediately, then the air conditioner, rolling up her window.

He knew she would wait until he was airborne and hurried to warm up Black Stealth One, not waving until his gauges showed readiness. With his wave, he engaged the wastegates and saw the hardpan fall away quickly in a swirl of dust. The sudden maneuver was not for show: if the intakes swallowed too many large grains of dirt, eventually Medina would have to replace more impeller blades. By that time, Corbett judged, he would be far beyond caring; but as long as he lived, he cared.

Moments later Petra jounced away in her tough little vehicle, and Corbett set his controls for an economical climb while scanning her route below. Presently he broke radio silence long enough to tell her he could see nothing as large as a jackrabbit between her and the Mexican highway, got her thanks, and banked toward the north. Her dust trail faded behind him within moments. *First item,* he decided, *is that old hangar I saw. Could come in handy for Speedy, one of these days.*

The border was only minutes away by now; the hangar, another few minutes. Corbett found the place by remembered landmarks and circled twice, checking the vicinity for IR traces, finding them only in reflections of sunlight from high windows. As a final precaution, he made the Hellbug hover above the sheet metal roof for a moment, battering it with his downblast before moving up and away. If people were inside, that should bring them out in a panic.

Dropping near again, he could see something like an aircraft through those high window openings; something dark and perhaps familiar. He landed quickly then, half in hope, half in fear.

Corbett pulled the shotgun from its clasps and hurried to the small side door, dropping to a crouch as he moved inside and let the barrel of his weapon swing across an arc. He recognized Medina's little Mini-Imp instantly.

"Speedy, it's me! Show yourself," he called, his bellow echoing in the big enclosure. In addition to his gut-tightening anticipation of ambush, the sight of the Imp triggered a wave of fury in him, much the same reaction he would have felt seeing a puppy strangled by a drunk. Though its nose wheel and one main wheel were extended properly, he could see that its left main wheel strut had been savaged and shards of carbon fiber glistened between puncture marks. The aircraft leaned crazily with one wingtip dented against the floor, and kneeling at the splintered strut, Corbett cursed. The punctures, and fresh gouges beyond in the concrete floor, revealed that someone had shot the strut away. It had taken several rounds, perhaps a burst from an automatic weapon. "You didn't do this, Speedy," he said aloud. Only then did he begin to suspect who would have done it. *They were here, Medina found them,* he thought. The logic of it all gave him a sense of vertigo.

A hurried check in the cockpit, and under discarded bundles of filmy black plastic, turned up no bodies. He allowed himself to begin to hope, then, that Medina still lived.

Corbett hotfooted back to Black Stealth One. Petra, he found, was still a dozen miles from Juarez but his Mayday to her must be an exercise in evasiveness. As he spoke to her, he was preparing to lift off again. "I want you to flip a *U* and take the first bad road you see without people nearby. Stop within a few hundred yards. I'll find you."

Her reply was tight with tension: "A malf in your machine?"

"No, I'm fine. But I may have to drop you a love note and I don't want to do it on the highway."

"Turning now," she said, as he sent the Hellbug skating forward, gaining altitude to better pinpoint the location. He continued his climb while scribbling on a lined pad, dealing impatiently with the charts he unfolded, taking time to follow tire tracks from the hangar back to a locked gate and thence to the New Mexico black-top some distance away. Then he turned southward.

He located the Cherokee in less than a half hour and kept his altitude while waiting for two cars to disappear on the highway. He folded his note around his Swiss Army knife, twisted the ends tightly, and brought the Hellbug down to within twenty yards of the scrub, directly in front of Petra and no faster than a man can run. He could see her through the windshield; saw her startled re-action as he flicked the pixel program off, then on again, giving her one fleeting glimpse of the craft with its familiar naked, predatory lines. He lifted his side of the canopy enough to hurl the note for-ward; saw it fall nearby; saw Petra swivelhip from her seat to re-trieve it as he began climbing again.

He did not wait for her to wave, but set off again toward the place where, he felt certain, Medina had surprised a brilliant mad-man. He had noticed a scatter of concrete blocks near the hangar. Maybe, he thought, he could stack them well enough to level the Imp for repairs.

THIRTY-FOUR

JUNE 1991

OF *COURSE* HE'S cleared," Ullmer barked into his phone. "No, he knows his way up to my office, I just didn't expect him." Placing the instrument into its cradle, he saw Marie Duchaine peering around her computer terminal toward him. His expression would have done credit to Oliver Hardy. "Would you believe Bill Sheppard's on his way in here?"

Patting the air as if it were a favored Great Dane: "Settle down, Ben, it's not worth a hissy fit. Shall I call the study team members in?"

"Naw, we need them on our birds today. If Sheppard wants 'em, he'll tell me," Ullmer said reluctantly, and ran a hand over his scalp. This could be bad news from a customer; why let your own people watch somebody smear egg on your face? He called up his most recent files on the NSA study, nodding to himself from time to time. If Sheppard wanted to halt the operation now, at least the paperwork was up-to-date.

He was still immersed in those files when he heard Marie welcome the little man into their office. "Go on in, he knows you're here," she added.

Ullmer made a show of pleasure he did not really feel: the smiles, handshake, the offer of coffee politely declined. "If you wanted to catch us napping," he went on, "you did. The team members are downstairs if you want 'em. Except for Leigh."

If a prime customer's smile could disarm Ben Ullmer, Sheppard's would do it. "No need, Ben. The fact is, for two years my brother's been trying to drag me out here to the Umpqua River for some fishing. I just sneaked away for half a day to see, firsthand, what went wrong with that equipment of ours. A vacation from my vacation,'' he said as if admitting a minor crime.

Ullmer tried not to show his relief but knew he had the world's worst poker face. "Most basic thing in the world sent my people home: a power lead with a bad solder connection. I guess it's my turn to ask whether you want the whole pod back now, or . . ." *In other words, Bill, is the operation scrapped or just in abeyance?*

"Keep it for now." Sheppard's canny gaze said he'd heard the unspoken question. The little man seemed, as always, unable to sit quietly for more than a few moments and now he was up and roaming again.

Ullmer would have told one of his own people to "siddown for God's sake" but Dr. William Sheppard, even a Sheppard in hiking boots and tan whipcords, was a man you allowed to roam. "If I'd known you didn't have a bow tie on, I'd have had you stopped as an imposter," Ullmer said instead. "Except there's nobody like you."

"Don't bet on that," Sheppard replied, with a sunburst grin that faded too quickly. He stopped to peer at a photograph on the wall; a Lockheed Blackbird, perhaps the little-known A-12 version, carrying a small unmanned aircraft on its back. Some of the Aurora technology, still deep black, had emerged from that lashup. "You had some wonderful ideas," he said.

"That one had a feature that didn't work. We lost an airchine, too. A wonderful idea that doesn't work is a shitty idea," Ullmer grumped.

"Didn't work is one thing. *Can't* work is something else. The surveillance we tried against the Butcher Bird could have worked, Ben. It's going to work, sooner or later. Either that, or Roland Clement is exactly what he always thought he was, a universal genius equal to da Vinci."

"You're all that sure it's ol' damn-his-eyes Clement, are you?"

"Close enough. We have a psychological profile of the man, thanks to the DGSE."

"The who?"

"No, that's a rock group," Sheppard teased. "Mitterand's people renamed their SDECE; now they're the *Direction Générale de la Sécurité Extérieure.*'' He shrugged, mangling his French a bit. "But they're the same sweet-tempered bunch, believe me. No matter on whose turf they found him, if they got Mister Clement in their sights they'd shoot him out of hand."

"Fuckers were always out of hand," Ullmer observed, recalling the assassinations and sabotage managed, over the years, by France's version of the CIA. "So what did they tell us about Clement that we can use?"

Perched on the edge of Ullmer's desk, Sheppard ticked items off on his fingers. "Son of an exiled felon with a ten-pound brain and a megaton of scores to settle. When he left France he was virtually unemployable there, and that gives him an international enemies list. Never forgets an insult but keeps his rage bottled until he can exact his price."

When Ullmer did not respond, Sheppard continued. "You remember what he looked like: medium height, solid build, deep-set eyes. Attentive to women, though I don't remember that he ever had anything good to say about them. Or anybody else. His profile says he's not a physical bully but if he felt the need, he'd put a knife in you without hesitation. The man who was taken out in French Guiana used to be one of Clement's few friends, but they had a falling out. We think Clement developed the Butcher Bird in Syria but there's no reason the French can find to implicate Assad in Didier's assassination. They think it was Clement's own agenda."

Ullmer stared at the wall for a moment, his head shaking. "No trafficking in drugs?"

Sheppard shook his head. "I know what you're thinking."

Ullmer: "Why would he go after that poor bastard Borges unless there's a drug connection?"

"Not a drug connection, a money connection," Sheppard replied. "Clement isn't a rich man. Wasn't," he amended. "A man like Clement might sell his services to the highest bidder. Borges might've been a saint for all he cares. And as long as he can get an injection of cash now and then—"

"He can zap away all the top frogs in Aérospatiale and Matra," Ullmer finished for him.

"If that's his agenda," Sheppard said. "Our political position is that we'd rather he was a French problem back there than our problem here. There was, ah, some sentiment to the effect that we might pay him to go home. A minority opinion," he added quickly, noting Ullmer's frown.

"Seems to me," Ullmer mused, hands clasped behind his head, "he might be a Syrian problem. If they're running the son of a bitch, they can stop him. We might pressure them into it."

Sheppard cocked an eyebrow and smiled, nodding. "I can't comment on that, Ben."

But you just did, Ullmer realized. "Well, I don't see how any of that helps us now. If you want us to continue the study, or the surveillance, we'll need direction. For all we know, Clement is lying low in Mexico."

Sheppard began pacing again, murmuring as if to himself. "There's no point in surveillance now, but we have to be ready for it at the first sighting. Your study team will be doing detailed design, just as if we *were* going to build one; no telling what shortcomings might pop up, and if that goddamned Butcher Bird has failings, we need to know them."

"You've got people who could do that," Ullmer objected, then cocked his head and guessed. "But you've been doing that right along. Shit, you're running parallel teams without telling either team the other exists!"

Offering empty hands, palms up: "It's not malicious, Ben. What would you do in such a case?"

"Use three teams," Ullmer admitted.

"We did," Sheppard said, catching Ullmer's eye, and both men laughed. "If it's any consolation, your study team made better guesses than our other two. Um—I don't know exactly how to put this, but, well, there aren't just a whole lot of people you could have hired to do that low-altitude coverage."

"Don't ask, Bill. Believe me, you don't want to know."

Sheppard proved that he could craft a pixie smile. "Not quite true, Ben; I want to know the capabilities of your people, but in a few specifics I wouldn't want to admit certain knowledge to a board of inquiry. So, if I happened to try and match a recent voiceprint to some very old ones, after hours and without one of my analysts looking over my shoulder, it would be deniable. It's not good business. It could retire me. So for the record, I haven't done it."

After a long silence, and a long intake of breath, Ullmer prompted him. "But?"

"But if I had, I might wonder if a man with a shadowy past and a damned-near invisible airplane had somehow made common cause with Clement."

Ben Ullmer needed a moment to fit all this innuendo together and, when he did, his face clouded. "I got it. Maybe there isn't any Butcher Bird, maybe there's a guy with a stolen NSA bird. Maybe he's carrying Clement's UV laser himself, playing both sides of the street and throwing us off by claiming he saw exactly what we hoped he'd see. Maybe I'm a patsy," he went on, his voice deepening, growing ugly, "or maybe I'm on the other side myself, and have been for years!" *Ever since Corbett stole Black Stealth One*, he wanted to add, but managed to keep that inside.

With an effort, the old man lowered his voice to a virtual whisper. "Okay, you have to consider paranoid shit like that. It's in your charter, I s'pose. I just wonder how you figure we've kept that airchine operating first in Syria, then in South America, and now here, without half my employees being in on it. Jesus jumping Christ, Bill!"

Sheppard bit his lip and failed to meet Ullmer's stare. His first reply was a shrug, followed by: "It's farfetched, I admit. It's my own private little demon and I'm keeping it that way, but I wanted to share it with you. Sooner or later, we're going to nail whatever it is that we call the Butcher Bird." Now he did meet Ullmer's gaze without flinching.

"We don't even have an issue there, pal," said the old man. "And when we do nail it, you'll feel better. I happen to know that my contract pilot couldn't fly his airchine at all at a time when the Butcher Bird was killing people. Never mind how; it was something I stumbled across."

"Nothing to do with replacement impeller blades, I take it," Sheppard suggested.

Ullmer's face went into his hands. Muffled: "Dead right, so you know who ordered 'em. That blew me away. How many others know?"

"Just the clerk who forwarded the data and promptly forgot about it. I sometimes initial things without thinking it out and double-checking my suspicions. Or so I would claim," said the NSA man with a faint smile. "Now you see what started me playing paranoid games about the kinds of work your shop does."

"Let me tell you something, what keeps me awake nights is figuring out how that guy does his own work. He's got a fuckin' skunk works somewhere."

"Maybe it's all he does. A lot of money disappeared in that operation," Sheppard said.

"Yeah, but still—all I know is, he makes noises like a patriot. And he's not a well man, Bill, I don't think he'll be flying a year from now. I think he sees this as a final hurrah, and for the love of God keep that to yourself."

"And Petra Leigh, of course."

"She doesn't know about that. He doesn't want her to."

The two old professionals shared a moment's reflective silence, broken by Sheppard's: "I guess I've done about all the damage I can for one day, Ben," as he made ready to leave. "Will Hardin and Morrison stay on call?"

"Until hell freezes. They're thoroughly pissed about that equipment letting them down."

"Well, I'm off. If you get a hot flash from us, it'll be my deputy for the next week or so while I'm on vacation. Clement evidently needs time to set up when he moves and I should be back in harness before his next operation." Sheppard turned and walked toward Marie's workstation. "Meanwhile, I have yet to catch a trout as big as David's."

Ullmer grinned at him. "Wish I could go along, but first chance I'll have to dip a hook will be August, in Lake Winnebago." This reference, an old joke between them, drew a smiling nod from Sheppard. Ben Ullmer did not fish. "You gonna spend the whole time on the Umpqua?"

Sheppard, with his hand on the doorknob: "No, we'll be heading for an annual family blowout in a few days. Maybe I'll catch something big when I go home to Pueblo."

THIRTY-FIVE

JUNE 1991

I T WAS SIMPLY astonishing, Petra reflected as she toured the El Paso hardware store, that with all the things he *did* know, Kyle Corbett didn't recognize morning sickness when he saw it. Her gynecologist had pronounced it all perfectly normal, nothing to worry about during her first trimester of pregnancy. Ecstatic as she felt to carry Corbett's child, these queasy mornings were a damned outrage. Did God in His infinite wisdom give female rabbits and guppies the same daily reminders? Some redesign of the system, she decided, was definitely in order. No stress analysis necessary; she was stressed, all right. . . .

By the time she began to lose her waistline in the fourth month, the doctor had said, her barf-ish mornings should be behind her. But that was still a month away and, meanwhile, she awoke every morning in hopes that this would be The Day her breakfast didn't go ballistic.

She had lost it again this morning, shortly before Corbett came ghosting over with his note. For some reason, one good look at that note had made her forget her queasiness: Black Stealth One, evidently, had a structural problem. Any decent stress analyst would know what to make of that shopping list: two yards of carbon cloth woven in Style 181, two more in the heavier Style 285, for example. Failing that, Kevlar or *S* glass cloth, and the glass was all she could get. The gallon of epoxy she could have taken for granted, plus shears, dropcloth, latex gloves, and that old standby, "etc."

Well, he could just be damned glad she knew what that "etc"

entailed in repairing advanced composites. Saturating pieces of drapery with a syrupy mess of poisonous glop was a mild way of putting it, and *mess* was the operative word.

The bill came to nearly two hundred dollars. She made a fruitless call to their Barstow place, filled the Cherokee's tank and remembered to pick up sandwiches in Las Cruces before turning south from the interstate on a road that might once have known a repair. She saw no traffic, but shortly before noon a vast shadow fell in place overhead, then outpaced her. When she looked up, she smiled; Corbett was leading her on that last leg.

Once past the gate, she could see recent tire tracks, and by the time she reached the old hangar, Corbett had landed the Hellbug behind it. He welcomed her with a kiss and, "You aren't going to believe this," as he led her by the hand to the hangar.

Standing at the narrow opening, peering inside: "You've found him," she squealed, reasoning that, wherever Medina's Imp sat, its owner could not be far away. "That's why I couldn't get him on the phone!" Corbett disabused her of that idea, explaining while he shoved a hangar door further open, bidding her to drive the Cherokee inside.

At close range she could see the damage to the tiny aircraft. "Damn, Kyle, it infuriates me to see such a thing! And where did those concrete blocks come from?" As she spoke, she was hauling her purchases from the Cherokee.

He had found the blocks outside, he said; had piled them up while waiting and, because the craft weighed less than many a sailplane, lifted the wing atop them with discarded plastic as a pad. "I make it a four-hour job," he said, setting out paper cups and duct tape near the epoxy, "which we're going to do in half that time. Just be glad Speedy made these gear struts from composite instead of metal. Oh shit, this isn't quickset resin," he muttered. "It's going to take a full four hours."

"Quit bitching," she rejoined. "Slowset is stronger."

He sighed and nodded, then found a rasp from the Cherokee's tool kit and attacked the wheel strut furiously. The entire aircraft vibrated with his work because a landing gear strut was linked solidly to the guts of its structure.

"I hope you set the orientation of each ply according to the manual," she cracked, drawing a cynic's grunt from him. An ordinary fiberglass boat patch bore the same relation to advanced composite repairs as a manicure does to brain surgery, but this job would look more like the manicure. Using successively finer sandpaper, Corbett studied the strut to discover how many layers of carbon fiber had gone into that part, and in which directions the strands had been applied. Though they had no vacuum bags, no heating elements and no carbon fiber, at least he could replace the layers of new material in the proper directions.

The repair would not be finished until additional layers had been applied, rather like adding a cast over a fractured arm. And ironically, if it got him home, he would then have to throw that strut away and do it right.

The repair, he told her, needed to survive exactly one takeoff and one landing. "I'll set it down at Barstow and we can made a new strut later."

She was using shears on gleaming white glass cloth, several plies of it, but paused to stare at him. "And leave the Hellbug here?"

A headshake. He attacked the strut again, using fine grit on the tough composite to improve the bond when the epoxy hardened. "We'll leave the Cherokee here," he said, panting with his exertion.

"Shit oh dear," she breathed, straightening as she realized the implications of what he'd just said. At first blush the notion struck her as ridiculous. "You want my first solo to be in the Hellbug, cross-country? At night?"

"If we can finish this in two hours and let it cure for another hour or so, you and I will fly wingtip to wingtip, love. We can raise Barstow in daylight. All perfectly illegal, I assure you."

She began to measure resin into a cardboard cup, knowing that she must not think about that flight at a time when she needed sure-handed dexterity. "In this heat, the epoxy will cure pretty fast," she reminded him. "How soon do you need the first short pieces?"

He had his reading glasses on, peering at her work like a schoolmaster. "Another few strokes. You can wet the two small angled plies out now."

Gloved and sweating, she moved behind him. "Hold still."

He must have heard the shears snipping. "What the hell? This is a perfectly good shirt," he complained.

She continued to snip, then to rip, and in moments had fashioned two sweatbands from his shirttail. She placed his around his forehead. "And you'll ruin a perfectly good resin bond if you drip sweat on it, and you sweat like a dray horse," she replied, unperturbed as she tied her sweatband in place. "And so do I."

He was chuckling as he finished preparing the strut. "Let me know before you start on my pants," he said.

"A tempting idea," she said, brushing more resin in, watching the cloth become almost magically clear as it lay on the dropcloth. Together they applied the flaccid stuff to the broken strut, layer after layer, working air bubbles out swiftly. The first stages of their repair were complete when Petra remembered their lunch and stripped her gloves off.

"I don't want to think about Raoul Medina," she said around a cheekful of chicken sandwich, "but I can't help it. How can you be sure he isn't off somewhere by himself?"

"I can't, Pets. But those holes in the strut were just about nine millimeter," he said. "Or thirty-eight caliber; whatever. And he wouldn't leave the Imp like this if he had any choice. Notice the tread marks near the front of the hangar? The Imp's gear makes little prints. Those are bigger. Somebody's been here in a light cargo craft, maybe as recently as this morning. There's trash in the corner, bread crusts and stuff, that's still fresh. As soon as I clear the ground safely and before you lift off, I want you to call Ullmer."

"Oh boy," she said, "this place will be wall-to-wall fuzz by sundown."

"Yep. So everything I touch has to be wiped down or go into the Hellbug. You're okay, you're legal. Let ol' Ben make up whatever he wants to, he's seen the Imp anyway, tell him you made a repair on it. The point is, you suspect Clement and his bunch were here before that. I'm betting some of those forensics guys will be able to prove it."

"This will be FBI stuff, won't it?"

"At least," he agreed. "I don't mind if they have questions; I just don't want any answers to spell out 'Kyle Corbett.' "

"Or Raoul Medina," she added, and burst out: "Oh my God, Kyle, what if they've—"

"Don't borrow trouble," he injected. "We have to think he's still alive. That's why I'm fixing up his boytoy, Petra, instead of getting the hell out of here."

She wandered over to the Imp, checked their initial repair, and then donned a fresh pair of gloves. "I'm not hungry," she explained, pouring more epoxy. "The first layers are beginning to set."

At Petra's suggestion they cut thin strips of heavy cloth for a helical winding around the first layers and followed this with more long gossamer layers. When finished, they looked down on a swollen strut that should have twice the necessary strength because it had three times its normal thickness.

"Looks like a clenched fist in the middle," Corbett observed.

"Speedy won't mind," Petra said. "It'll still retract." They set about removing all signs of their work, Corbett wearing his thin flying gloves to wipe down the hangar door. At one point, when the epoxy was already half-cured, she stopped and lifted her head, inhaling. "What's that smell?"

"Don't look at me," he answered. "The epoxy, maybe."

"No, something else. I keep getting a faint whiff of cheap perfume." Actually, she thought, it smelled pretty ritzy.

"Do Frenchmen wear that stuff?"

"French *women* do," she said.

"That's a mystery we'll just have to live with. How's the test panel we made?"

She tried flexing a foot-long piece they had laminated for the express purpose of testing. "Still a weenie. A watched epoxy never cures, you know," she said darkly.

He grinned and checked his watch, then made a third inspection of the dented wingtip, which, he hazarded, probably could wait for replacement. They topped off the Imp's tank from their reserve supply.

"You're sure it will start," Petra said in doubt.

Corbett nodded. "I tried it after I dropped your note this morning. It's rarin' to go and so, by God, am I."

"Let's fold up all our stuff in the dropcloth and put it in the Hellbug," she said. "If the FBI is going to be checking this place over—"

"You're right. Don't worry, you'll get the Cherokee back."

"I'd better." Then she squeezed her eyes shut, fists balled. "Damn you, Speedy, don't you get yourself killed," she demanded of the missing Medina.

Corbett moved nearer and held her, both of them rocking together in the mutual agony of fearing the worst. "You might suggest to Ullmer that he have someone fly sweeps around here in a helo," he said at last. "No telling what they might find."

They discussed it at length, moving outside in open shadow to catch vagrant breezes. Thanks to the furnacelike conditions in the hangar, in another half hour their test specimen was tough as a bed slat, and shortly afterward they rolled the hangar door wide. The landing gear took the Imp's weight easily and, when all was in readiness, Corbett fired up its engine.

Both of them winced when the tiny craft jounced over the uneven surface outside, but the repair held. Takeoff did not impose loads as heavy as landing, and before landing that composite would be more fully cured. Again they conferred, then Petra dropped her ignition key in the Cherokee's front seat and closed the hangar door.

Ten minutes later, the two shared a final kiss behind the hangar before she faced the raptor's bulk of Black Stealth One, hands on hips. "Behave, you big bastard," she warned it softly, "or I'll drop you right out of the sky."

"You got it scared now." Corbett chuckled, and opened the canopy for her.

The only way to do this is fast and by the numbers, she told herself, ignoring her lover, clambering in, starting her ignition sequence. She chose the right-hand seat because it was the one she had used most, and when she turned back to secure the canopy and wave to Corbett he was nowhere in sight. "Where the heck did he—" she began, and then saw a slender charcoal-black teardrop with a scythe whirling at its tail, already lifting from the old airstrip.

If he just sashayed off like that, who am I to worry? she asked, and planted both feet into the wastegate controls as hard as she could. In moments, she was rising in a dust devil, skating forward slightly, and with a hundred feet of air beneath her she closed the wastegates while moving at perhaps thirty miles an hour.

She felt the distinct punch-in-the-butt of a very light aircraft with a small pilot and excess power, and watched her airspeed indicator, and by the time Corbett slid into formation off her starboard wing Petra Leigh was doing a hundred and forty knots, grinning like a fool. Now she could take time for such things as her call to Ullmer. The one thing she dared not do was reflect on the relative ease of getting the Hellbug *up,* and the complex mechanics of getting the damned thing safely *down.*

THIRTY-SIX

JULY 1991

MEDINA KNEW HE had wasted hours in silent rage over the way Clement seemed to enjoy using that little burp gun against the Mini-Imp. Later the same day, however, he began to appreciate the problems that beset Clement, and to pray for more of them, after they flew away from that old hangar. From the way Mamzelle dispensed tabs and fresh dressings, and kept poking a thermometer in the Frenchman's face, Medina inferred that the slash on Clement's arm was not healing well. The man was a rotten patient in any case, using that arm constantly when a more cautious man would keep it in a sling. Still, he did demand a lot of toting on Medina's part.

In some ways, Medina realized, Clement's operation was similar to his own, depending as it did on avoidance of casual curiosity. It would have been asking too much for Medina to wish his own aerial mite could carry the cargo of a Cessna STOL, because then it would no longer fly aerobatics like an ultralight interceptor; but whoever had chosen that damned Cessna had chosen well.

With his language limitation, Medina failed to understand at first why only Mamzelle spent so much time absent in their newly rented Dodge minivan while the rest of them stayed in the arroyo. Having many years' experience at eyeballing his nation's geography, Medina knew that the site Clement chose lay within fifty miles of Pueblo, Colorado.

Raoul Medina studied the broken plain, the sun rising above rangeland that sloped gently toward Kansas and setting between a phalanx of Colorado peaks, and the nightly glow verified his guess; their little encampment in the mouth of that arroyo lay to the southeast of Pueblo. Mamzelle bought camping equipment as if money were no object. The smaller of their new tents was devoted to Clement and the woman; the larger, near enough to share tent pegs, housed much of their technical hardware in addition to Medina and the Arab.

As near as Medina could gather, their cover story would claim a wildlife study for European ecologists. Buffalo had grazed that miserly turf two centuries before, and a better than average pilot could use it as if it were a bumpy landing strip, mile after mile of it, dotted with shrubs and wild grasses. The nearest roads, he had noted from aloft in the Cessna, lay to the west. *That's where I'm heading when I get loose,* he swore. Not if, but when; Raoul Medina was not a quitter.

On the evening of their second day in the arroyo, Mamzelle brought an item that earned her a resounding kiss from Clement: an expanse of camouflage netting half the size of a tennis court, a huge bundle in the minivan, from a surplus store. It was the wrong color, but she brought latex paint and brushes, too. Medina and the Arab spent much of the next day anointing greenish cloth in the net so that it looked more like the rust and tan of their surroundings before they stretched it over the Cessna. They also managed to contract minor sunburns in the process.

Mansour took his sunburn philosophically. "It is what I deserve," he told Medina, "for spending so much time in caves and buildings. Allah gave me a skin that accepts the sun, and punishes me for becoming a creature of the shadows." His smile said that this was his idea of a joke, and Medina grinned back, halfheartedly.

This and similar utterances by the Syrian made it clear that Mansour was not a man to be easily understood by Westerners. Nor did Mansour seem to understand their captive very well. The surprise, to Medina, was that Selim Mansour retained a streak of compassion even for a captive. Medina learned quickly that the Arab's treatment of him depended greatly on whether his leader would notice. In fact, whatever Mansour did, he seemed to do with a weather eye for Clement's criticism. If Roland Clement was unlikely to notice some ordinary chore, it might be done in a slapdash way.

The fetters that bound Medina were things that Clement checked often. He allowed replacements of tape, to reduce chafing at Medina's wrists and ankles, only after he saw the abrasions bleeding. "If these get infected," Medina had said, "I may not be much use to you."

"When that happens, find a rosary," Clement had replied, smiling at his own cleverness. Yet he had spoken to Mansour about it, and the abrasions got attention. No one could deny that the captive was a worker. But during each task, Medina kept watch for a tool that might fit those *chingada* fittings. Given enough time, he might disappear into the broken plains, but without water or a decent stride that would mean only a slow and agonizing death. In southeastern Colorado, Medina knew, lay an awful lot of nothing and a man could die trying to walk twenty miles in hobbles.

On the third day, Mamzelle returned over her own tire tracks in midafternoon, fast enough to raise a dust trail and a snarled complaint from Clement.

That did little to dampen her mood as she brought her notes and perched on a camp stool, smartly dressed, one leg crossed splendidly over the other, to make her report. Mansour attended this as well. To Medina, sitting beneath the rain flap of the other tent, where they could see him, most of it was still gibberish. A few words were beginning to make sense and he could tell that her research had gone very well. When she began chattering with a new map, he saw that its largest print read CITY OF PUEBLO. With pencil and string, Clement measured off distances and direction, then sent Mansour to the Cessna for an air chart. *They're zeroing in on some poor bastard*, he realized. *And you, you sorry* maricon, *are helping them do it.*

Medina's natural optimism kept popping to the surface at times like this, telling him that when they finally made their big mistake he would help pound them into Colorado dust. He worked as slowly as he dared, stumbled and dropped things using his fetters as justification, even arranged the tent flaps so that when dust blew on the breeze it blew handfuls onto delicate equipment. Nothing worked perfectly for very long; surely some component would fail, or a rancher or flying state cop would come to investigate; if not today, then tomorrow, or . . .

He was still sitting there, enumerating his hopes as a spinster might caress tattered keepsakes, when he realized that Mamzelle was giving him orders, using that same sharp voice she always used when Clement was around. He scrambled to his feet, bewildered. He had not expected them to prepare their deadly little zapper for a launch this late in the day.

Evidently, Mamzelle's research had pinpointed something

worth a flight by the Butcher Bird. The little team no longer bothered with antiradiation walls, he noted, perhaps because they now had their miniature reactor loaded, covered by a heavy custom-sewn blanket that he supposed must be lined with lead. *Yeah*, he thought as he hauled the blanket away, *and they don't think I notice them peeking at those plastic cards in their pockets but I know a radiation dosimeter when I see one.* Would Mamzelle warn him away from the evil little robot if she found that it was leaking dangerous amounts of radiation? Maybe, maybe not; but she damned well wouldn't spend as much time near it as she was doing now.

As the time grew near for liftoff, they surprised Medina again by ordering him to remove the Cessna's camouflage net. This entailed an argument that Clement won—he always won—though it ended with a clenched jaw on Mansour's part and huffiness from Mamzelle. It was during the argument that Medina managed to catch the edge of that netting on a tool kit.

He squatted low to unhook the nylon, then withdrew one of several small C-clamps from the kit and thrust it between his trousers and his belly. He drew in a huge breath, perfectly aware that it might be his last if any of them were watching, then finished gathering the huge bundle of net together and deposited it near the equipment tent. When he turned, Mansour gave him a disinterested glance and waved him away, intent on the umbilical cables that must drop away before the flight.

Sitting quietly in the tent shadow, Medina fleshed out his plan. *I could just stomp shit out of that umbilical fixture when I get loose, but they might have a spare. I should stomp the whole fucking console but that would make noise, and the time to use that C-clamp on my cable clamps is when they're asleep. Do I really want to wake 'em up?*

Maybe not, he decided. He wanted to remove his hobbles and walk the hell out of there during the night. The glow of Pueblo's lights, even from this distance, would be a friendly beacon on his horizon.

This time, Clement did not wait for the Butcher Bird's takeoff but, assuring himself that the Pueblo map and his handgun filled his pocket, strode away to the Cessna during the start-up sequence. The Frenchman started his big turbocharged engine and watched the rest of the launch sequence closely, his smile broadening as his assistants spoke their litany together, and as the Butcher Bird's peripheral vanes began to blur he urged the Cessna forward. Mansour waited until Clement had climbed and circled before he spoke the magic word, the umbilical dropping, the whirring Butcher Bird a sizzling demon that dwindled rapidly in the dry High Plains air. Then both aircraft moved away toward the northwest, the Cessna visible for several minutes as it followed a far more lethal machine.

Selim Mansour waited no longer to vent his spleen, stalking about, kicking at clods, once raising both hands toward the dot that was Clement's Cessna and squeezing them as if a throat hung there before him to be wrung. Mamzelle spoke some French at him but it did not seem to help. Ever the opportunist, Medina ambled near her and sat down, arms folded at his knees. "The boss may be wrong, but he's always boss," he said. Whatthehell, if these two got mad enough, they might mutiny. *Right*, his cynical side replied; *yeah, ri-i-ight.*

Mansour was still talking, apparently to himself. Mamzelle began to take him seriously when the Syrian actually began to slap himself across the face, not little love-taps but good solid whacks. Medina had half a notion to laugh. *At a crazy man who carries a submachine gun*, he thought, and kept the notion at bay. With a gesture of dismissal toward Medina, the woman walked to where Mansour squatted like a Bedouin, talking to the dirt.

Moments later, she came back; actually, "sashayed" was more like it, visibly calmed by some knowledge. Only it was more like a need for knowledge, Medina found. "Speedy, you know that Selim wishes you no harm."

Medina looked at her and lifted one eyebrow.

Now she passed a hand behind her neck, fluffing the short dark tresses, raising her chin as if appreciating the breeze; as if the tightening of fabric over her breasts were entirely circumstantial. *Roughly as circumstantial as pulling a rubber out of her purse*, Medina thought. "Speedy, *mon petit*, you know that Selim is under great stress. We both are."

"And I'm not," he said. "Lady, my heart just pumps weewee for you both."

Now she squatted at Medina's level; and because she was still wearing the skirt and blouse she had donned for her day in Pueblo, the view for Raoul Medina improved remarkably. After one startled glance he thrust himself back in character, refusing to inspect the bait, looking off toward the late sun with a morose headshake.

"Speedy, you know many things that we do not."

Playing on his wisdom, Medina guessed, must be the kind of oil that soothed Clement. *She must think it'll work on me, too. I think she really despises the asshole. Whatever he is, I'm smart not to be.* "I'm just a dumb airplane jockey, lady. I don't speak your language and

I don't know what the hell you people are doing, and," he said, inspired, "your panties are showing."

She brought her knees together; called something to Mansour; then resumed her seductive wheedling. "Speedy, Selim is beside himself with worry. I might simply open a bottle of wine, but he is a Moslem and cannot drink alcohol. Did you know that *al-kohol* is an Arabic word? They first distilled it, but must not drink it," she injected, with a smiling headshake at this irony. "Some Moslems may not smoke hashish, either, Speedy."

Pause. Medina waited for the other shoe to drop. "Yeah?"

A conspiratorial smirk: "Speedy, Selim is not one of those."

Medina blinked; gazed toward the infuriated Syrian. "Whoa. You're telling me hash is okay? Hashish, pot, marijuana, grass, whatever you want to call it." He saw that her nod was serious. "Well hell, don't let me interfere, I'm not going to tell."

"You don't understand. He does not have any. He would have been insane to carry such things on his person while crossing several borders. Roland would kill him for that, I think."

"And after I've been searched several times you think I've got some on me?" This was too much, and Medina began to grunt with soundless laughter. "God, this is rich, Mamzelle. I've been known to, uh," he mimed an inhalation from between thumb and forefinger, letting his eyes pop, "take a hit, but I don't carry it around. I can get it at any bus station and most honky-tonks. Or ask a taxi driver. It's no big deal," he added.

A ululating cry from Mansour drew their attention. The man was now hurling every rock he could find as hard as he could in the general direction of the Cessna, and Mamzelle spoke quickly. "Then tell him how one finds it, ah, makes an insertion?"

"Connection," he supplied, and brightened. "I could go with him."

"No. That will not be allowed, do not imagine we are that stupid. What if Roland should return with you both gone?"

Medina thought the basic idea itself was pretty stupid but was not prone to argue. The woman coaxed Mansour into dropping his stones, brought him to the brink of good sense again with promises. Then, with Mamzelle listening, Medina explained how a man might find a source of marijuana without much risk.

With enough cash to pay a taxi driver well and making protestations that he could find his way back easily, Mansour took the minivan's keys. He drew the woman aside for a moment, handing her the stubby weapon he carried as they talked, and moments later the silvered van was spouting another dust trail in its wake. *It's crazy,* Medina thought. *But maybe Arabs are like that. Then again, I wonder if he'll come back smelling of booze. His ethic seems to work more on shame than guilt; what we don't see won't hurt him. Yeah, maybe ol' Mansour has agendas that only seem crazy. . . .*

Clement had been gone for a half hour now. Obviously they expected the flight to last a few hours. This was the time, he decided, to overpower Miz Mamzelle, to splatter all that high-tech hardware with a few well-chosen rounds, and to get the fuck out of here, in that order. "Come on, sit in the shade," he told her, patting the camp stool next to him.

"Perhaps I shall," she said, making no move to do so, opening a button on her blouse and shaking its lapels to fan herself. "But this is very confining. I need to change," she said, and tossed him an entirely different kind of smile as she ducked into her tent.

He did not want to be encumbered with those cables when it came to wrestling with an armed bimbo, and the instant she was out of sight he had the C-clamp out, tightening it against one of the fittings. It did fit, and he felt the nut begin to turn, now only finger-tight, and then he felt a breath tickling the back of his neck and turned his head, and stared into the muzzle of Mamzelle's little burp gun.

"Naughty Speedy," she whispered, holding out her hand for the purloined C-clamp. "What will I do with you?"

Though her finger lay in the trigger guard, and he could not hope to twist around before she blew him away, she was wearing only a halter above her waist, kneeling so near that by leaning to one side slightly he might kiss the upper swell of her left breast.

Under the circumstances, that was all he could think of, and he did it without moving his eyes from the gun muzzle.

THIRTY-SEVEN

JULY 1991

WHEN CHASING THE afternoon sun for six hundred miles, you get a bonus of daylight. Corbett had factored that in, so the headwinds they met over Arizona only raised their fuel consumption by a few pounds per hour. It turned out to be almost a few pounds too much. Without one of those nifty NSA comm sets in the Mini-Imp, and flying off Petra's right wing, he used up most of his pantomime routines before Petra finally understood that she should hang back a bit and let him land well before her. He greased the Imp in on their little strip outside Barstow as the sun touched the horizon, and had the hangar doors fully open when he saw Black Stealth One dropping toward him in the dusk, balanced on its columns of deflected air from the wastegates.

Petra tried three times to settle, wings rocking dangerously, the Hellbug's own downwash making its nose bob like a hesitant dragonfly as it came within an armspan of the concrete apron, before Corbett motioned for her to enter the hangar without settling. This, she would not do. He could see the tension in her face, the sinews corded in her neck, and judged at last that she was right to refuse. Landing too hard on what were essentially large casters, she might crack the Hellbug like an egg. Finally he ran near and motioned for her to open her side of the canopy. "I'm going for a ladder," he shouted above the airblast. "Coming in there with you!"

Her relief was almost comically obvious. "Do it," she called back. "I'm running on fumes, Kyle!"

Their final maneuver looked more like Buster Keaton boarding a ship on the high seas than modern flight technology. He brought out an aluminum ladder, mounted it, and stood teetering there with his head ten feet in the air while the Hellbug's bulbous nose nudged him like an overly friendly mare. He managed to get his side of the canopy open but, stepping toward the footwell, he added almost two hundred pounds to Petra's steed. Her correction knocked the ladder flat and for the first time in his experience, Corbett entered Black Stealth One flailing like a drunk. He flashed a smile and a gestured OK to Petra, who was more than willing to let him land his beast.

This kind of exertion shouldn't make me so faint, he thought as he took familiar controls in hand. But of course it might for a man dying of cancer. He had already taken up a notch on his belt to adjust for his weight loss, and as he settled his aircraft to the apron he thought for a moment that he might pass out. The Hellbug's wings drooped, letting the concrete apron take the weight.

Inside with the canopy shut, they no longer shouted. "Okay, let's try it again, Pets," he said, blinking, ignoring his dizziness. "You did great getting here, but landing this gossamer bitch is partly a process of feeling when the downwash bounces her nose up. So take it up a few feet and let's practice. One of these days you'll have to learn to feel it out. Why not now?" *While I'm still around to coach you,* he added silently.

He watched her face intently as she straightened the solid little shoulders, swallowed, and nodded. That was when the rotary engine stopped, the impeller blades spooling down. "Why'd you kill it?" he said, perplexed.

In answer, Petra held up her hands in innocence, then leaned forward and tapped the fuel tank's digital readout. "I didn't," she said. "It's fresh out of spit; me, too."

They sat back for a moment and shared laughter, fingers interlocked. Then, "We'll just have to push it inside," he said, and they did.

Because Corbett did not want to use their special communications gear from a base that must not be pinpointed, they decided against calling Ullmer. After moving the Imp inside and checking his answering device in the dwindling hope that Medina might have called, they tossed their clothes into one pile and showered together in the living quarters, lights out. He thought she was crowding him just to cuddle until she murmured into the warm spray, "If you let go, I'll fall. I must've burned a jillion calories today."

"Tension will do that. Want to sleep?"

"Later. I'm hungrier than I am tired."

"We'll fire up the tow truck and go for a steak," he said, and turned off the water. She let him towel her dry, eyes closed, luxuriating in rough terry cloth and tender treatment. He told her again that she had handled her first solo wonderfully well and asked if she wanted to try again. What she really wanted, she said, was liver and onions. With a glass of Mogen David and strawberry shortcake. He thought it a perfectly reasonable request.

They had to forgo the shortcake but the steakhouse near Barstow did have strawberry pie, and Petra fell asleep in their booth while finishing her second piece. Corbett let her snooze for a few minutes, finishing his second Negra Modelo in no hurry, surveying her features with a tiny smile that mirrored his pleasure in her. *Wonder how she'll look when she's my age. Probably more like her father, the patrician son of a bitch, but he gave her good cheekbones and a killer smile.* Oh yes, he knew Petra's family from way back, knew her bloodline better in some ways than she did. He wondered whether, after he was no longer in her personal loop, she would go back to them in Old Lyme, Connecticut, to sort her life out. *She'll have no trouble finding a good man. Not as good as me, but better than most. Raoul? Naah. One fugitive in her life should be enough. I'll have to remind her of that when I tell her about the big C. Man oh man, is she going to be pissed!*

It occurred to him, then, that one day soon she would not have his counsel; which, as he thought about it, did not seem such a shame. She did not need counsel as much as most people her age. A gutty, self-sufficient little bombshell, in fact, who would probably survive his passing with a minimum of grief. Only when her image began to blur did Kyle Corbett realize that their waitress was standing near, openly curious about the young woman snoring lightly with a fork in her hand, and the burly older man watching her while tears rolled down his cheeks.

THIRTY-EIGHT

JULY 1991

THOUGH HIS NEED for hashish was entirely bogus, a desperate ruse, Selim Mansour's need to reach civilization was agonizingly real. Though an Alawite Moslem, Mansour's formative years had been more traditional, and while the women in that household had raised little girls with strict punishments, little boys were always allowed honest displays of high emotion. Thus it was not too rare for a trained scientist, in that corner of the world, to throw an occasional temper tantrum. Mansour was only proving that the child is father to the man.

Far from playacting, Selim Mansour had simply given vent to honest frustration that had culminated with Clement's decision to chase his djinni and watch it perform a surveillance mission. That Syria's most talented mercenary would pursue his plaything across the sky like some—some *hobbyist*—was an absurdity so fraught with pointless danger as to stand beyond comparisons.

To Mansour it seemed that, with each success, the Frenchman was beginning to take more capricious, insane risks. It was exactly this sort of imponderable that had moved Syrian intelligence, long before, to enlist Selim Mansour. There were no telephones in that arroyo, no way for Mansour to reach his controller in Damascus. The poor fool Ashraf had been the obvious political watchdog for Assad, properly unaware that Syrian intelligence might place a second and more subtle watcher inside Clement's little team. So long as the muscular Ashraf had kept contact, there had been no need for Selim Mansour to activate himself. It was barely possible, he judged, that Ashraf had really knifed Clement and escaped on foot. It was far more likely that the Frenchman had killed him out of hand.

Mansour, a onetime student resident in Massachusetts, knew that he did not need to locate a communication center; with a quarter, he should be able to reach Damascus from any pay telephone in the country merely by calling the Syrian embassy collect. Once he struck Route 25 and turned north, he had only to find a truck stop and convert the twenty-dollar bill he had borrowed from the woman. It was not, he found, quite that simple.

He obtained change at the truck stop and sought the row of pay telephones away from the clatter of dishes. He found that he needed to change more dollars into quarters when the embassy receptionist simply refused to take the call. Because the hour in Damascus would be predawn, he could expect only some sleepy clerk on the other end of this tenuous link. And Mansour needed some high-level decisions *right now.*

To his surprise, he was patched through with unusual speed to a major who, unlike the embassy receptionist, made proper responses to his code phrases. Speaking Arabic, Mansour explained his predicament quickly, then found that the major wanted all the details while furnishing only a few in return.

"If Ashraf has not contacted you, he is almost certainly dead," Mansour replied. "My time is very limited at the moment. If our Frenchman knows I have left camp, he will immediately suspect many things, including the truth. He has evidently set himself the goal of killing every Western aerospace expert in his files, and most of them are in this country. I must know, either from you or your superiors, whether to help him or eliminate him."

The major was no fool, refusing to give such an order himself, and making it quite clear that one did not wake colonels in the dead of night without a national emergency. In any event, it would take an hour to obtain the answers Mansour needed.

"I beg of you," Mansour said, "to have answers for me when I call again. No, I cannot say when that might be; and he gives me little advance notice before we relocate. The best I can do is to give you the exact location for our encampment today." He sighed, and gave the chart coordinates he had memorized. "We have a small transport aircraft there. By the way, Clement has replaced Ashraf with a captive American who helps with the heavy work. I might slow this operation down in either of two ways: allow the American to escape, or kill him." He heard the response and sighed. "No,

I cannot sabotage our equipment without Clement suspecting me. If that is an order, please tell me now."

He listened again, glancing repeatedly at a nearby wall clock, certain by now that the major in Damascus was not going to take any risks with new orders. At length he said, "I shall report again at my earliest possible opportunity, Major. Meanwhile, my standing order is that I continue to support the Frenchman and until that order is countermanded, I intend to follow it."

Mansour broke the connection feeling no better than when he started and remembered to replenish exactly three gallons of fuel in the van's tank before driving south again.

While driving back to the arroyo, Mansour kept glancing into the sky. If Clement returned in time to see the van in motion, there would be the devil to pay. In any event Mansour himself must display all the signs of a man terminally relaxed by smoke laced with tetrahydrocannabinol, because that is what the woman would expect. If she were foolish enough to recount the story, at least she would believe his momentary defection was in search of hashish.

Mansour emerged from the vehicle with a languid smile, waving the ignition key gaily to the woman who was preparing their dinner, the weapon slung from her shoulder. The American, shuffling around their tents to tighten the tent stays, appeared as curiously relaxed as Mansour, humming a little tune to himself. "I must say it was easier than I thought," Mansour announced in English, which unaccountably set Speedy Gonzales to laughing.

Mansour gave up the key, located his prayer rug, and tucked it under his arm. The woman tossed him a vague smile, as if she had emptied a bottle of wine during the past two hours. Whatever her distraction, it had made her clumsy enough, or tired enough, to spill food. Mansour took the gun without another word and strode into the plain for his prayers.

The djinni returned at sundown, dangerously late for a device that depended on visual cues for navigation. Mansour waited until its vanes has ceased windmilling to make his first cursory postflight check: cracked vanes, overheated turbine exhaust, and the like. The djinni, as always, had returned without obvious problems. The Cessna was not far behind and Mansour stood near the van, feeling its hood for residual heat, thanking Allah for the way their various missions had turned out. He wondered, as he watched Clement taxi near, what excuse he must find for his next telephone call.

Selim Mansour's first ploy, as he chocked the Cessna, was an apology for his unseemly behavior earlier in the afternoon. "It is clear that you were right and I was wrong," he added.

Clement scarcely heard him, babbling on about the flight as he walked to the now-silent djinni. "I wish I had brought a video camera in the Cessna," he enthused, squatting, peering at his brainchild with the fondness of a doting parent. "I lost sight of the djinni several times but I knew its schedule and the spacing of its passes, and—well, Selim, it was magnificent."

Mansour smiled and nodded. Roland Clement was really congratulating himself; it took a brilliant mind to make mental calculations of such accuracy that he could anticipate the very moment and position when the tiny craft would make its next pass, mapping a portion of a city. A brilliant mind—but perhaps not an altogether sane one.

After dinner, with the American forced to sit outside and slap mosquitoes, Mansour and the woman crowded near Clement to watch the djinni's videotape on the console. Near a sweeping arterial that the map identified as Bonforte Boulevard lay a group of homes, some well fenced.

Odile Marchant picked out the target area with complete self-assurance. "There, with all the cars filling the driveway," she said. "Take it frame by frame."

The house was typically American, set well back with a useless expanse of front lawn that, in a more thrifty society, would have been choked with garden vegetables. Behind the house, children were playing with a dog. A large sunshade took up one corner of the back lawn, and Clement cursed. A sunshade could defeat the djinni by robbing it of visual cues.

"Wait, see all the chairs folded near it," said the woman. "They are preparing some kind of assembly near that smokestack."

"It is a cookout," Clement exclaimed, then chortled. "An American barbecue. And because I see no smoke, nor anyone busy around the thing, they were not preparing it for tonight. Tomorrow, then."

The woman nodded. "At first light?"

Mansour and Clement exchanged knowing smiles. "Not if I know Americans," Mansour explained. "They reserve such feasts for later in the day."

"Like mad dogs and Englishmen," Clement muttered, still amused, yet somehow not convinced of the scenario. "Their great feast day is the Fourth of July, which is the day after tomorrow. But this scene has 'tomorrow' written across it."

"Perhaps they intend to feast for two days," the woman suggested.

Mansour and the Frenchman traded glances; both shook their heads simultaneously. "It is not their way," Mansour said.

"I believe I know," Clement said. "Our man is there to celebrate his birthday, on the *third* of July. We shall send our emissary tomorrow at noon and, if necessary, again the following day. In direct line of sight," he added, pointing off across the starlit plain, "it is only a half-hour flight for the djinni."

Mansour could not resist. "And will you track it again as you did today?"

Clement's moods were always mercurial. "If I choose," he said smoothly. "And if I do, will you treat us to another fit of self-destructive Arab rage, Selim?"

Selim Mansour knew that he had given the Frenchman yet another chance to show his supremacy. "If I said yes, then you would probably do it," he said.

Clement nodded, teeth showing, eyes aglitter.

"I am not a man to tempt fate," Mansour said, and flushed because the woman laughed aloud. *Then let us say I have tempted it enough for one day*, he corrected himself silently. At such times as this, he loathed Odile Marchant. A Syrian woman, enjoying a man's guilty secret with such open laughter, would have earned a beating. Quite early in his employment on this team, he had realized that he must consider Odile Marchant as a neuter; virtually a member of another species. By this rigorous denial of her sexuality, he was able to deal with her.

They finished laying out the djinni's new flight pattern and enjoyed the fresh, High Plains breeze with coffee before arranging themselves in pairs for the night, the captive linked to Mansour as usual. The Syrian lay awake afterwards for a long time. With such a tight schedule, he could not figure out how he might make another telephone call before the kill, and the relocation that must follow it. And without new orders, he was bound to assist Roland Clement in every way he could.

THIRTY-NINE

JULY 1991

D R. WILLIAM SHEPPARD grinned when his mother asked, "Davey, will you carry the potato salad outside?"

"It's Billy, Mom, and sure I will," he said, pausing to kiss the nape of her neck, lifting the big bowl of potato salad from the kitchen table. Well, at eighty-six, Mom's eyes and ears weren't what they used to be and his brother David *was* wearing an identical T-shirt to his: DOUBLE YOUR PLEASURE, DOUBLE YOUR FUN printed across them in big block letters. The idea had been David's, one more joke to share with close kin. *It's a good thing the lads at Fort Meade can't see me like this,* he thought, loving every minute of it.

The Sheppard boys, highly regarded professionals nearing retirement in their fields, had missed these annual chances to be boys again only during their military service. Here and only here, at the family seat in suburban Pueblo, could they relax and answer to "Billy" or "Davey" again though their father was no longer alive to add his endorsement.

Negotiating the last of three steps down to his mother's back lawn into the noontime heat, he dodged the playful assault of the household's fat golden retriever, got sideswiped by one of David's grandkids, then lost his balance and spun completely around, managing somehow to stay upright, the bowl miraculously unspilled.

Catcalls, applause; and from David, as he drenched charcoal briquets with too much fluid, a low whistle of pretended awe. "Waltz me around again, Willie," David drawled in an Oregon twang that Bill envied. Once the two of them had been as close, their father had claimed, as deuces in a deck. These days, David twitted his brother for his dialect and made jokes about the "E cubed"—effete eastern elitist—syndrome. Bill Sheppard minded it less as retirement grew more imminent. David's kidding underlined an issue between them, but they had already agreed on the solution: to fly-fish every river in the west together, a project that should take the rest of their lives. In a few days he would be Dr. William Sheppard again but not just yet, he thought with an upwelling of deepest satisfaction. Thank God, not quite yet . . .

As Sheppard placed the bowl on a card table beneath the canvas sunshade, a nine-year-old boy darted a finger toward it and then, catching Sheppard's eye on him, paused and made a comic grimace. Because the boy's T-shirt read NOT TEDDY, and his ten-year-old brother's shirt said NOT ALEX, Sheppard was unerring. "So who's watching, Alex," he said, winked, and made a production of looking away toward David, who stood hatless in the sun with the beginnings of a three-alarm blaze before him. Somewhere nearby, a soft whirr dopplered past in a furious whisper, perhaps an illegal firework from a neighbor. Or perhaps not. It registered on Sheppard's memory only because he enjoyed watching fireworks, and while standing under the sunshade he'd missed this one.

Little Alex plucked a gob of the pickle-spiced salad, thrust it into his mouth, threw his other arm around Sheppard's waist and hugged his great-uncle Billy briefly before seeking the dog to cleanse his fingers for him.

Sheppard chuckled to himself, recalling last year when his mother had announced, "We're short of napkins, but from time to time a large shaggy dog will pass among you. . . ." And the kids had taken her at her word. Now he gazed across the backyard, with no grandkids of his own, yet perfectly happy at this moment with nieces, nephews, and their kids coalescing, breaking up and reforming in new arrangements as they renewed acquaintances.

And David, after all these years, still hadn't learned a damned thing about heat transfer. Popping a Frito into his mouth, Sheppard stood beneath the sunshade, his gaze drawn to the big fieldstone barbecue pit. "David, how many years have you done this?"

"Umm—twenty-one years, since Dad died. It's my right, I'm older than you are, bubba."

"Not by all that much," Bill said. "Twenty-one times I must've told you then: you drench the bottom layer of briquets and then add the rest. The dry ones have no fluid to evaporate, so they ignite faster. And you save on fluid, so—"

"By God, that's about all I'm gonna take from you," David replied. "Twenty-one years of nagging! You need to cool down a little, Billyboy," he went on in a parody of irritation, devilment shining in his squint. "Somebody toss me a can of Coors."

"Two can play at that," said Bill Sheppard, and darted toward the ice-filled washtub full of beer and soft drinks. David got there first by skirting the sunshade, but he fumbled his can while shaking it and then, popping its top too soon, took its spray full on his own breast. He stood only one fateful pace from the canvas sunshade while Bill, knees bent, remained in shadow.

Bill Sheppard shook his can exactly once and, while both of them were laughing at David's clumsiness, sent a spray of beer and foam unerringly into his brother's face. David jerked backward, and in that instant the spray seemed to divide vertically in midair with a distinct *pop*, steam spreading out and dispersing. David Sheppard spun, knees buckling, now sprawled in the shade of that canvas, and he was not laughing, nor cursing, but inert on his back. A hideous track of burned flesh had laid his face open from forehead to chin, the wound actually smoking, and a small oval spot on his T-shirt smouldered near his throat. The odor reminded Bill Sheppard of someone searing a steak in a very hot skillet with beer gravy. But the effect was as if a white-hot, invisible lightning bolt had speared down from heaven at the speed of light.

William Sheppard stood silent and transfixed for a count of two before he connected the whirr, a minute before, to the bolt from above. In labs devoted to particle-beam physics, a high-energy beam was sometimes called a "bolt." Sheppard leaped forward, lifting his brother's upper torso, dragging him further into shade, the table with chips and dips falling on its side. "Someone help me," he bawled, because a dozen of his kin were just beginning to react with shouts of alarm.

All right, it may still be up there, or maybe it comes down for another shot, he thought wildly. David was breathing; moaning, in fact, with blessedly little blood because the goddamned laser beam had cauterized the wounds it made. That spray of Coors had done more than just make David jerk backward; it had also made the beam expand, dissipating a fraction of its energy, not by much but just possibly enough to mean the difference between life and death.

David's oldest son helped Bill Sheppard lift. "My God, Uncle Bill, what's—shouldn't we put him down?"

Speaking quickly, as others crowded near, some of them crying, Sheppard said, "He's been shot. Get everybody in here under the sunshade, I'll explain later. *You've got to do it*," he insisted, his eyes burning into his nephew's.

In the hubbub that followed, Bill Sheppard studied the terrible wounds and felt his brother's body shake, thinking, *I can run inside the house holding the card table over me. They'll all think I'm crazy but I have to get to the cellular link-up in my suitcase.* There was no way to know how much danger the rest of them faced, so he must convince the men to keep the kids in the center of the sunshade.

Sheppard kissed his brother's unravaged cheek and made a silent promise. He knew, without the merest vestige of a hint of doubt, that the laser beam had been meant for him. It was simply one of those tremendous trifles on which lives pivot that Dr. William Sheppard's brother David was still, after all these years, his identical twin.

FORTY

JULY 1991

I F THE FBI had a football team, it could hardly choose a better fullback than Inspector Marvin Payson. The Bureau had chosen the big man for numerous major cases and picked him again, once it became clear that they needed a man already on good terms with the NSA's William Sheppard. Both men had been involved in the interagency sting that had captured Guillermo Borges. Further, the Bureau's El Paso office knew that the assassination of Borges was connected with their forensics work in that old New Mexico hangar, precisely because Sheppard had told them. That put NSA and FBI in the same corner.

Marv Payson was the kind of man who could, all by himself, fill the corner of a gymnasium. In the past year his bald spot had grown by two millimeters, his considerable girth by exactly zero. Payson still played chess, still wore out a pair of size thirteen Nikes a season, and looked it. He was pacing in deeply burnished wing-tip oxfords, as was his wont, in a room of the Denver Resident Agency when Bill Sheppard walked in.

"You look like you could bite a crowbar," Payson said, once the amenities were over. "Sit." Because the usually imperturbable Sheppard seemed ready to flap his arms and rise off the carpet, Payson added, "If you will, I will," and sat down. "Is your brother going to make it?"

"You know, then." Sheppard fell into a chair and rubbed his face with vigor. His demeanor suggested that this had been, emotionally, the longest day of his life. "Yes, he was even conscious when I left him an hour ago. They put him in Fitzsimons, the Army med center here in Denver. It wasn't the kind of trauma civilians usually get, and he's a vet, and so am I and," he sighed heavily, with a wave of hands and a wan smile, "I pulled a string or two."

"I saw photos of Borges. What hit him looked like nothing more than a cigarette burn, but it sure took him off. They tell me your brother took a hit that looked worse."

"So near me, I was spraying beer on him," Sheppard went on softly, staring at nothing.

Talking it out compulsively, Payson decided. *I guess he needs to.* The concern he showed in his face, though deliberate, was no less real. He prompted Sheppard with a simple, "Yeah?"

"You wouldn't think a spray of liquid that trivial could defocus an HEL, but I guess a high-energy laser you can stuff into such a small vehicle isn't in the multimegawatt range." Now something broke behind Sheppard's face, but he caught it before it could overwhelm him. "I could see the grooves in his skull and cheekbone, right down to his collarbone. A tenth of a second later it would've missed him."

"And a thousandth earlier—" Payson began, then cleared his throat and changed his tack. "And all this before noon today. I think you were both lucky, Sheppard."

"I've never believed much in luck," Sheppard said with a faint smile. "The laws of physics don't care whether you cross your fingers."

"Maybe; still, the thing isn't perfect because it missed *you.* But look, this can wait another—"

"No, it can't," Sheppard said, low in his throat. "David is my *twin* brother, Payson. Fitzsimons thinks it's me that's hooked up to life-support hardware."

Now Payson leaned forward, thinking at triple time. "That, I didn't know." He studied the ceiling a moment, then flipped a folder open. "Here's one for the books, though: your own communications people flagged a very special telephone call made yesterday afternoon, but they didn't get to it for a full day and nobody connected it to you. Someone made a call from a Pueblo pay phone to Syria. He spoke Arabic but the word 'Clement' was what raised the flag.

"The guy claimed Clement is out to bag any and all aerospace experts who're in his own league. I've got a translation here, if you haven't seen it." Payson selected a page from the folder; held it up.

"Haven't seen it. I'm—I was on vacation," Sheppard admitted, accepting the proferred page, scanning it closely. He muttered to himself in the process: "My God, they have a hostage," and, moments later, "They have an airplane too, no question about it." Eventually he handed the page back with a headshake.

As he took the page, Payson said, "We've checked out the coordinates this Arab gave, and somebody has abandoned a rental minivan in an arroyo southeast of Pueblo. The hostage is male but some footprints out there are almost certainly female, and that tallies. Looks as if they took off early this afternoon, Christ knows where they went. These folks are camping out, Sheppard, and the aircraft tread marks are identical to those in New Mexico."

"We think the Butcher Bird navigates and aims with highly sophisticated video equipment," Sheppard told him. "The damned thing probably made a record of that shot. Clement is the sort who takes risks. If he packed up immediately, he must've thought he had killed me."

"If he thinks he's nailed you, he won't be looking for you again. Frees you to move, if you do it right." Payson scanned a pertinent page. "I've just come from El Paso, supervising a team of local agents at an abandoned hangar your people told us about. We're not finding enough, but—I can fill you in later on that. Now you're telling me that, ah, Butcher Bird tried the Borges treatment on you today at noon, and got your brother instead, and," he paused with a wondering shake of his head, "you had the coolth to make it look as though they succeeded. I don't think I would've had the presence of mind."

"I am a walking nervous breakdown," Sheppard conceded slowly. "But that's a luxury I can't afford, so it will simply have to wait. I really came up here to make certain the Bureau has really changed its mind about taking this on. I want you to, you know."

"I've been on it for a few days now," said Payson. "And remember, you've been a little out of touch."

"That's true. Let's clear the air here just a bit: you know that your Bureau was *not* anxious to get involved with this. Or did you know?"

Payson let a judicious nod escape. "And I know why, and I agree it's picayune politics of a sort I don't condone, but can't afford to condemn, for the record." He passed a hand through his hair and made a wry grimace. "When people fear for their high positions, sometimes they aren't very aggressive in taking on new trouble. Almost makes you wish for a martinet again who's a law unto himself. I said, almost." He knew Sheppard would intuit the name,

Edgar Hoover. Some things you just didn't say out loud. "But the hit on Borges and the tip your people passed on amounted to something the Bureau can't ignore. It wasn't clearly our charter until then."

"And now it is," Sheppard said.

Payson held his hands out in an "as you can see" gesture.

"This has become very personal. For weeks I've been three nines certain who's behind it—oh. You'd know that too." At Payson's nod, the little scientist went on: "I knew Clement slightly. Never any hostility between us that I know of. Of course I may have criticized some of his work for its risky nature, but who didn't? He's killed an old friend of his who just happened to be one of France's best aerospace people. Now me—or so he thinks. Who's next?"

"I'm in synch, I think. The crazy bastard wants to be the only high-tech player in his field," Payson rumbled, noting that the NSA man seemed increasingly in control of himself when his mind was diverted from family tragedy. He waited for a sign of agreement, got it, and pursued the idea. "Now, I don't think it matters how many people are really his peers or his betters. The question is, who he *thinks* are. That's the list we should be worrying about. Could you provide me with such a list?"

Sheppard's head shook once; then, after a moment, several times. "I don't know how he thinks. The best I could do would be guesswork but if I were guessing, I'd look for men who get media attention."

"You get much of that?"

"More than I'd like." Sheppard shrugged. "Certainly more than is fair."

Time for a little pick-me-up for this guy, Payson decided. He leaned forward and covered one of Sheppard's hands with his big paw for an instant. "Let me give you a reality check. That's insightful stuff, and under the circumstances I don't know how you're doing it. I'm just glad you can. As for the media thing, I think we can do it but you're going to have to stay the hell out of sight. Few little cosmetic changes—a beard, we call it. You might keep in touch with Meade with scrambled communications routed through Fitzsimons to make it look good."

"I hadn't thought that through. I can do it, but I can't just sit on my hands, Payson."

"Didn't think you could," the big man said, and grinned. "You could do liaison. With me."

Now Sheppard showed the first sign of optimism. "A task force?"

"Not exactly. But it could turn into that, and as a full inspector I can organize teams, pull local agents in as I need them. Field ops can work that way, especially when we're likely to be chasing this maniac all over CONUS. I'm not belittling the Bureau when I say I don't think we have anybody with your grasp of what we're up against, and what high-tech countermeasures this nation can use. I can use you, Sheppard, big-time."

Sheppard nodded; almost smiled. "I'll try not to step on your toes."

Payson half-turned in his chair; elevated one big foot for Sheppard's scrutiny. "A wise decision; I have a pretty heavy tread myself. Now then: I gather you've already ordered some civilian contract aircraft into the area for surveillance this afternoon. I've had some people doing the same thing but it's obvious now that our," he spoke the name as if spitting out something nasty, "Butcher Bird has flown this particular coop. I'd say our next step is working up a media release."

"I'm, ah, not very good at talking about myself. If you took that on, I could start making up that list you wanted."

Payson fired his thumb and forefinger at the little man. "You've got it. Need clerical help?"

"No—yes! I don't bother to keep current on everyone who's getting media hype but you could have someone pull files on *Aviation Week* for the past few years, get a printout of who's been hot, both domestic and foreign."

"A tall order; that's going to be like the LA phone book, Sheppard."

"Just Pasadena," Sheppard said, smiling. "Besides, I imagine Clement's list will be skewed toward old-timers, and I have one of those irritating memories that won't let me forget such trivia. I can probably add names that won't be in the magazines. While you're at it, you might arrange that link to Fort Meade. Am I forgetting anything?"

"I don't think you've ever forgotten anything," said Marv Payson with feeling, and turned toward the nearest word-processor.

FORTY-ONE

JULY 1991

N O HARDWARE PROBLEMS," Colleen Morrison reported into her headset, resetting the trim on her Nemesis craft. "If you're worrying about the sensor package, don't. I checked the rewire myself." At seventy thousand feet, her circular flight pattern was so high above Pueblo she could see beyond the early evening lights in Colorado Springs, fifty miles to the north. "I'm afraid we got on station too late, Oversight Control, but we're recording light aircraft blips all over the place down there, over."

Ben Ullmer, querying her from Oregon, sounded dejected. *But when did the old wowser ever sound enthused?* she asked herself as he said, "Some of 'em are federals, flying close cover. FBI, if it makes any difference."

"Not the team you had before?"

"There wasn't time, they don't have your top-end speed. This was the best we could do. I know it's prob'ly an exercise in futility, Oversight One. But you never know; if one of those little airchines comes down where there isn't a road or a landing strip, and doesn't send a Mayday of some kind, it just may be our target."

"We copy," Colleen replied. "Since target aircraft is already in the air, pretty soon our station will be the least likely one in the world. Any idea where I should surveil next?"

"Not the slightest," Ullmer said.

"Me, neither," Wes Hardin injected from his place in the tiny sleeping quarters behind Colleen. "But we know this spot won't do us any good for much longer."

"Ah; you're patched in, are you?" was Ullmer's way of greeting Hardin.

"Where else would I be? Yep, I'm back in the 'pipe.' I'll relieve her from twenty-four-hundred hours to oh-four-hundred, but keeping this station seems mighty pointless from here."

"Like the old joke says, it seemed like a good idea at the time." For a moment the channel was silent. "Try east," Ullmer said suddenly. "It's the only direction from you without rocks sticking up in the sky, and whatever target aircraft is, it lands conventionally. So spend an hour southeast, then due east, then northeast. Judging from his previous landing sites he's got to be in a STOL of some kind. So he won't be doing over two hundred knots, but you can. Use up some fuel, see if your machmeter still works," he added.

Colleen donated a dutiful chuckle. Even at loiter speeds the machmeter gave accurate airspeed readings, and because the old man knew that, he was just being cute. In the same vein she said, "We don't know where we're going but we're in a terrible hurry. Why not try to outguess target aircraft; fly a picket line?"

Without a pause, all business: "Give me terminal points."

"Uh, Sioux Falls and Wichita," she said.

And almost simultaneously, "Lubbock and Omaha," from Hardin.

"Go for it." Ullmer sighed. "At four hundred knots you can each do your thing before morning. The hell of it is, you might get Clement on scope at some point but there's no way you'll know which blip he is."

"Unless he lands where he shouldn't," Colleen reminded him.

"Fat chance, but that's why you're up there," Ullmer said.

"I don't suppose you want to tell us exactly what brought this on," Colleen said, bringing her great gossamer craft around to a one-hundred-degree heading that would bring her high above Wichita. Given a modest fragment of jet stream and four-hundred-knot airspeed, she would see Wichita's freeway arterials below her, fluorescent veins in the body politic, in less than an hour. "I take it the Butcher Bird has been spotted."

"Naw, it did the spotting, and that's all I can tell you at the moment. I'll be able to brief you later, I think. Actually I can add a little: I just got word from a Denver hospital that whoever's been getting public credit for airchines like the Pond Racer and the Aurora and the Nemesis, had better wear goddamn wide sombreros for a while. We may be targets."

Something in that offhand manner set a phalanx of gooseflesh marching down Colleen's spine. "We, as in me and Tex here?"

"I doubt it. We, as in Rutan and Rich and me and some others," Ullmer growled. "I can't express to you how that's gonna cramp my style when I take my dip in Lake Winnebago."

Everyone on Ullmer's staff knew that phrase, Ben Ullmer's sarcastic joke at his own expense. No recreational swimmer, Ben had swum in the Wisconsin lake exactly once: the time a friend's amphibian sank while taxiing toward the seaplane slips. It was said that old Ben had dog-paddled the last fifty yards, refusing help and cursing the plane's builder with each breath. The tale had become part of what pilots called "Oshkosh lore" because Ben's swim had taken place during an annual fly-in. And not just any fly-in, but the Oshkosh event, late in July when the town's population of fifty thousand swelled to gridlock proportions. Seaplanes and amphibs moored on the lake; turf-whackers lined up wingtip to wingtip on the edge of town, at Steve Wittman Field.

And while the number of aircraft was numbingly huge, many thousands of flying machines from Monocoupes to MiGs, the paid admissions to the aerial shows might exceed a quarter of a *million* on a given day. In the same way that car buffs swarm to the Paris auto show, experimental aircraft enthusiasts will overwhelm verdant Wisconsin pastures for a week as they stroll miles to inspect new craft and moon over classics, some of them—in Ben's words—please-God unflyable.

In this circus atmosphere, builders meet under acres of tents to attend workshops, lectures, colloquia. Colleen Morrison had attended two Oshkosh Fly-ins. Ben Ullmer, along with most of his handful of peers, had attended most of them. She knew very well that nothing short of a coronary would keep the old fellow away from Oshkosh this year as she said, "Try and keep your feet dry this time, Oversight Control."

"Don't you read the media? These days, I walk on water."

"That's tellin' her." Hardin chortled, and then asked how long they might be required to keep up this wild-goose chase, and the moment passed.

But when she had signed off, and Hardin's snores added their timbre to the buzz of the Nemesis engine, Colleen kept thinking about Oshkosh. Ben Ullmer's devotion to the event approached the fanatical. And everyone who ever knew him—knew *that*.

FORTY-TWO

JULY 1991

ROLAND CLEMENT HAD viewed the djinni's videotape exactly once, an hour after noon, before dismantling its vanes for stowage while Odile supervised the American in loading the Cessna. "It is almost too easy," he boasted, "when you know their habits."

An hour later they were airborne, the minivan abandoned in their haste. Clement shrugged off the likelihood that, once found, the van would quickly be traced. He would simply destroy Odile's credit card and that would be the end of it. Using the American's identification, they could rent another vehicle halfway across the country.

Private aircraft in a nation three thousand miles across, Clement reflected as he followed the South Platte River into Nebraska, could not possibly be so popular without support of the finest sort. Among the Cessna's charts and manuals lay a tome the size of a small city's telephone book, entitled, *Aviation USA*. It was a year old, and well thumbed like the outdated air charts, but it listed virtually every commercial airport in the country with maps and lists of amenities. Clement had spent hours choosing from his options. The one he had chosen, according to this airman's encyclopedia, gave service around the clock and permitted camping on the premises.

Prevailing winds over the rolling plain favored them enough that the five-hour, eight-hundred-mile flight past South Dakota ended at sundown, with a fuel reserve that was barely adequate. To

Odile, sitting near him, he remarked over the engine's steady thrum that Texas might have its own Los Angeles, but Minnesota could boast both a Cambridge and a Princeton. In approved fashion, he circled the airstrip and noted that the little city of Princeton, Minnesota, lay within a mile of the field.

The American could have been a problem had Clement not ordered him to lie down atop the equipment below window height. Mansour saw to it, ignoring the man's curses, prodding him with his weapon as Clement lined up on the runway. Roland Clement never felt so alive as when he entertained a chosen risk and now, entering a new phase of his task and a locale totally unfamiliar to him, he felt very lively indeed. The sensation made him uncommonly alert—Odile might have said jumpy—and, with the pistol in his pocket, more dangerous than strangers could possibly know.

By the time he had obtained fuel, new sectional air charts, and permission to camp out near the taxi strip, Clement found his heartbeat slowing again, his heightened sense of danger abating. The Canadian border lay within two hundred miles and, if pursued, he could fly there in an hour. A man with flawless French and a bankroll could, according to rumor, find adequate haven in Quebec. The best feature of that scenario, he thought, was that while vengeful Americans might seek him everywhere, the local patois in Eastern Canada would help defeat them. Buoyed by this specious reliance on language barriers, he returned to his little team and told Odile to feed them all.

Of course Odile muttered vile things about her status as a kitchen maid, but while he and Mansour erected one of their tents, she prepared a decent meal. Gonzales was permitted out of the Cessna to eat after full darkness. Though Clement observed that a missed meal would do the man no harm, Odile thought otherwise. If they wanted the beast to pull his weight, she said, their donkey must have his fodder.

They retired early into the tent to escape mosquitoes. "The day has been long, and tomorrow will be longer," Clement warned as they spread their sleeping bags. "This region is quite different from the American West. It may take a week to find a site suitable for our purposes, perhaps longer, and the population density here is dangerously high. We cannot continue using these swollen limousines they call minivans."

"A gypsy caravan," Odile said.

"Here, they are called campers," Mansour supplied.

"Or recreational vehicles," Clement said. "Large enough for

our privacy, small enough for the meanest provincial road. Well, we shall rent one. Or at least,'' he added, smiling, ''M'sieur Gonzales will.''

The American's gaze flickered, and Clement knew beyond doubt what lay behind that impassive face. *He imagines that he will have a chance to escape among his countrymen. But I have no intention of taking that particular kind of risk.*

The following morning, Clement's little group was up with the sparrows. Clement needed at least a day or two to overfly the areas he had studied on his charts, and did not want the American with him if he needed to land, for whatever reason. Because Odile was naive in matters automotive, the task of locating a suitable vehicle fell to Mansour. The purchase would be made in person by Clement, later. Gonzales turned surly when he learned that he would not accompany the Syrian, and in fact must remain in the tent.

''You have no vote in the matter,'' Clement told him cheerfully as he gathered his charts. ''Mademoiselle may not enjoy your stink, but she may need you for donkeywork.''

Thanks to carefully phrased comments by Odile, it never occurred to Roland Clement, as he prepared to leave the two of them alone, that some donkeywork is at stud.

FORTY-THREE

JULY 1991

THREE DAYS AFTER the attempt on Sheppard's life, newspapers no longer carried brief stories headed by SPY SUBCHIEF INJURED and SCIENTIST IN COMA. Reporters were encouraged to believe that Dr. William Sheppard lay near death in an Army hospital, the victim of a shooting by persons unknown, perhaps a rifle bullet accidentally discharged by some fool in suburban Pueblo. By that time, the thirty-odd men and two women on Bill Sheppard's list had all received visits from FBI field agents.

On Payson's recommendation, Sheppard had the Nemesis "Oversight" team recalled. They had provoked one flurry of action near Wichita the first evening, when a small aircraft landed on a country road near Hutchinson, Kansas. It turned out to be a crop duster who had used the last vestiges of light to empty his tank of insecticide before taxiing to his patron's barn for the night. The FBI's Wichita contingent responded faster than anyone thought possible, and at least one AgriCat pilot in Kansas went to bed that night muttering about Big Brother. As an exercise, it lent optimism to the team.

Payson had taken it philosophically. "At least we know the Nemesis can help." He sighed. On the following day, however, Sheppard accepted the inevitable and recalled the Nemesis to Oregon.

On the fourth day of Sheppard's liaison, Mary Payson waved a sheaf of messages to the NSA man in the Denver office. "I've got a half-dozen queries about something called Oshkosh, Bill. I gather these folks on the hit list aren't too keen on missing it."

Bill Sheppard gave him a sad little smile, his cheeks still a bit stiff with their new silicone implants. "I'm not surprised, but it can't be helped. This year, Oshkosh is the last place they should be."

"When you say 'Oshkosh' to me, I think of bib overalls," Payson rumbled. "A brief adumbration might help me."

I'm getting used to him, Sheppard thought. *It hardly rattles me at all to hear academic words like that from a man who looks like a nightclub bouncer.* "To begin with," he said, "it's a week-long festival for aircraft buffs, run by the Experimental Aircraft Association in late July. Most of it happens in the open air at Wittman Regional Airport, and at a guess I'd say people will be wandering over, oh, a few square miles."

"Good God! How could we protect them?"

"No possible way, unless they stayed inside vehicles with reflective glass. And that would limit where they could go. We're talking about a third of a million people, you know." Sheppard went on to describe the place, its stunning crowds, the almost constant aerial displays of warbirds, stunt birds, and even antique racers ripping across the sky. Eventually he paused, noting that Payson's mouth hung slightly open below eyes that seemed to be glazing. "And that's just for starters," Sheppard added. "The workshops and lectures fill several acres of tents."

"It sounds like a high-tech Woodstock," Payson marveled.

"But better organized. Happens every year," Sheppard replied. "There's a major fly-in at Kerrville, Texas, every fall and a lot of enthusiasts think Oshkosh is like that: two days of low-key demonstrations and a few hundred aircraft." He shook his head, smiling. "Don't you believe it. Oshkosh looks like gridlock in pilot's Valhalla. I'm surprised it's not better known, but to get the flavor of it I suppose you'd have to be there."

Payson's gaze began to glitter at a point just above Sheppard's head. "Maybe I will," he said, and pointed at the sheaf of papers on his desk. "Maybe we all will. Because wherever the Butcher Bird is right now, intuition tells me it'll be looking for trouble over Oshkosh before the end of the month."

"That's been in the back of my mind. Roland Clement may even be an EAA member."

"I don't think the Bureau has an RA in Oshkosh. We've got

resident agents in Madison and Green Bay, and a field office in Milwaukee," Payson said, his tempo upbeat.

"You know, we just might get ahead of Mr. Clement this time," Sheppard mused. "But I still don't think it's wise for potential victims to show up at the fly-in."

"Neither do I," Payson said, pausing with a telephone halfway to his face, "and we'll say so in no uncertain terms. When I said we'd all be there, I had something else in mind. I don't even know if it's doable, but some people in Anaheim can tell us. There's also that bunch in the Bay Area; Industrial Light and Magic. For all I know, your own people can do better."

Sheppard, nonplussed, shook his head, and Payson lowered the receiver again. His explanation took perhaps thirty seconds, and by that time Sheppard's expression managed to mix delight with incredulity. "That's outrageous," Sheppard said, starting to laugh.

Payson, accusingly: "You don't like it."

Sheppard: "I love it. NSA isn't doing it, but as of tomorrow we probably will. It just—well, you'll admit it's an idea that takes getting used to. Very appropriate to the problem, when you think about it."

"Long ago, I acquired a taste for the bizarre," Payson said, waggling his brows. "But look here, if we *do* manage to sucker the Butcher Bird in, we'd better have something that can hit back."

"We do. DIRNSA could borrow a pulsed Army HEL that can raster an area."

Payson blinked. "Run that by me again, would you?"

Sheppard shook his head ruefully. "I'm sorry. The Director of NSA can probably get us an Army high-energy laser that fires pulses in a crisscross pattern to cover a wide area. Anything in that area will take at least one pulse, and one should be enough."

"Can you give me an idea of its size?"

"It's not something you can carry around, but it will fit in a truck. Not in production yet." His face clouded briefly before: "I'd better check into it further before we get too committed to one weapon." He, in turn, picked up a telephone.

Payson held up a restraining hand. "One thing you can bet on: someone's going to have to see the top names on your list, very, very personally."

"I expect you're right. And I think we should watch the process at least once." Sheppard beamed. "I know just the man most certain to be on the list."

"If it's who I think, he might show us the door."

"No he won't; he'll be nice to the folks who fund his surveillance teams. I can hardly wait to see Ben Ullmer's face."

"Faces," Payson corrected, deadpan.

"Now I know why you wanted me here: you needed a straight man," Sheppard remarked as he began punching digits on his telephone.

FORTY-FOUR

JULY 1991

L ONG BEFORE ROLAND Clement became thoroughly familiar with his new maps, he began to suspect that Americans named their towns for the express purpose of bewildering him. It was not enough that the state of Wisconsin had its own Belgium, Brooklyn, *another* Cambridge, Dallas, Denmark, and Montreal; within the fifty-mile radius he had drawn around Oshkosh lay a Berlin, a London, and to cap his vexation, still another Princeton.

Their rented camper, which navigated highways well enough on its Ford chassis, stretched some twenty-two feet and Clement thought it might be a near-perfect vehicle for them. It was roomy enough for their equipment, yet smaller than thousands of other highway leviathans, not of a size to provoke special interest. At first he ignored Odile's complaint that the thing wallowed alarmingly on inferior roads. As for the fine sand that lurked along the verges of some back roads, the stuff could entrap wheels like so many tons of sugar.

Clement did not realize how tippy the vehicle was for nearly a week because, day after day, he spent daylight hours flying patiently through the area he had circled with Wittman Airport at its center.

Penetrating further into Wisconsin, they found that the verdant, rolling farmlands had little in common with the open ranges of the West; its population density, even between the towns, was high enough to remind him of France. Local farmers seemed to have manicured their lands and maintained them too carefully for a camper to become lost on the premises. Nothing on his charts or in his previous American experiences had prepared him for the fact that, come summertime, the people of Minnesota and Wisconsin abandon cities and towns for their lakes full of redoubtable walleye. They seek lakes still clean, with rental cabins or space for campers, and from the air all those galumphing vehicles became a disheartening sight to Clement.

As he moved south in his search, Clement began to fear that he would find no site wild enough to hide his operation. This entire region, with its great expanses of ripening corn and innumerable small lakes scooped out by long-vanished glaciers, had so much shallow water that Clement was soon thinking about houseboats. Each night he would land at a predetermined small airport, take a taxi to the nearest town, and seek its post office where the white Menominee camper picked him up. By order, Odile drove while Mansour kept watch on the American in the camper's kitchenette.

During this time they discovered that their camper was known as a "gypsy rig," and that campgrounds of the KOA sort might have been tailor-made for their one-night stops. It was the morning after their overnight stop near Fond du Lac when Clement first flew over the Horicon Marsh area and knew that he had found a largely trackless wilderness. Here, there were no knots of campers or strings of cabins, and only a few small boats.

By noon, he had made his decision. This vast tract of wetland, flanking a gentle watercourse called the Rock River, must cover close to fifteen thousand hectares—as Americans would have it, over fifty square miles, surely among the nation's largest freshwater marshes. For long stretches the meandering Rock River virtually became a lake, or sometimes a connected series of shallow ponds. Here and there, as he studied the wetlands sliding beneath the Cessna's wing, lay expanses of open water traversed by the occasional canoe; but over a much greater area, marsh grasses grew thick as cane, some of it as high as two men, with sunlight glistening among the greensward to reveal that the grass stood in water. Flocks of waterfowl floated safely here, and once Clement spotted a small herd of deer, testifying that portions of these wilds could be navigated on foot. Indeed, he could see slender islands protruding, all oriented north-to-south as though turned up by some enormous plowshare. He realized with a start that glacial action had been the plow, scouring as it advanced, transforming the land on a scale almost too vast for understanding.

Best of all in Clement's view, a very few levees arrowed across the region, miles apart, with telltale vehicle ruts that ended where boats could be launched and recovered. Clement was no sportsman, and could not be certain what sort of floating platform he might find to enter this haven, but he knew that water left no tracks. He flew on, identifying the town of Horicon at the marsh's southern edge from the water tower that named the town in block capitals. Although he had planned to land at the airport near Horicon, that was before he realized he would be spending so much time nearby, and he let caution guide him farther away. He banked to the southeast and, twenty minutes later, landed the empty Cessna at West Bend. If the Americans somehow connected the aircraft with him, West Bend was so near Milwaukee as to deflect their search away from the marshlands.

Using his Algerian identification, he rented a blue four-door Oldsmobile sedan. The drive to Horicon took him only an hour, though his search for local literature on the wilderness area frustrated him for another half hour. "I guess this is the only town in Southern Wisconsin that's always out of brochures," a drugstore maven told him in apology.

Eventually he found a tourist folder and consulted it as he sat in the Olds, parked on a low rise that overlooked the marsh. The folder, on cheap newsprint, provided him with more than maps; it carried embedded warnings that he was quick to notice. Certain nesting areas were off-limits; though the southern stretches were controlled by the state, the northern part of the region was under federal government control; and officials patrolled the marsh from aircraft as well as boats.

For a time he reconsidered his scheme. A houseboat, he realized, would be almost impossible to hide from aerial surveillance. Their tents, however, could be hidden beneath a cover of marsh grass on firm ground. From the air he had seen vacationers paddling small boats down the open stretches of water. No single piece of his equipment was too heavy to move by hand, and stored in its container with its vanes removed, the djinni would be manageable. *And water leaves no tracks*, he told himself again. He backed the Olds out and pointed its nose along a parkway that flanked the marsh.

Not far beyond the village of Mayville, he found the levee that separated state and federal land. Bumpy and lined with rank grass, it supported a path that led him far into the marsh. A few small signs implied that he was on a public access road and therefore breaking no obvious law. The path ended in a loop in the shade of massive cottonwoods, and from scars in the levee embankment he saw that small boats were sometimes manhandled into the marsh at that point. Clement shut off his engine, got out, and strolled along the levee's edge. No sound of human activity reached him here, and to his surprise he was not attacked by mosquitoes. Perhaps the huge populations of fish and birds consumed bugs as fast as they could breed. Or perhaps the mosquitoes would come at dusk.

He stepped carefully down the embankment, squatted, and trailed a hand in the slow-moving stream. The water was tepid and brownish, but clear enough to reveal a silted bottom. He had expected a stinking, stagnant swamp but the sluggish current evidently made the marsh a living thing with a lively ecology. At his casual footfall, a frog piped in alarm and disappeared into the marsh; a vagrant breeze herded silent riffles across the water. Back along the levee, several kilometers distant, he could see farmland rolling into the far distance with one silo towering against the sky like some great monument, a cylinder of white rising from a base of light green, fading to darker green, backdropped by the horizon's blue. For a brief moment he was reminded again of central France with its carefully tended lands. Clement smiled briefly. Treated at the *Ecole Polytechnique* as a perpetual outsider and later as something worse, he had no love for France.

His gaze swept to the left, across a patch of open water. North of this point, the marsh was under federal control but the southern reaches lay under state jurisdiction. Roland Clement knew that the U.S. Government's resources were enormous, and naturally opted to seek his site on the other side of the levee. Somewhere to the south of where he stood, possibly quite near, he would find a suitable launch site from which he would strike his enemies.

Not once did Clement see another vehicle while he jounced his way back along the levee, and this, he felt, was the best of signs. Once back on a good blacktop he drove back to Horicon and parked just off Main Street within walking distance of the post office. Two automobiles and an airplane could become a damned inconvenience, but he would need to use the Cessna only once more before he could dispense with the Olds. Very soon, he decided, he would have a small boat that could be lashed atop the camper en route to the levee.

Because Odile and the camper were nowhere in sight, Clement drove the few blocks back to the northern side of town, where the watercourse became recognizably the Rock River again, its effluent regulated by a small dam. Here, too, some canny restauranteur had

built a place with a view overlooking the river—and, not inciden-
tally to Clement, the boats that plied it now and again. He finished
two cups of coffee there, taking his time, noting that two kinds of
boats predominated. The blunt-ended type, generally similar to
what the English would call a punt, often had small engines, and a
beam broad enough to accommodate his widest containers. Clement loved the idea of power-assists, but those little engines voided
visible smoke that was doubtless ripe with odorous fumes, and the
noise could give one's position away.

The canoes were more slender, but they slid along very smartly
even when paddled by obvious dunderheads. The canoes were
double-ended with sharp prows, too, a clear advantage if one were
pushing through tall grass and cattails; and at least one canoe that
he saw carried four idlers. Having made another important decision, Clement paid for his coffee and drove back to the post office
having failed to note one subtle detail: that those who knew how to
paddle canoes in anything short of white water did their steering
from the rear. He found Odile, a tanned vision in sunglasses and a
vexed expression, parked nearby and was gratified that she did not
notice him as he passed, quite near her, in the Olds.

After leaving the car two blocks distant, he strode briskly into
the post office for a moment, then out again, walking straight to the
camper. He hauled himself inside with, "Good news, *ma chérie;* I
have found it at last."

She brightened enough to flash him a pro forma smile that
winked off again immediately, then drove away. "I hope your day
has been better than ours," she replied, grim-lipped.

He could afford to cobble up a bit of synthetic sympathy and
asked, "Was it tiring for you?"

"Not until I stopped at a red light in a place called Watertown,"
she said.

"Isn't that far south of here?"

"Your instructions were to keep moving during the day, and to
obey traffic laws to the letter," she said, as if blaming him for whatever had happened. "You were quite explicit, Roland."

"I was explicit," he agreed. *"What did you do?"*

"I?" A gay, false laugh, with venom barely contained. "I
stopped when Mansour shouted. After I heard a thump from behind me. Just before a terrible noise that made me think someone
had struck us from behind. And after that, I had to help load Gonzales back into the camper."

Clement put fingers to his temples; shook his head. "Wait," he mumbled, "we are driving away from a car I have rented, which I need to use for an early flight tomorrow, but we cannot stay near here tonight because it is too near—and you are telling me the American fell out of the vehicle?"

"Not exactly. He escaped."

"*Mon Dieu.*" Clement gasped, with a mental image of his operation in ruins.

Judging by Odile's glance, she had hoped to startle him. "Oh, we got him back. A bit the worse for wear, the ungrateful *salaud*," she spat.

"Odile, the man is a prisoner. One does not expect gratitude from a man in hobbles."

He thought her face ran through an odd repertoire of expressions before she essayed a wry and very private smile. "Even so," she muttered. "Even so." Only when Clement threatened to go into the kitchenette and ask for Mansour's version did Odile begin at the beginning, and before she was done with the telling Clement could readily understand why she might be feeling less than cordial.

Early in the afternoon, near the edge of a township, Mansour and the American had been playing cards at the camper's table, curtains drawn as usual, Gonzales facing backward. When Odile braked suddenly for the light, Mansour grabbed for his coffee. The American, with a quick glance, had evidently seen forward via the passthrough that, when Odile stopped, it was to honor a traffic light. Because traffic lights imply a high population density, Gonzales must have realized that he was not likely to have a better chance than that.

Gonzales somehow managed to vault over the table with both ankles hobbled, head tucked, in a roll that brought him to the camper's back door. "You haven't seen the door," Odile interjected, breaking her own narrative.

"Why would I bother?"

"It is wired shut. The *cochon* brought both feet together and smashed it so hard it fell open. I thought we had been in an accident! Then Gonzales fell or leaped out, of course I could not see but Mansour was shouting, and somehow he managed to leap out and club Gonzales with a full wine bottle before the damned animal could regain his feet. This, you understand, in an intersection near the edge of a medium-sized town. Thank God it was a residential area."

Clement, by now, had hidden his face in his hands. The word

"no" kept emerging from him occasionally. As his buoyant mood filled up with despair and began to sink, perhaps even *because* of that fact, Odile Marchant's aspect improved. She seemed almost sprightly as she added that, to their amazement, not a car and not a pedestrian had been within a block of them.

Had the American fought? Like a drunken Lascar, Odile said, though Mansour had fetched him a blow early on that might have killed a more intelligent man. After several such wallops and a drenching with wine from the bottle, Gonzales had sagged to the pavement leaving Mansour to heave him back into the camper with Odile's help. And not one person had witnessed the altercation.

"I should have thought," Clement said, "the American's shouts would bring someone. Surely the clamor of it—"

"What shouts? I heard nothing of the sort except from Mansour." She shrugged.

"He should have simply shot the man. Though I admit we will need his strong back very soon."

"Oh, of a certainty, there is nothing like submachine-gun fire in a quiet neighborhood to pacify the gentry," she said tartly.

Begrudging it: "Selim seems to have behaved correctly, under the circumstances. Is he well?"

"Mansour's clothes are torn. I should imagine his nose has stopped bleeding by now. In any case, he trussed Gonzales like a goat while the man was unconscious. They may both be sleeping now."

Clement released a sigh from the pit of his stomach. If anyone had seen the fight from a hundred meters' distance, they almost certainly could not have seen those thin wires hobbling the American. And without the sight of those, the whole business might merely have been a family falling-out, a drunken battle among vacationers.

And yet— While directing Odile back to his parked Oldsmobile and establishing a rendezvous for their night's stop, much of his mental circuitry kept busy with a fresh riddle. Nothing was wrong with the American's voice, but at a time when almost anyone would have been yodeling like a Swiss, Gonzales had apparently made no outcry at all. *Perhaps because Selim hit him so soon with that bottle*, he thought, but the scenario did not play very well.

No, if Gonzales had not screamed for the police, it must have been because, while he wanted to escape so much that he would risk his life in an attempt, he did not want to face the police. There was also the matter of his piloting that tiny handcrafted aircraft of his near the Mexican border. It began to seem increasingly likely that M'sieur Speedy Gonzales was not only smarter than he liked to seem, but just as much an outlaw as his captors.

FORTY-FIVE

July 1991

CORBETT'S LAUGH, MORE in astonishment than pleasure, echoed through the Barstow hangar as he cradled his cordless phone between shoulder and ear, continuing to hand-sand a new wingtip fitting with four-hundred grit paper. "Are you out of your mind, Pets? Anywhere near that place I'd be a dead-slow buzzard at an eagle convention! All those aircraft buffs scanning the sky all day long, and he wants me flying close surveillance. I'm sorry, honey, but even if I stay in, ah, my feather mode, some sharp-eyed bozo in a fast stunt ship might get close enough to spot my canopy from above. Cut me some slack, there *are* limits."

Petra Leigh, calling from a pay phone in Coos Bay, continued to use the very careful phrasing of one who knew better than to use key words that might flag their conversation to NSA monitors. As Corbett had told her, it was one thing to make a personal agreement with Ben Ullmer, and quite another to give away his location to anonymous NSA—or NRO, National Recon Office—spooks.

"That's what I told Uncle Ben," she said; no doubt at all whom she meant by that. "I reminded him there'll be time-to-climb record holders, a lot faster than you are, boring holes in the blue all around you. He gave me one of those disgusted looks of his and said Granny doesn't need to be taught how to suck eggs, and that he doesn't expect you to hang out within sight of—uh, all the people." She had spelled out the site once using pilot phonetics—Oscar Sierra Hotel Kilo Oscar Sierra Hotel—while updating him, and once was all it took. "What he hopes to do is get a vector from the team flying high cover and give us an idea where to loiter, twenty miles or so away from the public show.''

Corbett shifted the workpiece in his hands; looked toward the chart pinned above the workbench; cursed as he had to catch the phone before it could clatter onto the bench. ''Damn. Let me think it out here.''

As he adjusted his reading glasses, he could hear her low, unconsciously sensuous chuckle in his ear. ''You're looking at that old IFR planning chart,'' she guessed.

He admitted as much, with a sudden sense of her nearness, as if Petra were standing at his shoulder. The rush of sensation brought a tightness to his throat. She had stood there many times as they discussed a route, a warmly silent, youthful intelligence beside him almost visibly soaking up nuances of flight that old hands took for granted. Two jet flight charts, taped together, formed a single map of the continental United States seven feet wide and five high. Because the ''heavies,'' big commercial airliners, flew so fast and so high on automated flight paths, they could generally get by without the wondrously detailed sectional air charts favored by pilots of lower, slower craft. On a big wall planning chart comprising the eastern and western charts, prohibited areas and flight corridors between cities took the place of geographic features. The western chart, with relatively few corridor lines, had the look of a simple map overlaid by a scatter of broomstraws. Kyle Corbett craned his neck upward, focused on the eastern chart, which looked more like the webs of five hundred spiders all competing for the same fly. *Competition is the word,* he thought. *Christ in a kayak, I'd almost forgotten how much traffic flies around the Great Lakes.* Michigan's peninsula, however, seemed a possibility.

''Look, luv, if you no like, I no like,'' she said. ''I'm not trying to—''

''Hold on, let me think.'' A moment's silence in which he could hear his beloved's breathing. ''A hundred sixty miles or so across Lake Michigan. Yeah, I think it might work. But listen, if I'm gonna risk buying the farm, ol' Uncle Ben will really have to let you buy one. You can hint we're thinking Wisconsin, but north of Grand Rapids looks better.''

''You mean a real, honest-to-God farm,'' she said.

''Honest to God. Whatever looks best to you, 'cause it'll have to be you who scouts the territory. I think your choice would be as good as mine, 'Course, it could cost a bundle.''

''I don't know how his budget looks,'' she admitted.

"A budget is a locus of power, and if the big boys are convinced this is important, six figures won't gag them. Even if they don't know what they've bitten off." He spoke up-tempo now: "I'm in, contingent on your finding me a site. I've got to finish some work here."

"I'll drive the Cherokee. What is it, two thousand miles?"

"Near enough," he agreed. "Take a few days; I don't want you trying that Wonder Woman all-night-on-uppers shit on the road alone. Plus a week to locate and buy the right place, one long-ass day for my cross-country—"

"You're cutting your fuel pretty close," she said, as if to herself, and then burst out: "Oh, honey, let's tell him no! There's not going to be enough time to do this right, and—and, oh hell, never mind."

"No, go on. And what?"

He heard small sounds from her throat, as if she were literally choking back her own attempts to speak. Finally: "You've always been such a cautious cuss, but recently you're not like that anymore. Damn the torpedoes, devil take the hindmost, go for broke; all that stupid crap that kills so many young men," she said in a rush. "But you've said yourself, and I quote, 'When you go for broke, bear in mind you just might break.' And I don't want you broken," she pleaded. "Let's give the old devil a flat 'no.' Please, for me?"

He could have been more diplomatic than, "And if I did that for you, what would I do for Speedy?"

"My God, I keep forgetting," she said, crestfallen. "But we both know, whatever you can do now it probably won't affect him."

"No, we don't." The hard-edged survivor in him surfaced now like the contours of some great implacable sea beast rising from the deeps. "We don't know how he is, or whether he still is, but we know who may have him, and if I get close enough to the sons of bitches you can bury them all in a shoebox."

"You might rethink that, and save them for questioning."

"That's the government's problem. They're so fond of analysis, well, let 'em analyze. My priorities are more direct."

"I hate hearing you talk like that; I can't always tell when you're exaggerating. One of them is a woman, you know."

"Her too," he said. "Without Speedy I'd be dead. I love him, Pets, that's easier to say when I know he may be—gone, but he is one of the two friends I have. I just love 'em differently. One I tow cars with, and one I sleep with."

"And what if he were a woman?" she asked slyly.

He barked out a laugh. "Not in a thousand centuries. She'd be a tramp beyond belief; with dirty fingernails," he added in afterthought.

"Well, I tried," she said in a long sigh. "I'll just carry the message and hope Uncle Ben won't buy us the farm. He's hosting a pair of mucky-mucks overnight, by the way. I think they're staying at his house. One is Foxtrot Bravo India, the size of a barn and sharp enough to be scary. He told Uncle they found that hangar pretty well wiped, but they got a few prints. And some of 'em match the prints of a body they just found this morning—"

"Nooo," Corbett moaned.

"Wait, it's not what you think," she went on quickly, perhaps divining his thoughts. "A body matching a description of one of the team, and the remains were a mess. White male Caucasian, weight-lifter type. He'd been shot at close range, and left in the desert without any sign of tread marks or footprints. The current guess is that he was dumped from an airplane. Maybe their seams are coming apart."

"Yeah, so maybe they'll kill for trivial reasons," he replied. "D'you suppose the other prints were Speedy's? They're on record, just like mine are."

"Uncle didn't say but I think, if they were, Unk would draw a bunch of the right conclusions. And I think he'd at least drop me a hint. I mean, he'd realize Speedy was working for him just like we are."

"Yeah, but I still worry. There's at least a twenty-five percent chance the second prints were Speedy's. We know damn' well he was in that hangar!"

"No we don't." Petra's logic, on occasion, could be as hard and incisive as his own; and just as uncompromising. "We know his Mini-Imp landed nearby. It's possible he never got captured."

Agonizing, in a rising pitch of frustration: "Then where the fuck *is* he?"

"I only said it's possible, and we have to consider it," she said softly. "Meanwhile, I'll go against my better judgment and try to promote some money from my uncle."

"Screw your Uncle Ben's money, I'll spend my own if I have to. Just don't tell him that, hm?"

He picked up the Imp's new fitting again, squinting as he held it toward the light, holding his connection to Petra against his shoulder again but gently, gently. He heard her say, "I hate to admit it, but I think we'll have time to get set before, uh, Uncle Ben takes his swim in the lake.''

At this, Corbett laughed softly, nuzzling the phone as if it were her ear. ''Did you ever hear that story?''

''Someone told me. Sounds just like him to ignore life preservers,'' she said.

''When he's pissed off enough he'd ignore a charging rhino.''

''Sounds like somebody else I know,'' she said. ''I want you to know I love that somebody else.''

''Same to you, honey. Oh,'' he added, guiltily because he should have asked before. ''How's the tummy?''

''Huh? Oh; better by a bunch. Must've been a bug or something,'' she said vaguely.

In common with many technical specialists, Corbett knew more about hardware than he did about women. Never having lived with a pregnant woman, he had a nebulous impression that morning sickness emerged promptly at conception and lasted for nine months. He had thought fleetingly of asking Petra the Big Question, but her latest response seemed to settle the matter. He did not try to analyze why her answer disappointed him and said, ''Good. And listen, keep me in the loop so I don't have to call your apartment from someplace in town. I've got a lot of details to cover before I leave here but believe me, soon as you're ready, I am.''

''That's my guy, always ready.'' She giggled.

''We wish,'' he muttered. ''But hold that thought.''

FORTY-SIX

July 1991

B EN ULLMER SELDOM invited visitors to his home in Coos Bay. His wife, Lorraine, filled her time so thoroughly with civic affairs she rarely gave the fact much thought, and Marie Duchaine hardly counted as a guest. On this balmy summer evening, however, Marie had phoned her with Ben's question. Would she mind conjuring up a meal for guests before they did some business in his workshop, or should he stop by the Taco Bell for a sackful of pseudo-Mexican mysteries? Lorraine gave a suitably tart response, defrosted enough chicken breasts for five, and broke out the good silver. Ben surprised her by bringing his guests home before six o'clock, wheeling the old Caddie past Ocean View Memory Gardens and showing off the coastal vista before turning in to his driveway nearby.

The woman, Erika Vernon, stepped out first, a fine-boned blonde with good lines and wonderfully frank eyes that seemed, much of the time, to be registering faint surprise. In her business, she must have met many a famous face and Ben felt gratitude that she seemed unperturbed among this particular little group. Vernon squinted into the late afternoon sun. "It's really lovely," she murmured, admiring their view toward the Pacific. "I envy you, Mr. Ullmer."

Old Ben, clapping his Stetson on as he emerged, gave only a glance toward the west. "Envy my wife, Miz Vernon. I don't see a lot of it. My own fault, I s'pose. Uh, don't forget your hat, Bill."

Bill Sheppard extracted himself from the car and put his new cowboy hat on as suggested, an addition to his clothing as incongruous as spats on Birkenstocks, while Marv Payson unfolded from the opposite door. The hats might be silly; might even be pointless. *But Sheppard underestimated that frog bastard once and with a wide-brimmed hat his brother might've been spared,* Ullmer thought as he led the way to his front entrance. Payson, who had insisted on carrying Vernon's two big equipment bags despite her objections, brought up the rear looking like a doctor on a major house call.

Lorraine, as elegant as Ben was scruffy, swept a hand over smartly done gray hair as she saw Ben enter; whisked her apron off as if it were a family secret; advanced on the group with her hand out. "You have no idea what an occasion this is," she said, genuinely cordial. "When Ben brings company home I know they're special."

Ullmer did the honors clumsily, stumbling on the word "cosmetologist" as he introduced Erika Vernon, and Lorraine offered drinks. Sheppard asked for a martini, not too dry; Payson, spotting the Laphroaig scotch, said he'd had a weakness for deeply smoked food ever since he pigged out on Texas barbecue. "My heart burned to the waterline," he said, "and I'd do it again in a second. Oh: no water; plenty of ice."

Vernon declined her drink with thanks. "I'll have to have steady hands later this evening," she said.

"Classmate of mine at Jawja Tech used to say booze made him steady, sometimes so steady he couldn't hardly move," Ben drawled, removing the cap from a Full Sail ale.

"Couldn't hardly." Lorraine tsk'ed, pouring the Laphroaig. "Can't take you anywhere, Ben."

"Well, you won't have to, I'm home," he said.

Sheppard, glancing at stairs that slanted over the living room, nodded in silent approval, and Ben knew he was admiring this worldly use of gossamer composites. "And quite a home it is. Built it yourself, did you?"

"Designed some of the interior stuff is all; floating stairs and such. Don't have time to do everything myself anymore." With that, the old man began showing them around while Lorraine headed for the kitchen and its mouth-watering odors. Most of the house, he pointed out, was to his wife's order, including the Jacuzzi outside the master bedroom surrounded by an impenetrable thicket of blackberries that happened, at the moment, to be in bloom. Each of them had a study upstairs—"but I also had a workshop built on the other side of the garage. A lot of the stuff I fiddle with isn't quiet, and it has odors. I'm translating from the original female, you understand," he said wryly.

"I'm with you: it's loud and it stinks," said Erika Vernon with a smile. "I'm not really a cosmetologist, you know, I'm a model-maker with Serendipity. It took me awhile to get used to all the lab stuff. I got started with Tim Barr's people—you know, Muppet stuff—and, well, I'm not sure there's any one proper name for it these days. Lots of chaos, overlapping crafts we teach each other, a combination of makeup, special effects, miniatures, closets full of stegosauruses and spaceships. When my daughter was young, she called the lab 'wonderland.' You can see why Serendipity Studio got the name."

Payson, in obvious disbelief: "You have an old daughter?"

Vernon, enjoying it: "Ancient. She's twenty-six. I'm—not."

Payson, persisting: "Your natural daughter?"

Vernon, laconic: "Oh, she's mine, but no twenty-six-year-old is natural."

Ullmer: "You're kinda supernatural yourself. Don't tell Lorraine, she would *kill* for whatever it is you do to look like that."

Evidently, Vernon was used to this kind of elliptical praise. "You'd be surprised how many people in The Business know makeup better than I do," she replied. "Maybe you were right about cosmetology, now that I think about it, but LA is brimful of men who can use cosmetics better than I do—in the mirror, every morning. My real specialty is in making things, copies of things, weirdly lifelike things. You'll see." She winked as if to confirm the promise.

Ben narrowed his eyes. "How well does it pay?"

"Look out, Erika," Sheppard said over the rim of his glass. "He's trying to hire you."

She named a figure, and the three men looked at one another blankly. "So much for that idea. She might hire me, though," Ben muttered. Grouped in the hall of the bedroom wing, they all heard Lorraine's call and trooped back to the dining area, which, like much of the house, depended more on ambience than on walls to separate a given activity.

Lorraine's chicken cordon bleu won special plaudits when Payson learned that he did not have to worry about its cholesterol. "The cheese is really a tofu of sorts." She smiled. "Ben doesn't notice the difference unless I tell him."

If the main dish was a new wrinkle, the dessert pancakes composed a very old one. Sheppard, taking seconds, wondered aloud if the basic material was some kind of concentrated San Francisco sourdough. "Sourdough, yes, but from up north. The starter's nearly a hundred years old." Lorraine smiled. "A few years ago, Ben got a batch of starter dough from a bush pilot in Alaska. Supposedly, it was from a batch a prospector started in 1898. The secret of making it extra sour is in letting the whole fresh batch become starter."

"You don't wants see it before she adds the baking powder and pours it on the griddle," Ben said, heaping homemade blackberry preserves on his own pancake. "Looks and smells like it needs tossing, but things aren't always what they seem."

"Speaking of which," Payson put in, and consulted his watch. "Erika, how long will you need to, um, immortalize the man?"

"It could take two hours or more," she said reluctantly.

Ben stared down at the ruin in his dessert plate. "Then I won't ask for another helping," he said, his expression mournful.

"You're right; one burp and we are undone," Vernon said.

Ben knew that Lorraine's understanding of the final use of her evening's work was, at best, vague. One of the reasons he remained so thankful in his choice of wives, after all these years, was that Lorraine did not insist on knowing everything he was doing. When he mentioned coffee in oversized mugs, she supplied it.

Erika Vernon declined again with thanks. "Caffeine gives me the shakes," she said. "That, we do not need."

Five minutes later, Ben Ullmer led his guests down a corridor that passed behind his garage, its external glass wall facing west— part of the solar climate control of the house, he told them—and tried not to show his deep satisfaction when the other three realized that the corridor had widened into a greenhouse. "This is where Lorraine grows our winter tomatoes and citrus," he said.

Sheppard's eyes were busy as he peered above a diminutive orange tree at the overhead ducting. "Let me guess: the wall behind me is a heat sink filled with, ah, water. Or mud."

"Gravel. You can pass air through gravel like a sponge. And on the other side of the interior wall, through that door, is my workshop. The coast around Coos Bay gets some lousy weather, but my shop doesn't need a heater."

The shop, some thirty feet on a side, boasted indirect lighting and, near the walls, various machine tools: lathe, shaper, table saw, bandsaw, drill press, and a hefty arc welding rig, with numerous portable machines depending from hooks, their outlines traced against the walls in orange flow pen. The big room was carpeted, already showing the spills and spatters of an oft-used workshop, and sheets of clear plastic film were bundled against flimsy ceiling girders so that, when released, they could drop like curtains to isolate a segment of the room. This kind of isolation, more essential than in the days of woodworking, served to minimize odors and airborne particles. Rolls and blankets of basic composite materials occupied one wall, the glass cloth white enough to dazzle, kapton cloth a light rich yellow, the carbon material a glistening black. Vernon seemed to recognize everything she saw, smiling, nodding.

In the middle of the room stood no fewer than four worktables, each movable on heavy casters and furnished with aircraft-type flush latches so that any or all of the tables could be locked rigidly together. "I'll remember this," said Vernon with another of those delicious winks, manipulating a latch. "Serendipity can use it. Well, hello there," she went on, her eyes lighting up, speaking as if to the broad flat slab taped and sandbag-bolstered to the nearest table. Though the panel of advanced composite lay under a dust-proof plastic film, she peered through the stuff, grinning wickedly. "You've got a better way than cardboard half-tubes to build stiffeners."

"Lighter, anyhow," Ullmer said. "Just an idea that has to be tried. Sometimes we only need to cobble up one prototype of a thing, but every extra milligram is an insult." He stepped aside so that the others could see. Erika Vernon had implied that, to stiffen a flat panel, Serendipity followed common practice by spacing a row of cardboard mailing tubes, cut in half lengthwise, on the roughened inside of a composite panel. The thin cardboard's only function was to support an overlaid strip of glass cloth or, in this case, the high-tech kapton, until the resin-impregnated stuff hardened to a stiff half-cylinder bonded to the panel. This trick enormously stiffened a panel that might otherwise prove too flexible. The cardboard remained inside, now useless but forever embedded as a minor weight penalty. In Ullmer's terms, that was a small insult to an otherwise ideal structure.

But Vernon had realized instantly that Ullmer's trick was to glue slender, snakelike toy balloons in place instead of cardboard. "Too bad you can't flatten the balloons on the bottom," she said.

"They've got barely enough air inside to keep their shape," Ullmer replied, "and the weight of the impregnated kapton cloth flattens them some." He saw her admiring grin. "Seems to work," he said.

Bill Sheppard pursed his lips, looked thoughtful for a moment, then said, "You might save half a kilo per square meter."

Vernon frowned. "That's all?"

Sheppard shrugged. "When Ben worked for me, he used to say that's one more pound of fuel his birds could carry. I'd say that still holds."

"Well, I guess that's my bonus for agreeing to do this," said the Californian. "Now, can we arrange a comfortable place for you to lie down for an hour or so?"

Ullmer nodded, then pulled a heavily upholstered recliner chair from its niche at an antique rolltop desk against the wall. The chair, too, was fitted with the kind of lockable casters that could have supported a wrecking ball. Over the upholstery, Ullmer had thrown a huge fluffy sheepskin, and with the chair removed, they could see a TV set half-hidden in the rolltop.

Ullmer saw the others exchanging looks; stopped; said, "What?" And then, with more force, "*What?*"

Marv Payson cleared his throat. "Um, well, it seems you have the trappings of an alternate home in here. No offense."

"Aw, don't make too much of it. Sometimes Lorraine entertains. Ever'body wants to look around the house and that's okay by me, but even if they stay out of my study I can still hear 'em squealin' 'three no trump' or 'gin.' This is off-limits."

Vernon, trying not to smile too broadly: "Your wife keeps them out?"

"Nope. But the locks do." And with that, Ben Ullmer trolleyed the chair further into the room's center.

Presently, Erika Vernon began to set her array of cans, bottles, and spatulas out on one of the worktables in a fashion that Ullmer saw was carefully ordered. "I hope you have a sink in here," she said, and nodded when she saw where he pointed.

"Have you ever had a life mask made?" To Ullmer's negative headshake she said, "It's an old technique but we've updated it with better materials. The flexible polymer won't bond to your skin, but it will feel like it's going to. It will cover your face entirely. Once in awhile, someone has a slight panic reaction but you can breathe through straws I put in place, and you can hear perfectly. You don't have a mustache or a beard, which makes it simpler. The first thing I apply when you lie down is an oily spray, a mold separator of sorts, and that makes it easier, but if you have even the beginnings of facial stubble you'll have to shave it now."

Ullmer rubbed his face, and announced his satisfaction. Then

Vernon stroked his chin lightly, and shook her head with a school-marm's sad smile. "Sorry, that might do in public but I don't think you want your whiskers pulled out bodily when my goo sets."

"Don't s'pose I do," said Ullmer.

She saw Ben eyeing the camera she extracted from one bag and said, "I'll mount a metering armature on your head, something like a ruler that folds in special ways, before I take the photos. You can shave while I'm setting up."

"Guess I can," said Ben. "I've got a virgin Bic shaver in this trash mine someplace so I can spiff up for you."

An hour later Ben Ullmer lay inert, the chair fully reclined. The top of his head was obscured by a pre-pantyhose stocking and his face was covered by a featureless mask with shortened plastic straws protruding from his nostrils in a way both comical and somehow sinister. As Erika Vernon mixed more of her magics before applying rust-brown creamy stuff over her earlier work, Payson cracked his joints in a mighty stretch. "I don't know how she does it," he murmured to Sheppard. "My neck's tired from just watching her."

In answer, Sheppard beckoned and led the way into the greenhouse. "Still, it's good to watch an expert doing what she does. Vernon takes pride in her work," said the little scientist, gazing through the glass wall toward unspecifiable lights in the distance.

"I hope Ullmer feels the same way." Payson chuckled. "Just between us, I think lying blind and vulnerable under that clammy stuff would send me up the wall."

Sheppard turned toward him, arms folded in repose, and considered the big man's statement. "I think perhaps your work has given you a slightly different paranoia from mine," he replied.

"Could be." They watched the lights for long moments before Payson continued: "I'm even too paranoid to put a move on our Miz Vernon. Or any other casual acquaintance, but usually it doesn't even cross my mind. Well," he said, defensive at Sheppard's doubting glance, "usually it doesn't stomp across. Nothing like a knockout in her forties to make you forget the young ones and remember your own youth."

"She's really something, all right. I wonder if she knows how devastating those eyes are."

"Uh-huh; like you wonder if Clement knows how devastating his laser beams are. She knows. She just thinks we're safe. She's right, of course." The big man sighed. "A lot safer than Ullmer's going to be, if this little scam doesn't work."

FORTY-SEVEN

JULY 1991

MEDINA'S HEADACHE LASTED for days with a ferocity that might have left other men sobbing, and no one else seemed to give a damn that he was bothered, during that time, by double vision. He had a goose-egg lump over his right ear and another high on the back of his head, but by God he'd nearly made it out of the camper. Without those manacles he *would* have made it; hell, who would've thought a man could tumble out of a vehicle at a traffic light without anyone rushing to investigate? The truth was, he felt honest surprise when he waked to see another day after Mansour sapped him repeatedly with that goddamn bottle and trussed him up for Frenchy.

Yet somehow he hoped that, as long as there was scutwork to do, and as long as he would bust his balls trying to do it despite dizziness and nausea, they wouldn't put a bullet in him before he could—somehow—rain on Clement's parade. So far, that hope was still alive but it promised nothing about his tomorrows.

He had lain trussed and gagged in the camper, only half-conscious, unable even to ask for a handful of aspirin while they drove all over hell and then bumbled atop the camper's roof to secure something up there. It had been two days after his attempt, he was fairly sure, when they finally allowed him to get up again and eat. And constipation hadn't helped.

By the third day, his bowels cut loose and his vision was improving. He did not know where the hell he was, but judging by the walloping jolts to the suspension, he knew it wasn't any road worthy of the name and he lost his breakfast into a paper bag before the ride was over.

When at last the jouncing stopped, Clement ordered him out of the camper at gunpoint and Medina found himself confronting a cattail marsh. He noticed one new item, lashed to the camper's ladder, as Mansour removed it: a motorbike, one of those ridiculous little Japanese velocipedes that might weigh sixty pounds and, if you weren't pretty spry at the handlebars, would sooner kill you than get you across town. His next impression was that they had reached a tidal swamp; Florida, or maybe Georgia. How long had he been in that stupor, anyhow? Then he saw the canoe, a midsized aluminum job, lashed on top, and realized just how far Clement would go to avoid strangers.

He changed his mind about the locale while teetering atop the camper, wrestling that aluminum canoe from its lashings. Both the logo and the quality of the rivets said "Grumman." He had done a little canoeing with Corbett and had known Grumman built some of them, and if the boat was anything like their airplanes it would be damn' near bulletproof. From his prominence atop the camper, ten feet above a rutted man-made levee, he could see for miles. The place didn't smell like a salt swamp and the cottonwoods had no big moss streamers, and before he climbed down from the camper he was pretty sure they were still in one of the northern states. And it had to be a state with a freshwater swamp, a morass that stretched before him as far as he could see. *Minnesota, maybe; isn't it the land of ten thousand lakes?* He had flown over the northern states often enough while in the service; but when you're making good time at thirty thousand feet you don't get all that good a feel for cattail marshes.

None of his captors seemed to know the first thing about canoeing, and Medina wisely pretended to be just as innocent of its most basic points. It wasn't a little hobbyist's rig, but not a twenty-foot cargo canoe either. He knew from the first that if they were going to ship all their equipment they'd need to make more than one trip. Maybe he could tip the damned canoe over; even though it had flotation compartments, that equipment might be ruined. In addition, Raoul Medina was a fair swimmer, but from the way Mansour eyed the water it was clear the Arab feared it.

Medina's optimism turned sour only after he had done most of the work up to his hips in water, loading the canoe to what Clement judged was its limit. Medina could have told them a canoe is more stable when heavily loaded down below the thwarts, but he

didn't. The Frenchman waded thigh-deep into water and urged
him into the canoe, then forced Medina to take the handles of their
power plant, and quickly twisted a loop of heavy wire between his
manacles and the heavy machinery. "You do understand, I think,"
Clement said. "If we capsize in deep water, I will try to retrieve the
generator last of all. By that time you will not care."

When told to remain alone with the camper—their gestures
alone said volumes—Mamzelle rattled off some pithy stuff, and it
would've been clear to a store-window dummy that she wasn't
happy about the arrangement. Clement's reply failed to draw any
smiles from her, but her eloquent shrug said that she would accept
the inevitable.

As Mansour and Clement tried to board their little vessel,
Medina caught the woman's gaze. She had treated him with silent
contempt since he bulldozed his way out of the camper, as if his bid
for freedom had been a swindle against her, personally. Now, as
their eyes locked, she bit her lip and turned away, struggling to load
the motorbike inside the camper.

He wished he could afford to tell her not to worry; wanted to
tell her to go fuck a duck; felt a surge of alarm as Mansour fell
bodily across the gunwales, tipping the canoe almost to the point of
shipping water; felt like snickering at the intensely serious antics of
two grown men unable to get into a canoe without falling in. He
remained expressionless sitting on a thwart amidships, maintaining
his balance, and let his captors take up their paddles.

Medina saw that the paddles were too short and tried to exult
over this small fact, the more so because the men were not wearing
gloves and would earn some fine blisters before long. If anyone had
told Clement about electric outboards that clamp onto a canoe, he
must have considered their hum too loud.

To make the travesty worse, actually better in Medina's view,
Clement had a compass and a marked-up map on newsprint, and
assumed that he should steer from the bow. The Frenchman gave
orders rapidly, reached far out with his paddle, and gave a mighty
pull into the water. The last part of his stroke sent a heavy spatter of
marsh water into the face of Mansour, who was ardently thrusting
away with his own paddle, and on the same side.

Naturally, the canoe made a brisk sally away from shore but
with both men paddling from the same side, it described an arc
before nosing smartly into cattails. More jabber from Frenchy, and
paddling in reverse by both men, and two minutes later they were
no farther from the camper than they had been when they em-

barked. Medina kept his expression blank with an effort, but a glance toward the camper proved that Mamzelle wore a smile that she made no effort to hide.

Presently, Clement realized that Mansour was aping his own motions, paddling when he did, and invariably on the same side. The angry jabbering then was wonderful to hear, but now the paddlers began to work opposite sides in a sensible way, Clement manipulating his paddle more efficiently, yet still taking great deep strokes that would doubtless tire him soon. And the man still did not use all his knowledge to intuit that in such calm water, steering should be from the rear, with final twists of the stroke to fine-tune their direction. To Medina it was as if they were flying without the faintest idea how to set a trim tab.

Clement evidently knew where he wanted to go, and made enough progress to leave the camper far behind them, but the watercourse snaked here and there as they moved generally south into this wilderness. Medina sat hunkered over the generator, trying to reach the twisted wire that linked his manacles to the heavy machine. Now and then, Clement would peer back over his shoulder and his glances toward Medina were obvious. When at last Medina did manage to embrace the generator enough that his fingers reached one tine of the wire, Clement caught him at it. He turned, the paddle whipping up and back, and it was only luck that its flat face struck Medina at the juncture of his neck and shoulder. "Sit up," Clement said without heat or anxiety, speaking English. "Selim, if he leans forward again, you are to beat on his head with your paddle."

After that, Medina sat erect. But he resolved, if they should meet another party in the marsh, to yell like hell and start unwrapping the wire while rocking the canoe like a tolled church bell. He thought it likely, with the marsh grass standing so high, that the bottom was not above his neck, if that deep. But it might be silty enough that his weight would sink him much further. *Would cattails support me at all?* With no idea of the answer, he would be taking a desperate chance. *Fuck it, that might be my last chance,* he thought. *But without help from utter strangers it would be no chance at all.*

Every five minutes or so, Clement shipped his paddle to consult his map and compass. Medina could see that the little map of newsprint, unprotected, already showed why newspapers are protected from rain by plastic wraps. Clement learned to thrust it inside his windbreaker, but not before it had torn in two places. Before long, whenever Clement brought the map forth, he did it with muttered curses. Medina understood enough of it to know he was cursing the ways of Americans.

Though a well-designed canoe is far more stable than most beginners think, it is a simple matter for a malicious passenger to rock it by subtle foot-pressure. This, Medina began to do after thinking it out for some minutes. Spreading his legs toward the upcurving sides of the hull, he exerted a sudden push with his left foot. The result was quite satisfying as both paddlers reacted, leaning to correct the movement. Presently, Medina did it again. He thought about trying it with his right foot but decided against it. Far better that they should think it was a peculiarity of this vessel, he decided.

Medina's game and Clement's incompetence caused the canoe to go astray twice before, immediately after one of Medina's efforts, he felt a poke at his back. He turned to see Mansour eyeing him grimly, head shaking in a silent message he could not mistake. *Okay, at least he didn't crown me again. I suppose there's a spark of decency in this guy. On the other hand, one more solid whack and I could be in a coma, and I don't think he wants to take over all the shit details.* Whatever Mansour's reason for the subtle warning, Medina knew that he must not continue his little sport. It only slowed their progress a bit, and wasn't worth the risk.

At last Clement pointed toward a line of tall grass to their right and began steering into it, and as they slid through the stuff Medina could see more open water to the west. All three men were startled by the sudden beat of big wings as a bird lifted into the air on pipe-stem legs, resplendent in snowy white and bluish gray, with a neck as long as its legs. With the first wing-beat, Clement's paddle fell into the water, his right hand groping in his windbreaker, but the bird was clearly no threat and the little pistol disappeared again as Clement reached for his floating paddle.

Mansour's efforts to help did more harm than good for a moment but the Arab seemed suddenly to reach a new understanding and, in moments, put the canoe's nose where he wanted it. He spoke to Clement for a moment, and received a curt reply, and Medina looked back to see Mansour give him a wan smile. *He knows who should be steering now,* Medina thought, *but Frenchy's too ego-involved to believe him. Could be that Clement's ego is my best ally, but not if he finds out I've been boffing his bimbo's brains out. Not that she didn't screw mine into my shoes too.* It had to be purely recreational humping for her as well as for him; it wasn't as if they had a lot to talk about. The time when Mansour had gone into a field with his prayer rug for ten minutes, for example: she was ready the instant she climbed into the camper. No woman had ever deliberately stuck her nose into his armpit and inhaled while hiking up her skirt before this, and while it might not mean True Love it was sure as hell sincere.

And so far, each time her approach was different. *I do believe,* he mused, *that little hotsy can do more tricks on six inches of schlong than a cageful of monkeys on a hundred yards of grapevine.*

During much of the canoe trip, which was long enough for his trousers to dry, Medina kept his eyes closed against sun glare from the water. His captors wore sunglasses but he knew they were courting headaches and hoped for the best. Even after an hour, they had not discovered that canoes are paddled most comfortably from a kneeling position. *Go ahead, sit up on the thwarts and break your frigging backs,* he urged silently.

They might have covered five miles before Clement pointed toward a stand of cottonwoods that loomed above the marsh grass to their right. Still making those long sweeps of his paddle, he aimed directly for a shallow embankment that identified relatively dry land. Instead of pulling alongside, parallel to the bank, he urged Mansour to greater labor so that the canoe obediently thrust its bow through muck and beached itself. He shipped his paddle, looked around with a triumphant grin, and stood up to climb over the bow. Medina kept still, his hands innocently in view, and waited for the debacle.

Medina knew that any canoe is at its tippiest with its narrow prow grounded and the rest of its hull floating, and that the experienced canoeist will step ashore sideways before pulling the vessel nearer. He added his shout to Mansour's when the canoe gave a violent lurch, toppling the Frenchman sidelong into the marsh and shipping gallons of water. Medina, fully aware that he must not show any pleasure, held on to the generator while Mansour scrambled forward.

But Clement would not drown in waist-deep water. He came up raging, pulled the pistol from his pocket, and leveled it at his captive. That was when Mansour spoke, unusually forceful for him, and his words seemed to dampen Clement's fury.

Medina: "What the hell? If you can't drown me, then shoot me?"

"I believe you did that," Clement replied, his sunglasses gone, water streaming from his hair.

"You're nuts, I could've been thrown out along with this steel anchor you tied me to," Medina answered with some heat, and as loudly as he dared.

"In your vernacular," Clement gritted with all the wounded dignity he commanded, "shut the fuck up." And with that, he waded to shore. He insisted that the others remain in the canoe while he strode, his shoes squishing at every step, up the gradual incline to vanish beyond the cottonwoods among brush and small oaks. Medina could not tell whether they had reached an island or a peninsula but, judging from the trees, this piece of land was rarely submerged for long. In any event it stood six feet or so above the water table, perhaps more beyond his view.

When Clement had disappeared, Medina turned toward Mansour, who had sat down again. "Whatever you said to him: thanks. No shit, I really didn't do that to him. It was his own fault."

"That is what I told him," Mansour admitted. "But do not imagine that I am your friend."

"Maybe not, but we can smile at the same things," Medina said.

"At your peril."

"I guess," said Medina, and then kept silent. Both men fell to watching the occasional passage of birds, some of them quite large, across the marsh. They recognized the cormorants, with their dark plumage and jet interceptor lines, and several varieties of duck. "I wonder where your fearless leader has gone," Medina said presently.

"To make sure we are alone on the island," Mansour replied. "You must pray that we are."

"Right," Medina said in irony that transcended language. *So it's an island. Sure, Clement must've found it from the air.*

"If we are not, you will be a problem that he can solve with a single knife stroke."

"And you wouldn't stop him."

To this, Mansour did not reply, did not even shrug, but simply looked away and swallowed hard. It was answer enough.

When Clement returned, he seemed in more buoyant spirits, helping offload the canoe and finally coming to realize that it was best done by pulling the boat ashore sideways. Once they had emptied the canoe, Clement simply stood and stared at Medina for a long while, rubbing his own injured arm. Then he said, "I shall show you where to set up the tents, and by the time I return you must have everything in place."

Mansour answered in French. From Clement's expression it seemed they were not arguing so much as discussing tactics, and the three of them lugged their tents some distance into the brush to a clearing of sorts.

When the Frenchman pushed off alone in the canoe, Mansour slung his little burp gun over his shoulder and took one side of the generator with, "You heard the effendi." Medina thought that might have been subtle irony, but made no reply. For the next half hour they moved equipment, and then set about erecting the tents. That done, Mansour set up the propane stove and made coffee for them both, sugared almost to syrup.

After a few sips: "He'll have a fine old time with that big case," Medina predicted.

"He should have let me gag you and leave you manacled to a tree" was the reply. "But he would have none of it. Once he makes a decision, it is cast in metal."

Medina shrugged. "If he gets lost, you and I may get to make our own supper."

"You may depend on that. It will take the two of them hours to load the boat, and more time while he takes the vehicle back to town and returns."

Medina thought of Clement, puttering down the ruts of that levee at sundown, and smiled to himself. "I guess Mamzelle will have a good story for anyone who happens along while she's waiting."

"I believe the woman is expected to paddle the boat into hiding. It is not difficult, I think, if one steers from the rear."

Medina raised his eyebrows and said, "No kiddin'," and the Syrian gave him a serious nod.

They spent the balance of the afternoon piling shrubbery against the tents, an activity that Medina viewed with mixed emotions. If it rained, the brush might cause a tent to leak. If it caught fire, they could all perish. Either possibility, however, had its bright side for Raoul Medina.

Dusk had reached the marsh, and frogs were calling with enthusiasm, when they heard familiar angry voices at the shoreline. Medina, walking ahead, was first to see Mamzelle's dull fury, her hair matted and dripping. Clement was no happier than she. They did not elaborate on their further misadventures but they were towing the biggest container, which floated as well as the canoe itself. After wading out to help beach the thing, Clement staggered off to fall onto his sleeping bag with no mention of a meal.

Manhandling the equipment to shore with the captive's help,

Mansour paused to survey the woman's waterlogged glory. "Will we eat tonight?"

"That depends on what you can find among the food we recovered," she said. "Most of the canned food is at the bottom of this cursed swamp and I certainly do not intend to savage my hands any further on this day."

Medina wondered for a moment why both of them spoke English, then supplied his own answer. *They're pissed at Frenchy, so they include me in his little society of victims.* It seemed a good sign. He wished to God he could have seen the Frenchman when the canoe turned over, as it almost certainly had, but a man couldn't have everything. He paused to look at the woman's hands. "You'll want something for those blisters," he said gently.

She drew her hands back, but not too quickly, and slumped away toward the tents. When Medina and Mansour finally dragged the canoe into concealing brush, they worked under starlight and neither of them said anything more about supper.

FORTY-EIGHT

July 1991

PETRA CHOSE TO remain on major interstate highways for her run to Michigan, and called Corbett from a pay phone after stopping for the second night. "North Platte, Nebraska." She answered his first question, managing to sound more chipper than she felt. "This trip is something of an education, luv. Did you know—oh, you would, of course—there are whole strings of what look like ocean-going barges up the Columbia River all the way to *Idaho?*"

The connection wasn't that great, but she thought she could hear exhaustion in his reply as well. "You can't really know the country," he told her, "until you've flown over it and driven across it, too. Just remember the rules for staying awake at the wheel," he added.

"Not too warm or too cold, no beer or heavy meals 'til you've stopped for the night, radio on, and you won't fall sleep while chewing gum." She rattled it all off quickly, having heard him say it a dozen times. "Did I get it all, Coach?"

His laugh carried a tinge of guilt with it. They shared details of their day; he recounted completion of the Mini-Imp's repair and she told him in some awe of a Wyoming truck stop "the size of Rhode Island," as she put it. She named the motel where she would spend the night, and after tender good-byes, broke the connection. *He really did sound bushed,* she told herself, but she had learned of Kyle Corbett's resilience long before this.

The following evening she stopped after crossing the broad

Mississippi at Davenport, Iowa, and this time made a pro forma call to Aerosystems instead of using the Cherokee's special comm set. NSA could get huffy, Ullmer had said, when you used their links for ordinary calls.

She got an answering machine. "Petra Leigh for Ben Ullmer, from Moline, Illinois, about twenty-hundred hours Central Daylight Time. No problems, I plan on turning north soon, will call again when I get work. Out," she said, and put down the receiver in her motel room. Corbett had warned that they could probably trace her every inch of the way if they truly wanted to spend the resources. It would be best if she simply ignored the possibility and trusted Ullmer's word that she was running loose. If he was lying, the two of them had a lot more problems than a trace on her Cherokee.

She did turn north the next day, but only after taking the bypass below Chicago through Indiana and into Michigan. To her great surprise, she found the southeastern shore of Lake Michigan to be a sparsely populated region with monstrous sand dunes, some of them over five hundred feet high, easily rivaling those of Oregon's coast. By the time she found a motel in Ludington that evening, she had traveled to a point that lay roughly a hundred miles directly east of Oshkosh. Mindful of the two-hour time discrepancy, first she had a leisurely supper, then called Corbett from the restaurant.

"You made great time," he told her, sounding as tired as he had two nights before. She could tell that the gaity in his voice was false, forced for her benefit. "Let me check the chart, I don't recall Ludington."

"Straight across Lake Michigan from Oshkosh," she supplied. "There are car ferries from here to the western shore. There's a national forest not far from here, humongous sand dunes, pines, lots of solitude. Not what I expected at all." She went on to describe the farms and orchards she had passed. The sum of it was that the farms seemed well tended, but not terribly successful. Old pickups and older farm machinery were the rule, not the exception.

"Look at the barns," he advised. "Many a farmer with a ramshackle house and a 'fifty-four Chevy has a million bucks or so tied up in his outbuildings."

She promised to remember, then paused. "Honey, will you do something for me tonight? No arguments, and no cheating?"

"Depends."

"It's easy, I promise, the simplest thing you can do, and it won't take you any time at all."

Silence, then a sigh. "You got it."

"Put on that Harry Connick CD I got for you, and maybe something like Ravel's *La Mer* to back it up, and please, please, go—to—bed."

"I sound that tired to you?"

"You sound like the living dead," she assured him. "Well, will you?"

"Maybe I will. Yeah, okay, for sure. Satisfied?"

"Not very, 'cause I'll be sleeping alone," she said gently. She replaced the receiver moments later, her intuition trilling for attention. Nothing that she could say or do would deflect him from this operation but just as soon as it was complete, Petra promised herself, she would hound him to go to a good internist. She had managed to hide the slight weight gain attendant to her pregnancy but knew that, simultaneously, he had lost a few pounds. And though he was accustomed to working at some favorite project through an evening, now he became haggard by suppertime. *Not good signs*, she admitted. *But it's probably some damned bug, we've just got to find it. Yeah, you'll be good as new, Kyle*, she promised him silently, because she did not even want to consider more sinister possibilities.

The following morning, Petra sipped bitter coffee as she drove straight into the early sun through Manistee National Forest, blinking fiercely against the intermittent yellow searchlight spearing at her from between conifers. With a fistful of charts, she found an ordinary highway map simplest to follow and, by noon, had completed a rectangle around the forest preserve. During her lunch in Muskegon, she checked the vagaries of a few secondary roads and, by the day's end, had plenty of notes for later study.

The following day she narrowed her search to farmland between Kent City and White Cloud, and in midafternoon she contacted a realtor in the area, introducing herself as Mrs. Lynn Castle.

Art Rossi, a tall natty dresser with artfully combed hair and a highly approving eye, remained no more than professionally friendly while she explained her mission. Her husband, she said, was recovering from a long illness and had conceived the notion to write his memoirs. What Mr. Castle needed, she said, was a place with a big barn or workshop where he could tinker with arts and crafts; could take long walks without seeing a strange face; in short, he wanted seclusion. A farm seemed just the ticket.

Rossi nodded sagely to all this, and asked a few questions while he leafed through his listings. Mr. Castle would not need a big house, she admitted, so long as they stayed warm and dry. Yes, they would consider a lease but they would want to occupy the place immediately. Improvising as necessary and bearing her own Connecticut accent in mind, she said they were from back East; had been college sweethearts.

Rossi gave her specifics of a few likely sites and stood very close as he showed her their locations on a wall map. Petra, as Mrs. Castle, vetoed the place within sight of little Kent City, and the one with only thirty acres of apple orchards. Two others piqued her interest: seventy-five acres where sugar beets had finally exhausted the soil, and a hundred acres of sandy loam with a potato shed that might serve as a workshop. "They're about thirty miles apart," Rossi said, "but if you have the time I think we can see them both today."

He opened doors for her and became even more friendly as he tooled his four-door Pontiac into the countryside. The beet farm, she saw immediately, would not do. "The house is practically falling down," she observed.

"It's rustic," he admitted. "Barn's got a good roof, though. You could probably pipe water to it." He saw her raised eyebrow. "No? Well, you're the boss."

"My husband is the boss," she replied, "and he wants immediate occupancy."

Rossi shrugged and ushered her into the Pontiac, and under his frank gaze she found herself wishing she had worn slacks instead of a skirt. Petra, no stranger to casual come-ons, put up with Rossi's palaver for the next hour as they toured undulating country roads.

The potato farm was untenanted, the farmhouse scruffy but acceptable, with indoor plumbing and a big propane tank for its stove and water heater. Its half-dozen planked outbuildings were small and unpainted. "I expected a nice big barn, though," she said.

"A shed," he reminded her as they strode behind the house.

"Not those little equipment sheds, surely," she said in irritation. The wretched things would not have housed chickens.

He grinned, evidently enjoying himself at her expense. "Well, a potato shed isn't like a toolshed. Here, I'll show you." And with that he led her to what, from the side, had looked like an ancient mound over two stories high with one precipitous face. She saw that a big corrugated metal half-cylinder, like a Quonset hut of fifty years before, had been erected and then ramped with an earthen berm, one end fitted with sliding metal doors. *Like a hangar; and my God, it's thirty feet wide,* she thought. "Is it full of things, Mr. Rossi?"

"As I recall, it's empty. Two forty-foot modules end-to-end, for storing spuds." He put both hands against a sliding door and shoved it a few feet, and Petra looked down quickly. The Hellbug could be slid in sideways with room to spare, and she did not want her expression to give her away after she glanced inside. "Got three-phase power for arc-welding equipment, overhead fluorescents, good floor, nice and dry. Don't let a few mice scare you," Rossi added as she stepped inside, his words echoing in this metal cavern.

Kyle will turn handsprings, she decided. *Or maybe not, depending on what else I find here.* She walked around as if aimlessly, hearing the faint scurry of four-footed occupants in the gloom, then emerged into the late sun. "It might serve," she said.

Rossi had put an arm around her with a quick squeeze-and-release before she could react. "I thought we could get together on this," he said.

He pointed out the property lines, and Petra judged that the nearest neighboring farmhouse stood a half mile away. "I'll have to check with my husband," she said. "It doesn't look very likely, but if you're sure we could move in right away . . ."

"No problem," Rossi promised. "This was a FSBO until recently, owner's getting anxious. You could probably lease with an option to buy."

"Fizzbo?"

"For sale by owner," he explained, taking her arm as she neared the Pontiac.

Rossi talked farm properties until they had reached town again. The lease idea seemed perfect to Petra. He promised to discuss terms with the absent owner and they agreed on an early morning appointment. "So where are you staying?" he said, too casually.

"Why would you need to know that?" she asked, heading for her Cherokee.

"Thought I might show you a quiet restaurant for dinner. You look like a girl who enjoys nice things."

Careful; mustn't squash this particular bug too soon, she thought. "I'll be busy tonight," she said, "but thanks."

She drove back to Grand Rapids in search of a first-rate motel and called Corbett with the good news. "We could walk the Hellbug in sideways on its casters. If you land with a shallow approach, you drop below trees on the fence lines."

Her optimism seemed to infect Corbett, who agreed that she should sign the lease, then prepare for his arrival, "—unless you can think of a reason why not."

"The only problem is, the real-estate man may try to hang around the place until you arrive. Art Rossi thinks he's Don Juan." She sighed.

"Is he?"

"I wouldn't know. But if we want to lease the place, I'll have to treat him better than he deserves."

"Name's Rossi," he prompted, and she reconfirmed it. After a moment: "Oh, I think you can treat him better, in perfect safety. You may want to jot down a name or two."

She listened, first with some doubt and then with growing delight. "I've got it. But if this doesn't work I'll just have to cut the silly ass dead and hope he'd rather have a cash commission than nothing at all." Corbett deferred to her judgment and said he'd had a good night's rest, and after leaving the phone booth she had supper delivered to her room where she finally fell asleep watching television.

She was late for her appointment the next morning and skipped breakfast, but Rossi's office colleague, a young man with a cowlick whose tie would have waked the dead, pointed her toward an assortment of doughnuts and a full percolator. Rossi breezed in shortly afterward and the two of them moved into his private office.

Petra's most complicated real estate transactions to date had been apartment rentals; and in her questions, she knew that it showed. Presently Art Rossi sat back and enjoyed a leisurely stretch, his grin insolent and knowing. "I think we can wind this up in a day or so to everyone's satisfaction. No matter what your real name is, Miss—ah, it *is* 'Miss,' isn't it?"

"Whatever gave you that idea?" she asked, drawing back.

"You married your college sweetheart, but young men don't write memoirs; and you can't possibly be over thirty. Your husband could be a very late bloomer in college, but I don't think so. You're from back East somewhere? Your accent's right, but—nah, not from your license plates. No wedding ring either.

"I know, I know," he said, holding up his hand as she started to respond. "You could find a way to explain every detail, but you wouldn't convince me, sweetie. You've got a finishing-school accent. You've got money, cash in fact, and you want a place to hide, probably with your boyfriend. Who from, your rich daddy? Your husband? No big deal, really," he said. "I just hate to get a con job from such a special little number. If you leveled with me—" He spread his hands expansively. "Who knows? I could help you out; be a pal; give you a shoulder to lean on."

Petra found it was actually possible, not merely to follow each step of Art Rossi's imagined progress, but to predict them in series. Corbett had given her a scenario and her first impulse was to follow it with uppity disdain. But there was a better way to follow it: as a latter-day Rappacini's daughter.

Petra let her chin quiver, but not too much. She swallowed; dropped her gaze. "There's no Mr. Castle," she said, very softly, and drew a Kleenex from her shoulder bag. *Damn, I can't shed tears on demand. Maybe I can snivel.* "But there's a Mr. Castellanuovo. Several of them, in Oak Park," she went on, naming a Chicago suburb sprinkled with fine homes.

"More like it," Rossi murmured, and leaned across his desk, forearms crossed. "Italian, like me."

"Not like you," she said, twisting the Kleenex. "He always makes a big point of the fact that he's Sicilian, not Italian. Point of honor," she said, with an eyeroll. "He scares me sometimes."

Rossi, almost whispering: "No shit."

"I'm doing this only because he wants a place to relax."

"Hey, if you can't relax in Oak Park—" Rossi began.

The Kleenex, twisted beyond its torque limit, snapped in a tiny soundless explosion of lint in Petra's hands. "Not if you want to live," she said. "It's a—a family matter."

"Waitaminnit," Rossi said, his mouth open slightly. "This *paisan* of yours, Castellanuovo, is a fugitive? You're bringing a fucking *fugitive* in here?"

"No, of course not, he's never been convicted, not once in all the, um, not even once," she repeated. "In fact he needs police protection but they won't give it to him. He's, well, not very tolerant of strangers, and you can see why. He can go anywhere he likes and bring a few soldiers along, but he's—tired. He just wants to be alone, walk in the sun, tend his garden," she said, hoping the god-father allusion was not too resoundingly obvious.

"Castellanuovo's your sweetie," Rossi guessed.

Petra frowned. "My patron. He thinks I have a future on the legitimate stage. Nobody would imagine I could find him a place, they think of me as some sort of china doll."

"And he's gonna bring some cannons along for company," he went on.

Petra nodded.

"And how long's this gonna go on out on the farm?" he asked.

"As long as Mr. Accardo is doing his time," she explained, all big eyes and innocence, firing her biggest gun quietly.

Rossi jerked back. His lips formed the syllables *ack card doe*, and then it was his turn to swallow. Corbett had promised that every Italian in the region would know exactly which Chicago family owed allegiance to an Accardo.

Evidently Corbett was right. The change on Rossi's face, from an expression of wry amusement and faint lust to one of ill-concealed panic, had worked itself through now. He drew a long breath, rubbed his forearms briskly, and sat back. "Well," he said, as if the two of them had just met this moment, "I think we can finish our business this morning, ma'am."

"I hope we can count on your discretion. Mr. Castle is a stickler for discretion," she insisted with a smile she hoped was naive.

"Count on it."

"He will," she reminded him.

As Art Rossi predicted, their business was finished that very morning.

FORTY-NINE

July 1991

T HOUGH THE OSHKOSH Fly-in was still days away, countless
volunteers had converged on the fourteen-hundred-acre site
and some of the exhibits were already in place at Wittman
Field. Well removed from the longest runway and not far from the
showy blond brick FAA tower, a fatigue-clad military crew had em-
placed a mobile missile launcher. A supreme irony in Marvin Payson's mind, the launcher was only for show, a scheduled display of
Patriot missiles that had so recently inspired public awe during Operation Desert Storm.

Payson wondered idly if a live Patriot missile might be a better
countermeasure than the one he was helping to prepare. *Probably
not,* he reflected silently. The last thing they needed in a huge public
throng was a half ton of debris raining down. One of the inert missiles lay in full view, though the Patriot launch modules carried
stencils proclaiming them EMPTY.

Two hundred yards from the Patriot battery, a huge NASA
semitrailer was disgorging equipment into a metal utility building.
Not far from there, a dozen huge canvas tents lay stretched across
grass, ready for erection in rows, most of them with canopies gaily
striped in green or yellow. Soon they would obscure the view of a
commercial exhibit some distance away where a half-completed
executive jet shuddered on its trailer as someone towed it into
place. Farther away, a forklift chugged away from a stake-bed truck
with another portable toilet stall. Over fifty of the white fiberglass

stalls already stood in line and several hundred more still awaited off-loading.

Payson, conferring with his people by cellular phone as he stood beneath a much smaller tent, waved as he recognized the brown sedan with the reflective windows. He ended his conversation and watched approvingly, the sedan stopping only when it was well inside that tent, Bill Sheppard emerging the moment it stopped. Even with the temporary cosmetic changes in his face, and a cover story placing the NSA man in a Denver hospital, Payson had insisted on maintaining extra precautions. "We're finally seeing some action," Payson said by way of greeting.

"I'm getting flack from my people though," Sheppard said grimly. "You would not *believe* the red tape attendant on training our technical guys to operate an Army laser."

Payson, studying the plywood sheath that workmen were applying over a sturdy steel scaffold already standing against their tent: "Serious delay?"

Sheppard, donning his cowboy hat as he moved nearer: "Could've been. I had to bend a few ears."

"Singe 'em, you mean."

"The National Security Agency does not indulge in rank-pulling," Sheppard said, and delivered a horsewink. He squinted at the scaffold, which was forty feet wide, towering three stories high, now almost hidden as workmen secured a plywood panel with bolts. "Do you know whether all the bits and pieces are on schedule?"

"Seem to be. The diorama robo—uh, models, are in place." Full-sized animated copies of human beings had a handful of names to confuse the unwary. Disney's folk had called their system Audio-Animatronics; government labs referred to their synthetic humans as robots, occasionally as androids, or in terms of telerobotics. To the experts of Serendipity, no matter how large or small the computer-operated robot it was still a model; and they referred to the setting, quite reasonably, as a diorama.

"Vernon's up there now, finishing the calibration," Payson went on. "When she leaves, all I'll have to do is flip a master switch to start it—you can call me Dr. Frankenstein. Plywood sheathing's nearly finished." Payson nodded toward the work in progress. "EAA's crowd control warned that people will try to climb anything that might give 'em a better view. Of course we'll stop them, but the sheathing may make it a moot point and I promise you, once the doors are hung, no unauthorized persons will get inside."

He did not need to say why; once the work was finished and the first crew had left, a very special laser weapon would move under the tent and then into the structure.

Sheppard took a step toward the interior stairs. "If Erika Vernon's here, why don't we go up and watch?"

"Because I'm a married man."

"Well, I'm not." Sheppard grinned, and headed for the stairs, followed by Payson. The NSA man paused before taking the last flight of stairs, peering into the gloom set off by pools of light from architect's lamps.

"That's her nerve center in the corner," Payson supplied, "with all that cabling and the console. She must be topside."

Sheppard went up slowly, and emerged beneath a canvas-draped top. Enough light came through crevices to reveal the diorama. "Good—God" was all he said.

"Hi there," called a familiar voice, and Erika Vernon straightened up, still on her knees. "With you in a minute."

Payson had seen it before, and kept his silence as Sheppard took a few tentative steps across the flooring. Dozens of human figures sat in neat rows of folding camp chairs, stunningly lifelike but silent, eerily motionless. One, a slender balding gent on the front row, had a curved pipe halfway to his mouth, frozen as if paralyzed. Like all the others, he was a product of Serendipity's genius, a perfect response to a robotic killer: a robotic decoy.

Sheppard laughed suddenly, then caught himself. "Erika, I know some of these fellows; I mean, I know them personally." He raised his hat and performed a mock bow. "Hello, Burt. Good afternoon, Ben, you never looked better." Clapping the hat back on, failing to mask his discomfort: "This is a psychedelic experience."

"Makes you want to administer CPR, doesn't it?" Payson rumbled.

"Well, not quite," said Sheppard.

The woman stood, dusted off the knees of her slacks, and took a tiny flashlight from between her teeth. "There, now, Mr. Rich can smile again. Would you like to see him do it, Bill?"

"I, uhm, well, I'm not sure. What do I do: tell him a joke?"

"Just stand there and watch. Please don't reach out to touch anything, some of our pneumatics are operating at near-capacity. I'll give you a moment's warning before I start the program," she added, brushing past him.

"I'll stand by with smelling salts," Payson put in, poised on one of the upper steps. "It gets to you," he warned.

A moment later, from below, came Vernon's call: "Ready animation; *roll* 'em." Instantly, a thrum from below; soft clicks and whooshes began to issue from the seated figures. Sheppard gasped.

The fellow with the pipe turned briefly to his companion, gesturing toward a big television set that faced them all. Across the aisle, the spitting image of Ben Ullmer folded its arms and took on a skeptical look. Another shifted in its seat and, with a brief whine of small gear-driven motors, crossed one leg over the other. Toward the rear, one of them adjusted its own straw hat. And all of it in near-silence, a startling imitation of human life, but attended by sounds more typical of locusts invading a cornfield. Gooseflesh raced from the nape of the NSA man's neck to his arms and legs.

Sheppard kept generally familiar with such work as the Aberdeen Army lab's powered suit of armor, and with telerobotics. He knew that the hum beneath his feet was a big hydraulic engine to power small actuators in the robots, and that Serendipity's technicians had programmed these manikins by literally wearing exoskeletons with strain gauge pads while they moved their own limbs, generating a program so that the robots faithfully copied every motion. *I'm not sure how they program the facial expressions, but I'm betting they valve pneumatic pulses like a player piano,* he thought. *And if genes are our personal programs, maybe DNA is God's big piano roll.* Serendipity's models, Sheppard decided, could do too many things for his comfort.

"You should all be wearing sombreros," he said to the throng around him, and heard only rustling in response. What they could not do, he knew, was get up and walk around. Yet. Somehow he preferred them anchored there by umbilical tubes that were noticeable only when he stood halfway down the steps. He decided he had seen enough, and hurried down those steps toward people who could talk back.

Sheppard's congratulations to Erika Vernon were heartfelt, and they lingered, discussing the diorama, for long minutes. Vernon knew better than to ask more questions than necessary. "But one day," she said, "I'd like to know exactly what I've been doing here."

"When I can, I'll look you up and tell you," Sheppard promised, noting Payson's eyeroll over her shoulder. Then the men excused themselves and navigated the stairwell.

In the ground-level tent again: "This is the first time," Sheppard confided, "that I've hoped the Butcher Bird's shots are all accurate. I wouldn't want any of them to miss the diorama."

Payson craned his neck upward and gnawed his lip, imagining the structure as it would appear when complete. He had seen the sketches: within featureless plywood-sheathed walls, the laser's power supply would squat at ground level, its turbine exhaust stack the size of a telephone pole. The Army laser itself would be mounted at one side below the top-level flooring, with an aperture for its unlikely-looking muzzle; and just above that diorama floor, hidden from the public by plywood walls but open to the sky, some of the world's top aerospace experts would tempt the silent blast of Clement's Butcher Bird. "If our diorama would fool a film camera from six feet," Vernon had said, "it should fool your mystery guest from a hundred yards away." By now, both men agreed.

"So far, Bill, the damned laser hasn't missed by much that we know of," Payson reminded him. "Even if it misses, all our target models are grouped so none of 'em is within ten feet of a wall. And there'll be steel plate bolted under the diorama's plywood flooring after Vernon leaves. It would have to be one hell of a miss to injure someone, wouldn't it? Unless it picked out the wrong person down here below the diorama," he muttered. "Just how good are the optics on that hovering assassin?"

"We don't know their exact resolution. We can start with some commercial components, though, as a baseline, and the Butcher Bird is at least that good. You know that newspaper photos are made up of dots, right?"

"Yeah, about a hundred to the inch, as I recall," Payson agreed.

"A hundred down by a hundred across, makes a grid of ten thousand per square inch," Sheppard went on. "Actually the dots on newsprint aren't square, but you get the idea. For comparison," he said, placing his thumb and forefinger a half inch apart, "Texas Instruments has made a standard CCD, a charge-coupled device, for years, almost exactly a half inch on a side. The CCD is basically the eyeball of modern electronic optics. Its resolution is far higher than what you get on newsprint: a grid of, um, something over two and a half *million* dots per square inch. The dots of a CCD are of varying tone, as well. That's good enough for orbital telescopes. And the numbers I quoted aren't even the latest technology."

Payson thought about that for a moment. "And the Butcher Bird is at least that good, maybe better." He saw Sheppard's nod. "So it can measure the width of a man's mouth to the millimeter, all the dimensions of his face, to the proverbial gnat's ass, from miles away and compare it with its stored memory of the guy."

"Maybe not quite that good," Sheppard hedged, "but it doesn't have to be. It's quick enough to nail you from a half mile, and small enough to escape notice unless you're looking right at it. That's too good for my comfort."

"You don't think it's good enough to spot our full-scale diorama for what it is?"

Now Sheppard looked down at his feet and scuffed the grassy turf uneasily. "I think we'll fool it, but we just can't know until the moment of truth. You've got to factor in the alignment speed of our bigger laser unit, which is limited by how fast a mechanical mechanism can swing our brute for the gross alignment. There's also the question of whether the Butcher Bird will dash away after each shot before it draws another bead, or will hover right where it is while it fires and re-aims at its second target, and its third, and so on. That's one reason why we've given it a target-rich environment, with targets sitting three feet apart. Even if it shifts position between shots, perhaps it won't shift very far for the clump of targets we're presenting."

"If I were the Butcher Bird I'd smell a trap," Payson said.

"No, I don't think you'd have the brainpower to harbor suspicions," Sheppard argued. "If you were the Butcher Bird you'd be an idiot savant, programmed to do certain things brilliantly, and you'd be absolutely incapable of thinking about some other things. You'd be as smart as all the subroutines Clement loaded into you."

"But not smart enough to hightail it when I saw all those targets lined up like an engraved invitation?"

Sheppard's smile was beatific. "We don't even know for certain that Clement will be within a thousand miles. But if he is, that's exactly *why* he is. He wants all those targets, the murdering son of a bitch. If anything, he'd think a dozen victims together would be," and here Sheppard paused to savor the word, "serendipitous."

Payson grinned to show he hadn't missed it. "I notice you lined yourself up a serendipitous date with Vernon. Nice going."

"One does what one can." Sheppard smiled, then looked around him. "I suppose you've got people doing surveillance here already," he said.

"Want to spot 'em?" Payson waved a hand. "Look for the workmen with blistered hands. And some wearing the togs of Wisconsin Bell, too; I set that up after I found out they install the world's largest temporary phone net here every year." He consulted his wrist quickly. "I've got to sign some authorizations. Want to go, or stay here?"

"There's not much to see here yet, and I feel a bit disengaged. Actually, I was wondering whether your area sweeps have turned up anything suspicious."

"Making progress," Payson replied, and made a friendly "come along" gesture as he moved toward the sedan. "That's what you say in the Bureau," he confided, "when you're utterly without a clue but damned if you'll admit it."

FIFTY

July 1991

ODILE MARCHANT SAT on a low embankment, cooling her feet in the lazy current as she waited for the djinni to return, and reminded herself once again that her mother had not raised her to become a swamp rat. Such a fate would have been among Odile's least likely guesses when, as a young computer programmer, she first linked up with Roland Clement. They had managed to avoid gossip, their affair a secret shared by two, and Odile had counted herself lucky to have the attentions of a man widely known for his brilliance—even somewhat unstable brilliance. To a young woman who craved both money and romance, Clement had seemed the ideal colleague. Small wonder that she had followed him secretly, romantically, to Syria.

Now it seemed to Odile that every time she took up different lodgings at Roland Clement's pleasure, her next location was worse than the last. From sun-blasted Syrian desert to a rotting, humid South American jungle. From there to another desert and in a broiling abandoned hangar, at that; then to camping on a dry plain. And now this, she mused, sharing eye contact with an extravagantly ugly little frog that had just emerged, with hardly a ripple, at the stream bank. She wondered suddenly whether frogs had a range of facial expression; this one, she believed, was glaring at her in a way both doleful and accusatory.

With a flirt of one alabaster foot, Odile sent the small amphibian on its way. The only part of frogs she liked were their legs, and in a restaurant that understood a decent sauté. Still, she would willingly have kissed the wretched animal if it had promised a single day, even an afternoon, of shopping in civilized surroundings.

Give Roland his due, she thought glumly, *he brought tins of pâté de foie gras and bottles of acceptable wine.* Much good it had done her, she thought with heavy sarcasm; most of it now lay a mile distant and more than a meter deep, in the muck of this infernal marshland. It had been Clement's own fault for trying to balance the djinni in its container across the gunwales of their canoe instead of towing it, as they had eventually done after their absurd capsizing.

Upon finding that the water could not quite drown him he had stood neck-deep in water, raging at her, and she had screamed back at him until he begged for silence, only because he could not get near enough at that moment to throttle her. She was, after all, the better swimmer.

Now, with several days of swamp camping behind her and still more of it to come, at least their primitive hidey-holes were well enough camouflaged that she could relax occasionally. The mosquitoes proved voracious only at dawn and dusk, but those were times when they dared not counter the insects with smoky fires. Clement's wound had, at long last, stopped suppurating and begun to mend. Once again, lying together at night, he was reminding her that they slept on bundles of American cash and that much of it, eventually, would be hers. Or so he said.

On the other hand, the healing of his arm was accompanied by renewed demands for her favors. Odile, wise in the ways of most men, regarded a flat refusal as a denial of her craft and knew as many ways to avoid sexual contact as to achieve it. She could manage a fit of giggles, or a strategic and apparently accidental pinch, with the best of them. What she could no longer seem to manage was any real enthusiasm for Roland Clement as long as she lived on the same tiny island with M'sieur Speedy Gonzales.

At first, she had felt outrage and shock at the American's escape attempt, an act that clearly said Speedy, unlike any of her former lovers, would rather be free than in bondage to her frequently offered charms. Well, he had paid dearly for that insult. Mansour, beyond earshot of Clement, had actually offered the American an apology for his own panic, and the vicious blows of his overreaction. After that, Odile began to consider whether she, too, had overreacted.

On further reflection, she decided that she had. After all, Odile had never shared dalliance with a genuine, manacled prisoner, and no doubt his bonds loomed as large in his thinking as his testicles did. She had never felt that way when past lovers had tied her up, but then, she admitted, her plight had been different: even bound with her own stockings to a bedstead, Odile had known that she remained mistress of every situation.

Yet she was never sure that she held personal control of the American, precisely because the man remained in bondage. He had little choice in his partners. Sex with Speedy—a misuse of language, for at least once, the man had shown that he had the stamina of a python—was a special treat, beyond his lithe male beauty. Very well then, she would admit the rest of it: the risk and the playacting in Clement's presence gave added charm to it. Each time she heaped scorn on Speedy for Clement's benefit, she promised herself another moist little gift for the American as soon as the opportunity arose.

But with all of them camped on an island less than a kilometer long, she had found no such opportunities recently. And for the first time in her life, she could not be sure of her welcome. Judging from his behavior, M'sieur Speedy was that alienated. No doubt much of his aloofness was an act, his way of manipulating her in exactly the ways she manipulated men. Perhaps, she thought, she had met her opposite number; *but it is such delicious algebra,* she admitted.

A distant whirr interrupted her reverie, endorsed by a thin whistle that was a call sign of Selim Mansour. Odile hurriedly snugged her loafers on and made her way around a wall of grass to see Clement staring upward, the djinni sinking at a steady pace toward its launch site after the surveillance flight. The little clearing had been scraped flat, innocent of so much as a twig, and the softness of the earth probably kept the impending failure from destroying the djinni outright.

Odile, still some distance away, did not notice that one of the djinni's three landing feet was only partially extended, but Clement saw, and even as he dived for cover he called a warning.

Selim Mansour did not understand the nature of the warning and spun on his heel, snatching the little submachine gun from his shoulder. To Odile it seemed that the Syrian was scanning the area for strangers. In any case he was standing, knees bent, within ten meters of the djinni when it began to settle, dipped to one side, and leaped like an animal as its whirling blades struck the ground.

Each blade on the djinni's periphery had been pressure-molded and fitted for far more delicate dynamic balance than, say, the tires of a racing car. A blade moving at high speed could survive contact with grains of sand or even small insects and, in fact, the blades were already spooling down so that they were not traveling fast enough to support the little craft. They were, however, moving at a fourth of their maximum velocity, roughly two hundred and seventy feet per second, when a few of them touched soft turf.

During Clement's damage assessment later, he was to remark with some satisfaction that only six blades needed replacement. But two of those blades, shearing off near their mounts, flashed away at the exact tangents to send them whistling into the body of Selim Mansour.

The Syrian staggered with the impacts, then sat down hard, with an expression that would have been comical had he not rolled onto his side, writhing in pain. Because this had been only a surveillance mission, they did not fear radiation leakage. Clement leaped up to approach the djinni, cursing, and called on Mansour to help.

But, "I am hit, you fool," gritted the Syrian in French so strangled that Odile could scarcely understand him as he struggled to sit upright. Odile cried out as she saw him clutch at the ragged rips in his shirt just above his belt.

The American, who had been sitting as ordered near their tents, came shuffling forward as fast as his ankle restraints would let him. He knelt beside Mansour, bidding him lie flat, pulling the man's shirt up carefully. "Well, shit," he muttered, more to himself than to the Syrian. "He's got some punctures, all right."

At this point Clement abandoned his inspection and went down on one knee beside the kneeling Odile, pushing the American's hands aside, pressing with his fingers around the wounds. Remarkably little blood issued from the rough slits in Mansour's abdomen, but with Clement's probing the Syrian jerked and moaned. "You have pieces of blades in there," Clement murmured. "They will be septic, of course, so we must get them out."

The American evidently did not understand Clement's French. "Better get him to a doctor, man. You never know with shrapnel wounds, he could be all torn up inside."

Watching Mansour's face, Odile knew that the man was capable of taking all this in, but his grayish pallor suggested that he might not be conscious for long. "We will take care of you," she said, running a gentle hand over his forehead. Then, switching to English: "Speedy, what experience have you had in such things?"

"Enough to know he's in deep shit, Mamzelle. If he has exit

wounds some of the pieces may have gone through. If not, they're all still in him.''

With a quick nod, and utterly without concern for Mansour's pain, Clement tugged the wounded man's trousers down and rolled him over to check for exit wounds. When there was no response, Odile realized the man had lost consciousness. "Well," said the American after a moment, "whatever they are, they're still in there, Frenchy. I think he's out cold, and that's good. We can load him in the canoe without him thrashing like a crazy man."

"The canoe? I am sure you would like that," Clement scoffed. "We take care of our own, Gonzales. But it is true that I must work while he is unconscious."

Odile thought for a moment that Speedy would, at last, attack Clement with his bare hands until Clement produced his little pistol and stood up. "And if I must kill you first, so be it," Clement went on. "Or would you rather carry him to his bed?"

Odile took the man's feet and helped the American carry him to the bough-covered tent where, very soon, Clement collected cognac, towels, and two pairs of needle-nosed pliers, which he rubbed down with a booze-soaked hand towel. Odile insisted on heating the tips of these outrageously primitive instruments on their camp stove before surrendering them to Clement. On the way, she retrieved Mansour's burp gun. *If Speedy had been less concerned with our Syrian at the moment, he might have noticed this first,* she thought with relief. She was even more certain when she saw their captive glance at the weapon and then look away in silent disgust, doubtless at himself.

Clement's work did not involve much blood at first, but the job became gory after he worked the first piece of blade out of Mansour's flesh with pliers. Odile was there to sprinkle the last of their sulfa powder into the wound, Clement having used most of it on his own arm. The real difficulty arose as Clement probed for the second, more deeply implanted blade fragment, and Mansour began to struggle in his semiconscious state.

By this time, Odile was sitting on Mansour's legs and holding the pistol while the American, impeded by his manacles, fought to hold Mansour's arms. When at last Clement tugged the offending blade out, a brief spurt of crimson followed, and with it a glimpse of the merest edge of something that was soft and purplish blue. Clement demanded more sulfa; Odile could only tear the empty sulfa packet wide and let him daub its pitifully few smears of remaining powder on the blue thing before he poked it back with a finger.

Then: "Bandage, quickly," Clement husked, and used more cognac to clean the victim's abdomen around the wound. Mercifully, Mansour ceased his thrashing then. As Odile placed cotton and adhesive strips tightly over the jagged hole: "He no longer bleeds," Clement said.

"Not on the outside," Speedy rejoined.

Clement took this as implied criticism. "Could you have done better?"

"A doctor could," said the American. "That was a piece of gut you pulled out and stuffed back. Hell, I don't know," he admitted, moving away to sit morosely, cleaning his hands on a towel. "You've either fixed him or killed him, Frenchy. I've heard that before modern antibiotics, most body wounds were death sentences. The least you can do is fill him up with medicine."

Clement, now furious, sprayed him with spittle as he snarled, "And if we have none?"

"Get some," said the American softly, wiping his face.

"I can see why you want one of us to go on such an errand," Clement said, eyes narrowed as he regarded his captive. "But why do you want this man to live?"

"Beats the shit outa me," Speedy admitted, taking Odile in with his glance as well. "I guess because he's a decent sort."

Odile had seen that look on Clement's face before. It said he thought he was being lied to. "And why would that matter to you?"

For a moment that stretched to its breaking point, the American said nothing at all, only staring back at Clement as one would study a perplexing riddle. Then, with a nod: "I believe you're serious, mister. So forget it, you wouldn't understand. I never met anybody quite like you." And with that, he shuffled away.

After that, no one said much at all for hours. Odile made a dinner that neither she nor Speedy could finish, though Clement ate with his usual gusto.

Later, after binding the American to Mansour, he studied the new videotape with Odile. "You see the long runway," he said at one point, freezing the frame. "In a day or so, to the west of it will lie aircraft of every possible description, and literally hundreds of thousands of gawkers. The serious scholars will be here, however, among the tents and open-air displays." As he spoke, he fast-forwarded the image.

"But if this event is as you've told me, Roland, there will be a stunning amount of air traffic overhead. We've never had to deal with that much of it before."

"You worked those subroutines in to my specifications, *ma petite*," he said easily. "The chances of a sighting or a collision are extremely low and the djinni will, of course, avoid any casual approach."

"It is not the casual approach I am thinking of," she reminded him.

"You installed the instructions yourself," he said. "A close approach triggers an avoidance. The second approach," he shrugged, "equals pursuit."

"And it will fire on a pursuer," Odile murmured. "Even a merely curious pursuer."

"Of course," Clement said. "It is only logical. Ah," he finished, slowing the tape as it registered the djinni's recent landing.

Odile thought he intended to study the botched landing until he stopped the tape three times. Each time, he brought cross hairs to bear on one of the faces below: the face of Speedy Gonzales, sitting alone, head cocked so that his eyes followed the djinni as it descended.

After a moment, Odile could hide her cynicism no longer. "I suppose you have told the monster to memorize us all."

"No. Only M'sieur Gonzales, during several takeoffs and landings. Our djinni knows him now, perhaps, better than anyone."

"I am sure you have a purpose in that big head of yours," she said, with a special use of her teasing smile.

"Let us say several options for sport," he countered, smiling, and Odile made herself smile back. *That is what he called it during those first killings in Syria,* she remembered. *A political victim was business, but the others were merely sport.*

FIFTY-ONE

JULY 1991

CORBETT TOOK THE sectional charts he needed in Black Stealth One, charts named for cities prominent on them: Los Angeles, Las Vegas, Denver, Cheyenne, Omaha, Chicago. Which was not to say they were all up-to-date; his Montreal and Halifax charts were years behind the times. Many a landmark drive-in movie theater had been razed to make way for suburbia, many a microwave transmitter erected with its red hazard lights, since Corbett had needed to know these details about the northeast.

His Chicago chart was only six months from current, however, and he had spread it across the copilot's seat for quick reference. When fully open the chart spanned four feet, printed on both sides, so peppered with special symbols that a neophyte might have stared in confusion. Its boundaries were roughly Waterloo, Iowa, to Battle Creek, Michigan, in width, and Green Bay, Wisconsin, to Champaign-Urbana in height. The most significant things about it, to Kyle Corbett, were its colors: the light green of lowlands and faint blue of lakes. Earlier in the day his charts had shown a lot of rust-red, and because the Hellbug was not a high-altitude craft he'd taken some rough air near mountain passes.

With a late start and an economy cruise of one hundred forty knots to conserve fuel, Corbett praised his tailwind and passed south of Oshkosh at eleven thousand feet shortly before sunset. Until recently he had routinely flown higher, but every week he found headache country a bit lower. Probably, he concluded, it had something to do with the cancer's side effects.

Though his path took him within twenty miles of Horicon Marsh, his gaze moved north, not south; and his thoughts peeled the years back to an Oshkosh of better times.

Though a veteran of several Oshkosh Fly-ins, Corbett had never taken time out from his work to fully enjoy aircraft as a pure sport. The same guys who built Long Ezes and Midget Mustangs and who envied him for his classified work, had not believed that he could envy them in turn. Much of what a real aficionado enjoyed, he had to enjoy secondhand. *Of course it's not like old times,* he told himself with a reflective smile; *and what's more, for most of us it never was.*

This year, according to Petra's EAA updates, a Lockheed Stealth fighter and a Patriot battery would be on display—perhaps already sitting in the open, a temptation for Corbett to fly nearer for a glimpse. But even more tempting were the rumors of prewar racers once flown by men like Doolittle, Le Vier, Chambers, Wittman, and the cavalier design genius, Howard.

Maybe I'll get a look at Howard's Mr. Mulligan while I'm working. That'd be a blast, he thought. Back in the mid-thirties, with the irrepressible designer Howard at the controls of his creation, the aircraft he named Mr. Mulligan once jumped a first-line Army fighter plane and outran it horrendously in full view of Wright-Patterson's Army brass. The Army had never, ever forgiven Howard for gobbling up a single-place P-26 with an enclosed, four-place sportplane. Nor had they stolen his design.

The present version of Mr. Mulligan was a replica, handcrafted like the original, but reputedly one so identical as to defy detection: virginally white, tiny with short curvaceous wings and teardrop fairings over its wheels, voluptuous in its broad four-place cabin where most racers had remained slender—and with a great thundering radial engine up front that could, almost sixty years before, haul its freight at nearly three hundred miles an hour.

To be sure, it had been a thirsty little bastard, but the fast ones usually were. And the Hellbug? Truly, comparisons were ludicrous. All but radar-proof, capable of vertical hover, and invisible in its pixel skin, the craft Corbett had stolen was infinitely more desirable. *But let's face it, I wish Mr. Mulligan were mine, too. Howard made only one mistake with it,* he decided. *That sexy little bomb should've been called Miz Mulligan. Which reminds me, I should be meeting my own miz in an hour.*

By now, with a few lights showing in Sheboygan off his starboard wing, the expanse of Lake Michigan filled his forward windscreen. Presently, with sunlight winking from beach-home windows far ahead, the Michigan shore slid into view. *That'll be Ludington,* he thought, and began to search for power lines shown by the chart.

An old jape claimed that IFR, a reference to bad weather conditions, meant "I follow roads," but rivers and even power lines could serve. Corbett kept his bearing, crossed the power lines at sundown, and climbed into headache country as dusk settled. He was watching for Petra's strobe.

The strobe lights on aircraft wingtips are tiny things, battery-operated curlicues of glass with halogen souls that shed light the way armor plate sheds BBs. Adaptable to many uses, a wingtip strobe can be fitted with a conic reflector and used as a ground beacon so that, while dust motes will give it away, the full glare of its ravening, winking beam can be seen only from aloft. Because Kyle Corbett was not a fool, he did not intend to use his NSA comm set above his base, even a temporary base. Petra Leigh had promised to hand-activate her beacon strobe from atop her Cherokee, roughly one wink per minute and definitely not on a precise schedule, at dusk. She had sworn to him, on the telephone, that fog would be no problem. And even a light fog fails to completely hide a strobe light.

He was studying one farm of likely size, wondering at the glow from two structures and wondering too just how damn' dark it had to be for Petra's idea of dusk, when a burst of light made its silent signal a few miles off. He began to descend, the Hellbug's impeller idling because he was now flying on reserve fuel. Another almighty blip reminded him of Vietnam and fragmentation bombs, not a seconds-long signal but a flare as brief and as powerful as a billion-watt flashbulb.

Rather than crank up the impeller, he simply inverted the Hellbug, dropping out as though from a loop virtually without power, now three thousand feet lower and headed in the opposite direction. Then he did the same thing again. This maneuver, the legendary Split S, can place an aircraft on its original heading but a mile lower, in seconds, with only its altimeter—and the pilot's lunch—any the wiser. If that pilot is not in good health, he may suffer a brief moment of vertigo. Corbett angrily shook his head against his dizziness.

He recognized the place from Petra's description then, saw the blunt boxy shape of the Cherokee, and cursed good-naturedly as another strobe pulse burst in his eyeballs. He came in without running lights at maximum distance from an adjoining farmhouse, lower than the tree line as he winked his own landing lights, and then realized that the faint light moving away from the Cherokee was Petra with a flashlight. She kept flashing its beam against a wall until he realized that it was the door of a storage shed that, at a guess, could swallow all the potatoes in creation. The apron outside it was concrete, made as if to order. Twenty seconds later, Corbett touched down, cut power, and popped his canopy door up. Ten more seconds and Petra, still squinting from the dust devil he'd raised, had flung her arms around his neck.

When he could get his breath: "Hi, Miz Mulligan," he said, enjoying a joke that only he understood.

"Hi, Pops," she replied, enjoying hers in the same way. "Don't look at me, I've been cleaning out your hangar and I need a shower in the worst way."

"How 'bout the best way? I could use one, too," he replied, very much aware that he was still suffering slightly from vertigo, unwilling to say so.

"There's hot water for it. But first, help me get those doors open," she said, as he exited his great bird. "If we don't get the Hellbug out of sight now, we might forget later."

FIFTY-TWO

JULY 1991

FOR TWO DAYS, Medina helped nurse the injured Mansour and pretended to ignore an increasing wealth of air traffic. He narrowed his suspicions as to his locale when he saw a half-dozen ultralights in formation, essentially hang gliders with angry little engines, their fabric wings butterfly-brilliant, migrating north. He knew for dead certain when, with a thrill that marched goose-flesh down his back, he recognized a fifty-year-old B-24 escorted by a bevy of gorgeous, howling P-51 Mustangs. *Oshkosh, by God! It's that time of year.* Some of the other ancient warplanes that passed overhead were still more powerful. Even the marsh birds, sup-posedly protected in this huge game preserve, became reluctant to fly when at any moment the stillness might be shattered by recip-rocating engines that could swing propellers two stories in diame-ter.

But most of the time, Medina listened to the wrangling be-tween Frenchy and Mamzelle. She had not forgiven the French-man for his attitude toward their Syrian. Medina heard without much enlightenment, because he understood so little of what they said. The little he did understand was because the woman tended, when preparing a meal or washing blood-soaked bandages for reuse, to mutter in English. This drew ever more sullen glances from Clement, and finally when the Frenchman stalked off beyond earshot during the second afternoon, Medina made an entreaty.

"I hope you realize you're going to get me shot, Mamzelle," he said softly, not looking at her.

"He suspects nothing. Believe me," she said, boiling bandages.

"Suspect, hell. He hears you bitching about poor Mansour around me, in English. That's gotta sound like you're more on my side than his. And if he thinks that, he just might decide to put me away. Lady, that guy is about one castanet shy of a tango."

"He is capable of anything," she agreed, and fell silent while she forked a steaming mass of cloth from the pot. "Poor Speedy. Then you would be forced to tell him about our little tangoes, hm?" She moved her hips in a way that could have suggested a dance—or not.

Startled, he looked to see her regarding him with a smile. "Jesus Christ, you think I'd hump and tell? What makes you think that?"

"Revenge," she suggested.

"Wouldn't help me a bit, Mamzelle. Know what I think? I think you wouldn't mind if I did."

"As you would say: What makes you think that?"

A shrug. "A little extra excitement, maybe. Just throwing in with that guy, you've got to have a touch of the risk junkie in you."

Still smiling, she hung the bandage from a sapling, but now that smile was tinged with deeper reflection. "Risk is spice, Speedy. But punishment is acid. Roland Clement has thrown enough acid in my face already."

"Then why not change sides?"

The smile was gone now. "I have invested much in Roland; everything, in fact. And you are as much a mystery to me as—" She paused as Clement returned, then switched instantly to a less damning topic. "—and if Mansour is willing to drink warm broth, crush two more painkiller tablets into his cup."

Bustling past them, his gaze darting from one to the other, Clement knelt at a container and spoke as he pawed among the tools. "Odile, I am securing the new blades in their sockets but we must run the djinni up for a dynamic balance test." Medina wondered why the man said it in English until Clement, looking straight at him, added, "Such tests are not without some risk, Gonzales. When the device is running, you will be wise to take cover."

Medina nodded, thinking, *Well, you must still need me for something*, and shuffled away to attend to the Syrian, whose grayish pallor and feeble motions suggested that his internal bleeding had not entirely stopped. Mansour was not enthusiastic about his broth, but accepted the cup, hands shaking so that some of the stuff trickled into the stubble on his chin. Medina daubed carefully, impassive as he watched the process. "You're hurting; right?" The only answer was from eyes that he judged were full of pain.

When he had drained the cup, Mansour sighed and lay back. "You are drugging me at every meal, are you not?"

"Just painkillers," Medina replied. "Or so they tell me. I don't know what the labels mean." At that point Medina realized that someone had walked quietly near the tents and was now rummaging for something inside. He did not glance away from Mansour.

"I shall die here, if I do not get medical attention," Mansour husked.

A shrug from Medina. "I told Frenchy that," he said softly.

From the Syrian, then, very clearly in a voice that carried: "He is a madman, you know."

"Take it easy. Relax," Medina cautioned. What he wanted to say was, "Shut the hell up if you value anybody's life!" And when he heard footsteps moving off, he turned to see the broad back of Roland Clement. He would not know until later whether Clement had heard Mansour's indictment.

The djinni's dynamic balance checks required several brief runs of the turbine that afternoon, with a lot of technobabble between Mamzelle and Clement. They had to run the generator for delicate grinding operations, but as dusk crept across the marsh and soft birdcalls ceased in the evening's hush, Clement finally pronounced the djinni operational.

Their supper was slapdash, but afterward, Clement did a curious thing. "Open that tin of pâté de foie gras, Odile, and some of those croutons of which you are so fond," he said, brandishing a squat bottle of brandy. "We shall celebrate today, and tomorrow."

When Frenchy speaks English he's including me, thought Medina, but remained uncertain until Clement urged him to take part and filled his cup brimful of some of the best brandy he'd ever tasted. The celebration seemed chiefly in recognition of *Samedi*, Saturday, which set Medina's mind to jingling like wind chimes. It seemed to him that tomorrow would be Saturday but he wasn't sure. The Oshkosh festivities always began on weekdays and rose to a crescendo on Saturday. Maybe Clement knew that someone very special would attend on Saturday. *Oh, shit, ol' Ben Ullmer himself never misses—but of course he knows this fucking maniac is loose. Surely, surely he'll be careful.*

He found his cup almost empty and jerked his thoughts to the present as Clement, attentive as any waiter, offered a refill. Medina took it in genuine surprise; raised the cup; sipped lightly and faked a gulp. *This isn't the Clement I know and love; he's already poured three jiggers in me and wants me to take three more.* The Frenchman attended to the woman's cup as well, refilling his own cup lightly, swirling and sniffing more than sipping. It was a damned shame to waste such heady booze, but in the next five minutes Medina managed to pour most of it onto shadowed ground. He was already feeling the ounces he'd swallowed and knew that he would have no trouble sleeping on this night.

Which sent an alarm singing through his wind chimes. *He's putting me and Mamzelle both under. If he intended to shoot us both he wouldn't waste good booze, so what the hell* IS *he up to?* Medina, not the most inhibited of men when cold sober, had no trouble slurring a bit, singing a dirty ditty that was a bit risky in its variant of "Froggy Went A-Courtin', He Did Ride, Uh-Huh," and allowing out loud as how ol' Clement wasn't such a bad guy at all, and he poured abso-*chingada*-lutely prime booze. Above all, Medina offered no objection when Clement helped him back to the tent he shared with the moaning, half-comatose Mansour.

Days before, Mansour had fashioned a cable that looped like an anklet around his own right ankle. It was the work of moments to engage the cable between Medina's ankles and now, with Mansour unable to walk, Clement simply linked them again using the wrench he kept in his pocket. Mansour moaned again. Because of the way the Syrian flung his arms about fitfully in what must be agonized sleep, Medina had learned to sleep with his arms crossed over his face. He turned partly away from Mansour and exhaled mightily as Clement stood at the tent flap. Perhaps a minute later, Medina realized that Clement was gone. But he might be standing near, listening, waiting.

No telling what the bastard might do, and Medina kept his body on full alert until he heard the muffled sounds of conversation from the other tent. Soon those sounds became suggestive of another kind of conversation, Clement unwilling to take any evasion for an answer, and the brandy slowly worked its tawdry magic, and for a time, Medina dozed.

He did not know what waked him; a moan, perhaps, or a jostle at his side. He was awake enough to see a darkened shape that sat astride the body of Selim Mansour. The little burp gun slung from his shoulder, Clement pressed something bulky over Mansour's head with both hands, something that crinkled softly as Mansour feebly writhed, his arms pinned at his sides.

Medina's first impulse was to rise shouting and fight against this ultimate indignity. Yet Mamzelle would probably come to Clement's aid and it was clear that Mansour was dying in any case, had been dying for days. *Maybe it's best for the poor guy,* Medina thought, *but when Frenchy saddles up on me next I'll be ready, gun or no gun.* Tensed, furious, with his frustration virtually to the bursting point, Raoul Medina made no sound as he waited for the Frenchman's attention. And waited, and waited.

Eventually, the crinkling rustle of cloth and plastic sounded again. From Clement came heavy breathing and a muffled belch, and then soft footfalls diminishing from the tent. *Goddamn,* Medina realized, *I missed my chance.* He felt for Mansour's wrist and fruitlessly sought a pulse. Yes, it probably had been a favor to the Syrian, but among Medina's feelings toward Clement, gratitude was absent. *I knew I was next,* he excused himself: *I was ready for him and I'm sick with disappointment.*

But it was not disappointment that sickened him, and he offered those excuses in vain. Lurking in his soul, flapping like banners, were the words *coward* and *gutless,* and one other. "Chickenshit," he breathed softly to the dead man beside him. And for that, he would forgive neither himself nor Roland Clement.

FIFTY-THREE

JULY 1991

FRIDAY EVENING, CORBETT waited until dark directly above the Michigan farm site before settling Black Stealth One vertically like a winged elevator in its hover mode. He knew that Petra had listened passively to his transmissions during his day on station near Oshkosh, so she had to know he had seen no sign of the tiny, murderous Butcher Bird. What she could not know was just how weak he felt after horsing the Hellbug around all day. It hadn't helped that, just as the doctor had said, whenever the tumor was producing those right-side headaches, he was likely to lose his vision on the left side of both eyes. Well, he was coping; by turning his head a bit he could still get a good visual field.

"But I had a fair seat in the bleachers for what I *did* see," he told her with forced gaiety, as they closed the big doors of the shed. "Mostly aerobatic teams today. I was too far away to see much, but you can't mistake that weird biplane with landing gear topside as well as below. Guy named Craig Hosking; it had to be him."

He realized he was chattering on like a kid, focusing on the good moments to avoid an admission that he'd thrown up twice during the afternoon. As they stepped into the rundown farmhouse he saw in Petra's fond glance of concern that she knew he was acting strangely. But she shot him a puzzled glance now. "Landing gear on top?"

"Hosking lands upside down and then rightside up," Corbett explained, grinning. "He flew the big iron for that film, *Rocketeer*, or whatever it was. Work I'd like to have."

"Those old racers were killers, weren't they?"

He shrugged, and then stumbled, and sat down hard on a kitchen chair. "Sorry. Give me a minute."

But she was on her knees now, her palm against his forehead, peering closely at his eyes. "Honey, what's wrong? I don't think you have a fever but—" She sat back on her haunches. "You lost your cookies, didn't you?"

"Me?" His frown denied it.

"Don't play macho bullshit games with me, I can smell it on your breath! Oh, Kyle," she crooned, and hugged him. "Do you have any idea what's wrong?"

"Not sure," he lied. "But I could use some rest, and some pills." If he'd been clearheaded he would never have mentioned the medicine.

"Pills for what?"

"Hell, I don't know, generic pills," he muttered, grinning crookedly. He sure as hell wasn't going to say, "Dexamethasone."

"Let's get you to a warm shower," she said, and helped him shrug out of his flying togs en route to the bedroom. While using the toilet, he managed to swallow his medicine.

The warmth of the shower, and Petra's care, buoyed him through the next hour, and though not at all hungry he dutifully downed the soup she warmed before crawling onto their inflatable mattress. "I've got a feeling tomorrow will be better" were his last words that evening.

"I've got a feeling about tomorrow, too," she replied darkly, but before he could ask what she meant, he fell asleep.

Never a man to be disturbed by thin electronic beeps, Corbett waked to the clangor of his old windup alarm clock and rolled out of bed near dawn on Saturday. He reassured Petra several times while he dressed, sipping instant hot chocolate and munching cookies, and thought he had surrogated a healthy man pretty thoroughly until he walked into the pantry door, edge-on.

"All right, that's it," she said firmly, "you're not going out that door in your condition."

"The hell I'm not," he said, reaching for his leather jacket.

She took a catsup bottle from the table; planted herself against the screened back door. "That's right, you're not. You'd kill yourself, Kyle."

He stared at her, glowering. "Have you forgotten I'm bigger than you are?"

"You're not bigger than this," she said, brandishing the bottle. "I could probably beat you up without it."

"Yeah, you probably could," he admitted with a sigh. "But I've got to go, Pets. You know that."

"Not without me," she countered, and darted to retrieve her own quilted jacket. "I don't know how I'd stop you and you know damn' well I wouldn't crown you with a bottle of catsup, but you can't stop me either. If you go, I go." He stood there, swaying, teeth gritted, and when he opened his mouth she added, "What if you pass out in midair? I can fly it; you know that."

"Not very well," he reminded her.

"And how about you? This isn't the best day you've ever had." She was pulling gloves from her jacket as she spoke, assuming command as though born to it.

And she probably was, he thought. At least he had that silvery blanket of stuff from Ullmer as a cockpit lining. "Shit. It's against our better judgment."

"Our? This is my best judgment."

"Ullmer's and mine," he explained with a wan smile. "We swore to each other that you wouldn't get involved in the flying part. We knew damn' well you'd probably want to."

"I don't want to, I *have* to," she said shortly. "I have a good imagination, and I've studied the Butcher Bird's specs. A person would be out of her mind to like this idea."

Zipping his jacket, he said, "Well, grab the rest of the cookies and that orange juice in the cooler; and don't forget your sunglasses. There's supposed to be a weather front building slowly, but this'll probably be another sunny day."

In moments, she was ready. "Cookies, juice, barfbags and those pills you don't think I know you're taking: I hope we've got everything," she remarked.

"Everything but fuel," he said. as she pulled the door closed behind them.

"I took care of that after you fell asleep last night," she said. "Did a postflight and all. What would you do without me?"

"It's not a pretty thought," he said, and pinched her rump as, together, they walked toward a potato shed full of Black Stealth One.

FIFTY-FOUR

July 1991

FOR A MOMENT while waking, Medina forgot that he was shackled to a corpse. But that brandy, he decided, must have been awfully pure stuff because within seconds he had his mental marbles lined up and, sober as granite, realized his opportunity. Realized, in fact, that the opportunity had hovered within his reach for much of the night.

Of course I couldn't wake up before dawn, oh no, not me. Well, I was pretty fuzzed out, thanks to Frenchy. But still . . . Lambasting himself for events he could not control, Medina listened to the mutterings and movements in the next tent while he tugged furiously at the ankle of poor Selim Mansour.

A light sleeper, Mansour had not fashioned that cable loop around his own ankle very tightly. It had been enough to know that, if Medina tried to remove it, the process would bring the Syrian wide-awake. But nothing would ever wake Mansour now, not even an amputation. For a few moments Medina held out hope that he could force that loop down over Mansour's heel but, after pulling until the skin tore down to cold white flesh without bleeding, he gave that up.

The Syrian had kept a small box-end wrench for Medina's nightly shackling, just as Clement did. But where? *Think, dammit,* he told himself, patting the rigid body down without result. He forced himself to crawl across the corpse and rifled Mansour's fanny pack, which lay next to his rolled prayer mat. And when he lifted the mat, a little wrench slid from inside the roll.

As he attacked the shackle bolt between his wrists, Medina could hear a verbal donnybrook erupt between Frenchy and Mamzelle. A couple of turns was all it took with the wrench, leaving the bolt only finger-tight, and then he was fumbling at his ankles, clumsy with haste. It sounded as if Frenchy were losing the argument. And then Frenchy's voice, no longer muffled, made it obvious that he was outside the tent. Medina froze for an instant. *He'll come in here to unshackle me and he'll be armed.* He abandoned his attempt on the bolt at his ankle and thrust the wrench into his hip pocket, struggling back across Mansour's corpse in an effort to feign sleep again. That is how Clement found him, dragging himself backward against the boardlike stiffness of Mansour.

Clement's shout was melodramatic. "What are you doing, Gonzales?" And then, quite convincingly, bringing the little burp gun up: "What have you *done?*"

"I'm trying to get away from a dead body, goddamn you," Medina shouted back. "What would you do if you woke up tied to a corpse?"

In the recesses of his mind, Medina had assumed the Frenchman would pretend to think Mansour had died during the night from his wounds. Evidently Clement was more subtle than that. "What did you do, strangle him?" On hearing this roar from Clement, Mamzelle vented a cry of despair and came hurtling from the tent, pistol in hand.

I can't jump the sonofabitch while I'm still linked to Mansour, Medina thought. They were only a few paces from the water, but the odds against getting Clement out there were simply too high to be thinkable. "I didn't do the poor devil in," Medina barked, no longer able to control his anger. "What for? So I could drag this—this statue around with me?" He turned his glance on the woman, who gazed on the tableau in horror. *"You* tell *me* how long he's been dead," he added, his eyes boring again into Clement's. "The man is hard as a carp, for Christ's sake!"

"That is true," Clement replied grudgingly, defeated by this logic. Backed by the woman and the pistol she held, he knelt with his own wrench to separate the corpse from its unwilling companion. "There. Now make yourself useful and find stones to weight the body. Poor Selim," he said with a sigh as Medina began to put on his shoes.

"Poor Selim," Mamzelle echoed, but in a tone that drew a hard glance from Clement. "How did you know it was true, Roland?"

The Frenchman said something undecipherable to her.

"How did you know," she asked, very slowly, "that poor Selim was, in that hideous vernacular, hard as a carp? You had not touched him."

"Why, I assumed it," Clement blustered, and snicked his weapon's safety off.

"You knew it," she replied stonily. "How did you know it?"

"You would question me," Clement said in wonderment.

Medina stood up fingering the loosened bolt between his wrists. In all probability, he was moments away from a burst of parabellum slugs as he spoke. "He knew it because he got you and me both drunk last night, and then gave you a hump you didn't want—don't forget I could hear you both—and then he came in here later and smothered Mansour when he thought I was asleep because the poor bastard had outlived his usefulness. Just like he'll do to you, Mamzelle, sooner or later."

Clement's snarl came an instant before he swung his weapon up, and in that instant Medina jerked his wrists apart. The severed wires at the end of the loosened cable became bunched needles on the end of a short but exceedingly tough flail, and they lashed Roland Clement full across his face in a whistling snap. Medina followed this with more of the same, the cable end slashing Clement across his head and shoulders in a furious volley.

Clement staggered sidelong, his weapon pointing briefly at the woman, and before he could recover Medina was grappling for the weapon, butting his own hard head into Clement's face repeatedly.

Both men could clearly see the woman as she pointed the little pistol first at Medina, then at Clement, then back again in an agony of indecision. Though fit and wiry, Medina lacked the upper body bulk of the Frenchman and felt himself losing this struggle of weight against weight. That was when he brought both feet off the turf, gripping Clement's weapon like a trapeze, and slammed both feet into Clement's shins before regaining his footing.

Clement screamed like a woman, pitching forward onto Medina, who bunched his legs beneath him and began a backward roll, using all the power of his legs to catapult the Frenchman over him. Though the violence of Clement's short arc tore the weapon from Medina's grasp, it also brought Medina halfway to his feet scarcely two paces from the water's edge, where Clement, facedown at the muddy verge and still holding his weapon, streamed blood and writhed in pain from that pitiless double slam into his solar plexus.

The woman still stood, mouth open and aghast, now pointing

her weapon at Medina but still unable to bring herself to fire. Medina's fierce grin became his only farewell before he hit the water in a shallow dive.

The fetters at his ankles restricted his desperate scissors kicks, though not as much as he had feared. He could see no more than a few feet in the turbid water and stayed beneath its surface as long as he could, moving beside canelike stands of reeds near the shoreline, the sluggish current adding to the distance he managed before surfacing. He could not avoid gasping for breath and expected to feel the bite of bullets at any second, though he found that Clement was now out of direct view. And then he heard the shouting match begin anew.

As long as they wasted time arguing, Medina reasoned, he could use that time to good advantage. The only way he could use that little wrench of Mansour's in neck-deep water without shaking the cane and giving his position away was to take a deep breath and let the current carry him as he felt blindly for the damned bolt. He stirred up bottom sediment too much to see, and needed several breaths before he felt the bolt loosen. He had developed a fine hatred for that little cable but remembered his military survival training: you don't throw away anything you can sensibly keep.

He was fifty yards downstream from the point of his escape when he heard a crashing through the cane and saw tops of the stuff waving hard, and it had to be Clement coming nearer. A short burst of gunfire snapped through the cane and into water ten yards upstream, and Medina knew that he could still die at the Frenchman's hand. Another burst, five yards downstream. *He's firing blind, but his guessing's too good,* Medina thought. For a moment then, breathing quietly through his mouth, he glimpsed Roland Clement as the man wiped at blood that dripped from his forehead into his eyes. Clement cursed in French and fired again, a bit farther downstream, then continued his stalk. Maybe going with the current was no longer such a good idea. Maybe it was time, Medina decided, to move sideways and put a few of those tussocked little islands between himself and the burp gun. He brought up a double handful of mud and applied it to his head as camouflage and then, slowly, keeping arms and legs beneath the surface to silence his progress, he began to swim toward an inlet across the short stretch of open water.

FIFTY-FIVE

JULY 1991

WHICH OF US would you have shot?" Clement asked after his return to camp, standing above Odile who sat on a log, her face buried in her hands.

Her response did not quite qualify as an answer. "You both deserved it," she said, damp-eyed and listless. Clement was not certain of all the nuances in that, but let it pass as she continued. "The American told the truth, did he not?"

"Where is the crime in putting a man out of his misery?" Clement growled, dropping his weapon carefully, running his fingers with care over the gory mess at his brow.

Odile had still not looked up. "I suppose you killed poor Speedy as well," she said.

He thought that very unlikely but chose not to admit it. "I could not be certain," he said grudgingly. "Your poor Speedy came very near to blinding me."

Now she did look up, and gasped. *"Mon Dieu,* Roland, that needs attention."

"How touching that you finally noticed." A month before, he thought, she would have been fussing over him like a mother hen.

"I do not know why I could not fire at him," she said, "but I simply could not."

With a curse, Clement backhanded her across the cheek, hard enough to send her sprawling. "A reward for your incompetence," he said. "Come. After we tend to this head wound, I need your help in reprogramming the djinni before we launch. With any luck we can be out of this morass before dark."

The cable had laid his face open but, as with most head wounds, the bleeding had made it seem worse than it was. After she had bandaged him, and without so much as a decent cup of tea for breakfast, Clement folded and stowed the protective plastic from his console, then from the djinni, which squatted some distance away. Odile took her time about it, but by the time he had his systems booted up with recent videotape running on the screen at a fast scan, she took her place near him. "I thought you already had your next target inputs," she said after watching for a moment.

"All but one," he muttered. "Thanks to your squeamishness, I must now improvise a double mission. Ah; here we are." The video image, as he slowed the display to real time, showed the same landing sequence in which he had identified Medina for the djinni's electronic memory. "Here is your target," he said, placing his finger on the screen. That finger shook with controlled rage.

She began tapping her keyboard. "I see. You are not certain about Gonzales, but you will be," she murmured, checking the video's cross hairs on the upturned face of the escaped American, not daring to sabotage Clement's ploy when he stood at her side half-mad with fury. Because the system needed several perspectives of a victim for its best target matching, they used three images of the man during the tape of that landing. *Ah yes, I shall be certain,* Clement said to himself. He noted that Odile was capable of marking the American for death now, so long as she was removed from the immediacy of it and fearful of Clement himself. Why did ordinary mortals seem to share such problems? They had never been problems for Roland Clement. No, indeed . . .

To make doubly certain that every detail of the escaped American's face was in the djinni's memory, Clement made her run the tape further and took more images of the damned American, this time mostly in profile. As Odile reluctantly completed her input instructions, Clement watched without comment, a savage smile creasing his cheeks. He could have done those operations himself, but Odile's work was quicker when rage palsied his fingers. Besides, it was infinitely more satisfying to see Odile targeting the man who, he felt glumly certain, she would rather entertain than Roland Clement. He had not missed those glances between them. He wondered idly if—but no, he had given them no opportunities without Mansour's presence. He was certain of it.

Their last instructions to the djinni were complex enough to require brief consultations with a manual they had generated themselves, a year previous. The flight required an initial scan of the immediate area, a square mile or so, in search of the escapee. After that first kill the djinni was ordered to proceed to the Oshkosh site. If no kill was recorded after an hour, the djinni was to break off the search for its single victim and proceed to Oshkosh anyway. *Why squander fuel on one target, who may already lie on the bottom of this stinking swamp, when so many others are begging for attention?* Clement stroked his chin and approved Odile's inputs.

When at last Odile stood up and waved a hand at the display as if to say, "There you have it all," Clement queried the djinni's magnificent visual memory to be absolutely certain that he *did* have it all. The djinni duly provided recognition of its next victims, with the computer-developed images of familiar enemies rotating on the screen like the busts of a Who's Who in Aerospace Technology, and Clement ended the display in good spirits. He called Odile back from her attempt to make tea. "Time enough for that after the djinni is aloft," he explained.

Shorthanded as they were, the launch took longer than usual. Clement completed all of the preflight checks himself and, less than two hours after the American's defection, saw his little craft sizzle into a morning sky that, though overcast, promised a perfect view for killing. "Now let us have an emperor's breakfast," he said to Odile. "I am famished."

He was also in more pain than he would admit, and kept the djinni in sight as long as he could as it began its search for the unspeakable Speedy Gonzales. Very soon he found himself watching the spots before his eyes, and rejoined Odile who, by now, seemed to be doing woman's work more grimly than she ever had before.

Clement, while waiting for his breakfast, did man's work: he dragged the body of Selim Mansour to the water's edge, and chopped the hands off with their wicked little camper's axe before sticking them into mud-filled tin cans. He weighted the rest of the body down by slitting the body open and filling the cavity with dirt. He watched as his assistant sank slowly, inexorably, into murky depths, the eyes still open in impassive reproach. None of this ghastly work bothered Clement in the least, save one thing. He wondered whether decay would produce enough gas to bring the remains back to the surface, sooner or later. As for identification, Mansour's teeth had been perfect, unsullied by fillings. And fingerprints would never be a problem because, before acknowledging Odile's call to breakfast, Clement walked upstream and hurled those two mud-filled cans far out into the water. As he strode toward the tents Clement heard the familiar whistling passage of the djinni for one brief moment. *It spotted us and came down for an identification pass,* he thought, failing to see it as it swept past. And for one timeless moment, he felt the sensation of the hunted man staring into a gun muzzle.

FIFTY-SIX

JULY 1991

CHRISTIAN CARLSSON PUT down his phone, snagged his windbreaker on his way out of the office, and stuck his head around the adjoining office door. "Well, this is what I get for coming in on a Saturday," he said to the young woman inside. His face, "leather from the weather," as his colleagues put it, became younger as he showed teeth in a rueful smile. "Got a squawk about some idiot firing an automatic weapon on DNR turf. Most likely not turf at all, so I'm taking a flatbottom."

She snaked a clipboard from the wall behind her without rising as he started down the hall. "Chris? Don't go zooming off without a time and location."

He returned, shrugging into his jacket with the DNR—Wisconsin State Department of Natural Resources—conservation warden patch. "Oh, shoot, I dunno; back by eleven, I guess. The firing was somewhere east of the canoe trail, north of Steamboat Island." He ran a hand through plentiful dark hair a bit longer than regulation cut, suddenly reminded that he'd intended to get it trimmed this very morning. "Uh, call my wife, will you, and tell her to back off my date with the barber, but I'll still take Nels to the Little League game."

"Can do," she called, as he hurried from the long brown bungalow-style DNR building. Its view was from a rise overlooking not only the town of Horicon, but the lower reaches of the wilderness area as well. Somewhere to the north, some fool was probably playing war with an illegal weapon, most likely sighting it in but, just possibly, poaching. Firecrackers? A definite maybe. Chris Carlsson hoped it was firecrackers that had spooked the couple on their early-morning canoe trip.

Across the parking lot lay the garage, a cavernous barn, really, where several boats and decades-long accumulations of equipment waited. He might have taken an airboat with its big Lycoming aircraft engine, but for a man alone it was easier to manhandle one of the little flatboats with a go-devil engine and the kind of extension-mounted propeller they called a "mudlicker." Those rigs had proven themselves in the shallows of Southeast Asia, and they worked equally well around Horicon.

Chris backed the Blazer quickly to the trailer's tongue, hitched up, and checked the go-devil's fuel before taking that final moment to consider every possibility. Then, without any fuss about it, he went back into the bungalow for his two-way radio and a Remington 870, the kind of shotgun that had a tube extender as long as its stubby barrel. A twelve-gauge, it would pump seven rounds of buckshot. Even facing a fool with an assault rifle, the Remington gave a man a certain air of authority. The Smith magnum on his hip, added to that Remington, made Chris look very businesslike indeed.

He debated putting the boat in near the park on the south end of the preserve but reasoned that any guy spraying ammunition around would also have left a set of wheels somewhere at the edge of the marsh. That sent him north, to the levee near Kekoskee, and a half hour later he backed the Blazer at the turnaround, careful to put the trailer within a few feet of the water.

When he had wrestled the flatbottom halfway into the shallow flow, he parked in a way to avoid hogging what little room there was, and when he locked up he noticed, for the first time, the tread marks of big dual wheels that had recently sunk deep into the turf. Some pickups had duals, but this had been one heavy mother, maybe not a pickup but a camper. He also spotted the spoor of something very much smaller, probably a scrambler bike from the look of it, with the tread patterns of new tires. Might mean anything or nothing; merely data to file away. Meanwhile, there were no vehicles in sight but his. Chris Carlsson donned his rubber boots, levered his wiry body expertly into the boat after shipping the Remington, and started up the snarling little go-devil.

While a man can virtually plane a flatbottom with a go-devil at full throttle, Chris knelt in approved fashion and steered cautiously, the prop extension working as a rudder. Puttering along, ears tuned for gunfire, he almost immediately noticed a place where something big and very clumsy had flailed through the cane grass to a tiny island, hardly more than a hummock. Closer inspection revealed a flash of color in the reeds at ground level, not a tint of waterbirds, but the bright synthetic hue of paint. Floating alongside the hummock, his engine silenced, Chris did not have to leave his boat to see that he had resolved a piece of one small question: someone had stashed a small, spanking new motorbike there in the belief that no one would spot it behind those savaged grasses. Either the bike had been brought across by boat or carried bodily across the water. Strong and fit for his size, Chris thought about that for a moment. If someone had carried that bike across neck-deep water, it had been someone a lot bigger than Christian Carlsson. No doubt the bike had been boated across.

Maybe those are the wheels our war-game player is using. But maybe not, and its existence there was no serious infraction in itself. Instead of deflating its tires, Chris brought his radio to his mouth and called his position in, then mentioned the vehicle hidden on the hummock. Looked to him, he said, as though somebody had found a new way to foil bike thieves.

Puttering downstream again, Chris passed into the shadow of a big cottonwood and eased the throttle still lower as he saw the heron rookery, with slapdash nests scattered in the tops of smaller trees to the left of the open channel. A man could disturb the very birds he was trying to protect if he wasn't circumspect. Suddenly, though he was taking great care to keep his noise down, several herons unlimbered their great wings and fled the treetops. *Damn and blast, some warden I am,* he told himself as still more of the birds stretched sticklike legs out and flapped away. And because he was watching and listening so intently, Chris Carlsson saw the thing almost the instant he heard it, the thing the herons had discovered before he did, a finned discus that arced overhead coming toward him with a sound like a fluttering steam nozzle.

FIFTY-SEVEN

—

JULY 1991

THE DJINNI'S EYE resolved a pattern that its circuits knew: *potential target*. It sent commands to its canted rudders and monitored the results, dipping for a rapid low-level pass, if not pleased with its own performance—for it was incapable of such emotion—then perhaps "satisfied" with the result. As the Arabs had said of ancient legendary djinn: while it might do the bidding of a human, its perceptions were inhuman; alien.

Its emergency circuitry flickered into readiness as several small obstacles rose almost into its path. Those flying objects had eyes, a crucial datum to the djinni's programs, but eyes set on the sides of the heads, unlike a hawk's. The djinni's creator had considered the possibility of hawk attacks from the first, so a simple subprogram in the djinni equated objects with wings and eyes as potential attackers. And a potential attacker became a potential target. Because the herons fled instead of attacking, the djinni was not compelled to identify any of the birds as active targets, and maintained its focus on the potential target that knelt on a flatbottom boat.

The staring face below opened its mouth as the djinni flashed overhead. By the time the little predator began to climb again, it had already completed some of its comparator tasks and continued to run the remainder as it soared higher. *Width ratio, eye sockets to nostrils: 3.16.* Not a good match, not even close. The ratio of the head height to width, and the exact shape of the ears, also failed to tally with the djinni's electronic needs and these failures of congruence, combined with a dozen less important differences, overwhelmed the few ratios that did match to three digits of accuracy.

The question had been answered. *Negative match.* The djinni's circuits kept their memory of this facial pattern briefly, to avoid wasting energy on it a second time, but meanwhile the rudders and fuel flow valving received new commands. The djinni surged forward, its eye shifting to a wider field of view, seeking more potential targets connected to necks, torsos, arms, legs.

Ineffably brilliant by some standards, the djinni was horrendously stupid by others. It was capable of scanning and memorizing the patterns of thousands of faces for a brief period, thousands of megabytes of data, but it would obediently blow a hole in a decapitated head if that head was a positive match for enough critical ratios. And once a laser had penetrated that target, the djinni no longer retained any interest in it, was in fact not capable of further interest in it. The target had been struck. It would not be engaged again without reprogramming.

Cruising at surveillance altitude, the djinni completed its southward run, reversed its course, and returned on a path a kilometer east of the run on which it had, unknowingly, astonished a set of patterns called Christian Carlsson. Its internal clock allowed it another seventeen minutes, twenty-four seconds before this single-target mission was replaced by another, and at that instant the djinni's eye reported another potential victim. Rudders deflected, fuel valves shifted, and the djinni made its identifying pass, hungry for congruence with its memorized patterns.

Each set of human patterns had a name, a fact the djinni neither knew nor cared about. This set was named Raoul Medina, and it did not form a complete shape with legs because it was only half out of murky water, waist-deep as it struggled to walk between hummocks, over a mile from the tree line on the eastern side of the marsh.

The head jerked around as the djinni sizzled by, a behavior familiar to the busy circuits, and with a wealth of perspectives in temporary memory the djinni began to match patterns on its way to firing altitude.

Several critical ratios matched perfectly. Several more did not; the face seemed to have no forehead and the cheekbones did not project as they did in its electronic reconstruction of Raoul Medina. Not only that, but the bridge of the nose was far broader than any pattern the djinni had ever memorized. *Negative match.* Sixteen minutes, forty-three seconds remained in this mission as the djinni accelerated away from Medina, still searching for him. Scant seconds later, unnoticed by the receding djinni, a piece of drying mud fell from the face of its most recent potential target, and the bridge of Raoul Medina's nose regained its true shape.

Roland Clement had never taught his brainchild to see through this kind of camouflage. Medina waded on, unaware that his mud pack had bought him a kind of temporary salvation.

FIFTY-EIGHT

JULY 1991

ON STATION," CORBETT was reporting on the NSA channel, "orbiting west of, ah, Ripon this time unless you have a hot tip I don't know about. Getting much nearer without an immediate reason would definitely be uncool for us."

"Roger that, Yucca One," replied the voice from the command center while Petra, monitoring them with her own headset, scribbled *Sheppard himself* at the upper margin of the chart spread between them. Sheppard went on: "Oversight One is still in place in a much wider orbit. Actually they're curious about you, but rules are rules. I've assured the Nemesis crew that somebody is really on station down there even if they don't have you on radar. Ah, you said 'us'?"

"Roj," Petra said in her best simulation of the lazy good ol' boy accents of yore. "I'll be riding shotgun up here today."

Sheppard again, after a few hurried words off-mike: "Ullmer's here, against my better judgment, controlling the team flying high cover. We both wonder why you're there. That's hazard duty, Yucca Two. We thought you were on wheels for emergency backup."

Corbett gave her an inquiring glance. *She'll think of something; she always does,* he thought, and made no effort to reply, banking the Hellbug slightly in its mile-wide circle.

"Well, I'm Yucca One today. Sorry; it's a little problem with contact lenses," she said with a shrug to Corbett that said, *So, I lied.* "His lenses, not mine. His distance vision seems to be sharp enough. He's watching those old trainer hulks do aerobatics from here," she said, balancing her lie with a slice of truth.

"You may not know it, young lady, but some of us learned to fly in an AT-6," Sheppard's voice said laconically. "Hulks indeed!"

Corbett's bass chuckle filled their headsets. Though he had trained in the later, heavier and faster T-28, he knew the kind of loyalty still commanded by the T-6s that were zooming so playfully over Oshkosh at this moment, totally unaware of the deadly game whose players were converging on another quadrant of the sky.

Moments later Corbett signed off, pleased that the Dexamethasone seemed to be doing its work. It was a damned nuisance when he had to sit beside Petra and pretend he was comfortable while fighting nausea and a splitting headache, but momentarily he felt that he was on the mend. Still, "You want some stick time? Take over for a few minutes if you like," he said to Petra, who was only too happy to comply.

He did not know how long he sat there dozing, the Hellbug continuing its gentle circles east of the little town of Ripon, before his headset brought him fully awake.

"We've drawn a laser strike," said Sheppard, his voice tight with excitement. They could hear him snapping to someone else in the command center, his fingers cupped over his mouthpiece: "You have our bogey? Well, find it, you know it's up there." Then, into the mouthpiece again: "Wait one, we're contacting Oversight."

"I wanted our transmissions separate, but this is not working. We need to know what they're picking up," Corbett said. Petra nodded. He pointed over his shoulder, toward Oshkosh. Solid contact with the Butcher Bird was all the immediate reason he needed to send the Hellbug skating out on thin ice. "I'll take it, we've gotta get closer than this," he said, hauling Black Stealth One around so abruptly they could hear creaks in its monocoque structure.

Sheppard's voice crackled with tension. "Yucca One, Oversight detects a trailing radiation plume that's just begun to spread above us, fifteen hundred feet AGL, south end of the long runway. And we may have it on scope. Wup! Another laser strike. Lord, but that thing is accurate." Without bothering to muffle his mouthpiece he raised his voice, obviously talking to someone near him. "Aren't we going to fire back?"

Petra, her face a study in rapt attention, covered her own mouthpiece. "I've never heard him like this. They must be going bonkers down there."

Corbett nodded and firewalled his gossamer brute, now aiming

south of Wittman Field's long runway. "Hold your horses," he said
to no one in particular. He was only minutes away now, his speed
above the normal maximum because they had been cruising several thousand feet AGL—above ground level—and when descending he could get a slight boost in velocity.

The Hellbug leveled off at two thousand feet, Corbett typically
choosing an old fighter pilot's option of superior height. Sheppard
again: "All *right*. We've returned fire by rastering the beam. I don't
know what to make of this, but Oversight One claims the Butcher
Bird is now orbiting tight circles, same altitude, and it has spewed
hard radiation four times. It has also hit four targets. Ben thinks it's
just trying to cool down its internals between strikes but I believe
we may have hit it. We're having an overheat problem on this end,
too. Do not, repeat *not*, enter the immediate area, you could get
rastered into confetti. What's your position, Yucca One?"

"Over Highway Forty-one, damn' near in Wittman's takeoff
pattern," Corbett replied, and added his altitude for good measure.

But it was a very bad measure. "Lower, or you could take our
strikes," Sheppard said. "This Army HEL delivers almost the same
energy at five miles as it does from five yards and we should expect
no less of the Butcher Bird."

Cursing, Corbett obeyed, both he and Petra searching for any
sign of the Butcher Bird on their scope. They had fine healthy blips
from the half-dozen T-6s cavorting innocently to the north, both
on IR and radar, but the yellow false-color image of a radiation
plume was not yet showing on their screen.

Though the NSA equipment had high fidelity they could still
tell when Sheppard had switched to their channel, and because the
channel was open they heard another voice that must have been
thunderous in close quarters: "Well, shut it down then!"

Another unidentified voice: "The diorama just took another
strike, sir. Some of those goddamn dummies are bleeding fluid
when they're hit, throwin' their arms around; Christ, it's scary!"

The big voice again; not Sheppard's or Ullmer's: "And we can't
shoot back? That thing's spraying rads and we've got two hundred
thousand civilians out there and damaged robots on my monitor,
jumping around like loonies! I'm pulling the plug. Get those fucking dummies out of sight, cover 'em with a tarp, *any*thing! Pull the
cables and—"

At that point, perhaps mercifully, the channel went dead.
"Boy, I'm glad we're here and not there right now," Petra said.

"Don't be too sure, luv," Corbett cautioned, one gloved finger pointing at the scope. "We're picking up that plume."

Faintly showing now, as they banked to avoid coming too near the enormous crowd west of the runway, they could see the false-color image Corbett had seen once before. The yellow line curled, pretzeling and shifting with the breeze, dispersing as it broadened. Stunned, fascinated, Petra made adjustments to the screen as Corbett brought the Hellbug to a stop in midair, hovering on its exhaust columns. "Jesus Christ, *there it goes,*" she exclaimed.

She had not seen the Butcher Bird itself but stared at its trailing plume on the scope, now a hard bright yellow, and though the radar's track remained dim the infrared trace led that yellow line. Its turbine exhaust yielded a strong red dot just ahead of that yellow tail. And it was streaking toward the south, across the bow of Black Stealth One.

Sheppard in their headsets: "Yucca One, Oversight has your bogey, course one eight five at—"

"Got it on scope," Corbett replied tightly, horsing the Hellbug around, demanding emergency power from the engine. For a few seconds, acceleration pressed them into their seats.

"Stay out of its wake," Sheppard warned, a second before the radiation Klaxon began its rhythmic hooting in the cockpit. "We may have hit it with our return fire. If we penetrate a reactor of unknown design—well, it's not a pretty scenario."

"Turn that goddamn Klaxon off," Corbett said over the hooting that set nerves on edge. "The scope tells us all we need to know."

Petra: "Where's the switch?"

Corbett: "No switch. Jerk the wires, I installed it near the pedals."

After a moment's confusion, Petra found the offensive little horn and ripped a wire loose, bringing instant quiet. She resumed watching the scope. Corbett, who had kept pace with technology without relinquishing his seat-of-the-pants preference, chose to peer ahead through his windscreen with brief glances toward the scope. "Pursuing, Yucca Control, but I still can't—yes, by God, I *can* see it. Quick little bugger for its size, but we're closing."

"Yucca One, I can't overstress this," said Bill Sheppard. "Stay out of that radiation plume, that's an order; over."

"You think I'd forget who's in here with me? Get off my back. Aaaand *out,*" Corbett finished. He did not shut down the channel but his terminal *out,* spoken as an expletive, could not be misunderstood.

As the pursuit stretched southward past Fond Du Lac, the Hellbug drifted in still nearer, closing on its quarry from a position slightly above and to the right, and when a vagrant wisp of cloud interrupted his visual contact, Corbett brought the Hellbug even closer. Then their view became clear again and most of the Butcher Bird's details stood out starkly from a distance of fifty yards. The vague bulges on its upper carapace were as Corbett remembered, but the sun's reflection no longer bounced from a smoothly contoured shell. To one side of its centerline, that shell seemed to have a new swelling, as if a pimple had erupted from inside, subtly buckling the surface. It had not been jittering or taking evasive action until now, arrowing straight for home, but as the Hellbug drew a fateful five yards nearer its quarry darted off to the left in an abrupt maneuver.

Petra, who could now see the thing clearly: "What's all that about?"

"I'm not sure," Corbett replied, "but I think maybe it's seen us." He would have left matters as they were but for the next cloud, which obscured their visual contact for much too long. Now they sought their quarry over farmlands that became marshlands, and trusted their electronics to keep them in close pursuit. On their scope it seemed that they were flying virtually on top of the quarry, and as their view cleared once again, Corbett found that it was no illusion; they had been gradually closing on it from the right, and were now dangerously near. He was in the act of sideslipping away when the Butcher Bird, performing several operations at once, slewed sideways. Something massive and boxlike protruded from the aerodynamic shell, which turned its belly toward them.

They did not see the beam itself, but when a small hole appeared through the bulging left window they both heard the sizzling *pop,* followed by a steady whistle of wind through the hole. Corbett's mind flashed on a new scenario: either the Butcher Bird had finally missed a target, or the Hellbug itself had become the target. The faint, sweetish tang of burned Plexiglas drifted through the cockpit for a moment.

For Corbett, time dilated as he demanded that Petra slide down; saw on his scope that the radiation trail had suddenly bloomed; gained a few feet of altitude; noted that the Butcher Bird was still streaking southward over a marsh that stretched for many miles.

"Goddammit, that's enough," he muttered. He might still be able to trail it back to its base now, but that NSA hotshot Sheppard had reminded him that a laser strike could be just as dangerous at long range; and the damned thing had already taken a good shot at them. *If it had hit Petra* . . . he thought, and a sudden rage boiled in his veins. "Pets, pull my Streetsweeper from the footwell and take the stick."

She unsnapped the bulky weapon from its Velcro and pulled it quickly upward. The Streetsweeper, Corbett's highly modified drum-fed shotgun, was an ugly and brutal piece of hardware. It demanded a sturdy user for rapid fire and had never been popular enough for mass production. For Kyle Corbett, however, it was a natural weapon of choice. He snapped its folding stock into place. Its magazine held a dozen cartridges and when firing repeated rounds of double-aught buckshot the thing could literally sweep a street of rioters.

But this was no paved thoroughfare. Corbett knew that his only warning of another laser burst would be that quick deployment of the laser cannon's muzzle. "If I tell you to jink," he said, sliding back the small transparent port in his window to thrust the shotgun's barrel out, "present our belly to that damned thing. This cockpit blanket liner of ours just might absorb some of its energy."

The blanket had been designed to intercept radiation, but not the kind of tightly focused beam of a high-energy laser. *At least Petra's on the other side of me*, he reasoned, and ducked down a bit to aim through that little port as wind hissed through it.

"Throttle back." She did. "Port a little. More." She did that, too, as well as he could have done it himself. He knew that buck-shot pellets, metal spheres the diameter of a medium-caliber hand-gun slug, spent their energy quickly and would be of no use beyond fifty yards. That was why he continued to hold his fire until he was virtually alongside the murderous little weapon system, perhaps thirty yards to its right.

When he did fire, it was not a single squeeze of the trigger because the weapon operated as a very fast spring-driven revolver. He aimed ahead of and below his target, hoping that some combi-nation of luck and Kentucky windage would send at least one group of buckshot pellets into a vital spot. He had the Street-sweeper angled at his shoulder so that, with his first shot, its own recoil would begin to force its aim for succeeding shots not only upward but back. The reports inside that bulbous canopy became repeated hammer blows on their eardrums, four, five, six, seven walloping blasts within a few seconds, and the acrid odor of powder residue surrounded them.

Without warning, the Butcher Bird's entire shell began to spin, rudders and all, as it swept across the bow of the Hellbug. Corbett barely had time to shout, *"Jink!"* as he saw, not ten yards away, what he took to be a hellish glow flickering within the Butcher Bird, just below its centerline.

FIFTY-NINE

July 1991

THE DJINNI COULD not feel pain. Yet its circuits had registered something akin to concern when, for the first time in its synthetic life, it took a ravening bolt of energy from somewhere below. The bolt had come, at relativistic speed, from a point very near the group of targets that sat and shifted in their seats and turned their heads now and then, and tallied precisely with the djinni's memories of such men as Ben Ullmer.

Though the djinni's own marksmanship had been perfect, none of the targets had slumped or fallen after its perfect strikes. Three of them, in fact, had begun to move like crazed marionettes, two spewing fluid the color of summer wheat. The djinni was not programmed to care about that; its CCD video optics would show that its targets were accurately struck—yet incapable of dying, remaining wildly active until four very nervous technicians hurriedly covered them all with tarpaulins.

But that laser bolt from below had been just as accurate. It penetrated the djinni's skin, damaged sensors inside, and showered still more energy, *heat* energy, into the guts of a system already dangerously overheated from firing its own weapon several times. It had been Selim Mansour's pleading that gave the djinni its ability to loiter between firings, long enough for thermocouples to signal that the on-board nuclear reactor had vented enough heat to be fired again.

Firing, circling while ram air flushed excess heat and hard radiation, then firing again, the djinni obeyed all instructions as well as it could while radiation began, insidiously, to generate false signals in circuitry Mansour had tried so hard to protect.

By the time the djinni began its dash for home, it was already flying erratically. It could still recognize a potential attacker, and while it had never seen any winged creature remotely as large or as fast as the one that dogged it on its way south, it could still react to what seemed to be an attack. When the gigantic Hellbug loomed near, the djinni tried an avoidance. And when that failed, it counterattacked.

Its CCD optics registered a perfect shot directly into the huge, gleaming left eye of the creature. One perfect hit had always been enough; the djinni had no further interest in its victim afterwards, and would not have fired a second time even if the pursuing Hellbug had involved it in a midair collision. It simply had not been programmed to cope with a victim that, moments later, launched its own counterattack with a spray of double-aught buckshot.

The carbon composite skin of the djinni, no longer structurally sound after that laser strike, still deflected several pellets. It did not deflect the one that struck a rudder actuator, sending it briefly spinning on its axis before regaining partial control; nor the one that shattered its charge-coupled device to blind it and then impacted its particle-bed reactor.

Now the djinni lacked sight, overheat sensors, and controls for the reactor. It knew, however, that it had already located its landing site in the marsh below, and must begin its descent.

In technical terms, it retained most of its flight controls but suffered from multiple malfs—malfunctions—that released a narrow spray of hard radiation that continued long after it had, somehow, managed something like a survivable descent path. But now it lacked vital sensors and some of its power controls. In layman's terms, the djinni had been driven insane.

SIXTY

—

July 1991

J UST CRAWL IN easy or you'll swamp us both," Carlsson insisted, coming forward on his knees in the flatbottom to help. The man slid in to the boat on his belly, moving slowly as if exhausted, and who wouldn't be after wading across mud-floored miles of open water up to his armpits? "You don't look that heavy; let me lift you in."

At last the man lay in the boat, rolling onto his side and gasping, face caked with mud as he tried to speak. Carlsson went on, judging the distance: "You know, I'm not sure you'd have made it all the way by yourself; people don't realize how tough that is with silt dragging at your ankles. Mind telling me what the devil you were doing out here?" He tried an encouraging smile.

The man tried again to speak, nodding as he did so. Yes, he would try to explain? Or yes, he minded? Either way, he didn't seem to have any spare breath just yet. "Okay, relax. I'm Warden Christian Carlsson. First order of business, I guess, is whether you're all right. No broken bones or anything."

A headshake, while lungs pumped long labored inhalations. "Be okay" were the first words from the mud man, in a hoarse, determined whisper.

Carlsson scratched his head, thinking it over. "Uh, where are you parked?"

Negative headshake again. "Not," said the man, whose swarthy features marked him as late thirties or so. "Hiked." More heavy breathing.

"Then we can puzzle this out later. You won't mind if I finish poking around before I take you back in the pickup," Carlsson said, moving back to start up the go-devil.

It was at that precise moment that heavy gunfire began to echo across the marsh, its origin mysterious, six or seven concussive booming reports in quick succession. "Shotgun, and too many rounds in that magazine to be legal. Firing it at all is illegal, around here," Carlsson said aloud. "I thought somehow you were part of that, but whoever it is—*good God*," he finished, his head swinging up.

A buzzard floated high above, its wings unmoving though it wheeled away in a tight arc before leveling off. And unless his eyes were playing tricks, Carlsson saw faint puffs of smoke barely visible in that buzzard's wake. Both men watched, thunderstruck, as something came tearing downward from the buzzard's vicinity, its path a long slanting descent toward a distant island, and it was moving at the pace of a peregrine falcon. The sound of its passage became a hissing flutter as it passed them, and while it dived out of sight beyond a distant line of trees there was no doubt that its landing had not been a gentle one. And Carlsson had seen that thing very recently.

"Yesss. Oh, yes," breathed the guy lying on his side, eyes closing as if in prayer; or rapture, maybe.

"Where the hell are we; the twilight zone?" Carlsson asked in genuine fascination, suspecting that his passenger could enlighten him quite a bit about this weirdest of all possible Saturdays.

"Couldn't tell you; stranger here myself," the guy croaked. Now he was sitting up, leaning against the front thwart and using his fingers to comb half-dried dried mud from his hair. He was still in no shape to run a ten-yard dash but managed to grin as he answered.

But Carlsson persisted. "Look, can you tell me what *was* that—that thing up there? It went zipping over me an hour or so ago, flushed all the herons from a rookery. Not what we like to see in our marsh, buddy." He did not wait for the answer before starting the go-devil, steering toward the place where that big Frisbee had gone down.

Now the guy up front was shaking his head and talking. Carlsson throttled back. ". . . armed and dangerous," the guy was saying. "That Remington pump won't get it, pal."

Nodding more to himself than to the other man: "So you do have some answers," Carlsson said.

"Not many. Uh, watched them awhile. They're lunatics, Warden."

"Watched them, did you? What were they doing?"

"Launching that thing we saw. Lots of equipment. Tried to bag me with a burp gun," said the man, now getting his wind back.

"Jesus. No wonder you took a long hike," Carlsson mused. *Burp gun? But that was no small-caliber weapon we heard a minute ago. Okay, so whoever it is, maybe they've got several weapons.* He jerked a thumb toward where that big Frisbee disappeared. "How many of them were there?"

"Three. Let me out somewhere if you're heading over there," the guy said.

Carlsson nodded and thought it over. Alone, he would have continued to investigate. It was, after all, his job. An exhausted, unarmed civilian in the boat made an entirely different equation when approaching a bunch of armed fruitcakes. "I'll take you back to the pickup," he said, "and you can wait there." Seeing the guy's firm nod, he turned up the wick on the go-devil and headed back toward the levee where he had left his pickup and trailer. That little engine made so much racket there was no point in trying to use the radio until they stopped.

When they reached the embankment with its big cottonwoods, Carlsson had to help his passenger out. As he brought the radio up to his face, something in the guy's face said he was growing, suddenly, more alert. Maybe wary was more like it; and that made Carlsson wary, too. "I'll need your name and ID," he said.

"Juan Gonzales. If you find my ID out there in the marsh, I'll be a happy camper," the guy said laconically.

This did not seem a proper moment, Carlsson decided, to pat him down. He wasn't really a suspect and it wasn't against regulations for a man to hike a mile or so in water up to his neck; merely weird, perhaps suicidally stupid. "Look, Gonzales, if those people were shooting at you, maybe you know why. You know them?"

"No. And don't want to." He was walking toward the pickup on rubbery legs.

"It's locked," Carlsson said.

"Want to unlock it?"

After the briefest pause: "I don't think so. You just sit tight there until I get back. You want them in custody for shooting at you, right?"

"Do I ever," said the guy, sitting down heavily.

Carlsson went over to him, dropped to one knee. "Well, you're the only guy who can swear they did it. Ah, you *can* identify them?"

"You goddamn betcha," the guy said slowly.

Carlsson clapped the guy's shoulder. "It's a deal. You rest up, Gonzales; I'll be back sooner than you think."

"Not if you face that bunch down by yourself," Gonzales warned.

"I'm calling for backup. Don't worry." Carlsson went back to the flatbottom and began to radio for help, keeping his voice down as he described Mr. Juan Gonzales. He signed off, then paused before starting up the go-devil, thinking a small white lie wouldn't hurt Gonzales any. "Should be more wardens along in a couple of minutes. You'll be okay."

"Be careful," Gonzales warned. "They're nuts, and so are you."

Christian Carlsson grinned and waved, and started the engine, and Gonzales waved back. And, as he said later to the feds who dusted the flatbottom in efforts to find a decent unsmeared print from those muddy fingers, that was both the first time and the last time he ever saw Mr. Juan Gonzales.

SIXTY-ONE

July 1991

RESPONDING TO PETRA'S quick reflexes, the Hellbug dropped its starboard wing and veered away, plummeting until she brought it level again. The scope showed her that the Butcher Bird was descending much faster, in a slanting rush, and only then did she notice that Corbett had slumped against the side of the canopy. "Kyle? *Kyle!*" He was moving, but said nothing for long moments as she shook his arm and pleaded.

She contacted Sheppard then, watching the path of their quarry as long as it remained on the scope. "Yucca Control, bogey is down, repeat down, at a high rate of knots but it may have hit Yucca One. I can't tell. We took at least one strike on the canopy. Over."

"Down? Impacted? Give us a fix," Sheppard demanded.

"That's, ahh," she consulted the console. "Forty-three degrees, thirty-three minutes north; eighty-eight degrees, thirty-seven minutes west, lost in ground clutter now." She repeated the coordinates again, quickly, fighting a cold sweat to maintain at least the sound of professional calm.

"Got it. You didn't have a visual sighting of a crash?"

"Busy with evasive action," she snapped. "I'm pretty sure it augered right on in but I suppose it could have made a soft landing." Hers was a reluctant admission; she did not *want* to think of the Butcher Bird surviving, but with no pilot aboard it could pull a lot of g's, perhaps even land safely after diving very near ground level. "Look, I've got a casualty in here. That's what I'm interested in right now, and *you owe him*, Doctor Sheppard!"

Now Corbett was wrestling himself back to a sitting position, his muttering vague. Then he said, quite clearly into his little mike, "Hell with that, just—headache. Goddamn but it's the worst yet," he finished.

"Switching," Sheppard noted, and the channel went dead.

Corbett's face, normally tanned, was more florid than usual. "Kyle, honey, you're all flushed. Are you having some kind of attack?"

Negative headshake. Then, "Remind me not to do that when I'm this dizzy. Listen, Pets, my personal compass is uncaged; you're gonna have to get us back. I'm out of it," he added. He slid the shotgun from its slender port until Petra could grasp it, then collapsed shaking against his seat back. "Jee-*zus*," he mumbled, gloved hands clasping at his temples.

Sheppard's voice winked back into their headsets. "Oversight One confirms a strong radiation bloom at coordinates you gave, Yucca One. Do you need medical help?"

"Nope," from Corbett.

"Absolutely," from Petra. "If he didn't take a laser strike then it must be something else, at a range of a hundred feet. He nailed the damned thing, you know."

Plaintively, almost in falsetto, from Sheppard: "With what?"

"The mother of all shotguns," Petra replied. "Point-blank."

"Holy God," Sheppard muttered. "I think he could've taken a spray of hard radiation. You both could have."

Black Stealth One was now climbing, its tachometer registering maximum revs as Petra set her course back toward Oshkosh. "I feel okay," she announced. "We were both masked by that protective blanket lining the cockpit. But from the nose up he looks like a man with a third-degree sunburn just starting to swell. Oh, *dammit*," she said. It sounded like whining, even to her. "I need clearance to land somewhere near," she went on, controlling her anxiety. At this pace and from her commanding height, Wittman Field was emerging on her horizon. "He did more than you ever asked of him. You've got to get him to medical help."

"Yucca One, listen carefully," Sheppard said, voice low. Apparently he was still not alone. Not only that; but Petra felt certain Sheppard knew that, somewhere in this communication loop, a tape was recording every word. "I can promise only so much. There are other agencies involved now, and I can make no promises for them. If your vehicle is seized—and you can't hide it from all angles simultaneously—you lose it, and a lot more, and so would someone else." That someone, she knew, was Sheppard himself. "If you put your man off and tell me where, someone can help."

"Take me to the farm," Corbett said suddenly. "Take the Hell—"

"Shut up," Sheppard interrupted in the tones of a rasp, "and let us work this out. I'm having a hard time justifying this already and it doesn't help when you remind me who you are, and what you've taken."

Petra: "There's a set of small hangars to your west, Control. Near a grove of trees, practically a forest. Very protected, nobody I can see near them."

"Adjacent to Wittman?"

"Affirmative. White roof with a sign. I can't read it."

"Pioneer Airport," Corbett put in. "Know it by heart."

"He's right," Petra confirmed.

"It's a kind of museum, off the beaten track a mile or so from me. But there ought to be at least a few people hanging around it," Sheppard protested.

"Then they're hiding in short grass" was Petra's reply. "We're putting down immediately west of it. Look for my guy, he'll be—"

"I know what he looks like," said Sheppard with a glimmer of wry humor.

Now Corbett retched, a dry heave at first. "I'm not going," he managed to say.

"Shut up," said Petra and Sheppard together. Petra went on, now bringing Black Stealth One over a nearby highway in its eye-deceiving pixel plumage, bleeding off velocity with enough expertise to surprise herself: "On final approach, Control. Never forget this: he put your Butcher Bird down."

"I'm on my way; Control out," Sheppard said quickly, and then the channel went silent.

Petra realized that Corbett's heaves were no longer dry, but the very act of tending to her lover at this precise moment might cause her to make a misjudgment that could hasten his death. She cloistered her mind into two parts. The major portion said, *Hit those damned deflectors hard over the trees, watch the tach, don't catch a wingtip; forget the airspeed indicator and let treetops be your guide, thaaat's it, settle beyond the trees, get down into ground effect before you chop the throttle. There are a few people a quarter of a mile away but with the trees as a background maybe they won't spot us.*

The remainder of her awareness said, *You have to trust Sheppard now, he knows how much we owe Kyle Corbett. Yes, and he is also a deputy director of an alphabet soup agency with a career to lose and why should I trust him?* And the answer slid into place as sweetly as the Hellbug wafting onto grass: *Because if Kyle goes down, so do I, and I'd take Sheppard along for the ride, and well he knows it. My God, he practically told me so himself!* Another complication suddenly flooded her thoughts: *But Sheppard's at the top of the old-boy network, and maybe his neck isn't as far out as he wants me to think. Trustworthy, or treacherous? It's a coin-toss.* And she was betting Corbett's life on the way she called it.

"Not going," Corbett mumbled, as they felt ground contact.

"And I'm not moving until you do, and I can see people looking this way," said Petra, folding her arms, sitting back instead of hugging him as she longed to do, barfy jacket and all.

"Goddammit anyway," he burst out, with a glare that frightened her because his eyes were horribly bloodshot and, from the bridge of his nose upward, his face was dreadfully red and swollen. She glared back, then turned her face away, stolid, hoping he could not see the tears coursing down her cheeks.

His side of the canopy creaked open. "Don't know if I can make it," he said.

Now, a tiny figure in the distance had begun to walk in their direction; now two. Intuition said that this was no time for her to reveal any lack of decisiveness. "Yes you can, you macho bastard; if you're going to die, don't do it in here," she quavered, hoping it was the right note of a toughness she could not feel.

Then he was rolling out sideways, hitting the turf with a grunt, and she did not reach across that empty seat to latch the laser-damaged canopy until she had the Hellbug skating along beside the tree line, a fleeting glimpse of tomorrow's triumphs for a pair of curious onlookers four hundred yards away.

SIXTY-TWO

JULY 1991

FOR SOME MINUTES before the djinni's return, Odile had been listening to the intermittent sputters and wails of a small high-speed engine somewhere off to the east, and not all that far away. She continued to seal up some of their crucial equipment while Clement made decisions on items to take, items to abandon. As much as he wanted to view videotape of the djinni's foray, Roland Clement wanted more to be under way again by noon and he was willing to sacrifice camping equipment in the process. She had assumed that no matter how they packed, they would have to make two trips.

Clement had what he thought was a better idea. "Someone with a powerboat," he said, "is not far off. I think perhaps we shall become lost, *ma p'tite.*"

"I do not want to hear that."

"You must believe it enough to convince a stranger," he said, striking an anguished pose, forearm flung across his forehead in what Odile realized was his parody of a distressed damsel. "Oh, m'sieur, you must help us," he implored in a tone that cooed, and ground his hips in a way that disgusted her.

But that is how he sees me, she reflected, her face impassive. *His summary of woman's work. It is his version of the truth.*

Now he dropped the pose and knelt to snap a container shut. For a moment they both fell silent. The boat engine, if that was what it was, no longer echoed across the marsh. Then Clement was working again. "So make yourself useful and lure another boat if you can. Shout for help. Wave your arms; scream, if you must. But if we can commandeer a second boat it will save an hour. If any of our operations is to bring an air search quickly, it will be this one."

"I suppose you will want me to shoot them," Odile said.

"Oh no. No, I cannot trust you to do that. Leave man's work to me; I will leave the seductions to you. I must say you played the role well enough to Gonzales—for all the good it did him," he finished with an infuriating chuckle.

The booming reports, a half dozen of them in rapid succession, shattered the morning stillness. "*Mon Dieu*, they have guns," Odile exclaimed, already striding off from camp but now turning.

"Go on. They will not see mine until too late," Clement replied, and waved her away.

Odile had walked no more than a dozen paces out of sight when she heard a familiar whirring, but not at a pitch appropriate for a gentle landing. She looked up, saw nothing but a carrion bird wheeling in the sky, and then caught one glimpse of the djinni. She could not hear its final approach over Clement's howls of dismay, but she knew he must have seen it and heard its terrifying impact through the reeds not far from their encampment.

And now a new realization flooded the mind of Odile Marchant. *It is finished, there will be no repair this time. Roland will know that as well as I and he will be raving like a lunatic, waving that damned weapon around. It would seem that I have been tugging on the wrong sausage much too long for my own good.*

The discovery filled her with a sense of freedom, indeed of deliverance, and before reflecting on it she called, "Roland! Can you hear me?"

His reply was immediate, over the sounds of his heavy body crashing through marsh growths. "Come immediately, *m'aidez*, help me rescue the child; Odiiiiile," he bayed.

She hurried back to their clearing, dropped to her knees before Clement's personal baggage, and found what she sought. The irony was that she found more of it than she could readily carry. To judge from the waving reeds and all the sobbing, Clement could be no more than thirty yards away, and a fresh howl told her that he had reached his pitiless killer; his intellectual child. "Gonzales was far more man than you, Roland, an infinitely better lover," she called.

"*M'aidez*, help me," he called back brokenly.

But Odile turned on her heel and trotted as far as the canoe, wasting not a second in pushing off, paddling briskly away. "It is man's work, Roland. Help yourself," she murmured; but softly, softly.

Odile Marchant smiled a gentle smile as she left the island behind her, heading south. Her mother, she decided, would have approved her decision.

SIXTY-THREE

July 1991

I F MARVIN PAYSON thought the tumult in that command center had become a Chinese fire drill, he needed another term to describe his experiences getting to the Horicon Marsh. Thanks to Sheppard's foresight, the NSA's huge amphibious Sikorsky helo was on hand for just such an event as recovery of a damaged Butcher Bird. Its trained crew had winches, grapples, even a plenum of the big helo's cargo section surrounded in antiradiation blankets that must have weighed tons.

They did not, however, have a radiation suit big enough for the hulking Payson. "I'm sorry, sir, but we're going to land where we can pick up whatever's left, and we don't know what we'll find down there," the pilot told the frustrated Payson, "and if you were president of the United bloody States I couldn't let you aboard." The Sikorsky's blades were already moving as he spoke.

Payson accepted the refusal and radioed for another vehicle, anything that could put down in a marsh, as he watched the big Sikorsky thunder away. Sheppard had already disappeared in a car, God knew where or why, leaving Ben Ullmer at the command center to operate their communications link. A local agent had concluded that the Butcher Bird had crashed on marshlands controlled by the state of Wisconsin. While waiting for another helo near the landing pad some distance from the milling crowd, Payson got through to the state office in Horicon. It seemed that no one in the Oshkosh crowd had noticed anything worrisome.

"That's right," he told the woman who seemed at first to think she was being hoaxed, "the Bureau is sending a team your way in several vehicles; should be there soon. What we need is experienced wardens to cordon off the northern part of your land for the public's protection. A whopping big Sikorsky will be landing there in a few minutes and nobody else, I mean *NO* body, should be in the vicinity."

He listened for a moment. Then, "The loud-hailers are a good idea. The airboats as well; I'd estimate a dozen agents will show up in the next hour." A pause. "No, it's—we believe the problem is some kind of highly toxic substance. It could be deadly from hundreds of yards."

No point in starting a panic by telling too much, he thought as he heard her reply and responded to it. "Yeah? Is your man in a car or a boat?" Pause. "I wouldn't recognize a go-devil if it bit me on the ankle, ma'am. Do you have radio contact with your man?" He nodded at her answer. "Tell Warden Carlsson it might be wise to abandon the area. Can you patch him in? I'll need to talk with him."

When this proved impractical, Payson bent his energies to memorizing what the woman told him. Lacking a highly detailed map of the marsh itself, he let his radio talk to his Nagra recorder and hoped that he would recognize the landmarks she mentioned. He ended the link with, "And ask Carlsson to detain any foreign nationals he finds in the area. They could be armed and dangerous. In fact, anyone in the area is a suspect."

The Kaman Seasprite that blew his hat off minutes later was a vintage Navy vehicle half the Sikorsky's size, but the pilot assured Payson that it would float in calm water. Payson clambered aboard with two agents and, moments later, felt the drag of gravity as the craft gained altitude. "Just be glad," he called to the pair over the rotor noise, "you're dressed as maintenance men." He pointed down to his wing-tip oxfords, the size of handball racquets. "I didn't expect to go swamp-strolling this morning."

The Kaman's pilot homed on the Sikorsky's radio signal, sighting it moments before Payson recognized the levee with the state pickup parked near a big cottonwood. The copilot called back: "They say we might take a rad or so of ionizing radiation if we landed near them at the moment, but they'll have the source sealed up shortly."

"Have them let us know when it's sealed. Meanwhile, let's take a swing along that island—and keep some altitude, we might be somebody's target," Payson advised.

The Sikorsky squatted at the end of an island on a bed of reeds like some enormous swamp creatures in its nest, rotors swinging lazily. A stone's throw away lay another kind of nest: two tents blown into the shrubs by the helo's downwash, with numerous containers lined up neatly nearby as if for loading. Payson did not think anyone could hide in that stuff. He darted a forefinger ahead.

The Kaman wafted southward down the island's length, flushing enough birds to reach Payson's guilt threshold, but if anyone was hiding there he was doing a damned good job of it. Payson suggested that they continue their sweep.

Now they saw a man and a woman in a canoe, cameras trained on the Kaman; now a lone woman in another canoe, imperturbable in a wide-brim hat as she paddled at a leisurely pace; then a trio, one of them a child, rowing slowly in a flat-bottomed boat. In the distance, more boats dotted the surface of the marsh, their numbers growing with proximity to the town of Horicon. The state troopers and agents were still nowhere in sight, and a lot of suspects could wander off before this place got a decent cordon around it.

When at last they had finished their recon sweep, Payson reached the state office again. He found that Warden Carlsson was in contact with the same woman by radio, and the broad levee became their rendezvous.

Christian Carlsson, a leathery younger man eager to help, nonetheless had a haunted look about him by this time, and a story to explain why. "The thing actually buzzed you?" Payson asked at one point. *It was trying him on for size,* Payson guessed.

"Yeah; panicked a heron rookery," Carlsson said, and laughed nervously. "I thought, 'What is this, a movie set?' But I knew better. This is my turf, Inspector. Then there was the failed Jesus who couldn't walk on water, and after that this damned flying buzz saw shows up again and goes down south of here, where that big chopper is, and later I get a call from the office about you. Thanks, by the way."

"Let's, um, backtrack a moment, Warden. Where does this failed Jesus thing fit in?"

"Oh; damnedest thing you ever saw. Some citizen, swarthy WMA calling himself Gonzales; I found him wading—if you can call it that—through chest-deep water with a foot of muck on the bottom. He must've walked more'n a mile unless he swamped a boat out there. If he did, we should be able to see it from the air." Carlsson's tone suggested that as long as his Saturday was already shot to oblivion, he wouldn't mind a short hop in a Kaman.

"Maybe later. Religious fanatic?"

"No, it was simply the kind of thing you'd expect only from a man who thought he could walk on water. Poor devil could've drowned. Claimed the people who launched that thing shot at him."

"Did he sound foreign?"

"No-o, not exactly. I mean, well, maybe Mexican-American, but his English was pretty standard. He sure wasn't anxious to meet our suspects again."

It was only then that Payson began to realize he was hearing a description of a desperate man, and knew that at least one of the people he sought had reached dry land. Some foreigners managed perfectly idiomatic English. The Butcher Bird people were supposed to have taken a hostage but if the man had been Clement's hostage, Payson reasoned, surely he would have said as much. The one thing he could not figure out was why a member of an assassination team would not smash the window of a pickup truck in an attempt to steal it. Payson tried on a lot of scenarios for that one. He never thought about the possibility that white male adult Gonzales, the failed Jesus, might have shown innate decency or gratitude for Carlsson's help. In Payson's own assessment later, this operation ended with an embarrassment of unanswered questions. It had, he would admit, more loose ends than a worm ranch.

SIXTY-FOUR

AUGUST 1991

THE BUTTONED-DOWN GENT who ushered Petra Leigh, Ben Ullmer, and William Sheppard from the Hotel Martin and then through two tiers of security seemed to have his speech down by rote, but no concept of good humor. If one believed his spiel, the innocuous building they finally reached could boast the best care anywhere for victims of radiation accidents; and Petra wanted to believe it. He was very careful—perhaps *too* careful, Petra decided—to point out that while this facility smack in the middle of Rochester, Minnesota, was reached by a warren of underground passages between the Mayo, Charlton, Plummer, and other medical buildings, it had absolutely no connection with the Mayo Clinic. None, zip, nada; it was merest coincidence that the towering aqua-tinted main building of the Mayo *fils* nearby blocked out most of the view of Rochester's smokestacks.

"You've convinced me," she said, unconvinced. "I'm just glad we were so near here when, ah, Mr. Doe needed you." It had been one hundred and ninety statute miles. Sheppard had never said how he commandeered a blisteringly fast helo so quickly but Oshkosh was, after all, Oshkosh; and Rochester boasted more than one landing pad for medical emergencies.

The elevator was the sort that would easily swallow a gurney with attendants, or four people swinging tennis rackets. Once inside it, Sheppard spoke for only the second time since they'd entered the building. Petra got the idea that he and Buttondown were already acquainted. "Is room surveillance operating?"

"Of course," the man murmured.

"Shut it down, please. Shut it *all* down in that suite," Sheppard said casually. "Now."

"Irregular," Buttondown said.

"Yes, it is," Sheppard agreed, and stared until he got the man's nod. The visitors went through one door into a tiny anteroom leaving Buttondown outside; heard locks engage; then the second door opened into a hospital suite that was nothing if not private. Petra forced herself to walk, not rush, to the side of the absolutely bald man who waited there.

She stopped at his bedside, hands out, blinking away tears of joy, then burst out laughing instead. "I'm sorry," she said. "Is it okay to kiss you?"

"Damn' shame not to," he growled, with a glance at the men standing behind her, and reached out to clasp her. After a long moment: "I know how I look," he said. "Sometimes when I shave, I laugh too. For awhile I didn't need to shave. Afternoon, gentlemen," he said, extending his free hand to be shaken. Petra thought his normal wariness might be cranked up a notch; he looked as though, after the handshakes, he was tempted to count his fingers.

"I have to tell you why I laughed," Petra said in self-defense. "I've wondered how you'd look when you were older. Suddenly I know," she said. "Telly Savalas's barber."

"I'm getting my eyebrows back. We'll see about the rest," said Corbett. Petra noted that his color seemed good, and yes, he did have a stubble of hairs where eyebrows should be.

"He took about two hundred rads, you know," Ullmer put in. "Or is it rems? I forget."

"Roughly the same," Sheppard replied. "Just enough to do him a major favor."

"Not funny," Petra said.

"I don't think—" Corbett began.

"I wasn't joking," Sheppard said quickly. "Of course by now you know about his brain cancer, so what I meant was—"

"No, I certainly did *not*," she interrupted, a hard edge on her voice. Her look toward Corbett was not pleasant. The tears were there again, ready for deployment, yet she fought against them. "But he knew, I'm sure."

"He had to. He had special medication for it in one pocket," Sheppard explained.

"Thanks a goddamn million," Corbett flared, "for all the domestic assistance. I'd say you've just made us even, Sheppard."

"Not even in your dreams," Sheppard replied, but he was blushing as he said it.

Now Ullmer coughed for attention, like a schoolmaster before quarreling scholars. "The thing is, Petra, when he blew a hole in the Butcher Bird, it gave him the biggest reward a man can get."

Petra's glance toward the old man was disbelieving, and Sheppard hurried to redeem himself. "A one in a million shot," he said, nodding; "just enough radiation to zap the tumor without killing him. No specialist would have dared hitting a patient with such a blast of therapy."

"In the words of one sawbones," Ullmer said, "he rode the razor's edge. Well," as he saw Petra's grimace, "he said it, not me."

Petra's hand flew out, gripped Corbett's on the blue coverlet. "The headaches, the weight loss," she said. "No more?"

Corbett, with a faint grin: "No more, Pets. You'll need another reason to get rid of me."

"Oh, I've got a long enough list," she warned, pulling her hand away as punishment for his secrecy, knowing it was a childish ploy, doing it anyway. *But if he didn't tell me, I haven't told him either.*

Perhaps, she thought, Sheppard just wanted to change the subject when he said to Corbett, "Well, there are lists, and then there are other lists. There's one I'd like to ask you about. Don't worry, there's no surveillance tape running. It seems the FBI has been going over all that equipment they recovered in the Horicon Marsh."

"Nobody's told me yet whether they got everybody responsible," Corbett complained.

"Well, yes and no," Sheppard admitted. "Actually, no. We have some transcripts that make it pretty clear Damascus thought it was running the operation; they just lost control, that's all. What we do to chasten Mr. Assad is anybody's guess. Maybe nothing.

"Or maybe we tell him a whopper; claim we're ready to teach the Israelis how to build a Butcher Bird of their own." Sheppard smiled beatifically. "As to the Syrian team here in CONUS, first we recovered that body in southern New Mexico. Another, with its hands removed, from the marsh when it floated to the surface." Sheppard shook his head sadly. "Whoever dispatched the man was—a human monster, is the best way I know how to put it. And of course we found that maniac Clement, hugging the Butcher Bird as if it were a cracked egg he had laid himself. I suppose, in a way, he had."

Corbett's desires were clear from the way he said, "Alive?"

"Oh, dear God," Sheppard said with a pained and mirthless chuckle, "the man was virtually a clinker. You took two hundred rads; he embraced a few *thousand*. He might as well have hugged a nuclear furnace. No, he couldn't have lived two minutes. But he had to know he was frying," he said.

"But the list was longer," Corbett prodded.

Sheppard held up two fingers, looking at them as though mystified by their existence. He turned one down with, "The woman. She simply disappeared. From complete prints we know she got away and abandoned the canoe they used. We finally located a Cessna STOL with the right prints on it, but logically there must've been a truck or a van as well, and we never found one; she must have found it first. We'd love to know more about her. And finally," he turned the other finger down, "fingerprinting sometimes depends on putting partials together, and Forensics came up with a few that seemed—impossible." He shrugged, after searching fruitlessly for a better word. "Impossible," he said again, ever so softly.

"I'm supposed to guess," Corbett said.

"Raoul Medina," said Sheppard in accusation. Petra kept her face impassive with an effort.

"The body in the water," said Corbett, nodding glumly. Then he saw Sheppard's headshake and raised both fists in triumph. "God*damn*, he got away!"

"He got away from us, all right," Sheppard agreed.

"From you? From *THEM*," Corbett bellowed.

"Easy," Petra cautioned.

"Pets, he thinks Medina was on the other side," Corbett said, looking at each face in turn, more animated than she had seen him for months. "He was my wingman on this—or was until they grabbed him at that New Mexico hangar. Tell 'em, Petra."

"How could you believe that, Doctor Sheppard?" Petra asked the little man whose gaze was now switching between her and Corbett. "We found his Imp damaged in that hangar. No one was even looking for him, he had everything to lose and only patriotism driving him. Well, that plus a hope that if he was ever found, this mission would square him."

Sheppard: "And you expect your government to take that on its face?"

"I know better than that," Corbett said bitterly. "But we both used the same Mexican lakebed for refueling and bivouac. Lago Santa Maria, near Guzman. Make a note, goddammit."

Petra knew of Sheppard's trick memory and was not surprised when the little man tapped his forehead. "I have it here."

Corbett: "If you think Medina was in Syrian pay, you have shit up there."

Petra: "Stop it, Kyle."

Corbett: "Well—no offense, Sheppard."

Sheppard laughed merrily. "Oh, certainly not." Brows elevated as he looked toward the ceiling, he laughed again.

Now Ben Ullmer snapped his fingers. "Sure. You two will have left tread marks all over the place. I know you were on our team. If Medina was with you, he couldn't very well have been on theirs." To Petra it was obvious that the old curmudgeon wanted to give Medina the benefit of any doubt.

Corbett frowned now, and made an iffy gesture to Ullmer. "I just thought of something. It still won't convince Sheppard, Ben. He doesn't know those are Medina's wheel marks. I tell you this flat-out: wherever Medina is, he's not *ever* gonna fly his little Imp someplace and let a bunch of feds check his tread marks."

"Won't have to," Ullmer said, sucking a tooth, grinning. "You left a nice little set from that airchine yourself, on my property. The ones in the shed should be good."

In wonderment: "By God, I did," said Corbett.

"Unless Bill, here, thinks I'm part of the Butcher Bird crew myself," Ullmer went on airily, starting to enjoy himself. "Which is perty reasonable when you think about it. I'm actually an Ayrab, but—"

"Will you stop, Ben," Sheppard begged. "We'll do that little checkup, never doubt it. I've known about those fingerprints since I was with my brother last week, and I still can't believe Medina was alive all these years! Probably still is."

Petra said nothing as her glance strayed to Corbett, but with her head turned just—so, she lowered one eyelid. She could not be certain Corbett had caught it. *Poker-faced old devil, I love you,* she thought at him.

"I could never figger him as a turncoat anyway," Ullmer said. "But then, I can't understand why he officially upped and died on us."

"He went private for the same reason I did," said Corbett. "Working for his government nearly got him killed. And he wasn't really sure which side tried to nail him."

"All right, all right," Sheppard said in exasperation, "I'll do what I can. I know I can take the heat off of Medina. He only terminated his employment without notice, as the euphemism goes. You?'' He pointed at Corbett. ''You're still a jondoe until you get a medical release; a few more weeks, I understand. After that—well, just don't get caught with your stolen billion-dollar toy, that's my only advice. Mine is not the only agency you'd be dealing with.''

Solemnly, the two shook hands again. Then Corbett looked across at Ben Ullmer, and his expression drew Petra's glance. Until this moment she had never realized the old man had a silent tear in him.

''Ben,'' she said tenderly, ''he's going to be all right.''

''It's not for this asshole in bed,'' Ullmer grumped, licking at the edge of his mouth. ''It's for Medina.''

''Never doubted it for a second,'' Corbett said.

''If he turns up again, and needs a good job, Aerosystems could use him. I think my top assembly people may be about to jump ship, maybe even start up a shop to compete with me. Lotsa luck,'' he added with ego-driven sarcasm.

Petra had caught no hint of this at work. With an audible gasp: ''Hardin? But why?''

''Morrison too,'' Ullmer said gloomily. ''I think they're fed up with folks like me who can't resist working with,'' and his nod was toward Sheppard, ''folks like him. Purely pissed off about the Butcher Bird thing, they didn't like the mushroom treatment.''

Petra nodded and sighed. She knew the old saying about the mushroom treatment: kept in the dark, covered with crap. And the Nemesis crew had been told too little about their mission to be properly used, because Ullmer had promised to satisfy secrecy demands of Petra and Corbett. ''I guess you can't satisfy everybody,'' she said, with a gentle hand on Ullmer's sleeve.

''That's what I tell my wife,'' he answered gruffly, and Petra knew better than to expect any more softness from that old man, not in the immediate future.

''Now if you jello-hearted old farts don't mind, I'd like some privileged time with the lady,'' Corbett said, breaking the mood.

''You're a piece of work, Mr. Doe,'' said Sheppard, and turned to leave.

SIXTY-FIVE

August 1991

I WISH YOU WOULDN'T cuss me in public," Corbett said as the door snicked shut. *Let's get this over with up front,* he thought.

"I should've, but I didn't," Petra rejoined.

"Hell you didn't. When satchelmouth Sheppard told you about that tumor, your look said, 'Corbett, you son of a bitch,' plain as day," he said.

"Well—then you heard right. I'm a big girl, you can tell me things like that." Hands on her hips, she loomed at him.

"You've put on a few pounds," he said, and leered. "Big girl is right. I like it."

"You are *such*—an—idiot," she fumed. "It still has not crossed your alleged mind why?"

Pause. "Why I'm an idiot? Sometimes," he admitted.

"Why I'm fat and ugly," she stormed.

"I guess," he said, "so nobody but an idiot would want to marry you." *Say it now or never,* he told himself. "So I'm qualified. So I'm asking."

She let her arms drop, like a puppet suddenly unstrung. He wondered if he had ever seen emotions chase one another across a face as rapidly as this. "I haven't much choice," she said at last, "if we're going to be a family."

"Sure. A kid, maybe; the whole nine hundred yards," he said agreeably.

"Maybe? Let me, uh, let me see if I can put this as subtly as you need." She pursed her mouth, then nodded to herself. As if he were deaf, she called out, "I'm four months pregnant with your daughter!"

Well, I will be a dirty son of a bitch, was the only thing that came to mind. Then: *And a happy one, at that.* He let his grin say it for him and when he was through goggling at her, he asked, "Are you absolutely sure?"

"Yes, a girl. Sorry 'bout that, don't you just hate it when that happens? I ordered a boy but this is what we get," she said, patting her firm little belly. He held his arms out and she leaned in to them, laughing. "Such an idiot you didn't know morning sickness when you saw it."

"And you, little bastard that you are, wouldn't tell me."

"I didn't think you wanted to marry," she said.

"Not with a death sentence," he said. "Things change, lady."

"Our kid is going to have one weird upbringing, you know that, don't you?" she said.

"Mom a stress analyst, Pop a hunted animal, kid soloes at eleven, a Nobel at sixteen—pretty ordinary, I'd say."

"You just remember that when she asks to take the Hellbug out for a late date," she warned him.

He used his elbows to sit up, his glance wary again. "Hey, go turn on the water in the sink. Let it splash," he said.

She did as he asked, tossing a mystified look at him, then made a little mouth as the white noise of rushing water filled the suite. "Doctor Sheppard told them to stop surveilling this suite. I heard him."

"Yeah, and maybe they did. And maybe it's on again."

"They're giving you the best free care in the world," she reminded him, "and you still don't trust them."

An old journalism adage, *All governments are liars,* flickered through his mind but why start a philosophical argument with Petra now? Instead, he said, "When I start entirely trusting those fuckers, you can rent out my head for a bat sanctuary. Humor me, okay?"

"I'll humor you," she said, sensuously enough to be almost a threat. She eased herself onto the bed and swung one leg across him, the way they slept on cold nights when the wind howled across Barstow straight, it seemed, from Alaska.

He turned so that his mouth was near her ear; kissed her in that nibbling fashion that always made her shudder with delight. It worked this time, too. "You gave me a big wink," he said in a very soft rumble. "About Speedy."

"I called, and called, and got humping *sick* of that answering machine," she replied softly. "And then at noon one day I tried, and Speedy's Tow Service was in business. I cried, Kyle; I couldn't swallow another bite, had to throw away a perfectly good egg sandwich."

"Oxymoron," he said. "Good egg sandwich; conflict in terms."

"Screw you, you want to hear this or not?"

"There's more? I want to know about my Hellbug."

"I flew it back nonstop the day after you were hurt, while I was immune to fear. Seems like a dream now, I'd be petrified to do a cross-country alone. But you might die, they said, and I was simply numb. You do funny things then."

He felt a small female hand rubbing him. "You're doing funny things now. Don't start with me in this goddamn video arcade, luv."

"When can we start, then?"

"When they let me out. Another two weeks, they say."

"I'll weigh half a ton," she cautioned.

"I'll give special attention to every ounce," he promised. "Besides, I know you have too much willpower to get sloppy. And you've got a metabolism like Medina's. Speaking of which: is Speedy okay?"

"Him? Never better; I think he's saving some details for you, good ol' boy that he is. He's hungry for every word about you. I went to Barstow last weekend; helped him vac-bag a new strut."

"You wanta watch that wetback, he'd get you in a bag if he could."

"Not now he wouldn't. Anyway, I was sleeping with a Strectsweeper."

"A *who?* Oh," he said, with a bass chuckle. She'd had him going there, for a moment. "That, he would definitely understand."

"Yes, but what I mean is, he has a new miz; from Quebec, she says. He caught a ride with her all the way from Wisconsin, and sweet-talked her into looking for a job in Barstow. I met her in town; that accent has just got to be a fake but she's one snappy dresser. I think she must have money," she went on, as if to herself. "Calls herself Odette. Odette, brunette, coquette, bimbette. Probably from Cleveland."

"You telling me he's serious about her?"

"Oh—as serious as he gets. If you mean, is he using his real name or showing her the Hellbug, no fear of that. But he told me, as long as she's happy with Speedy Gonzales, the tow-truck keeng, he'll give her a bouncy ride."

Goddamn, ol' Speedy's back in harness. "Sounds like him," he said, laughing gently.

"But you know, sometimes I wonder," Petra murmured lazily. "Now she lives in a Winnebago; they came from Wisconsin together; and that suck-the-logo-off-a-lightbulb French accent of hers just might be genuine. The Butcher Bird team had a woman. You don't suppose . . ."

She turned her head, and for a timeless moment the two of them shared a suspicion. Then: "Naaaah," they said together.

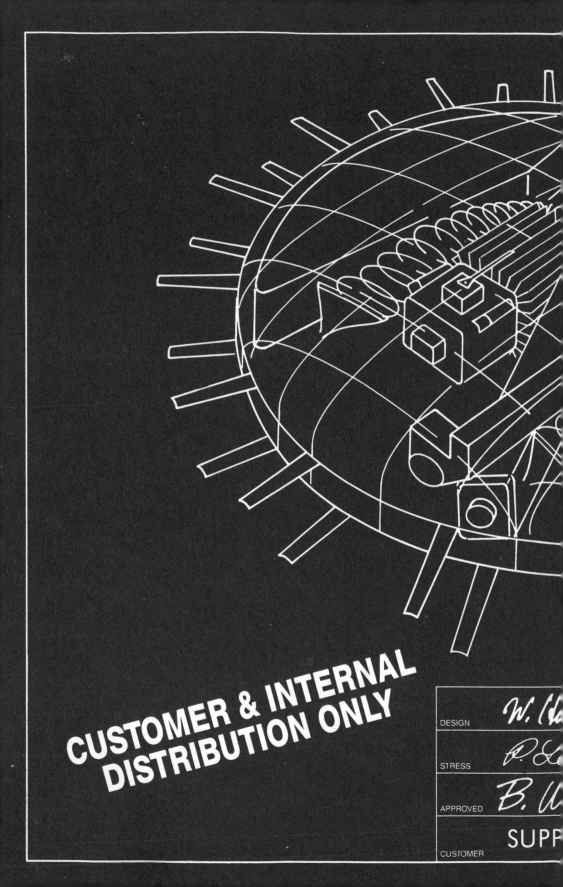

DESIGN	W. Id
STRESS	R. L
APPROVED	B. U
CUSTOMER	SUPP